HIS KIND OF TROUBLE

TERRI L. AUSTIN

Cover designed by Dawn Adams/Sourcebooks, Inc.
Cover image by Shirley Green

Published by Sourcebooks Casablanca, an imprint of Sourcebooks, Inc.
P.O. Box 4410, Naperville, Illinois 60567-4410
(630) 961-3900
Fax: (630) 961-2168
www.sourcebooks.com

Printed and bound in Canada.
MBP 10 9 8 7 6 5 4 3 2 1

To Gretchen Jones, Czarina of All Knowledge. Thanks for being so patient with all my car questions. You are awesome in every way.

Chapter 1

Monica Campbell eyed the refreshment table, ignoring the appetizers and zeroing in on the champagne. "Why ruin a perfectly good Saturday night with a wedding?"

Evan Landers flicked a piece of lint off his green-and-black tartan jacket. "This isn't the way I want to spend the evening either, and I'm not even related to the groom."

"Don't remind me." Monica uncrossed her arms. "Okay, I'm going in for another glass. Keep a lookout for Allie." Monica's sister had already pulled her aside once and told her to slow down. Not happening. Even Allie's disapproval couldn't keep Monica away from the booze. It was the only thing this party had going for it.

Not party. Wedding.

So her dad was getting married. Great. Monica was happy for him. Really. He was moving on, and good for him. That's what people did, right? They moved on, got remarried, started over. Totally natural. But the cloying smell of all these flowers reminded Monica of that hot, cloudless day when they'd buried her mom. Patricia Campbell had loved gardenias. Her casket had been covered with them. *You'd think he would have remembered that.*

Yeah—definitely time for another drink.

Stepping forward, Monica threw a smile at the cute

waiter manning the table and trailed one hand across her bare shoulder. "How are you tonight?"

His gaze dipped to her cleavage. She showed quite a bit of it. Allie had bitched about that too. Along with the color of her dress. What was so terrible about wearing red to a wedding? It was a joyous occasion. That's why they were all here—the bride's small family, Monica's tribe—to celebrate her dad's new life.

"Good," he said. "I'm very good." He leaned forward and stage-whispered, "Technically, I'm only supposed to serve you sparkling cider."

Ugh, Allie. Monica might have been a few months shy of legal, but since when had that ever stopped her? "I hate getting technical. Don't you?"

After glancing over each shoulder, he reluctantly nodded. "Go ahead," he said. "I won't tell."

Monica plucked up two glasses. "Thank you. You're sweet." As he blushed at her words, she spun around and did a quick scan of the room. Filled with bright, delicate flowers and dripping in candlelight, the glass-walled conservatory reeked of romance. A perfect setting for a perfect couple. Yep. Happy, happy.

Monica tipped back her head and chugged the expensive champagne as if it were tap water. She ignored the burst of fizzy bubbles that tickled her tongue. Barely tasted the dry, cool flavor. She needed to get her buzz on—ASAP.

"Easy there, slugger. This isn't a kegger," Evan said.

"God, I wish it were." Monica set down the empty flute and stood shoulder to shoulder with him. He'd come as her "acceptable date," per Allie's instructions. Evan lacked a criminal record and attended college, although *attended* might be a liberal use of the term. He deserved a best-friend award for suffering through this with her.

Monica had met most of Allie's requirements for this event. Appropriate date? *Check*. Mandatory attendance? *Check*. Stone-cold sober? *Not for long*.

Allie had commandeered Monica's day from the time she'd woken up this morning until now: breakfast with the bride and her family, mani-pedis, hair and makeup, pictures. Monica had reached her snapping point. She just wanted out of here.

She missed her mom all the time, but today that grief was a persistent ache. It sat in the middle of her chest—a hot, painful burn that never let up, not for one minute.

This time, Monica didn't bother to look around before she drained the champagne. If Allie didn't like it, tough shit.

"How long do we have to stay?" she asked.

Evan patted her arm. "I'm not sitting through all this without getting a piece of cake."

"I'll buy you a cake. You can eat the whole damn thing."

"Come on, Monnie. It's one day. You're tough, suck it up."

She might be tough, but she was restless and unhappy, and *oh shit*—

"Uh-oh," Evan whispered. "Incoming."

Allie Campbell Blake headed toward them, her long white-blond hair flying outward with each step. At five months' pregnant, Monica's sister had never looked better. The bright blue dress she wore matched the color of her eyes. A fake smile she'd perfected over the years graced her lips. That smile fooled most people. Not Monica.

"Hey, Evan, do you mind if I speak to Monica for a few minutes?"

"Sure."

He turned to leave, but Monica snagged his arm and refused to let go. "He can stay."

Allie's smile grew brighter. That always spelled trouble. "I thought we talked about the champagne."

Monica raised her brows and attempted a look of innocence. "I've been drinking sparkling cider."

Evan nodded. "Yep. I can vouch."

"See?"

Allie stared at Monica until she nearly squirmed. "Okay. I won't nag you anymore." *Right*. "But this is Dad and Karen's special night, Mon. Please don't ruin it." Then she walked off to greet the officiant.

"Thanks, Ev." Monica gave his forearm a quick squeeze. "Do me one more favor? Keep her away from me."

"I'll do my best. But you could at least make an attempt at being subtle."

"I don't do subtle."

He laughed. "No kidding."

After a few minutes, Monica began to feel it—that nice little sensation starting at the base of her neck, the one that numbed her brain. She welcomed it. One more glass, and she just might make it. But before she could reach for it, Evan nudged her arm.

"And I thought you were underdressed. I think that guy stumbled into the wrong place."

Monica followed Evan's gaze. *Whoa*. Her restlessness

disappeared, blown away like dust in a windstorm, and in its place stood the best diversion possible—a smoking-hot bad boy.

Monica may have been inappropriately dressed, but he took the jackpot. Long brown hair brushed his jawline. His leather jacket appeared battered, worn at the cuffs and rubbed bare at the elbows. His faded jeans fit him just right, showcasing his long legs. On his feet—black motorcycle boots. Whoever he was, he'd be right at home in a biker bar, but he looked completely out of place among the well-behaved guests.

"Who is he?" Evan asked.

What does it matter? This night had just taken a turn for the better. Her body responded to him. Attraction tugged at her, pulling her toward him. Straightening her shoulders, Monica started across the room, intent on finding out more.

Before she could take another step, the officiant walked to the front of the room, and the string quartet began the opening strains of "Pachelbel's Canon." Damn. That was her cue. Time to find a seat.

Evan grabbed her wrist and drew her back to him. "Come on," he whispered. "The wedding's going to start."

For the next thirty minutes, while her dad and Karen exchanged vows, Monica's eyes kept straying toward her mystery man. He sat across the aisle, two rows back. She tried to take Evan's advice and do subtle, angling her chin and glancing at him from the corner of her eye. Finally she gave up on subtle. Twisting her head, she openly studied him.

She tried to guess his age—late twenties maybe? Excessively badass, that much was obvious. Who strutted into a wedding like that, completely at ease with himself, unapologetic? Monica could respect that kind of *fuck you* attitude.

Every time he moved, that leather jacket creaked, just a little bit. Her eyes slid back to him once more. He had a strong profile—straight nose, square jaw. As if he felt her staring, he turned his head and looked her right in the eye.

And then he gave her an uneven grin.

Completely charmed, she smiled back. Monica wanted to talk to him, find out his story. *Who are you kidding, Campbell? You want to fuck him.* Absolutely. But exchanging a few words first wouldn't hurt.

She tapped her fingers against her bare thigh. This ceremony couldn't end fast enough. It just dragged on and on—rings, candle lighting, pouring sand into a glass jar for some reason. All the cheesy, clichéd symbols. Was it really that easy for him to forget her mom? Commit to another woman?

Whatever. Maybe that guy would give her a ride on his bike. Then she could give him a ride back at her apartment. That seemed fair.

The next time she glanced at him, he'd slipped his jacket off. Nice arms—tanned, muscular. He threw her a broad wink, and it earned him another smile. God, he was hot. Flirty. Cocky. Just her type.

When Evan lightly slapped her arm, Monica returned her attention to the front of the room. Her dad and Karen kissed. Then, hand in hand, they gazed at each other and walked up the aisle, stopping to greet people along the way. When they reached the row where Monica sat, her dad leaned down and pecked her cheek.

"Congratulations, Daddy." It almost physically hurt to say the words.

Yet, he did look happy. Content. One chapter closed and another one opened. That was life.

The sadness that pierced Monica's chest burned a little hotter. She tried to ignore it.

Once her dad and Karen left the room, Allie took front and center. "Just a few announcements." Monica suppressed a groan. Like a flight attendant, Allie gave directions, complete with hand gestures, about the buffet dinner in the dining room.

Monica looked back once more. This time, the stranger was waiting for her. He lowered his head a notch, and his eyes traced over her face. No smile. Just heat.

Monica stood, her gaze unwavering. They simply stared at each other, ignoring everyone else. People began filing out of the conservatory. Chatter filled the air, and the quartet played a chipper tune. Hardly any of it registered.

Evan leaned down and spoke in her ear. "Are you coming?"

"You go on," Monica said, keeping her eye on the prize. "I'll catch up later."

"Okay, but whatever you do, don't get caught." He sidled past her and left the room.

Soon, everyone cleared out, even the musicians, until only the two of them remained. Monica and this stranger. He kept his eyes locked on hers as he moved forward. Every step brought him closer. Finally, he stopped in front of her, the tip of his boot resting against the toe of her stiletto. He stared down at her with the greenest eyes. They danced over her, lighting on every part of her, eating her up. Monica breathed it in, loving the attention.

"And who are you, then?" he asked. He had a British accent. A bad boy Brit. Too perfect.

"I'm the daughter of the groom. Monica Campbell." She held out her hand.

"Cal Hughes. I believe your sister married my cousin, Trevor." He took her hand and didn't let go. His skin felt hot against hers. "Felicitations on the wedding and all that." His deep voice made her nipples tighten. His gaze kept darting from her face to the tops of her breasts.

"Thanks. You have very interesting taste in wedding attire."

He glanced down at his clothes. "Sorry about that. I rode into town this afternoon. Didn't think to pack a suit."

"Rode? As in motorcycle?"

"Yeah."

Ha, she knew it.

When Cal let go of her, she missed the contact. Wetting her lips, she watched as he dropped his jacket in a chair. A hint of ink peeked from under the sleeve of his black T-shirt. Tattoos made her weak. Pretty much everything about this guy checked all of her boxes. He even smelled good. Woodsy and fresh.

"Is Cal short for something?"

He took one step closer, so her breasts brushed his chest. Now she had to lean her head all the way back to look up at him.

"It stands for Calum."

"A British name, huh?" She swung her head so that a curl bounced off her shoulder. "Do you live in Britain?"

"Some of the time. And what do you do, Monica?" The way he said her name made her skin heat up. She wanted to hear him say it again. Monica could use a good distraction tonight, and Cal Hughes was the man to give it to her. Hopefully, he'd give it to her twice.

"I'm a student." Using one finger, she lifted the edge of his right sleeve.

"Like ink, do you?"

Still feeling the effects of the champagne, she gazed up at him, a smile hovering over her lips. "I love ink." A Celtic knot. She fingered the bottom edge of the design.

"You're a student at university?"

She dropped her hand and nodded, pulling her bottom lip into her mouth. He watched it hungrily. "I haven't decided on a major yet. Have any advice?"

"No, school was never my strong suit. So what do you do when you're not studying?"

"I like to dance. Club dancing, for fun. Not pole dancing, for profit. Just so you know."

Cal threw out a surprised laugh. "You're a bit of a wild card, aren't you?"

"Sometimes." His wide shoulders blocked out the fountain. The flickering candles cast a shadow across the left side of his face, making him appear even more mysterious. He represented all of her fantasies rolled into one tasty package.

"I suppose we should join the others," he said.

Monica didn't want this moment to end. "I'm not interested in joining the others."

He lifted his hand and looped a strand of her hair around his finger. "What are you interested in?"

"Do you want a list?"

"Yes, I do. We'll fit in as many as we can."

"We could start with Trevor's garden. Have you seen it?"

"No, but it sounds as though I should." He unwound her hair and ran his finger down the side of her throat. His whisper-light touch made her tingle. "If you'd show it to me, I'd be *really* grateful." He grinned again, and that smile was her undoing.

Monica pointed to the garden door, tucked in the corner behind a potted orange tree. Cal shrugged his jacket on and followed her outside.

The night was cool. The new moon didn't offer much light, and only a few stars dotted the sky. The vast garden wasn't dark though. Tiny white lights hung from tree branches and lit the pathway.

Cal stopped walking and looked around. "This is exactly like my grandfather's garden. Except for the grotto."

"That's a Vegas thing." Monica followed the pathway past the rosebushes. From here, she could see into the dining room. Two dozen people sat at the long table. They could probably see her too, if they were paying attention.

Cal wrapped his hand around her waist. "Want to go back inside?"

"Not at all." She turned to him and splayed her hands across his chest. The knit material felt soft, like it had been washed a thousand times. Monica stood on her toes and ran her tongue along his jawline. "You know, I've never been kissed in a garden."

"Haven't you? What a terrible shame. We should fix that." Cal leaned down, but instead of kissing her, he gently bit down on the place where her neck and shoulder met.

Monica grabbed a handful of his hair. "I like that."

Cal lifted his head and nodded toward the house. "Is there somewhere a little less out in the open?"

Being out in the open made it that much more exciting, as far as Monica was concerned. But if he needed privacy, she'd go along. As she led him toward the pond, she cast one last glance at the house, glad she wasn't stuck inside. The fresh air felt good. The flowers in the garden smelled fragrant and sweet, rather than overpowering. And she could be herself out here, without everyone watching over her and disapproving.

Once the path ended, Monica walked across the thick grass to the back wall. The garden lights didn't extend this far. It was dark. Private, like he wanted.

She swung around. "What do you—"

Cal didn't let her finish. Cupping her jaw with his free hand, he bent down and kissed her.

As his mouth moved over hers, Monica felt it clear down to her toes. They curled inside her shoes. Her belly fluttered and her knees grew weak. And it wasn't the champagne. Cal Hughes took her breath away.

He let go of her hand in order to cup her breast. Monica's nipple strained against the rasp of his thumbnail. Her panties grew damp and her pussy clenched. Fuck being on her best behavior. She needed this rush of desire, this instant attraction. She felt so alive right now.

Parting his jacket, she ran her hands up his torso. Solid. Muscular, but lean.

Then his hand tugged on her bodice and palmed her bare breast. The cool air picked up a curl, and it tickled her cheek.

Monica tore her mouth away from his. "You don't have to be so gentle."

Cal's grip on her breast tightened, and his lips slipped down the column of her neck, taking little bites while he grazed her nipple with his thumb.

She reached for his dick, rubbing her fingers along the edge of his fly, getting a feel for it. "Yes," he murmured against her neck, "more of that." Then he shoved his hips against her hand. He grew under her touch. Hard and long—Monica couldn't wait to see it. Maybe taste it.

"Mon?" *Allie*. "What the hell are you doing?"

Monica peeked over Cal's shoulder. Standing at the edge of the path, Al stared at them. With a hand at her belly, she shook her head. "Oh, Monica."

"Shit," she whispered, pushing out of Cal's arms. She quickly shoved herself back into her dress.

Cal straightened. He gazed down at her, looking dazed, and ran a hand along his jaw. "Damn."

Monica stepped around him. "I…we just needed some air."

"Get in the house." Allie used a soft tone, one that spoke of disappointment rather than anger. Monica could handle anger, fight against it. But this… *Pack your bags, Campbell. There's an extended guilt trip in your future*. "Stop by the powder room and get yourself together. Your hair's a mess."

"I don't want to go back inside, Al." Cal stood next to her, silent. Waiting. She could still ride away with him, lose herself until tomorrow.

Allie dropped her hand. "Dad won't cut the cake until you're there. Please do this for him."

As upset as she was, Monica didn't want to ruin his perfect day. She took another peek up at Calum Hughes. "Maybe next time, huh?"

"Definitely." Cal bent down and gave her one last, hard kiss.

Then Monica ran toward the house without looking back.

Chapter 2

Five years later…

MONICA CAMPBELL'S CAREFULLY PLANNED SCHEDULE was shot to hell. Not just her schedule—her entire morning. She needed a do-over. If only those worked after the third grade, she'd be golden, because this day was shaping up to be a real pisser.

She'd woken up at six, bleary-eyed and in desperate need of coffee, but her machine had refused to give up the dark roast. Then her sister, Allie, had texted to switch the location of their eight o'clock meeting. Now instead of a ten-minute drive to the office, Monica had to hightail it from Vegas to Henderson. Hastening her routine, she'd sped to the nearest coffee shop and stood in line with all the other caffeine addicts in the throes of withdrawal—thirty-two minutes wasted—before heading straight into rush hour.

Allie had given no explanation for the change in locale, no apology. But since she was the boss, it was her call. And she never let Monica forget it.

One thing Monica resented above all else was having someone dick with her schedule. And today the universe had her in its crosshairs. *Roll with the punches. Go with the flow.* People uttered the trite phrases as if they were actual philosophies. But if time didn't mean anything, why had clocks been invented? *Yeah. Argue that one, slackers.*

As the coordinator for the cancer foundation named in honor of her mother, Monica kept busy; her job was one big blur of back-to-back meetings. Allie's little hitch threw everything into chaos. So as she sat behind the wheel in bumper-to-bumper traffic, Monica sipped her sugary black coffee, called the office to reschedule three appointments, and left detailed messages for two separate committee chairs.

By the time she pulled through the gates of Allie's sprawling mansion, Monica had regained a small measure of control. She'd still have to scramble to fit in all of her appointments, but if she could keep Allie on point, Monica might finish everything on her to-do list and make it out of the office before midnight.

After parking in the circular drive, Monica walked at a brisk clip to the side of the house, her mind spinning in ten different directions. But when she rounded the corner and neared the freestanding garage, her feet stopped moving altogether.

"*Bloody fucking hell.*"

Monica didn't bat an eye at the crude words. It wasn't the masculine British accent that brought her to a standstill, either. No, it had everything to do with that deep, raspy voice. It sounded very familiar, but this man's timbre was lower, much rougher than the one she remembered.

He stood bent beneath the hood of an ancient Mustang. The light gray Bondo filler spread along the car's body was as faded as his jeans—so faded they'd turned white in the well-worn creases and at the seams. The denim wasn't artificially distressed. It was the real deal.

Sounds of metal clanging against metal emanated from the engine where the stranger worked. "Fuck," he muttered.

Monica didn't know much about British accents, but she recognized a posh one when she heard it. And despite the rumbly tenor and foul words, his accent was as high-end as it got.

When he retreated one step and rose to his full height—well over six feet—Monica's heart thumped hard against her ribs. His torso was bare, without an annoying shirt to mar the smooth expanse of deeply burnished skin.

She licked her dry lips and adjusted the collar of her blouse. As she continued to gawk, he shifted his weight from one foot to the other, causing the muscles of his back to contract ever so slightly. Monica swallowed as she took in the line of his broad shoulders. When he raised a hand to brush the hair off his forehead, powerful muscles bunched and rippled in a graceful, fluid motion. Monica blinked slowly, practically hypnotized. Oh crap, he had a tattoo. Starting at the cap of his right shoulder and ending on his bicep, a set of interconnecting Celtic knots and swirls decorated his skin. Wait. She knew that tattoo.

Calum Hughes was back in town.

Fan-fucking-tastic. Monica's disastrous day just took a nosedive.

She inhaled deeply in an effort to slow her racing pulse, and reminded herself she was immune to bad boys now. Well, not immune so much as on the wagon. Though after Cal, it had taken Monica awhile to her get her shit together, she had been a bad boy–free zone for four years. Four very long years. She only went for nice men now. Respectable men. Men with real jobs and life goals. Like her ex, Ryan.

That reminder helped dispel the lusty fog that clouded her mind. With firm resolve, Monica pulled herself together, straightened her spine, then averted her gaze, forcing her feet to move.

She resumed walking to the house, but he must have heard the click-clack of her heels this time, because he spun around quickly. Determined not to be diverted again, Monica kept moving. But she couldn't help giving him one last side-eyed glance.

"Good morning," he said.

Now that he'd spotted her, Monica couldn't just ignore him. Adjusting her sunglasses, she stopped and turned to face him fully.

Monica may not have immediately recognized Cal's back, but she'd know that face anywhere. With a stubbled jaw and angular features, he was more arresting than handsome. Shallow grooves formed brackets around his mouth, which tilted noticeably higher on the left side when he smiled. Deep, pleated lines framed those spring-green eyes. Time had only made him more attractive.

No, not attractive. That was too benign a word. He had a strong, masculine presence, an attitude of casual self-assurance mixed with sex appeal that would entice any woman with a pulse. Monica definitely had a pulse, and hers was approaching the red zone.

She remained silent for a moment, waiting to see if he would recognize her. And as she waited, her gaze traced downward. While his biceps weren't bodybuilder huge, they were well defined. He had the look of someone who developed them in real life, not by pumping iron in a gym. His solid, carved abs stood out in relief, the tanned skin molding over them, contouring the hollows between each distinct muscle. God save the Queen, it was getting hot out here.

A trickle of sweat slid from the back of her hairline, working its way down her neck and disappearing beneath the collar of her white blouse. *Immune*, the sane part of her brain protested.

"My God, it's you." He strode forward, tight jeans riding low on his hips, pulling at his thighs with each step, and stopped just a foot away. He smelled of motor oil and sunshine. That shouldn't be such an intriguing combination. "Monica Campbell." The way he whispered her name sent a quiver shooting through her belly.

Now he stared at her, his body motionless—then without warning, he reached out and whisked off her sunglasses in a lightning-fast move. His gaze held hers, searching—for what she couldn't say—but his grin kicked up a notch. "I wondered if I'd remembered correctly. If your eyes were really that blue. They are. Your hair's different though, shorter. As I recall, it used to be curly." With his free hand, he reached out and rubbed a strand between his fingers. "Still soft," he rumbled low in his chest.

Monica forgot to inhale for a few seconds. Okay, so he still remembered her. It didn't mean anything, not really, not to a man like him—a man who probably had sex as regularly as he drank beer: each night, after a full day of hammering on a dilapidated engine. Monica was probably just a notch he couldn't add to his undoubtedly high pussy count, and that made her stand out. Still, the fact that he hadn't forgotten *that* kiss flooded her with relief. His tongue stroking hers, his hand hot on her breast, squeezing with just the right amount of pressure…she'd never forget it. That night in the garden, the smell of roses crossed with Cal's woodsy scent—epic.

Cal's gaze flowed over her again, but slower this time, like an intimate stroke up and down her body. He took in everything, from her plain white blouse to her black jacket and slacks, all the way down to the sensible pumps on her feet. "Who died?" he asked.

"What?"

"You look as if you're in mourning." As he dropped her hair, he dipped his chin, nodding over the length of her. "Are you going to a funeral?"

Funeral? This was a perfectly acceptable pantsuit—black, classic cut. From Nordstrom. The sale rack, but so what? "No one died. I'm a professional. I wear clothes that reflect that." She jerked the sunglasses out of his hand and settled them back on her nose. She felt less exposed with the dark lenses covering half her face.

"A professional what?"

Monica wasn't going defend her life choices to Calum Hughes. She'd kissed him five years ago, and it was never going to happen again. Time to move on. She had a to-do list two miles long. Her schedule was all fucked up. Right. She'd actually forgotten about it for a moment. The sight of Cal had scrambled her brain. "I need to go, or I'm going to be late for my meeting." There. That sounded in command and unaffected. Of course, she clutched her computer bag to her stomach like it was a shield. Monica tried to subtly loosen her grip.

Cal's laugh was gruff, jagged. The sound made her nipples strain against the lace cups of her bra. She ignored them, glad her suit jacket concealed her breasts so thoroughly.

"The Monica I met a few years back wouldn't give a toss about a meeting. You *have* grown up, then."

So had he. Five years ago, he'd still retained a hint of boyishness, a softness in his face, a twinkle in his eyes. But now his face was leaner, his cheekbones sharper. And his eyes were a bit more wary. "It happens to the best of us," she said. "I take it that's your car?"

"Yeah, just bought it." He glanced over his shoulder. "What do you think? It's not much to look at right now, I'll grant you, but it has potential."

One of the many losers Monica had dated over the years had owned a Mustang. Dustin Something. According to him, Mustangs were money pits. For every one problem he'd fix, three more popped up. Since he talked endlessly about it, she recalled more about the car than the guy who drove it—air-cooled engines and drippy cowl vents and lots of rust. "If you say so."

He glanced back at her, eyes zeroing in on her lips. "I'm good at spotting a diamond in the rough."

"Well, I'll leave you to it. Good luck." She forced herself to glance away. The fine sheen of sweat coating his muscle-carved chest was starting to make Monica a little light-headed. She couldn't retreat to the house fast enough. If she didn't go now, she'd be tempted to do something stupid, like trace her fingers across Cal's tattoo, then follow it up with her tongue. "Good to see you again."

She turned on her heel and took one step before Cal's

big, callused hand snagged hers, pulling her closer to his side. She looked down, noticed how large and tanned it was in comparison to hers. His nails were super short and clean, despite the fact that he'd been toying with an engine only moments ago.

"Why don't you skip the meeting, and let's sneak off to the garden. For old times' sake?" His grip tightened just a fraction. Where he touched her, every nerve ending tingled.

Without responding, Monica jerked away and kept walking.

"Was it something I said?" he called after her.

Monica didn't look back, but she knew his eyes followed her every movement. She could feel his gaze wander over her, and despite the heat, a shiver skidded up her spine. Shit. Cal Hughes was trouble. Handsome, hard-bodied trouble.

Once Monica reached the house, she flung open the side door and bolted inside. The cool air felt good against her clammy skin. Leaning against the wall, Monica removed the glasses and closed her eyes. She rubbed the back of her neck, where heat crept under the surface and worked its way upward, toward her cheeks. She needed to calm the hell down. He was just a guy. *A guy you've never been able to forget*. That night, under a sprinkling of stars, Cal Hughes had made her feel exotic, untamed. Desired. But that was five long years ago—might as well be a lifetime.

Monica struggled to find her center, to compose herself and assume the calm demeanor she'd worked so hard to acquire.

After a few deep breaths, she strode past the glass

cases that held various objets d'art, but she didn't pause to look at them today. Instead, she headed straight into the breakfast room, hoping she'd have a few minutes alone before facing anyone. But luck was not on her side this morning. Her brother-in-law, Trevor Blake, sat with phone in hand, tapping out a text message. With his dark, overly long hair combed back from his face, he wore a perpetual haughty expression that made him seem cold and remote. Except with Allie and their twins. Somehow, Monica's sister smoothed out Trevor's harsh edges, made him not softer, but more approachable. Allie and Trevor shared something unique, and Monica sometimes envied the connection they had.

She plopped down next to him. "Hey, Trev."

He didn't speak until he'd finished texting. "Hey, yourself. Are you quite all right? You're a bit peaky."

"I ran into your cousin outside. What's he doing here?" Other than throwing Monica's world completely out of whack.

"Still tinkering away, is he? Wonder how long that will last." Like Cal, his accent was posh. Arrogantly so. But where Trevor's voice was cool and clipped, Cal Hughes sounded husky, like he'd smoked too many cigarettes the night before, or had just woken up. Monica closed her eyes in an effort to banish the images that kept flashing through her mind. Cal lying in bed naked—white sheets tangled around his legs, a contrast against his sun-kissed skin. With strong arms crossed behind his head, his crooked smile would beckon her…

When she felt a hand clamp onto her shoulder, Monica's eyes popped open, and she nearly jumped out of her seat. Allie stood behind her holding an enormous black binder. With messy blond hair falling over her shoulders, Al wore a pink T-shirt and ripped jeans, managing to look sexy and disheveled. "Good morning."

Monica placed a hand on her chest and willed her heart to slow down. "God, Al, are you trying to kill me?"

"What's wrong with you?" Without waiting for an answer, Allie glided to Trevor and gave him a kiss…one that lasted so long, Monica felt as if she were intruding on a hot round of foreplay.

She cleared her throat. "You two done over there?"

Allie raised her head, with a playful smile on her lips. Trevor's gray eyes were darker now, and Monica had no doubt if they'd been alone, he would have nailed her sister right there on the table, next to the blueberry muffins.

Allie settled into a seat. "We have a lot of ground to cover today."

Get it together, Campbell. Keep your mind off Calum, and force Allie to stay on point. "I have an hour before I need to head back to the office."

"It'll take as long as it takes," Allie said.

"That may be true, but I'm leaving in an hour." Monica pulled the tablet from her bag and turned it on.

Before Allie could respond, Monica's younger sister, Brynn, walked into the room. "Hey, Mon, Cal Hughes is here. Do you remember him from Dad's wedding? Because he remembered you." She parked herself in a chair.

"What do you mean?" Surely he hadn't mentioned their garden grope to Brynn? She felt Allie's appraisal but refused to look up.

"He asked how you were. Wondered if you still lived

in Vegas. He just jetted in from Australia two days ago," Brynn said.

"Fascinating." And now he was looking for a fuck-buddy. Well he could look somewhere else. She refused to spend one more minute talking about Hot Ass Hughes. Monica switched her attention to Allie. "Why couldn't you come to the office for our meeting? I've had to rearrange my entire afternoon."

"Because Cal's here," Allie said. *So much for changing the subject*. "I didn't want to be a bad hostess."

"You're not a hostess, because he's not staying here," Trevor said, glancing up from his phone. "He's staying at a hotel. I've not changed my mind about that."

Brynn plucked a muffin from the platter and peeled back the paper. "He's not staying at a hotel, he's staying at one of *the* villas." Her dark hair and delicate bone structure weren't the only things that set Brynn apart from her sisters. She was also incredibly shy with strangers. But apparently Cal didn't qualify as one.

Monica gave up trying to change the course of the conversation and indulged her curiosity. Only movie stars, whales, and foreign zillionaires stayed in the exclusive casino villas. "What does Cal do for a living anyway, run a country?"

"He fixes cars," Brynn said.

There had to be more to the story. Monica had dated her fair share of motorheads in the past, and none of them had been rolling in expendable income. Cars were a pricey hobby.

"According to English here"—Allie wagged her thumb in Trevor's direction—"Cal's *the shit* of the old-car world."

"Not old cars, darling, vintage cars," Trevor corrected. "Classics. And he is *the shit*—an artist, really, when it suits him. He doesn't just fix them, he restores them to their former glory."

"He's working on the Mustang here because our garage is so tricked out," Allie said.

"Yes, lucky us." Rising from the table, Trevor threw down his napkin and gave Allie a final kiss. "See you later. And remember ladies, play nice." He patted Brynn's head on his way out of the room.

Shoving aside her empty plate, Allie opened the binder and clicked her pen. "All right, let's get started. The gala's less than eight weeks away, and there are details we need to go over, starting with the linens."

Monica had an urge to bang her head against the table until she was semiconscious. "Al, you know I don't care about this shit. My priority is fund-raising."

Allie raised one pale brow. "Since we're all a part of the foundation, we all need to decide these things."

"Isn't this what the event planner is for?" Monica didn't care if they used white tablecloths or pink, had tea roses or calla lilies. She had one goal: to raise more money than last year. She needed to tap donors and contact sponsors. The rest was just a time suck.

"Do you want to bitch, or do you want to get through this as quickly as possible?" Allie asked. "Because if you want to bitch, it might throw off your precious timetable." Her tone remained pleasant, but Allie was on the verge of a full-blown snit fit—that placid, disingenuous smile gave her away.

Brynn sighed. "Stop it, both of you. I didn't take time off work to listen to another argument. Monica, we're already here—let's plow through this. Allie, we don't need to approve each and every minor issue. We trust your judgment. Just give us the highlights."

Allie's gaze clashed with Monica's. Finally, Monica nodded. "That sounds like a good compromise."

"Agreed," Allie said.

For the next thirty minutes, Monica tried to pay attention to Allie's concerns about lighting and who should be allowed to sit at the front table, but she couldn't concentrate. Against her will, her mind kept drifting back to that night with Cal.

Monica had just broken up with one of her deadbeat boyfriends—she couldn't remember his name. When Cal had swaggered into the room with his brash attitude and disarming smile, Monica had allowed the immediate attraction she felt to override her grief. And after the ceremony, she couldn't remember what they'd talked about, only that she couldn't wait to get him alone. She'd nearly dragged him out to the garden.

The way he'd kissed her, touched her, set Monica on fire in seconds—the man had some wicked skills. If Allie hadn't come thrashing through the hydrangeas, Cal would have been just another entry on Monica's long list of past mistakes.

Now she was a completely different person from that brazen, irresponsible girl he'd kissed in the garden. She no longer hooked up with strangers, or stripped on top of pool tables, and she didn't put herself in compromising positions. She had a serious job, a life, a home of her own. Cal was right about one thing—Monica had grown up.

"Mon?" Allie's voice derailed Monica's train of thought, pulling her back into the moment.

"What?"

"I asked how many donors you've contacted," Allie said.

"I'll send you a copy of my master list, along with the spreadsheets. Anything else? I need to go."

Allie closed her binder. "I thought we'd have a family dinner tonight, since Cal's in town. Seven o'clock? Trevor's parents are coming, along with Pixie and Paolo." Cal's mom, Pixie, went miles past eccentric and took a left toward loony. Her much younger Italian husband, Paolo, didn't speak much, but his lack of communication seemed to work in their favor.

"That sounds like fun," Monica said, "but I have too much going on at the office." Actually, it didn't sound like fun at all, and while she did have a mountain of work to do, in reality, she wanted to stay as far away from Cal Hughes as possible. As soon as he left Vegas, Monica would breathe a little easier. She wasn't sure if she could trust herself around him. The fact that she'd been struck immobile by the sight of him was a knock to her hard-won self-restraint. Plus, Monica had been on a sex-free diet for three months now. And like all diets, it sucked. Calum was more tempting than triple-chocolate cake. *Just one taste.*

She wouldn't stop at one taste—that was the problem.

"I know how busy you are," Allie said, "but you can take the night off, Mon."

"Nope, sorry."

Brynn rose from the table and stretched her arms above her head. "I'll be here, but I may be a little late. I've been putting in some overtime."

Monica and Allie exchanged a glance. "At least tell me you're getting paid for it, Brynnie," Monica said.

Brynn's eyes slid to the sideboard, where yellow roses filled an antique crystal vase. "My boss bought me lunch the other day. Does that count?" Brynn was a wonderful person—sweet, kind, funny. Assertive? Not so much.

"No, it doesn't," Allie said. "Quit letting her take advantage of you."

Brynn crossed her arms. "Cassandra is helpless, you guys. She's not a bad person, she's just flaky."

"You're doing all the work, and she takes all the credit," Monica said, feeling frustrated on Brynn's behalf. "Which is why you should demand a raise."

"I will, okay?" Brynn pushed her chair beneath the table. "Just not today. And stop ganging up on me. I like it better when you're fighting with each other." She walked out of the room with a wave. "See you later."

Allie poured herself a cup of coffee and stared after Brynn. "She worries me."

"Yeah. She needs to stand up for herself."

They sat in silence for a few minutes. Monica had some things she needed to discuss with Allie, but the quiet was soothing. If Monica broached her ideas about the foundation, the peace between them would come to a record-screeching halt. So much for giving Brynn advice about standing up to her boss. Monica needed to grow a pair herself before dispensing wisdom to her little sister.

So instead of getting into another argument with Allie, Monica shoved her tablet into her bag and stood. "I'll give you a status report next week."

"Why don't you just cc me on everything?" Allie said. "I think we should set up another food tasting too. I'm not feeling those salmon puffs. Also, make sure our emcee is booked for the right date. We don't want a repeat of last year."

"You're never going to let me live that down, are you? He was only an hour late." Yeah, that silence thing was nice while it lasted. "I'm on top of this, Al. I've got it covered. You need to trust me."

"Don't get defensive, I'm just double-checking. Also, we have a meeting with the event planner on Thursday. And I'd like you to contact every media outlet. We need coverage."

"The PR committee is in charge of media. Why don't we let them do their job?"

"Because if you don't stay on top of people, details can fall through the cracks. Please contact everyone again? You know how crazy I get with these events. I want it to go smoothly."

"Fine, if it'll shut you up, I'll do it." With a sigh, Monica turned toward the door and tried to make a clean break, but Allie asked one more question.

"Have you talked to Ryan?"

There it was. "No, why would I?"

Monica had dated Ryan for over a year. Her family loved him, and her friends adored him. Monica's feelings didn't go that far. And while she still had occasional moments of doubt for breaking up with him, she'd done the right thing. Monica had desperately wanted to take his ring and build a future together. It sounded so good in theory, but when it came down to the execution, she couldn't go through with it. Which was a damn shame, because Ryan was nearly perfect.

Since their breakup, Monica had done a lot of soul searching, thinking about her old, destructive patterns, the ones that had tripped her up in the past—saying yes to the wrong type of guy when she needed to say *fuck off and get a job*, and her inability to settle down with Ryan, a man who truly loved her.

Monica suspected she was defective. For certain, she had a broken picker. Given a room full of decent men and one bad boy, Monica chose the latter every single time. Tatted-up asshole? Two scoops, please. Unemployed heartbreaker? Bring it on.

And now Cal Hughes. If that kiss five years ago was anything to go by, he was all kinds of wrong for her.

"Ryan called me last week," Allie said.

Monica blinked. Twice. Familiar anger churned in her gut. Allie simply couldn't stop herself from sticking her nose into Monica's business. As director of the foundation's board, Allie may be the boss at work, but Monica's personal life was just that. "You need to stay out of this, Al. I mean it. I can handle my own relationships without your help."

Allie rubbed her fingers across her forehead. "He just wondered how you were doing. He's so sweet, I didn't have the heart to hang up."

"Commiserating won't help him move on."

"He's so good for you, Mon."

Defective. "I have to go." Monica adjusted her grip on the computer bag and strode out of the room.

Allie trotted after her. "Hey listen, I'm sorry I overstepped. If he calls again, I won't talk to him. It's none of my business." It never was, but that rarely stopped Allie from interfering.

Monica briefly closed her eyes. "No, it's fine. Do what you want, just leave me out of the conversation."

"No, I shouldn't have butted in. And I've been meaning to tell you, you're doing a great job. I see how hard you work. I'm really proud of you." Allie lightly squeezed Monica's upper arm. "Mom would be proud too."

"Thanks." She appreciated Allie's peace offering, even though she wasn't buying it. Monica seriously doubted her mother was looking down on her with pride. If Trisha Campbell watched over her from some celestial cloud, she was probably shaking her head, wondering why Monica couldn't get her shit together. Her mother would have loved Ryan. And she definitely wouldn't approve of men like Calum Hughes. He was the equivalent of doughnuts or fried cheese sticks. There was zero nutritional value in the Cals of this world. Sexy junk food.

And Monica was on the wagon for good.

She smiled for Allie's benefit. "Before I leave, I'll tell Trevor good-bye."

"Okay." Allie dropped her hand. "And think about coming for dinner tonight. The twins have been asking for Aunt Monnie."

"That's because I sneak them chocolate when you're not looking."

Allie grinned. "I know. And they love you for it."

Monica nodded and walked down the long hallway to Trevor's office. She didn't just want to say good-bye, she needed to run her idea by him. He probably wouldn't be receptive, but it was worth a shot. Rapping her knuckles on the thick wooden door, she opened it and peered inside. "Did I catch you at a bad time?"

Trevor glanced up from one of his computer screens. "Yes, but come in anyway."

Monica always felt as if she were breaching the inner sanctum when she walked into Trevor's office. Like the rest of the house, it overflowed with antique pieces, paintings, and oddities, but this room was command central, where Trevor made his fortune.

She took a chair in front of his desk. "I wanted to talk to you about the foundation's goals for next year." A big part of Monica's job entailed whittling down grant applications. She spent a lot of time staring at statistics and cost projections. Not her favorite part of the gig, but necessary. "I've been doing some research." She pulled a folder from her bag and handed it to Trevor. "Take a look at that. Developing countries are in desperate need of oncology training and equipment. They're lacking the most basic care. We could open up the grants next year, go international. Spread the wealth a little."

Taking his time, Trevor read through the file. Monica could almost see his big brain processing all the facts as his frown deepened. "You'd be broadening the scope of the foundation's agenda considerably. You'd have to develop relationships with individual clinics, hospitals, medical schools. That's a lot of extra work, and it would strain our resources."

"The payoff would be worth it. We're on target for more donations this year. It might mean taking on a consultant, hiring a couple more employees, but it would put us on the international map."

His eyes met hers. "Have you talked to Allison about this?"

"Not yet. I was kind of hoping you might mention it. Pave the way for me."

He shut the folder and tossed it on his desk. "Forget it. Do your own dirty work. I'm not going to get involved in a squabble between sisters. Especially you two."

"Trevor, please—"

"No. She'd be angry with both of us if I approached her instead of you." He held up his hand to stave off her words. "I like fucking your sister. When she's angry with me, I don't get to do that. Sorry, darling, you're on your own."

"First of all, eww. I'd prefer not to know the details of your sexy time. Second, you're pussy whipped. I expected more from you, and I'm deeply disappointed." Pressing her lips together, Monica slowly shook her head.

With a laugh, Trevor stood and handed the folder back. "I'm utterly pussy whipped. And I quite enjoy it. Talk to Allison. If you believe in this, convince her."

"Thanks for nothing. You know she won't listen to me."

"Sorry." Pity filled his eyes.

Monica looked away and grabbed her bag. Feeling deflated, she let herself out of Trevor's office and, instead of leaving by the side door as she usually did, headed to the front in an effort to dodge Cal and his bare torso. She felt like a complete coward for not wanting to face him, but she did it just the same.

As Monica walked outside into the hot morning sun, Calum Hughes sat fully clothed on the hood of her Honda, waiting. When he saw her, a wide grin broke over his face.

Well, hell. She just couldn't catch a break today.

Chapter 3

HE'D BEEN SITTING HERE FOR OVER FORTY MINUTES, waiting. How long could one meeting last, for God's sake? And what kind of meeting? Did Monica work for Trevor? She dressed like a bean counter, that much was certain. The suit, that horrible, boxy black jacket—it didn't fit her at all. Oh, it looked fine, dull as dishwater of course, but it didn't suit *her*, Monica Campbell, the girl with the wild hair and devilish eyes.

Cal remembered her clearly, had thought about her from time to time over the years. He fantasized about what would have happened had they not been interrupted.

Her father's wedding had been a small, intimate gathering—just family. Afterward, as he'd stood in the conservatory chatting her up, she'd been lively, flirtatious. Her hair tumbled down her back in thick honeyed waves, and occasionally she'd toss her head, causing them to bounce. The perfume she'd worn smelled lightly sweet, with a hint of spice. It reminded him of a winter he'd spent in Germany for some odd reason. And Monica had worn a red dress—*rosso alfa*, almost the exact color of a 1968 Alfa Romeo Spider. Not just any red, but a deep, dark scarlet. Strapless and glittery, it had showed off her tits, and was short enough to give him a glimpse of her fit legs.

Yeah, he remembered her—had almost total recall of the event. How she'd felt in his arms, the weight of her breast in his hand. Her lips had tasted sweet, fresh, with a hint of champagne. And if Allison hadn't stopped them, he'd have fucked Monica Campbell against the garden wall and enjoyed every bloody minute of it.

However, looking back, that may have been taking advantage of her. The thought never would have occurred to his younger self. Cal had simply seen a girl looking for a bit of slap, and he'd been eager to provide it. But she'd teetered on the brink of recklessness that night. He hadn't understood it at the time—he'd simply enjoyed being on the receiving end of all that attention. Now he realized how hard it must have been for her, watching her father marry a new woman. In essence, replacing her mother. He couldn't say he was *glad* they hadn't shagged that night, but perhaps it was for the best.

One thing Cal did know: he wanted another chance with her. Monica was older now, in control of her emotions. Too much so for his liking. She could do with a bit of loosening up.

This morning he'd barely recognized her. Her hair was several inches shorter. She'd forced it into behaving, taming the waves into a more manageable style. And while her eyes were the same crystal blue, he sensed something like unease in their depths.

While her voice had been cool and impersonal, she'd held that bag in front of her as if she were hiding behind it. The dreadful suit she wore was a buffer as well, camouflaging her amazing curves.

Ah, those sweet curves. Cal remembered them fondly. Firm, high breasts. Ripe, round ass. And her upper lip, noticeably fuller than the bottom one, drove him wild.

He wanted to kiss her again, see if she tasted as untamed and sweet as she had that night.

Probably not. She was different now, more serious, less impulsive. At least outwardly—the suit, the chic haircut, the sensible shoes. But when Cal removed her sunglasses, he saw a flash of vulnerability cross her face. He still sensed a feral wildness running through her. It called to him. She may want to deny her true nature, but he suspected that delightfully fun girl with a wicked smile was still in there somewhere, hovering beneath the surface.

Cal found himself utterly fascinated. What had happened to the fearless Monica he'd met a few years ago? Where had she gone, and why?

Although Cal never claimed to be clever, he knew one thing: no matter what a vehicle looked like on the outside, it was what lay beneath the hood that told the real story. Monica was like that Mustang he'd just bought. The outside had been tampered with, its beauty hidden by filler and some rust. But inside, it still had heart, and with a little time and effort, he'd have it up and running again. Monica had a lot going on inside of her too. He could see it in her eyes. This prim and proper exterior wasn't the whole picture. It couldn't possibly be.

Finally, the front door opened, and the woman who'd infiltrated his every thought for the past hour walked out of the house. "Hello, again," he said. Though he might be unable to read her features behind the dark glasses, her body language was wary. Monica held herself immobile, like a frightened animal on the verge of running. In an effort to calm her, Cal shot her his friendliest smile.

"Hello," she finally said. With jerky movements, she

headed down the steps and walked toward him. "What are you doing here?"

"This isn't an existential question, is it? I'm afraid I'm not contemplative enough for those."

She remained quiet a moment, her hands tightening on the handle of her bag. "Brynn said you just got into town?"

Had she lost her sense of humor, as well? "Yes, I'm here for my mother's anniversary party."

"What anniversary party?"

"Quite. Turns out Pix's anniversary was six months ago. My fault, I suppose, for not remembering the date, so here I am."

The edges of Monica's mouth pulled downward. "Why would your mother lie to you?"

"Pixie has her own reasons for doing things. It's best to go along and not ask too many questions."

Monica turned to the large stone fountain, where water trickled over the tiers and into the basin. It made a splashing sound and sent droplets sputtering onto the paved brick drive. "How long are you in town?"

Why wouldn't she look at him? Was he covered in grease stains? Cal swiped a hand over his cheeks, felt for sticky residue, but didn't find any. "Don't know, really. I rarely make plans." Vegas was as good a place as any to park his bones. London didn't appeal, even though his garage and showroom were there. Yet for the first time in his life, Cal wasn't eager to get to it. He sure as hell wasn't going back to Australia. The very thought of it filled him with a deep sadness he couldn't shake. At least Vegas had the mystery of Monica Campbell going for it.

"How does that work, exactly?" she asked. "Living life with no plans, no rules?" She inclined her head upward, and he assumed she was looking at him. Tough to tell with those dark lenses.

"Works out quite nicely. When I'm ready for a change of scenery, I hop a plane and see where it takes me. Haven't you ever wanted to do that? Just take off on a moment's notice and have yourself an adventure?"

Monica threw back her shoulders. "Some of us have jobs and people who depend on us."

Ooo, that prim, judgmental tone scraped along his nerves. He should be used to it—had gotten an assful of it from his father over the years—but still it stung, coming from her.

And what was so fabulous about having someone depend on you, anyway?

Glancing away, Cal planted his hands on his thighs. His lips slid into a grin. It felt stiff and forced. "Why don't you have dinner with me tonight? You can tell me all about your important responsibilities and this meeting you've just had." Which should take approximately ten minutes. After that, he planned on seducing her. A genuine smile replaced the false one. The thought of spending the rest of the night fucking Monica Campbell, watching her shed that uptight persona and fall to pieces as he buried himself inside her—it excited him like nothing else had in a while.

His cock became rigid just thinking about it. To hide his hard-on, he leaned forward and rested his elbows on his thighs.

"Allie's planning a family dinner for you," she said. "Your mother and Paolo are coming."

Well, shit. He didn't feel up to socializing, but if he could stare at Monica throughout the evening, he might be able to suffer through. "You'll be there?"

"No, I have to work."

He studied her carefully. Her shoulders hitched up ever so slightly, and her lips flattened into a straight line. She was lying. Did she have other plans, or was she avoiding him? If so, why?

Hopping off the car, he slowly crossed to her. When he reached striking distance, he once again snatched the sunglasses from her face. When she tried to grab them back, he held them aloft. He wanted to see her eyes, read what was going on in that head of hers.

"Hey, stop doing that." She placed a hand on his forearm and tugged. "Give them back."

Cal bowed down until only a few inches separated his face from hers. Truly lovely. Her skin was flawlessly pale, except for a grouping of four freckles scattered above the arch of her eyebrow. They were tiny and covered with powder, but up close, he could count them. Such white skin was unusual for someone living in a sun-drenched desert. She must spend all of her time indoors. "If you agree to have dinner with me, you may have them back."

Her wide eyes flew to his, and he detected a hint of fear. *Fear?* Of what, of him? That seemed unlikely. Women liked Cal, adored him, actually. He put them at ease, not on their guard. Had been doing so since he was a lad.

He gazed down to where her hand gripped his arm. The back of it was delicate with longish, pretty fingers and buffed nails. Nothing so frivolous as a pop of colored nail varnish for grown-up, responsible Monica.

Then a thought struck him—perhaps she no longer found him attractive. Could that be it? He took one deliberate step closer.

She audibly swallowed, and the pulse at the base of her neck fluttered like a trapped bird. No, she wasn't immune to him. Not at all.

She took a half step backward. "I'm not having dinner with you, Cal. I'm busy."

"Oh dear, this happens occasionally," he said with a tsk.

A little vertical crease appeared in the middle of her forehead as her brows drew together. "What does?"

"Some women can't control themselves around me, you know," he whispered, "sexually. It's my cross to bear. But I promise I won't give in, no matter how much you beg."

He expected her to laugh. But her blue gaze became darker, sharper, as her jaw muscles tightened. He stared at the little dent in the center of her chin, wanted to sweep his tongue over it. He'd ignited her anger. Good. At least she could still feel something.

"You're not half as charming as you think you are," she said.

"Right, but all in all, that's still pretty charming, isn't it?" Gently, he placed the glasses back on the bridge of her nose. Then he moved around her, and with a long-legged gait, walked to the house. "See you tonight, love," he said before slipping inside.

Shutting the door, Cal grinned. As of this morning, he felt more alive, more engaged than he had in months. He actually looked forward to something: teasing the bloody hell out of Monica Campbell.

Seducing her might be more difficult than he'd first thought. And getting her to drop that straitlaced image would be a challenge. But he was up to it. There was something truly horrifying about a naughty girl turned saint. It offended his delicate sensibilities.

Cal pushed off the door and strode from the foyer into a hallway, intent on finding Trevor. Turning a corner, he almost ran headlong into Allie. "Whoops," he said, reaching out to steady her shoulders. "Sorry about that."

She smiled. "No problem. How are you?"

"Very well. You're looking beautiful. Pink suits you."

"Thanks. I was just about to come and get you, see if you wanted a cup of coffee." She led the way to the drawing room, where Grecian busts and porcelain bowls covered almost every surface. "You know you don't have to stay in a hotel. You're welcome here. Don't let Trevor's bark fool you. He's a softy." She sat on one of the sofas and poured coffee from a silver pot.

He could call Trevor many things, most of them less than complimentary, but *softy* wasn't among them. "Thank you, Allison." He took the delicate china cup in one hand and sat across from her. "I'm perfectly happy in the villa." He rubbed his earlobe between his thumb and forefinger. "I chatted with your sister outside just now. She seemed..." He deliberately left the conversational door open, hoping Allie would walk through it. He wanted to know more about Monica. Was she seeing someone? Surely not, or she would have used it as an excuse not to have dinner with him.

"She seemed what?" Allie asked.

Well, so much for that ploy. "Grown-up, very professional." *Really, Cal? That's the best you could come up with?* But what the hell was he supposed to say? *Your sister still looks shagirific, Allie. I do hope she'll allow me to fuck her until her knees wobble this time.* Compared with that, professional didn't seem half-bad.

Allie nodded. "She is. Monica takes her job very seriously."

"What is her job, exactly? Funeral director? School marm?"

Allie's pale brows rose a fraction. "She works for the foundation."

"What foundation would that be?"

The smile slowly faded from her lips. "Pix didn't mention it?"

"Of course she did. I just forgot. Very important work, foundations."

Allie broke out laughing. "You have no idea what the hell I'm talking about, do you?"

He grinned. "Guilty."

"We run a breast cancer foundation, and Monica's our coordinator. She spends a lot of time looking over grants and helping organize fund-raisers. She's come a long way."

How very fucking dreary that sounded. Sexy Monica had turned into a glorified office drone? He refused to believe it. "What do you mean she's come a long way? From where?"

With her eyes cast downward, Allie used her thumb to stroke the saucer's edge. "It took Monica a while to figure things out, but she's on a really good path now." Her gaze lifted to meet his. "Do you understand what I'm saying?"

"Not really. Explain it to me." Allie was warning him

to stay away from Monica, clearly. But he wasn't going to be put off that easily. When Cal wanted something badly enough, he became rather persistent. It once took him two years to track down all the original parts for a '56 Arnolt-Bristol Roadster, but in the end, he got what he wanted. And he found himself very much wanting Monica Campbell, and not just sexually. He needed to know what made her tick.

"Monica used to have a wild streak," Allie said. "In the past few years, she's calmed down. She's working hard, making good choices. I know the two of you had a romantic moment the last time you met, but I'm asking you to leave her alone, Cal. I don't think you're right for each other."

"Right for each other?" he repeated. What the hell was she on about? Had he suddenly wandered into a Jane Austen novel? Cal wasn't some naff off the street—he was Trevor's cousin, for God's sake. Cal naturally fancied Monica. Wanted to fuck her senseless, but he didn't need Allie's permission for that.

He set his cup and saucer on the table between them. "I appreciate your sisterly concern, but Monica's a grown woman. Surely she can make her own decisions."

When he'd seen Monica this morning, so dowdy and buttoned up to her eyeballs, he'd been gobsmacked. Yet Allison sat here like butter wouldn't melt in her mouth and talked about good choices, as if her sister were a schoolgirl. Obviously Monica needed to break out of the cocoon she'd encased herself in. For whatever reason, she'd turned her life around so dramatically, she must be miserable. Tempting the proper Monica to embrace the fun-loving side of her nature sounded more marvelous with each passing minute.

Allie slowly nodded. "Of course she can make her own decisions. Look, I like you, Cal. You're charming and handsome and seem like a decent guy. But I don't want to see my sister get hurt." Her baby-blue eyes turned serious. "So let this be a warning to your balls. I assume you *like* them attached to your body?"

Cal stood and thrust his hands into his pockets. "They're quite happy where they are, thank you for inquiring." He fought a sudden urge to cup his jewels in case she decided to make a dive for them. "Message received." It didn't change his plans about seducing Monica, but one always appreciated advance warning.

Cal tipped his head and, turning, made his way from the room. It wasn't the first time a girl's overprotective loved one had warned him off. Probably wouldn't be the last. But Monica was a big girl who could take care of herself. He didn't want to hurt her—he wanted to liberate her.

As Cal wandered through the house in search of Trevor, he glanced through the various displayed collections of antique whatnots their grandfather had accumulated over the years. Trevor was now the keeper of all this rubbish, and good luck to him. Everything from cigar boxes to Japanese swords to birds' eggs. The old man had been the original eccentric.

Cal finally found Trevor's office and, after giving a perfunctory knock, strolled in. "What are you up to, then?"

Trevor's eyes flashed on Cal before returning to the computer screen. "It's called work. You should try it sometime."

"No thanks." With a grin, Cal fell into the chair in front of Trevor's massive desk. "Sounds painfully boring. By the way, your lovely wife just threatened my bollocks."

"I'm sure she had her reasons. So when are you leaving town?"

"You're the second person who's asked me that in the last half hour. Why is everyone so anxious to get rid of me? I was made for Vegas."

"Personally, I couldn't care less what you do. I just wondered how long you planned on keeping that rusty shitpile in my garage."

The Mustang. Cal had bought it on a whim. As the taxi had driven him around the city, he'd seen it parked in someone's driveway, and made an offer. It needed a lot of work, but tinkering gave him something constructive to do. Kept his mind occupied, at any rate. "I could rent a place to house it if you'd like, and get it out of your hair."

Trevor shot him a glance. "How was Australia? You don't seem keen."

Although Cal hadn't clapped eyes on his cousin in years, Trevor had an uncanny way of seeing what no one else did. "Me, I'm brilliant. And Australia was sunny. It's always sunny down under."

"According to Pix, you were there for over a year. That's unusual for you. And as soon as you get into town, you buy a car to work on, which suggests you plan on staying long enough to fix it. Did a girl finally figure you out and give you the heave-ho?"

Instead of getting defensive—his first instinct—Cal relaxed in his chair. "Since when do you dole out advice to the walking wounded? Has marriage turned you into an agony aunt? As for Australia—it's loaded with fast cars, faster women, and a wicked surf."

"Fine, I'll stay out of your business. And no, you don't have to rent a garage. You can work on it here. For some reason, your bollocks excluded, Allison likes you. And Mags would have my head if I kicked you out."

"How is your mum, Trev? Still shacking up with your father?"

Trevor briefly closed his eyes and inhaled deeply. "Don't get me started on those two. Now go. I need to work." Turning his gaze to the center screen, Trevor dismissed him.

Cal left the office and walked outside, back to the car. He grabbed a wrench and ducked under the hood. The last thing he wanted to think about was Australia. So he thought about Monica instead, and all the ways he wanted her. She wouldn't be a pushover—she'd proven that this morning. But Cal could be very persuasive. Monica Campbell would be in his bed sooner rather than later, if he had anything to say about it.

On her drive to work, Monica couldn't get Calum Hughes out of her mind. Why did he have to show up now, when her resistance to inappropriate men was so low?

Irritated with herself, she pulled into a parking spot and slammed on the brakes. She had a million details to worry about with this gala coming up, and she didn't have time to pine over that hot piece of British ass. She wasn't going out with him either, although it had taken every bit of willpower she had to turn down his dinner invitation. Especially when he kept walking toward her slowly, each step deliberate, like a tiger stalking his next meal. Or when he'd lowered his face to hers. An inch closer, and she could have lifted her chin, spanned the distance between them, and tasted him. She could have seen for herself if his lips were as talented as she remembered. But she hadn't.

Congratulations, Campbell. You showed a modicum of restraint. Do you want a gold star?

Monica grabbed her bags and strode into the building. Hopping on the elevator, she pulled out her phone and glanced at her revised schedule. A meeting with a sponsor, cost projections to go over with the accountant, a staff meeting later in the afternoon.

When she'd started as an intern at the foundation, Monica had done everything, from stuffing envelopes to brainstorming new ideas for fund-raisers. What she loved most was interacting with people—everyone from recipients to donors. After she'd earned her master's in public administration two years ago, Allie had put her in charge of running the show. Well, in theory anyway. In reality, Allie kept a very tight rein on both Monica and the foundation. Now Monica spent her days not only pacifying her big sister, but six other board members as well.

Walking down the hall and into the suite, she found Stella Greene waiting for her. "Good, you're here." The office manager twisted the pink scarf knotted at her neck. "Things have been crazy this morning."

"What happened?" Monica glanced around the open space at her ten employees. They all appeared busy, not harried.

Now in her fifties, Stella had spent the last thirty years

working for some of the toughest people in Vegas—tourists. As a hotel concierge, her job had been to remain unflustered and make the guests happy, so seeing her have a mini-freakout gave Monica pause.

"The printers screwed up the date on the gala tickets, two donors called and asked to speak to you specifically, and Mr. Stanford is here. He's been waiting in your office for over an hour."

Ah, so that's what caused the panic. Marcus Stanford was a pain in Monica's ass, and her most difficult board member. He asked for ballsy favors, tried to co-opt the foundation's staff for his own business purposes, and had a remarkable knack for showing up on hectic days. "What does he want?"

"No idea," Stella said. "I'm sorry I let him into your office. He tends to steamroll right over me."

"Don't take it personally, he does that with everyone." She moved past Stella and waved at Carmen Jimenez. The thirty-year-old mother of two was talking on the phone, but when she spied Monica, she placed her hand over the receiver. "The liquor company wants their name on the signage. Too tacky for a cancer event?"

Monica lifted one brow.

"Fine," she said, "but they're going to bitch about it."

Jason West strolled up to her with a half-eaten doughnut in his hand. "We need a new server, because ours is shit. Should I call Allie? And I hid a doughnut for you in the sweetener box, but it's blueberry. Stanford got the last chocolate."

A tide of frustration rose inside Monica—not about the doughnut, although blueberry was her least favorite. As the foundation's coordinator, Monica held the title, yet none of the power. Every decision needed to be filtered through Allie. Monica's crappy morning had drained her of patience, and she was feeling a little rebellious. "Just get what you need, and I'll authorize it." She could defend herself at the next board meeting. And if Allie didn't like it, too bad.

Jason toasted her with his Bavarian cream. "Excellent."

"What about the misprinted tickets?" Stella asked.

"Tell the printer to do it again. And he's paying for it. If he gives you grief, I'll talk to him myself."

"I'm on it." Stella gave her scarf one last tug and hustled to her desk.

Immediate fires now doused, Monica made her way down the hall and slapped a smile on her face before opening her office door. But when she saw Marcus Stanford sitting in her chair with his dirty work boots propped up on her desk, it threatened to slip.

With graying hair and skin the color of red brick, he wasn't unattractive, but he was arrogant and overbearing. His construction company was worth millions, and he had ties all over Vegas. He'd given a hefty donation in return for a board seat, but he hadn't done a bit of work since. He also liked to throw his weight around, and today, he was throwing it in Monica's direction.

"Mr. Stanford, how are you, sir? Can I get you some coffee? You take it black, right?"

"No thanks. Good memory, though."

"Is there something I can do for you?" *Extra gift bags for the wife, donors' private phone numbers?* He'd asked for that and more. Her answer was always the same: *No, it's against foundation rules.*

"Of course there is, why else would I be sitting here?

We're getting ready to vote on next year's budget, and I want you to open up the grants. Cast a wider net, so to speak."

That was a surprisingly thoughtful request and coincided with her own goals—providing funds for impoverished countries. "I'll consider it. The board would have to go along with any changes."

Stanford lowered his feet to the floor and stood. "Count me in. My wife's charity, Parents for a Healthy Tomorrow or Today or some such bullshit...anyway, they'll fill out an application. Make sure they get a cut."

She should have seen it coming. Monica really was off her game this morning. And she blamed Cal Hughes. His tight ass and uneven smile made her lose perspective.

Monica stared at Stanford, amazed at the size of his brass cojones, then simply shook her head. "You know I can't do that—it's a conflict of interest." Besides, grant approval was an exacting process. Monica spent months scouring through hundreds, sometimes thousands of applications, carefully examining each possible charity. "Is your wife interested in cancer prevention? We'd love to have her help—"

"Nah, my wife's just trying to get kids off the junk food." He strutted to the door. "You wouldn't believe the lengths I have to go to to sneak a burger."

She swiveled her head to follow his movements. "Mr. Stanford, I'm sorry. I'm not going to award funds to your wife's project."

He paused with his hand on the doorknob. "Look, you seem like a good kid, but let's face it, you got this job because you're related to Trevor Blake's wife. It keeps you occupied, and that's great. But this is a tax write-off, and nothing more. Just give my wife a few million. I'll consider it a personal favor." He winked and left the office, shutting the door behind him.

Monica let out a shaky breath. True, she had gotten the job because she was Allie's sister, but Monica had worked her ass off for the past two years to prove she could handle the responsibility, and yet everyone looked at her like she was Allie's lapdog. And that didn't sit well at all.

"What a fuckwad," she said to the empty room.

Ultimately, the nepotism didn't matter. Not if she continued to work hard and successfully tackled the demands of the job. Monica had made so many mistakes in the past, she needed this, needed to show Allie that she'd changed.

Monica swiped her palm across the desk blotter where Stanford's big feet had left behind a clump of dirt. After booting up her laptop, she put her self-doubts and Calum Hughes from her mind. She had work to do.

Chapter 4

Monica plowed steadily through her day. Stella brought her a salad at noon, and Monica took bites in between phone calls. She met briefly with the staff to make sure everyone was on task, and she touched base with the local media outlets about the upcoming event. Finally, Monica wanted to shore up her international grant proposal, so Allie couldn't shoot her down for not having all the facts at her fingertips.

She was so engrossed that when Stella knocked on the door and stepped into the room, Monica blinked in surprise. "Hey, what's up?"

"I'm leaving for the night."

"Oh God, it's six already?" Stretching her back, Monica tried to ease her stiff muscles. "I guess I should order some dinner."

"Not tonight," Stella said. "There's a man in the outer office asking for you. And, honey, if I were ten years younger, I'd be all over that."

"What man?" A trickle of apprehension slid through her.

"Tall, tan, and British. That voice. Mmm, *mmm*. I'll send him in."

"Wait—" But Stella had already gone. Monica had spent the entire day pushing Cal out of her mind, and now he'd popped up in person. Why wouldn't he just leave her alone?

Quickly, she pulled out a compact she kept in her desk. Gazing into the tiny mirror, she ran her fingers through her hair, then snapped it shut in disgust and threw it back in the drawer. She wasn't going out with him. She'd firmly tell him no and get him to accept it this time. And if her makeup was a mess, so what?

Monica's hand flew to the hollow of her throat as she stood. With shaky fingers, she fastened the top two buttons on her shirt. She probably looked Amish, but she didn't care.

Cal walked in a moment later. The tattered jeans from this morning had been replaced by a slightly less faded pair, which he teamed with a black button-down. He'd rolled the sleeves up to reveal his lean, tanned forearms. The stubble from this morning had disappeared, leaving his face smooth. Groomed or not—the man looked sinfully hot either way.

"Had a good day, love?"

"What are you doing here?" In spite of her best intentions, Monica's gaze slowly slid over him. He even wore a pair of black motorcycle boots. Goddamn it. Was he trying to make her come on the spot? If he flashed another glimpse of that tattoo, it was a real possibility.

She forced her eyes back up to his face. To that irritating smirk he wore.

"We were having dinner, remember?"

"No, we weren't. I told you I had to work."

He snapped his fingers. "That's right, so you did." He glanced around, taking in the picture window that framed the orange sun hanging low in the sky. "You spend all day, every day, in this little box, do you?"

"It's called an office. People work in rooms like this

all over the world." Being in such a small space with him made her muscles tighten. Tension, electric and immediate, thrummed through her body. She needed to be on her guard, ready for combat.

"Reminds me of a zoo," he said and began wandering around. He took in the framed photos of various distinguished events and tapped the glass of one picture. "You look good in blue," he said with his back to her. When he turned, his leaf-green eyes flickered in assessment, taking in her high-collared blouse. "I think I like you best in red, though. Dark red."

Monica's gaze traveled over the pictures on the wall. She wore subdued colors in all of them. She hadn't worn red in years, unless lingerie counted for something. With both hands, she tugged on the hem of her jacket, hyperaware of the way he kept staring at her.

After a few drawn-out seconds, Cal pivoted and continued to peruse the room. He sauntered to the opposite wall and stopped in front of a large oil portrait. "*In loving memory of Patricia Campbell*. You named the foundation after your mother?"

"Trevor did." Monica faced the desk and adjusted the angle of her laptop. She couldn't look at him. If she did, her defenses would weaken. Hell, they were threadbare as it was. Her stomach fluttered every time he rumbled something in that deep, sexy voice—Jason Statham crossed with James Bond. And he smelled good too—crisp and woodsy. His aftershave came wafting toward her with each step he took.

Immune. Immune. The word kept running through her mind like a chant. She clung to it as if it were a talisman.

"You look just like your mum, except your lips are

fuller, especially the upper one." He faced her then, and her eyes sought him, as if they had a will of their own. Cal's were riveted on her mouth. When she nervously bit her lower lip, that steady gaze never wavered.

"Thank you," she said, then cleared her throat. "Look, I still have work to do, so..."

With long, graceful strides, he walked over and dropped into her guest chair. "No worries, I'll wait."

How was she supposed to get any work done with him sitting there, looking at her as if he were starving and she was a T-bone? She desperately wished she hadn't buttoned her shirt all the way up to her neck, because the scratchy, stiff material was starting to itch.

In an effort to regain some control, she sat down and placed her hands flat on the top of her desk. Monica focused on his Adam's apple. If she looked too deeply into those eyes, she'd fold faster than a lowball poker player with a handful of aces. "Cal, I'm not having dinner with you. I'm going to finish my to-do list and go home."

"Oh my, I think I popped a bit of a boner just now." He grabbed his chest with one hand. "To-do lists have that effect on me."

Monica rolled her lips inward to prevent a grin. "Remind me not to show you my spreadsheet. You'll never be the same." Oh God, why was she flirting back?

"You, Monica Campbell, know how to put the sin in Sin City."

He was the tiniest bit amusing. Still, if she gave him half an inch, he'd have her flat on her back in under a minute. She knew herself too well to pretend otherwise. That bad girl part of Monica had been hibernating for the past few years, but the minute Cal Hughes blew into town, it had started to wake up and rattle around inside the tight little cage where Monica kept it. Cal represented Old Monica—the shot-slamming, bad boy–loving, promiscuous girl she used to be. *Immune, remember?*

"It was so nice of you to drop by, Cal, but I really have a lot of work to finish."

"Are you seriously going to sit here and cross off items on a list, rather than have dinner with me?"

"Yes."

He shook his head in mock sadness. "I'm profoundly disappointed. Wouldn't you rather take in a show? Or better yet, we could hit the craps table. Ever wonder what it's like to place a ten-thousand-dollar chip on one roll of the dice? I'll give you a hint," he whispered, cupping both hands around his mouth. "It's thrilling."

Monica set her jaw. "Do you know how much good you could do with ten thousand dollars?"

He rolled his eyes. "Oh God, I can't bear the earnestness. Fine, I'll make out a check to the foundation. But only if you come play with me tonight. You'll have fun, I promise."

Monica knew she sounded sanctimonious. Trevor had a boatload of money, and she never begrudged him a penny...mainly because he gave a ton of it away. But Cal was so tempting, she felt like Eve staring at a bright, shiny apple.

If he gave a donation, then that would make this a legitimate business dinner.

Sort of.

And the foundation could always use the money.

"You're rather stubborn, aren't you?" he asked. "Tell

you what." Standing, he dug into his front pocket and pulled out a silver coin. "Heads, you come out with me. Tails, I pick up takeaway and we'll eat here." He flipped the coin a foot into the air and caught it in his right hand. Holding it in his fist, he smiled. "Can you stand the anticipation? My breath is absolutely bated."

"Cal..."

He slapped it on the back of his hand. "Oh look, Her Majesty's lovely face. Out for dinner it is." He stuck the coin back in his pocket without showing it to her.

"That's cheating," she said, pointing at him. "It could have been tails."

"You'll never prove it." Placing his hands on her desk, he leaned in. "Since I took a cab, we'll have to drive your car. The Mustang's still not running properly. Hurry now, chop-chop."

She thought about arguing some more, but he was just as determined as she was. And she'd never get anything done with him sitting across from her, smelling so good and looking even better. Giving in to the inevitable, Monica shut down her computer. "Just dinner. Then I'm going home."

Cal watched her pack her bag with a look of smug satisfaction. "If that's what you really want."

"It is." Monica clicked off her desk lamp and walked to the door. "What happened to Allie's dinner party? I thought your parents were supposed to be there."

Cal huffed. "Pixie may be my mother, but Paolo is only ten years older than I am. He's not even a proper stepfather. Never took me fishing, not once." Though his tone was light, a hint of something darker colored his voice. She refused to ask him about it. Cal's life wasn't any of her business. "Besides, I told Allison I had plans with an old friend."

She gazed at him before hitting the light switch. "We're not old friends—we met once."

Before she could walk out of the room, Cal grabbed her purse strap and gave it a pull. He used it to swing her around until she faced him. Through the open door, a soft glow from the hallway allowed her to barely see his face. He looked serious in the half-light, more predatory than ever.

Monica's heart stuttered as he stepped closer. He was so much bigger than she remembered, his shoulders wider. Maybe she was misremembering their seven minutes in heaven. Maybe she'd built it up into something special when it was nothing more than a simple kiss.

But then Cal framed her face with his large hands, and she felt powerless to move as he lowered his head. She watched him descend toward her, then her eyes drifted closed. When he softly brushed her lips with his, it was all Monica could do not to give in. She wanted to open her mouth wider, stroke his tongue with her own. At his brief touch, heat pooled low in her belly. For a split second, Monica wished she was still the girl whose default was set to *yes*, because she missed this feeling, this rush of excitement. And she hadn't been imagining things. Though Cal had barely touched her lips, the effect was potent. That kiss in the garden had been epic after all.

When Cal dropped his hands and took a step backward, Monica's eyes fluttered open. "I remember snogging you that night, Monica, and touching you right here." He reached out, and with a careful, light movement, drew his finger from the edge of her collarbone down to the center of her right breast. Even through the heavy fabric of her jacket, her nipple pebbled. "If that's not friendly, what would you call it?"

At his mocking tone, desire flickered out, and humiliation took its place. He'd had her so easily, with barely a kiss. It took almost no effort on his part, and she was practically falling at his feet. She smacked his hand away. "I'd call it a mistake." With hurried steps, she scampered to the outer office.

This time when she turned off the overhead lights, she made sure she stepped out of the suite and into the lighted hallway first. She didn't want to be caught in the dark with him again—it fostered a false sense of intimacy.

Who was she kidding? Cal could have pulled that move in broad daylight and the outcome would have been the same—damp panties and limp-noodle legs.

Cal strolled out a couple seconds later. "Almost broke my toe in there," he said cheerfully. "Fumbling around in the dark is more fun when you're naked with a partner. Just a little tip for you."

"I'll keep that in mind the next time I want to fumble with someone."

He didn't offer a comeback, but followed her to the bank of elevators. "So, we'll head to your place, then off for dinner. What do you fancy?"

Monica punched the down button. "We're not going to my place."

His eyes widened, and he looked momentarily bewildered. "Don't you want to change?"

She glanced down at her pantsuit. "What is your issue with my outfit? I look fine."

"You look like a missionary."

"I'm not changing." Not her clothes, not her stance on bad boys, not her rigorous self-control. She could white-knuckle her way through one night. She was not falling off the bad-boy wagon because he'd copped a feel. It was time to get a grip.

The commas on either side of Cal's mouth deepened as his lips grew thinner. "Whatever you say. I am curious about something, though. In the office, you said what happened between us in the garden was a mistake. Is that how you really see it?"

"Absolutely." And she'd made enough to know—some more egregious than others. Cal wasn't the worst mistake she'd made, but getting felt up by a stranger at her dad's wedding wasn't her proudest moment.

"You think mistakes are failings, then? You're wrong on that score."

"Really? Please, enlighten me." She punched the elevator button again, harder this time.

"'Mistakes are the portals of discovery.'"

Monica tossed her head to displace a wisp of hair dangling on her forehead. "Life lessons by Cal Hughes. Let me get my notebook, Professor. I don't want to miss a word."

"Not me, James Joyce."

That made her stop for a minute. Cal Hughes, quoting literary giants? Or he could be jerking her chain.

He must have read her expression. "Stunned, are you? Didn't expect someone like me to know that?" Although his expression hadn't changed and he still wore a tilted smile, his eyes hardened.

"You're a big fan of Joyce?"

"Not really. I was fourteen and heard there were sexy parts in *Ulysses*, but by the time I slogged through it, I was too bored to care."

Monica fought back a laugh. She didn't know what to make of him. If he secretly wrote poetry on the side, she was a goner.

"Do you want to know what I think?" he asked.

"Not really."

"I think mistakes are missed opportunities. Being afraid to make a mistake is being afraid of life." The elevator doors opened, and he gestured for her to enter first.

"Mechanic. Gambler. Philosopher. Any other talents?"

"Scores, darling." His eyes were full of sexual heat. "Would you like me to elaborate?"

Crossing her arms, Monica shifted her glance to the closed doors. "Nope." *Yes. God, yes.* She paused for a second. "And for your information, I'm not afraid of anything."

"Hmm, I must have got it wrong then. From where I'm standing, it looks like you're trying to avoid me. And there's only one reason for that."

"You're annoying?"

"Because you want to finish what we started, but that wouldn't mesh with this rather dull, professional image you've created for yourself." The bell dinged at the seventh floor, and the doors slid open. When two men and a woman climbed on board, Cal moved to the back of the car. He tugged on Monica's sleeve, pulling her back with him and crowding her into the corner.

"Not true," she whispered. *So true.* "I don't want to finish anything with you." Just standing next to him in this small space was a test of her self-restraint. She fought the urge to gravitate toward him and take another whiff of his fresh, earthy scent.

"Prove it," he whispered back.

Monica tried to hold her tongue, but she liked having the last word too much. "I don't have to prove anything to you," she hissed. *Fantastic argument. What's next, Monica, the old I'm-rubber-you're-glue line of defense?*

Once they hit the lobby, everyone filed out ahead of them. "I'm not avoiding you, Cal. I'm busy." She peered up at him. "And I don't want to finish what we started five years ago. I barely remember it."

"You're a terrible liar, Monica."

Monica was a fairly decent liar. As a teenager, she'd told a lot of whoppers, most of which never came back to bite her in the ass. A good thing, because Allie had a very long memory. "I'm not lying."

"You are, actually. It's adorable." Cal kept pace with her to the entrance of the building. He held open the door and walked next to her as she crossed the lot to her car. "Look, I obviously make you uncomfortable. Probably because of your massive attraction to me. But I won't force my company on you. Just drop me off at my villa, and we'll call it a day."

She came to a stop in the middle of the parking lot, held up her keychain, and pressed the fob. "I'm not uncomfortable, nor am I attracted. I'll go to dinner with you, if you'll just *shut the hell up*."

Trying to suppress a grin, Cal shoved his hands into his pockets and strolled beside her. She was easy to wind up, which made doing so impossible to resist. He hadn't been able to resist kissing her, either. He'd only gotten a brief taste, but he wanted more. Cal wanted to strip her out of that suit and see what she wore underneath. Monica could make plain white cotton look fuckable.

He moved around her to open the driver's side door. "In you go."

She shot him a glance and mumbled a thanks.

"Where are we headed?" he asked after climbing in next to her. And that's when he noticed the fuzzy steering wheel cover. Hot, vibrant pink. "Did you skin a Muppet?" He pointed at the furry wheel.

"Yes. I'm sadistic like that. You should see what I did to Miss Piggy."

Cal leaned his head back and chuckled. This was a glimpse of the true Monica. It was the only sign of frivolity she'd shown all day, and he was heartened by it.

She reversed out of the parking spot and sped off. "What sounds good? Steak, sushi, Italian?"

"I'm flexible. Tell me about this foundation. Apparently, it keeps you so busy that you can't take time to eat a proper lunch."

"How do you know that?" She stopped at a red light and glanced over at him. "Has Stella been tattling on me?"

"Yes, she was quite vocal. Goes from zero to doing a ton in three seconds flat. Her engine doesn't idle, either."

Monica shook her head. "Are you saying she talks a lot? At least I hope *engine* isn't a euphemism for something else."

He shuddered. "It's not. Stella is an attractive woman,

don't get me wrong, but not my type. She gave me an earful about you, though. You've not been taking care of yourself, not since breaking up with Reggie."

"Oh my God, she told you about Ryan?" Monica slapped her palm onto the stick, slammed the car into gear, then tore out at the green light. "Stella and I are going to have a little talk tomorrow."

"Oh, do stop. She didn't mean any harm, she's worried about you." He hadn't meant to get the poor lady into trouble. After all, Cal had peppered Stella with questions like a chat show host, and used his most disarming smile to do it. The older woman had given Cal all the dirt. How wonderful, handsome, and successful Ryan was. Everyone adored him. Ugh. The dismal chap sounded like a right Herbert.

"Well, she can worry silently next time," Monica said, "with an idling engine."

Cal shifted in his seat. "So what was wrong with him?"

"There's nothing wrong with him. He's a really great, wonderful guy."

Cal narrowed his eyes. "According to Stella, you broke up with him."

"Wow, she really did fill you in, didn't she?"

"Was he a snorer?"

"Wha—"

"A bit of a slob?"

"No." She took her eyes from the road for a moment to throw a glare in his direction. "Calum, I'm not going to discuss my boyfriend with you."

"Ex-boyfriend. What does he do for a living, this paragon?"

She remained silent.

"Is he a vicar or something? Is that why you dress the way you do?"

"He's not a minister, there's nothing wrong with my clothing, and I'm not talking about him."

"Solicitor? That's almost as bad."

Monica tapped her fingers on the steering wheel. "He's an accountant."

"Dear God, an accountant. He did this voluntarily? That's a thousand times worse than a solicitor."

"I don't want to discuss him—are we clear on that?" She slowly turned her head to stare at him.

"I'm just curious, love. No need to be so cross."

"Are we clear?" She didn't look away from him, not even when the cars behind them started to beep their horns.

Her gaze met and locked with his. Monica was so lovely, especially when she was angry. Her stubborn little chin jutted out when she became well and truly hacked off. He reached out and caressed that cleft with his thumb. "Clear."

Her breath caught at his touch. She wasn't as unaffected by him as she pretended. Good to know.

Jerking her head away, she faced forward before speeding through the intersection. They were only a few blocks from the Strip now. Tall neon signs became visible, shooting upward toward the night sky. Blue, pink, purple, gold. All of them vying with one another for attention.

"Did he squeeze toothpaste from the bottom of the tube?" Cal continued. "I hate those people. So superior and smug about their dental hygiene." When she didn't respond, he carried on. "Didn't put down the lavatory lid?" Still, she kept schtum, not uttering a word. "Wait, I've got it. He didn't reciprocate with the oral, did he?"

As he watched her, Monica's lips flattened, and her eyes narrowed slightly. "I said—"

"Because personally, I like performing oral. Knowing my partner's satisfied makes me satisfied. I'm a giver, but not every man is. Was that your Brian?"

"Ryan," she said through clenched teeth. "And he was perfectly satisfactory in the sex department, since you're so freakishly curious. I was always very, very satisfied."

"Ooo, two verys—he must have been dreadful. And you're doing it again."

"What?" She'd turned onto the Strip, and they hit another red light.

Tourists lined the street up ahead, staring at a casino fountain. Its pastel-lighted jets of water were synchronized to Beethoven. Opus 15, if he remembered correctly. Cal had always liked that one. "You're lying."

"One more word, Cal, one more, and I'm kicking you out of the car."

He opened his mouth to say something, but closed it again just as quickly. He'd pushed her to the limit. And Cal couldn't remember the last time he'd had such fun.

Chapter 5

Monica parked at the front door of a casino and couldn't get out of the car fast enough. Cal had finally shut up about Ryan, after she'd threatened to dump his ass on the side of the road. She'd been halfway serious too. What was Stella doing, spilling all of Monica's personal business? Cal had probably acted all charming and winsome to get the information, but Stella should have more discretion.

Monica didn't want to talk about Ryan. Not to anyone—especially not to Calum Hughes. But he was relentless. Normally, she appreciated tenacity in a person, but not when all of that determination was directed at her.

After handing her key to the valet, Monica silently entered the building with Cal by her side. Inside, the sights and sounds were jarring at first. Machines jangled and strobed bright lights. People yelled and laughed, and a Bon Jovi song blared overhead.

Monica had spent a lot of time hanging out in casinos—the restaurants, pool parties, clubs, and blackjack tables. Not so much in the last couple of years, though. She sort of missed the atmosphere.

As they began moving down a long corridor lined with shops, Cal stopped and placed his hand on her upper arm. "Hang on a mo, I'll be right back." He left her to jog into the gift store, where all sorts of memorabilia filled the front window—T-shirts, coffee mugs, shot glasses. Monica watched people drift in and out of bars and the sportsbook as she waited.

Cal came back a few minutes later, empty-handed. "Ready." He laced his fingers with hers and brought them to his mouth for a quick kiss.

Holding hands with him made her heart patter like a teenager's on her first date. "What did you buy?"

"Mind your own business, nosy parker." His tone was chiding, but his eyes sparkled.

He was pushing every one of her buttons tonight. He seemed to have a knack for it. And all that sex talk in the car had her thoughts heading in one direction—imagining herself with Cal. It wasn't hard to do. She'd seen his bare chest this morning. Did he have any other tattoos? The old Monica would have made it her duty to find out. The new Monica tamped down her raging curiosity.

"Where are we headed?" he asked.

"Surf and turf restaurant. I've never been here, but I've heard it's good."

They took the elevator to the fifth floor, to a very trendy spot owned by a celebrity chef. Cal kept hold of her hand the entire way.

After they gave their name to the hostess, they slipped into the bar brimming with people. There were no free tables, and all of the bar stools were occupied, so Monica found a narrow space against the wall while Cal left to get her a drink. He came back a moment later with a glass of wine she'd requested, but hadn't ordered anything for himself.

After he handed off the pinot, he angled toward her.

Cal placed his forearm along the wall next to her head, shrouding her with his tall body, then lowered his lips to her ear. "You were at university the last time I saw you. How'd that go?" His breath stirred a lock of her hair. Their cheeks were practically touching, and delectable heat radiated off him.

"How do you remember that?"

He pulled back to stare into her eyes. His darkened to a deeper green. "I remember everything about that night. Don't you?" He arched one brow, waiting for her answer.

"Not everything." She remembered the best parts, the important parts. How he made her feel—hot and wet and excited. She felt that way now, and he wasn't even touching her.

"So did you finish school?" he asked.

When she nodded, her hair brushed against his arm. "Yeah. Got my master's too."

"Clever girl." He smiled, and she couldn't help but return it. His jawline was rugged, his neck muscular. She watched the vein at the side of his throat and clenched her glass to keep from reaching out and brushing it with her finger. "I know you have to work in that little cell of yours," he said, "but what do you do for fun?"

What did she do for fun? It had been so long since she'd had any, Monica could barely understand the concept. "I don't have time for fun right now."

Cal leaned nearer, traced his lips along the outer edge of her ear, causing Monica to shiver. "There's always time for fun." His gravelly voice shot a bolt of pleasure right through her. "And if there's not, you're doing something wrong."

"What do you do for fun?" she asked, sounding winded. He was so near. She felt cocooned from the crowd, his body shielding her, blocking everyone from view.

She'd hardly gotten the words out when he gently bit down on her earlobe. Shutting her eyes, Monica had to work to stay upright, but she couldn't stop herself from touching him. Lifting her hand, she lightly rubbed his cheek. His skin was hot to the touch, and smooth against her fingers.

Cal released her ear and raised his head to look at her. His pupils were large, eating into the green surrounding them. Slowly, he leaned even closer, giving her time to push him away.

Monica didn't want to push him away. She wanted his mouth on hers again. This time for a longer, deeper kiss. Her good-girl voice sounded a distant warning, but she ignored it.

Eyes wide, Monica remained still. His lips touched hers, and unlike the soft kiss in the office, this one packed a sexual punch. Placing his hands on either side of her head, Cal kissed her full-on. His lips coaxed and demanded at the same time.

As Monica clutched the placket of his shirt with her free hand, she kissed him back, and everything else fell away. The people, the noise, the fact that they were in public. None of it mattered except this moment with Cal. Her breasts felt heavy, achy, and her nipples were taut.

When his tongue met hers, Monica moaned into his mouth. She craved his touch, needed more of him—this kiss wasn't enough. Not even close. Her pussy contracted each time his thumb brushed across her cheek. Suddenly, something vibrated between them.

Cal's hands fell, and he broke the kiss. With his forehead resting against hers, he took a shuddery breath. "Bloody hell, I thought that was you for a minute. I think our table's ready." He pulled the pager from his front pocket. "We could skip dinner and get a room instead."

Monica stared at his flushed face and slammed back into reality. What the hell was wrong with her? Brushing her fingers across her mouth, she wordlessly shook her head. She'd just made a fool of herself. In public. What if someone she knew had seen her?

"I'm not getting a room with you, Cal. I agreed to have dinner, and then I'm going home. Alone." She plucked the pager from his hand and staggered past him, out of the bar. Walking toward the hostess, Monica didn't look back. And she couldn't even make eye contact with any of the diners—she was too shaken by what had just happened. Cal only had to stand next to her, throw a few kisses her way, and every scrap of resistance evaporated.

Well, no more. Monica wasn't a slave to her hormones. She had been a bad-boy-free zone for the last four years. She could withstand a kiss or two. She was made of sterner stuff.

Once they were seated, Cal's intense gaze darted over her face, her heated cheeks. "Are you all right?"

He wasn't teasing for a change, and she was glad. If he mocked her right now, she didn't know if she could stand it. Taking a deep breath, she squared her shoulders. "I'm fine."

She shook out her napkin and dropped it on her lap. Time for a neutral topic. No ex-boyfriends, or sex, or the past. And no more kisses. "Brynn said you flew in from Australia."

Cal picked up the menu and opened it. "Yeah, I did. Beautiful country—you should go someday."

"Which part of Australia?"

"Cairns."

"What did you do there?"

He looked up at her and grinned. "Hung out, surfed. Bought a wreck of an Austin Healey and had it shipped back to London. Have you ever seen one up close?"

"I've never seen one from far away. So is that all you do, fix cars and surf?" She wasn't being dismissive, she was curious, but a chill settled behind his eyes.

"What more is there?" He sounded flippant, but his grip tightened on the leather-bound menu. He was putting up a front. She recognized it instantly, because she was a master at it—acting nonchalant to get people off her back.

So what was he hiding? "Is there a girlfriend in Australia?"

"No." That deep, husky voice became clipped, like Trevor's. Monica was good at reading caution signs, and right now, Cal flashed a bright red warning: *Off Limits*.

But Monica couldn't leave it alone. "What about a wife?"

When he raised his head, Cal's lips curved downward, and that chill in his eyes became permafrost. "You think I'd be snogging you if I were married? Lovely opinion you have of me, darling."

"I don't know you. Not really. And Australia seems like a touchy subject."

"It's not a touchy subject. Not like you and the ex-boyfriend."

"Did you leave a job behind?"

He signaled a passing waiter. "Scotch, single malt, please. Better make it a double." Once the waiter left, his eyes pinned Monica. "No job. No wife. No girlfriend. Now your turn. Why did you break up with what's-his-face?"

"You don't have a job? I thought you were *the shiz* with cars." This felt very familiar—same old song, second verse. Monica always fell for the ones without a job.

"I *own* an auto restoration business, but my garage is in Britain, not Australia."

"How long were you in Australia?" She placed her hands on her unopened menu and leaned forward.

Cal closed his and mirrored her movements. "Why do you give a toss?"

"I'm just being polite."

"Hardly."

Her mouth popped open as she leaned back. "Really? You ask me about oral sex, and *I'm* the impolite one?"

A wide grin broke across his lips. "Well, perhaps we're evenly matched."

Monica decided to give up on Australia. "What's so special about an Austin Whatever?"

"Healey." He dug into his front pocket. "It's a piece of automotive beauty." He pulled out his phone and touched the screen. "It's a classic piece of British machinery. To restore a car like that is bringing a piece of history to life."

"Like Trevor's antique knickknacks," she said.

Cal's smile dimmed. "No. It's nothing remotely like the decaying shit Trevor's got lying all over."

"Actually, it's exactly the same. I saw that Mustang, remember?"

"But I don't hang on to cars the way Trevor does with jade Buddha figurines. I find classics, restore them, and give them a happy home." He shoved the phone under her nose. "Here's one I did three years ago. Take a look."

She glanced at the pic of a shiny, sexy red roadster. "It's very nice."

Cal barked out a shocked laugh. "Nice? No, love, that car is not nice. It's a marvel." He scrolled across the screen before handing it to her. "That's how it looked when I found it."

Now it was her turn for surprise. "This is a wreck." Literally. The car looked as if it had been cut in half. The front fender had sustained major damage, and the finish was completely eroded. To her, it looked like a piece for the salvage yard. She gazed up and saw pride in his eyes.

"I know. Just the chassis. That's all I had to work with. I rebuilt that car, every single piece, from the drivetrain to the seats."

"How long did that take?" She stared at the picture for a moment longer. When she started to scroll through to look for more, he snatched the phone from her hands and shoved it in his pocket.

"A year and a half. I was a bit obsessed. Normally, it takes much longer."

"So you finish a car, find a buyer, and move on to the next project?"

Cal nodded. "Precisely."

He probably did the same thing with women. Picked one, fucked her until she was ruined for every other man, then left her for a different model. Which explained Monica's attraction to him. *Along with that body, those eyes, and his sense of humor*. Maybe he had a little more going for him than all of the other losers she'd fallen for in the past. That didn't mean he was good for her.

"When did you start fixing cars?" she asked as the waiter wandered toward them and set a glass in front of Cal. He offered to freshen Monica's wine, but she shook her head.

"We'll need a few more minutes," Cal said, and the waiter disappeared. He turned his attention back on Monica. "When I was nine. One of my mum's boyfriends had a motor collection that was astounding. I was immediately hooked. The chauffeur, who also happened to be a fairly decent mechanic, taught me how to put together my first carburetor. I spent every day learning as much about cars as I could."

He took a sip of his scotch, and her eyes followed the movement of his throat. Cal seemed to do everything with an elegance that must be an inherent trait. Monica could practice forever, and she'd never possess that air of refinement.

"I travel often," Cal said, "I work when I feel like it, and I live my life. You should try it."

"Some of us don't have that luxury. Some of us have to work even when we don't feel like it." Cal might talk about living life and not being afraid to make mistakes, but that was easy to say when he didn't have any obligations.

The waiter returned, and Monica ordered grilled chicken and vegetables while Cal got the prime rib. Damn, that sounded good. But she'd made the healthy choice. She could do that with Cal too. Just as long as he kept those lips to himself.

"How about after this, we hit the roulette table?" he asked.

"No thanks, I have a busy day tomorrow."

Deep creases bit into the corners of his narrowed eyes as he studied her. Reaching into his back pocket, he pulled out a new deck of cards that bore the name of the casino. That must have been what he'd bought in the gift store.

"High card gets to decide what we do next."

With a breathy laugh, she looked away. "I'm not letting a card decide my future."

"Not your entire future, just the next two hours. My God, you've gotten prickly." He threw out two joker cards and shuffled the deck.

Monica's posture stiffened. "If I'm so prickly and boring, I don't know why you'd want to spend another minute in my company."

He leaned in. "I never said boring, darling. Besides, I like staring at that little divot in your chin." His eyes followed her movements as she involuntarily reached up to stroke the cleft. "And the way your eyes darken whenever you become pissy, like when I ask about the ex." He wagged a finger at her. "They're doing it right now. And you may have everyone else fooled into thinking you're a saint, but you kiss like a sinner. So no, I don't find you boring."

That last one struck a little too close to home. Cal sat back and watched her with a grin.

"You don't know anything about me." In fact, he seemed to know too much. How could he read her so easily? It was irritating, and a tad scary. What else did he see?

Cal placed the cards on the table. “Draw high, and you can go home to your lonely bed and dream of me.”

She shook her head. “You’ll be dreaming of me. I’m not the one who kissed you. Twice.”

“I didn’t hear you protesting. You could have slapped my face. Instead, you stuck your tongue in my mouth. Which was very enjoyable, by the way. You actively participated. That counts.”

“Sorry, Calum, we’re not compatible.” She sat back in her chair and crossed her arms. “I only date responsible grown-ups with real jobs.”

His taunting grin ratcheted up. “Who said anything about dating? And I don’t need a job, I have a trust fund. You had a responsible grown-up in Reggie—”

“Ryan.”

“But you kicked him to the curb. Why don’t you try having a little fun instead?”

Cal watched with satisfaction as pink filled her cheeks. Monica didn’t like to be reminded that she was human. But when he’d kissed her in the bar, she’d responded. She was so into it, she’d clutched his shirt in her fist. Despite what Monica said, she wanted him. He could see it in her eyes. They were a good gauge of her emotions. Stormy and passionate one minute, dismissive and superior the next.

The shade was very like the water surrounding the reef at Cairns—clear, light blue—until her emotions ran high. Then they turned to Meissen Blue—the color of a ’58 Porsche he’d restored some years ago. Her eyes were gorgeous. Like the rest of her.

His gaze drifted to her sensual upper lip—so completely at odds with her conservative exterior, and another naughty reminder of who she really was. When she caught him staring at it, she slid the tip of her tongue along its lush edge. Cal imagined those lips wrapped around his cock, and heat pricked his forehead. He wanted Monica Campbell in the very worst way. Wanted her beneath him—naked, open, and willing.

"Why are you looking at me like that?"

Cal attempted to relax his facial muscles. His desire must have shown clearly, because Monica appeared on the verge of panic. "When was the last time you went dancing?"

She blinked at the change in topic. "Where did that come from?" She fingered the spoon handle, picked it up, and started tapping it against the table. He was making her nervous. Good. He liked knocking her off balance. She revealed herself in all sorts of interesting ways.

"Last time I saw you, you told me you loved to dance."

"Cal, what do you want from me?" She glanced down at the table, and her shoulders hunched forward. "No matter what you choose to believe, I'm not the girl you remember. I don't stay out late partying, and I don't sneak off to the garden to dry-hump strangers. That girl's gone for good."

"You and I are no longer strangers, so I think we're past the dry-humping stage. However, I could be persuaded to a mutual wank-off."

She dropped the spoon and clenched her hand into a fist. "We're not wanking."

"Fine," he said, then sighed deeply. "No wanking.

We'll play for something that really matters. A good-night kiss." He gestured to the cards. "Pick one. Draw a high card, and I'll never bother you again. Draw low, I get a proper snog. Go on, I dare you."

She stared at him for a full minute. "Fine." She cut the deck and drew a card. Glancing at it, she closed her eyes for a moment, then showed him the two of spades. "Shouldn't be hard to beat."

Cal kept his eyes on her as he drew. He didn't look at the card, but showed it to her. "What is it?"

"King of hearts."

He nodded. "That sounds about right."

Just then, the waiter started heading their way. He set the dishes before them and gave a few more details about dessert. "Can I get you anything else?"

Cal stood and removed his wallet. He shoved a couple of bills in the man's hand. "We both need to make a phone call. Is there a room around here we can use, an office or a private loo?"

Looking down at the cash, the waiter nodded. "There's a supply closet in the bathroom hallway." He looked around as he slipped a key out of his pocket. "Don't get caught."

"Thanks, mate." Cal patted the man's shoulder and grabbed Monica's hand. Pulling her from the table, he ignored her expression of horror as he strode through the restaurant, hauling her behind him.

In the darkened hallway, past the loos, he found the narrow door. Without giving her time to make a dash, he slipped the key into the lock and had them inside in mere seconds.

"Cal, this is ridiculous."

He flipped on the light and glanced around at the rolls of paper products. Monica stood with her back to the door, staring at him with wide eyes.

Flattening both hands on either side of her head, he hemmed her in with his arms. "Tell me your heart's not racing right now. Tell me this isn't fun."

She opened her mouth, but nothing came out. Then she stuck her chin in the air and stared at his nose. "This isn't fun."

"If you want to go, I won't stop you. But if you stay, I intend to kiss you thoroughly. And I'm going to touch you. Here." He moved one hand and placed it over her breast.

Monica glanced around the room. "I can't believe you're doing this. We're too old to make out in a supply closet."

"We can't very well do it at the table. The other diners wouldn't be able to concentrate on their entrées. So what do you want to do, Monica?" He swept his lips over her cheek. "Stay?" He trailed tiny kisses up to those four freckles scattered above her eyebrow. "Or go?"

She placed her hands on his chest, her fingers restless as they turned inward, like talons, and skittered down to his waist. "Stay." It was barely a whisper, and her lips hardly moved. But it was enough.

Before she could say anything else, Cal placed his hands around her waist. The fabric of her jacket was stiff and unyielding. He very slowly slanted his body over hers, and angling his head, began to nibble the side of her neck above her collar. She smelled heavenly—sweet, yet spicy. Her skin was silk against his lips. A strand of her hair tickled his forehead.

Monica's body remained tense for a few moments, but gradually, as Cal ran his lips across her jaw, she relaxed and slid her hands up to his shoulders. Letting out a soft sigh, she tilted her head, giving his lips better access.

Yes. He'd been waiting five long years for this. Another go at Monica Campbell. Not his top pick for locale, but he'd take it. That girl in the garden had been eager and out of control. He wanted to make her that way again.

Cal trailed kisses up to her ear where he caught her lobe between his teeth. He bit down as he had in the bar, but not gently this time. Monica gasped, her breaths growing ragged as he pulled it into his mouth and sucked.

Cal let go of her waist and, with shaky hands, peeled the jacket from her shoulders and down her arms, dropping it at her feet. That damned blouse was still in his way. He wanted to rip it off and bare her skin. He hated that demure white shirt—unimaginative and puritanical, it was the antithesis of everything Monica was. As he tried to undo the top button, his fingers felt awkward and clumsy.

Monica batted his fumbling hands away, making quick work of the buttons. When she was done, Cal parted her blouse and stilled, gaping at her—at her full breasts pushed high above two peachy, lace-covered cups. The scanty material barely covered her nipples at all, and the dark pink areola of one breast peeked above the lace. Fucking hell. Her tits were plump and pale, nearly the same color as her bra.

Cal had been momentarily dazed by the sight of her, but suddenly, he was impatient. He jerked the blouse farther apart and shucked it off her completely, until she stood before him, looking seductive and angelic at the same time. “Lovely.”

Giving him a coy glance, Monica ran one finger along her breast, where the lace met her flesh. “Do you think so?”

He palmed those luscious tits, squeezing them tightly, raising them a little higher. The textured lace felt stiff against his fingertips. “No, I take it back. Not just lovely—gorgeous.” Monica Campbell was heady. Exciting. He wanted nothing more than to fuck her right here, against the door. Make her come with hundreds of people sitting out in the dining room, eating their steaks.

With his thumbs, he tugged at the bra cups and freed those stunning tits from their confines. They were full and heavy in his hands. He couldn’t stop staring, and her nipples budded beneath his gaze.

Cal was actually touching Monica Campbell. Finally, after all these years. And she felt even better than he’d imagined. Her skin felt so fucking supple, like the softest chamois. Her trim waist was a pale contrast against the black trousers.

She allowed him to stroke her like this—intimately. The fact that she arched her back and licked her lips said how much she liked it. When he brushed his thumbs along the underside of her breasts, then flicked her nipples, she moaned low in her throat. That sound, along with her short, breathy gasps, made Cal’s cock so hard it almost hurt.

Monica reached up and threaded her fingers through his hair, pulling his mouth to hers. He kissed her roughly. He wanted her to remember this moment, to come to terms with her passionate side. This woman, the one kissing him back, slipping her tongue into his mouth, biting his lip—this was the sensuous, untamed nature she tried so hard to suppress. This was the Monica from his fantasies.

Her lips were swollen and tasted faintly of mint from her lipstick. For the first time in months, Cal ached from something other than grief. He ached for release. Monica could give it to him. He needed to be inside her, feel her pussy, hot and wet and slick. He wanted to lose himself in her, forget the past and live in this moment. With her.

He'd never forgotten Monica Campbell, or the way she tasted. But this time was different somehow, better than he remembered. He didn't analyze it, but simply enjoyed the delicate flavor of her skin, the feel of her breasts in his hands.

He thrust his hips against her, torqued them slowly. The friction was almost too much for his sensitive cock.

"Cal," she whispered. "That feels really good. Do it again."

He obliged and roughly kneaded her tits at the same time. This was only meant to be a good-night snog—one that had gotten completely out of hand. Back at the table, when she'd drawn the low card, Monica hadn't been able to mask her troubled expression. Cal knew she'd fret about it all through dinner, so he'd acted on instinct. So glad he had, because kissing her, fondling her, grinding his prick against her was bloody brilliant.

Keeping one hand on her, Cal pulled back slightly.

"What?" Monica asked, her voice thready.

"I want to touch the rest of you." He wrangled with her trousers, unfastening them and lowering the zipper.

Incapable of finesse at this point, Cal thrust his hand into her knickers. *Slow down*. The thought was short-lived, because Cal couldn't slow down, couldn't stop his hand's path. He wanted inside of her, and if it couldn't be his cock, his finger would have to do. A thin strip of downy hair covered the top of her mound. The rest of her was bare and soft, like velvet. Cal's finger traced lower. Her pussy was wet, ready for him.

His heartbeat sounded so loud, he was sure Monica could hear it as well. His middle finger grazed across her slick entrance. As it did, Monica grabbed her other breast and pulled her own nipple. Cal's cock jerked at the sight of her touching herself.

Before he could slide that finger inside her, someone pounded on the door.

"Hello? This is the manager. I know you're in there. Come out right now."

"Shit," he muttered.

"Oh my God," Monica hissed and let go of her breast. Then she yanked on his wrist until he pulled it from her trousers. "Perfect," she whispered and zipped them up. "If we get dragged out of here by security, I will never live this down." Although she kept her head lowered, Cal noticed her pale cheeks as she shoved herself back into the bra.

"Just calm down." When she didn't look at him, he took her chin in his hand and forced her head up. "Trust me."

Cal stepped away, but kept his gaze on her. Monica's eyes were wide and worried, her lips cherry red. She was beautiful—a combination of strong and fragile at the same time. He wanted to protect her from this asshole pounding on the door, keep her from being humiliated.

He dug out his mobile. Unlocking the door, he stuck his head out. "Do you mind, mate?" he whispered. "I'm about to close on the biggest deal of my life. What, is my girl complaining that I've been in here too long?" Behind him, Monica silently buttoned her blouse.

A tall man wearing a moderately priced dark suit stared at him from the hallway. "Sir, this is not the place—"

Cal held up his finger and spoke into the phone. "Yes, that sounds great. No, it's never too late to call, sir. I'll send over the proposal in the morning." He smiled at the tall man and shoved the phone back in his pocket. "Sorry I commandeered your storage closet. I know it's not appropriate, but I had to take that call. You're an important man, surely you understand business." Cal pulled out his wallet and shoved a few bills into the man's hand. "I'm sure that will cover any inconvenience and the meal, eh? We're all friends here."

The man stared at the money. "Yes, sir. But you need to leave. Now."

"Just one more call? I'll be out in two shakes." With a wink, he shut the door in the manager's face.

When Cal turned back to Monica, anger burned in her eyes. "You're so full of shit. You think you can weasel out of every tight spot using charm or money?" She kept her voice pitched low.

"Quite. What's wrong with that? It's called problem solving."

"Not everything's for sale." She moved around him and opened the door. The manager had left, and the hallway was empty.

With his hands in his pockets, Cal lagged behind, watching as Monica charged into the dining room and grabbed her bag. Hastening his steps, he followed her out of the restaurant. When Cal caught up with her, he placed his hand beneath Monica's elbow, but she jerked away.

Drawing to a stop in the middle of the bustling corridor, with its shiny marble floors and gilded accents, she craned her neck to look up at him. "Leave mc alone, Cal. I'm going home."

"You're my ride."

"This town is full of cabs. If you're not smart enough to find one, walk."

She moved to storm away, but Cal gently snagged her sleeve and held her in place. "Enough of this." Her attitude was starting to wear on his nerves. "You may pretend that what happened back there didn't involve you, but it did. You were right there with me, loving it. You wanted me every bit as much as I wanted you." He softened his voice and lowered his lips to her ear. "Your pussy was aching for me. So stop acting like a fucking bystander in your own life. Now, I'm going to walk you to your car, and then you can slink home and make believe I'm the big, bad wolf. But you and I both know the truth. You've become a coward, Monica Campbell."

This time he stormed away, leaving her to scramble after him. That priggish bullshit might go down with her family, but Cal had had enough. He wasn't the villain here, and she wasn't a virgin at the stake. She could lie to herself all she wanted, but he was getting goddamned tired of her lying to him.

Chapter 6

"Pick your poison." Evan stood on Monica's porch holding a bottle of tequila in one hand and a carton of Ben and Jerry's in the other. His tousled, dark brown mane gave every indication that he'd just rolled out of bed, but Monica knew otherwise. He spent an inordinate amount of time making it appear disheveled. Evan was a peacock and a label whore with a closet full of fugly designer clothes to prove it. The combinations he put together usually made her eyes water, and tonight's microprint lavender shirt and skinny-legged green pants were no exception.

"Chocolate Fudge Brownie." She grabbed the ice cream and headed to the kitchen. "I think I've made enough bad decisions tonight. You know what tequila does to me."

Evan trailed behind her and slouched elegantly against the dated laminate countertop. Setting down the bottle of Patrón, he lifted one brow. "Does this bad decision have a name?"

Monica pulled a plastic spoon from the drawer. "Calum Hughes." For four years she'd been on the right path, only dating men who fit at least eighty-five percent of her strict criteria. One night with Cal, and she'd almost thrown it all away. For what? A quickie?

The worst part had been her level of enjoyment. Monica hadn't just *liked* kissing Cal and letting him feel her up, she'd reveled in it. Her breasts still tingled like he'd branded her with his touch. If that restaurant manager hadn't shown up when he had, Monica would have fucked Cal right there in the supply closet. Old Monica, rearing her ugly head.

What the hell had she been thinking? Well, obviously she hadn't been thinking. She'd been feeling—feeling his big hands wander all over her. And even now, still angry at her lapse in judgment, she felt keyed up and anxious. Monica's body longed for the sexual release that had almost been hers. Cal's finger had been close, so damn close to slipping inside her. With a sigh, she shoved a spoonful of ice cream into her face.

"That name sounds familiar." Evan grabbed a red Solo cup from the cupboard and poured himself a shot of tequila.

"Trevor's cousin, Cal? In the garden, after my dad's wedding?"

"Right. Tall British guy. You almost boinked him that night." It took a minute for his brain to put the puzzle together, then his jaw fell open. "Oh my God. Did Monnie get her groove back?"

"Almost. I'm slipping backward, Ev. I almost nailed him in a restaurant."

"Good for you." He toasted her and took a sip.

She glared at him. "What about my face says this is a good thing? You're here to talk me down, to set me straight, not raise a glass to my stupidity."

"Getting laid isn't stupid, it's human. You and Ryan have been apart for months now. You need to loosen up—otherwise, you're going to dry up." He pointed at her crotch. "Down there, I mean."

"I'm out of control. Next thing you know, I'll be lying on a bar with a shot glass wedged between my boobs. Or waking up with a guy whose last name I don't know." Monica grabbed the ice cream and stalked to the living room. "Cal said that I was afraid of life. I'm not afraid, I'm cautious. You know why I'm cautious, Ev."

He fell onto the sofa. "Yep. You've told me. Several hundred times. And while I get it, I miss the old Monnie. Remember when you used to be fun? I do." He finished off his shot. "We used to dance on tables, kid. We've gotten thrown out of places that wouldn't pass for a dive."

Monica swallowed a cold lump of chocolate so fast, she got an ice cream headache. "Ow. I'm still fun. I'm tons of fun. I'm just more mature now." Rubbing her forehead, she sat down next to him. "He accused me of that too. Of being prissy and prim. I run a cancer foundation, for crying out loud. It's serious work. Am I supposed to go to the office dressed in a halter top and Daisy Dukes?"

Evan sighed. "Why do you go to these extremes? There's a lovely place called Happy Medium. Find it. Live it. You'll like it there."

Monica had never been good at finding middle ground. She tended to be an all-or-nothing type of person. She came out of the factory that way.

"Mon, listen to me, okay?" Evan patted her knee. "I'm about to give you a dose of reality. Number one, because I love you. Number two, my girlfriend's getting jealous. If she hadn't been working tonight, I may not have been able to answer your distress call."

Monica frowned around the plastic spoon and pulled it from her mouth. "What's there to be jealous about?

We're like sibs. I'd never touch you. The mere thought is repulsive. No offense." She'd met Evan on her first day at UNLV. He'd been impossible to ignore in a pair of rust-colored slacks and an argyle sweater. The other girls on campus had thought he was harmless—sweet, caring Evan and his silly sweater vests. He'd totally used that to his advantage, but Monica had figured out his game from the start. When she'd asked if he and his grandmother shared clothes, Evan had schooled her on American casualwear, then informed Monica that if her skirt were any shorter, he'd be able to see her uterus. They went out for a beer using fake IDs, became each other's wingmen, and never looked back.

"None taken," he said. "I feel the same way about you. But Heather's a little insecure. It brings out these jealous rages. Last week, she thought I was flirting with a waitress and threw all my hair product into the trash compactor. Anyway, since tomorrow is our anniversary, you're lucky this crisis happened tonight. The point is this—"

"Anniversary? You two have been dating for a red-hot minute." Monica hadn't met Heather yet, but she had no doubt Evan's new girlfriend fit his exacting standards. Long dark hair, unnaturally orange skin, boobs so big they could poke someone's eye out, and an IQ barely hovering above a cactus's. A typical Vegas party girl.

"She likes milestones."

"Did she bronze the used condom after your first time together too?"

He threw back his head, laughed, then sobered just as quickly. "Hey, I have an idea. Why don't we talk about your love life for a change? Oh, that's right, you don't have one. Which brings me back to my point. Get a love life!"

"I need to avoid him, not fuck him. Cal is…" She slammed the melting carton on the coffee table. "He's everything that's wrong for me." And yet he was everything she craved. Handsome in an unconventional way, sexy, funny, smart. "And I *am* afraid. There, I admit it. I'm terrified I'll wind up in the same situation." Rock bottom. In a deep, dark hole she'd have to claw her way out of. Monica had no intention of finding herself there again.

Evan wrapped his arm around her, pressing her head into his shoulder. "You won't," he said against her hair. "You're stronger now, smarter. You need to have a little faith in yourself."

Follow your heart. That's what Monica's mom had told her before she died. But Monica's heart was as fucked up and defective as she was. "I can't. When I'm with him, I feel like the old me—reckless and out of control. It's scary."

"That's a good thing. At least you're feeling again."

"What are you talking about? I feel things. I have emotions. You make me sound like a robot. Don't you remember what a total mess I was back then?" She covered her eyes with one hand. "Ryan is the perfect guy for me. Why did I screw that up?"

"Stop it. He's not perfect. Although he's a nice guy and all, he's the most boring person I've ever met. You're so worried about past mistakes, but marrying Ryan would have been the biggest one you've ever made. Brynn and I made a pact that if you agreed to marry him, we'd do everything we could to talk you out of it. And if that didn't work, we planned sabotage."

She pushed out of his hold and scooted away. "You and Brynnie were conspiring against me?"

"Yes, and by any means necessary. Look, you're young, and you're reasonably attractive. There's no reason for you to be alone. This Cal guy fires you up. I haven't seen you this animated in years. *Years*. Treat him like a vaccine. Give yourself a little dose of the wrong kind of guy, but stay in control this time."

Monica lightly punched Evan's arm. "You're supposed to be my best friend, and that's the list you come up with? Young and reasonably attractive?"

"It's time to get back on the horse, Mon."

It wasn't time to get back on the horse. She couldn't be trusted in the saddle. It was safer to make a date with a glass of wine and her vibrator.

She hunkered in the corner of the sofa and came very close to sulking. "I don't want to talk about it anymore."

"Of course you don't. You never want to talk about anything that really matters. You're so predictable, it's sad."

Monica's gaze fluttered to his. She'd never heard that exasperated, disgusted tone in his voice before. Evan was disappointed in her. That hurt more than she cared to admit. He'd been her touchstone all these years. He knew everything about her and loved her anyway. "Any more grenades you want to lob my way tonight?" Her voice cracked a bit, so she swallowed past the lump in her throat. "Because I don't feel shitty enough right now."

He sighed and rested a hand on her calf. "I don't mean to make you feel that way. But I think I've been coddling you too long. And I can't do it anymore."

Now anger crowded out the hurt she'd felt moments

ago. Monica sat up and planted her feet on the floor. "Excuse me? *You* coddle *me*? I'm there for every nasty breakup you have. I'm a great friend to you. Who talked you down from buying those patent-leather Gucci tennis shoes last week?"

A long silence ensued.

"Oh my God," she said. "You bought them, didn't you? They have Velcro straps, Evan."

"They were on sale," he defended. "And you're trying to change the subject. Again. This conversation is not about me, or my shoes, or my crazy girlfriends. This is about you." He drew a circle in the air near her head. "You're not twenty-one anymore. You're not going to get stranded in Mexico, alone, penniless, and pregnant. You're too smart to let that happen again."

Shocked, Monica jerked her head back. Pain and humiliation shot through her, as if the wounds were brand new. The powerful emotions took over her body, expanded in her chest, made it hard to suck in air.

Monica jumped from the sofa and walked to the corner of the room, wrapping her arms around her torso as if she could ward off the past. She'd woken up that morning alone in Mexico—frightened and ashamed. She was used to being alone, even in a crowd, but that morning, as the sun shone through dusty motel windows, showing dark stains on the ancient green carpet, Monica had never felt so desolate. Now, closing her eyes, she pushed the pain down, shoved it away until she could breathe again. "We promised we'd never talk about that. Never."

Dropping her arms, she lowered her eyes as she walked back to the coffee table. She shoved the lid on the carton and picked it up, along with the spoon. "It's getting late, Evan. You should probably go."

"Monica."

She didn't acknowledge him, but shuffled to the kitchen, numb and detached, like her own body didn't belong to her. He followed and watched as she threw her spoon in the trash and stuck the carton in the freezer.

"I didn't mean to upset you. I'm just tired of seeing you so miserable."

Her head shot up. "What are you talking about? I'm not miserable." Sure, her job wasn't everything she'd hoped for, and since ending things with Ryan, she'd been a little depressed. But she wasn't unhappy. Monica felt Evan's warm brown eyes on her, but she couldn't bring herself to look at him. "My life is structured. I'm in a healthy place."

Evan remained silent. The pause drew out, became awkward. "Just think about what I said, okay? I didn't mean to hurt you." He stepped forward and picked up her hand. "Don't be mad at me."

Just like that, the anger drained out of her. "I'll talk to you tomorrow. Thanks for the ice cream."

He bent down and kissed the top of her head before leaving.

The next morning, Cal experienced a sense of disorientation when a buzzing sound woke him. At first, he thought he'd overslept. Panic ripped through him as he threw back the covers and leaped out of bed.

Babcock.

He stood naked in the middle of a dim room. Sunlight

filtered through a crack in the drawn heavy, red curtains. Cal gazed at the bed—king-size, Egyptian cotton sheets. Not a rollaway cot with a lumpy mattress.

Vegas. Not Cairns.

His mobile fell silent. Cal ran a hand down his chest, covered his racing heart. It all came flooding back. Why he'd left Australia—the emptiness, the loss. Then last night and his snog with Monica. *More than a snog, you idiot—practically a full-bodied knee trembler.* He'd spent most of the night drinking scotch and giving himself hell for letting things with Monica go too far too fast.

Cal had made a tactical error, sneaking off with her to the supply closet and yelling at her afterward. Not the way to win her trust, snapping at her like he had.

The phone started ringing again. Blowing out a deep breath, Cal strode to the bedside table and glanced at the screen. "It's eight o'clock, brat," he answered. "Why're you ringing me so early? Are you just staggering home?"

"Hardly. Why haven't you answered my four previous messages, you twat?" Jules had a delightful way with words, much to their father's chagrin. And despite the fact that his baby sister—half sister, if one wanted to be technical—had lived in America for the last eight years, her British accent was as strong as ever.

"I've been busy," he said around a yawn.

"With whom? And don't tell me some slag is more important than me, or I'll kick your ass."

Slag? Just the opposite, in fact. Monica was more prudish than anything.

"Daddy's thrown a wobbler."

Cal rubbed his gritty eyes. "What's got his knickers in a twist now?" His father didn't have the cheeriest disposition to begin with, so really anything might set the old man off. "Is he still cross about school?" As a financial wizard and maths genius, his father had very specific ideas about what his daughter should be doing with her life. Ideas that included studying something other than the latest copy of *Vogue*. Jules, on the other hand, had her own plans, like dancing all night, sleeping until noon, and giving her credit card a good workout.

"Not exactly. But I think he may wash his hands of me for good this time."

Cal fell onto the bed and stared up at the ceiling. The ivory-and-brushed-silver pendant light fixtures hung about the room like stalactites. "If you want my advice, shape up for a few weeks and you'll wiggle your way back into his graces without too much fuss."

"No." Jules's voice was quiet, serious. "This is different."

Alert, Cal sat back up. "What happened? What did you do?"

"I wasn't even driving. Not really. I barely tapped the car in front of me as I pulled out of a parking space. Since when does that count as a DUI?"

"You were drink-driving? Tell me you're not serious." He gripped the phone so hard he thought it might crack. Cal had worked on cars his whole life. He knew exactly how much damage one could do to a human being. And his sister, one of the few people he had left in the world, had climbed behind the wheel while drunk. "Are you fucking kidding me, Juliette? You're brighter than that, or at least I thought you were."

"Hello, this is L.A. Everyone has a DUI. It's like a rite of passage."

"You little idiot," he bit out. "You could have killed

someone. You could have been killed yourself. Don't you ever stop to think?" He ran a hand through his hair, so thoroughly angry, every muscle in his body locked down.

"Oh. My. God," she said. "You sound just like *him*."

He refused to take the bait. If one thing pissed him off, it was being compared to his stuffy, judgmental father. "You're not even the legal drinking age."

"I'm twenty."

"Again, not legal." Cal stood and paced to the window, parting the curtain with one hand. He gazed out at the private garden. The pool glistened blue in the early morning sun, but Cal was too brassed off to appreciate it. "I'm so disappointed in you, Jules. You could have called a cab or hired a driver for the evening."

"*You're* disappointed in *me*?" she yelled. "You've been a crap big brother. You're never here, I don't hear from you for weeks at a time. Every time I need you, you're off in Zimbabwe or Taiwan or Australia. You don't get to be disappointed, okay? That's my job."

That was fair. Cal hadn't been there for her, not when it really counted. Phone calls and presents weren't the same.

Cal fought the urge to yell at her some more, lecture her, berate her. But under all that anger was fear. He'd be absolutely gutted if anything happened to Jules. "Please promise me you'll never do anything so stupid again. I adore you, you know that."

She sniffed a couple of times. "I know it was stupid, and yes, I promise. It was mortifying, being driven away in a police car. I had to be fingerprinted and everything. Daddy was so angry he didn't speak to me for two whole days. Then he started with the screaming. I can't take it from you too."

Cal didn't understand why Jules expected anyone to be sympathetic. But he kept his mouth shut. She needed someone to listen right now, and pointing out the obvious wouldn't be useful.

"My car's been impounded, and I'm not meant to drive anywhere until we go to court. It's a bloody nuisance."

Again, Cal refrained from speaking. It was tremendously difficult, but he managed.

"Daddy made me give up my apartment, and I've been staying at their pool house, like I'm a gardener or something. It's dreadful."

"I'm sure it's not the best situation, but I've seen dreadful. You're the furthest thing from it." He tried to be gentle with her, but Jules was so terribly spoiled, she had no idea about life outside her little bubble. During his travels, Cal had witnessed deplorable living conditions. The slums of Brazil, the polluted Ganges River, poverty in the streets of Belarus. Staying in a comfortable pool house on a Beverly Hills estate wasn't a hardship. But in Jules's eyes, she faced a true crisis. "What are your plans?"

"I don't know. I'm bored silly right now."

"Why don't you find something constructive to do? Maybe you should enroll in school. Make the old man happy."

"God, you're such a bloody hypocrite," she lashed out, causing Cal to flinch. "You never went to school. Why should I?"

"First of all, Pix's father left me a trust fund that you don't have. You're still completely dependent on your parents. Secondly, I'm not clever like you." And the old man never missed an opportunity to rub Cal's nose in it. "You can do whatever you want, Jules—be whoever you want. If not school, then find something you're good at."

"I'm not good at anything."

"You are the most persistent pain in the ass I know. You're bright and funny, and you can do whatever you put your mind to." A vision of Monica came to mind. Perhaps Jules should take a page from Miss Prim's book. "What about charity work? Helping those less fortunate? And let's be honest, that's almost everyone."

"Don't start. Mummy's trying to get me to help her save blackbirds, or something equally stupid."

"You'll figure it out. I believe in you, Jules." The irony that Cal was trying to get Monica to unwind while encouraging his sister to straighten up wasn't lost on him.

"Oh God," she said. "You sound so keen right now, I need to hurl. Good-bye. Twat." And she hung up.

Cal stared out at the garden a moment longer before his phone buzzed again. This time, his mum. Cal didn't want to talk right now, but if he put it off, she'd hound him relentlessly. She was good at that.

"Morning," he said.

"Darling, where have you been? I've been calling for days. I thought you came to Vegas to spend some time with me, and I've barely seen you."

Rubbing his ear, Cal thought about all the responses he could make, but decided to remain civil instead. "I came to Vegas because you lied about your anniversary."

"Yes, but how else could I get quality time with my only son, eh?"

"You could have come to Cairns, but I suppose that

would have cut into your very busy schedule. I know your boy-toy husband keeps you terribly occupied."
Well, that wasn't civil at all. Despite Cal's best efforts, his vitriol leaked through. He had his reasons. After all, poor Babcock had spent her final days staring at his stupid face when she'd really needed Pix. Babs had to have felt betrayed. The woman had spent her entire adult life trailing after his mum, and Pix hadn't even bothered to make an appearance when it mattered most.

"Calum, please don't be angry with me, I can't stand it. I'd have given anything to be with Babs at the end. It simply wasn't possible."

Pixie had given a string of excuses about conflicting events and unspecified aches that made a long flight to Australia out of the question. For seven months? No, Cal wasn't buying it—he knew his mother far too well. Pixie simply hadn't wanted to be inconvenienced by taking care of Babcock.

Honestly, what was the point of arguing? It would simply wind him up with no resolution. "Right. Was there something you needed, then?"

"Come over for brekky. Your Aunt Mags is desperate to see you. I'll pop a bottle."

When she hung up, Cal stared at the phone. He could rail at Pix until he ran out of breath, but it wouldn't do a bit of good. There was no changing her. But now Cal knew when the chips were down, he couldn't count on his mum to be there. Fair enough. Cal had spent most of his life alone. Not so bad, really, depending on oneself—less disappointment that way.

He hadn't been awake fifteen minutes, and already Cal had wrangled with Jules, been put on the spot by Pix, and he had another problem—Monica Campbell. Cal owed her an apology, although she probably wouldn't accept it. Still, he needed to make amends, but how? What would appeal to her?

He stretched his neck from side to side and spent the next half hour planning a campaign to win over Monica Campbell. What he finally settled on was iffy, but he couldn't think up anything better.

Using the house phone, Cal dialed Mr. Lawson, ordering a car and driver. The villa came with around-the-clock butler service, which was most convenient. While Cal lectured Jules about helping those less fortunate, here he was sprawled across the lap of luxury. She accused him of being a hypocritical twat, and maybe that was true, but honestly, though this place was lovely, Cal felt equally at home in a tent with nothing but a bedroll and a sturdy pair of boots.

After dressing, Cal gave careful instructions to Mr. Lawson and dashed off a note on thick ivory stationery before heading to Pixie's house. During the drive, Cal thought about Monica. He'd been close to making her come last night, his finger mere centimeters away from slipping inside her. And she'd been so ready for it.

Monica may act uptight, but every movement she made was graceful and lithe—sexual in a natural way. After he'd stripped the blouse from her body, she'd stood before him, unashamed. He'd been spellbound by those lovely breasts. She liked his touch, grew breathless when he kissed her. It was bloody obvious Monica liked sex, so why couldn't she just admit it? The way she behaved afterward, as if they'd done something wrong or disgusting…well, it not only took him by surprise, it had bruised his pride.

Cal still didn't have any answers, and he needed to focus on something other than his cock right now. Thinking about Monica Campbell and her soft, full tits did him in.

They drove through aged wooden gates studded with wrought-iron hinges. It gave the faux palazzo a look of authenticity. In the circular drive, the car drew to a stop. Cal shoved a few bills in the driver's hand and didn't wait for him to open the door. "Pick me up in an hour, mate, and I'll double that."

As the car drove away, Cal stared up at the colossal house. He'd stayed in Venetian palazzos many times, and while this house bore the markings—white stucco and arched, narrow windows surrounded by delicate traceries—it lacked the aged patina of real plaster. And mold. Authentic palazzos always had mold.

He strode to the front door and used the ornate knocker. A moment later, the maid answered. Why his mother insisted on putting the woman in a black uniform was anyone's guess. Babcock would have wadded up the dress and told Pix to stuff it up her bum. Babs's wardrobe revolved around track suits and bright white trainers. *How else am I supposed to chase after you? Never in one place for long, the pair of you*. She'd said that often, usually while packing.

Cal followed the maid through the house and out the back door, to a multileveled terrace that overlooked rolling green hills. Brown mountains were a hazy mirage in the distance, far beyond Pixie's vast estate.

Tipping his head to the maid, Cal jogged down the winding stairs. Pix and Paolo, his aunt Mags, and her ex-husband, Nigel, sat at a rectangular table overlooking the pool.

Upon seeing him, Pixie rose and strutted toward him. Her silky purple dressing gown flowed outward to reveal matching pajamas. Her heeled slippers were purple as well, and encrusted with crystals. "Look who's here, everyone." With shoulder-length dark waves and carefully applied makeup, she appeared a decade younger than her sixty-plus years. "My darling boy, how are you?"

Cal bent down and kissed both of her cheeks. "How are you, Mum?"

"Better now that you're here. Come, sit."

Before grabbing a chair, Cal kissed his aunt. Where Pixie was petite, her sister, Mags, was taller, more voluptuous, and a few years older. Trevor had inherited his mother's gray eyes and too little of her charm.

"My dearest, how handsome you look, and so very tan," she said. "All that sun in Australia must have been lovely."

Cal wouldn't describe anything about his time in Cairns as lovely. He said nothing as he shook hands with Nigel. An older version of Trevor with his dark-turning-to-gray hair and a stubborn chin, Nigel didn't bear the same attitude of cool superiority his son had perfected. Instead, he possessed a ready smile, and though he'd gathered a few more wrinkles since the last time Cal had seen him, the older man wore them well.

"How are you, my boy?" Nigel asked. "Up for a game of golf while you're in town?"

Cal fell into his seat. "I don't really play."

Nigel looked momentarily dumbfounded. "Why ever not?"

"Hello, Calum," Paolo said. Dressed in a pink knit shirt

that strained at his biceps, and a light green sweater tied at his neck, he cradled a yappy white-haired dog.

When Pixie had first announced her engagement to Paolo, a man decades her junior, Cal had been concerned. He figured the waiter his mum had met while on vacation was a gold digger. But they'd been married ten years. Quite happily, by all accounts.

"Do you want an egg?" Paolo asked in Italian-flavored English, which had much improved in the last few years.

"No, thanks."

"Darling," Pix said, "what have you been doing with yourself? I've only seen you once since you've come to Vegas."

"I wonder why." Cal wasn't over his irritation at being summoned to the States. When he'd arrived on his mum's doorstep with a bottle of champagne, only to find there was no party and he'd been duped, Cal had been furious. "You lied to me? You dragged me halfway around the world for nothing?"

In the face of his anger, she merely shrugged. "I had to get you here some way. I've been so worried about you. You're becoming a hermit."

She wasn't wrong. After Babcock's death, Cal had been apathetic, listless. He sat on the beach, staring at the water all day, and nursed a beer on the veranda every night. He'd gotten himself into a rut, and he couldn't seem to shake the grief that had left him numb.

Now Pixie stabbed a blueberry with her fork. "I've apologized for lying, Calum, but I'd do it all over again."

Cal narrowed his eyes against the sun. "Oh, I know you would. Whatever's most convenient, that's your route."

Mags's glance darted between the two of them. "Trevor says you've been using his garage, dearest, which I hope means you're staying in town for a while?"

"I have no idea." Why the hell did everyone keep asking about his plans? Damned annoying of them. When Cal figured it out, he'd send them all a group text.

"Come along, Nigel," Mags said, "we should go. Cal, I hope to see you again very soon."

Nigel glanced down at his plate. "I haven't finished my kippers. What's the hurry?"

Mags stood and tugged at her tight blue dress. Then she whisked Nigel's plate from the table. "It's kippers on the go this morning. Spit spot. *Ciao*, Paolo."

Nigel pushed back his chair. "All right, woman. I'm coming." He turned to Cal. "Good to see you. If you change your mind about a round or two, do let me know." He trailed Mags up to the house.

Pix pursed her lips and angled her head toward the tennis court. "That was rather rude of you."

When the little dog began to whine, Paolo stood and swept it under his arm, then he leaned down to kiss Pixie's cheek. "Play nice." He shot Cal one last glance before taking the sunglasses from the top of his head and slipping them on. With a swagger, Paolo walked with the tiny dog past the pool and down the hill.

"He's a man of few words."

Pixie smiled. "He says all he needs to with his body."

"Oh God. Spare me the details." Cal's eyes wandered to Pixie's throat, lined with fine wrinkles. It betrayed her true age. Silence stretched between them until Cal said, "She asked for you, at the end."

Pix straightened her shoulders. She remained quiet

for a few minutes, then she turned to look at him. "I miss her every day, darling."

"Do you?"

Clearing her throat, she shook her head. "Don't do this to me, Cal. Please."

He slouched back in his chair, draping his hands over the armrests. Cal could continue to pick at her, but he'd only feel worse, and it wouldn't change anything. Searching for some topic to fill the space, Cal said, "Jules called this morning."

Pixie's face brightened as she grabbed onto the subject like a conversational life jacket. "Oh, lovely Juliette! How is she? She must be what, fourteen by now?"

"She'll be twenty-one in a few months. And she was just arrested for drink-driving."

"I can't believe she's that old. Where has the time gone?"

"That's what you're fixated on—her age—and not the fact that she was snockered and trying to drive?"

Pixie threw her hands into the air. "I can't say anything without you jumping down my throat. Honestly, Calum."

"Sorry." Sitting up, he leaned his elbows on the table. "Why didn't you leave me with him—after the divorce, I mean?"

"Who?" Pixie's dark green eyes widened. "Your father? What does it matter?"

"I don't know." Since he'd first learned of Babcock's illness, Cal had become introspective and out of sorts. The only time he'd felt himself in months was with Monica Campbell. Which was ludicrous, because she was quite obviously going through her own identity crisis. "It just does."

"Darling, men like your father live small lives." Pixie

placed her hand on his arm. At least two million pounds' worth of diamonds glittered on her fingers. "You would have withered under all of his rules."

"If he was so bloody horrible, why did you marry him?"

"I thought it was time to settle down. Your aunt Mags was married, and she seemed happy."

"Aunt Mags is always happy. Until she isn't."

"Your father was mad about me. Unfortunately, that wore off rather quickly, and we wound up rowing constantly. One day, I just couldn't take it anymore. You were only six and so terribly unhappy. So was I. If you'd stayed, you would have been miserable. I wanted better things for you."

"What better things?" *Like drifting from one place to the next, never fitting in? Feeling like a ghost in a world full of real people?* Where was this coming from? Cal liked new places, new people. Australia had skewed his worldview, and he wasn't sure how to regain his old perspective. "Why the constant moving around?"

"I get antsy. You're the same way. Staying in one place for too long, it made me irritable, like I was bursting out of my skin. There was always a new adventure to be had."

A new adventure. That's what she'd always said to him when he was a boy, but it was simply code for *Pix is bored now*.

Cal stared out at the mountains, the only thing breaking up the skyline. He couldn't fault Pix, because he'd done the same thing—traveled from place to place, staying put in London only when he had a car to obsess over. Now Cal didn't know what he wanted. One place was pretty much like another. Different beach, different country. Same sky.

His life was a carousel, going round and round, but never heading anywhere. At thirty-two, Cal felt weary.

"Would you have preferred being stuck in some dreary boarding school?" Pix asked. "I don't think so. We have good memories, Cal. Remember that little tavern in Minsk?" Pix quirked her head to one side. With her pointed chin and delicate features, she really did look like a sprite. "That pretty waitress made such a fuss over you, and you were only thirteen. Every time she pinched your cheeks, you turned bright red. Or the time we watched the fireworks on Bastille Day from a boat on the Seine?"

She was right. He'd have been bored to bits at school, and he wouldn't have done well anyway. Cal liked working with his hands. He probably never would have known that if Pix hadn't had an affair with Yurgi. That Russian had more classic cars than ex-wives.

"Darling, what is this about?"

Cal raised one shoulder. "I was curious, that's all. Babcock had no family. No one. Not a cousin or an uncle tucked away somewhere. Terrible, that. Not having anyone."

"Calum, you have someone. We have each other."

He looked into her eyes then, saw a hint of desperation there. She needed him to let this go, let go of the hurt and disappointment he'd been hanging onto. But he couldn't. He simply wasn't capable of forgiving her.

He stood and shoved his hands into his pockets. "I need to dash. I'll talk to you soon."

"Calum."

"I'm sorry." Pixie's eyes shimmered with tears, which she quickly blinked back. She was hurting in her own way, and he was a shit for causing it. But he didn't know what to do, how to fix this rift between them, if it was indeed reparable. "I'll call you next week, Mum."

Cal jogged up the stairs and strode through the house. Hopefully the hired car would be waiting for him. His skin felt tight, and he was edgy. He hated arguing with Pix. It rarely happened. She'd always been the good cop. Babs was the one who'd forced him to do his maths and eat his vegetables. Pix let him do whatever the hell he wanted.

When he walked out the front door, the car wasn't there, but Paolo was. He leaned against a yellow Lamborghini. He pushed off it and straightened when he saw Cal.

"What's up?" Cal asked.

Paolo thrust his hands into his pockets and nodded toward the house. "Make up with Pix. She misses you."

"I'm here now, aren't I?"

"You are not alone. She is sad about Bab too."

Cal's mood went from introspective to angry faster than that Lamborghini went from zero to sixty. "If she's so fucking grieved, she should have gone to Australia when she had the chance. And it's Babcock or Babs, if you must. She was probably the best person I've ever known, so get the name right, will you?" This rage blindsided him. He'd been a zombie for months, and suddenly he was lashing out, making Pix cry, yelling at Paolo. What the bloody hell was wrong with him?

Paolo appeared shocked. Before he had time to respond, the hired car pulled through the gates. "I'm sorry. Please forgive me." He needed to get out of there. Now. He strode to the car, flung open the door, and slid inside.

What a fucking disastrous day. And it wasn't even noon.

Chapter 7

Monica finished her fifth call of the morning when Stella walked into the office carrying an enormous vase of flowers. A profusion of freesias, peonies, and lilies filled the air with their sweet aroma.

Stella placed them on the small credenza across from the desk. "These came for you." She adjusted the vase this way and that before handing over an envelope bearing Monica's name, written in a bold scrawl.

Cal. Monica dropped it on her desk like it was radioactive. "Thanks."

"Well, aren't you going to open it?"

"Yep." She gave Stella a pointed look.

"Fine, I'm leaving," she said, rolling her eyes. "I assume it's from that sexy British guy?"

"More than likely."

"Monica, my dear, I'm going to give you the same advice I'd give my own daughter, if I had one. Get out and have fun. The girls"—she pointed to her chest—"they only stay perky for so long. Take advantage of it."

As soon as she left the office, Monica picked up the card—probably an apology for acting like an ass last night, for giving her the third degree in the middle of one of the busiest casinos on the Strip. *You weren't exactly tactful yourself, Campbell, blaming him for your foolish choices*. Well, there was that. Perhaps there was the slimmest chance she owed him an apology too.

Monica ripped at the adhesive flap and pulled out the note. She glanced over the words written on the heavy cardstock, then read them again. It wasn't an apology. She looked at the check. One hundred thousand dollars to the foundation.

Hope this helps. —Cal

Of course she was thrilled about the donation. But still, no apology, no request for forgiveness. Not a word about a second date. She would have turned him down, of course, but Calum Hughes had just taken another bite-size chunk out of her ego.

Monica's gaze returned to the flowers. Why send them? If he wasn't sorry, why send an arrangement that was damn near as tall as she was—what game was he playing?

She set the check aside and was about to drop the note into the trash can, but instead slipped it into her desk drawer. She'd have Stella send Cal a thank-you note from the foundation. A personalized note. He'd given her his phone number last night, but she wasn't going to use it. Ever. That would just be asking for trouble.

Monica worked steadily throughout the day. As she accomplished tasks, she crossed them off her list—and stared at those flowers. Every time the phone rang, her body tensed as she wondered if Cal was on the other end. Every time her email pinged, she checked it.

But he never called, never showed up. Then it occurred to her that maybe he wasn't playing a game. If he'd taken her at her word and was leaving her alone, good. Great.

Then why did she feel so restless? Monica shook her

head at her own stupidity. What was wrong with her? *What wasn't wrong with her?* If Monica started cataloging all of her character flaws, she'd be here all night, but falling for Calum Hughes wasn't going to be one of them.

At six, Stella walked in carrying three plastic takeout bags.

"You must be hungry tonight. These things weigh a ton. Don't stay too late."

It smelled divine. Chinese food, if Monica knew her Szechuan. Garlicky and spicy. Her stomach rumbled. "I didn't order anything."

Stella shrugged on her way out the door.

Monica peered into one of the sacks. Resting on top sat a hand-wrapped fortune cookie. She plucked it out and gave it a wary gaze, then broke the cookie in half. Cal's handwriting.

> *I wasn't sure what you liked, so I got a little bit of everything. Have a good evening.*

She pulled out containers filled with spicy beef, chicken, a steamed vegetable dish, and rice. There were egg rolls and dumplings and cartons of soup—easily enough to feed the entire office.

She'd refused to call Cal this afternoon to thank him, but now she had no choice. She was simply being polite. It had nothing to do with the fact that she wanted to hear that deep, raspy voice of his.

Who the hell are you trying to convince, here? Fine, she wanted to hear his deep, raspy voice. But nothing would come of it. Just a simple thanks, and she'd hang up.

Monica dug into her purse and retrieved Cal's number. Nervously scraping the surface of her thumbnail, she dialed and waited. When she finally heard his voice-mail message, disappointment hit her, swift and sharp. Where was he? On another date? A tight coil of jealousy wrapped around her chest and squeezed.

Whoa. Time to slam on the brakes. What Cal did, and with whom, was none of Monica's business.

Thanking Cal should be just another item on her to-do list, but she couldn't be objective. Last night had been much more than a good-night kiss. It had left her shell-shocked. If he could make her feel this fluttery and possessive after a semiclothed fumble, what would happen if they actually had sex?

Grateful—that's what she should feel. Grateful he hadn't answered the phone with that growl that left her stomach feeling like it was made of Jell-O.

Monica left a hasty, impersonal message, thanking Cal for the flowers, check, and food. There. Done. No need to think about him again.

Except that with every bite she took, he floated through her mind. His smell, his skin's texture. The way he'd touched her breasts and fondled her pussy. And she'd thought that kiss five years ago had been unforgettable.

Disgusted with herself, Monica boxed up the rest of the food and stuck it in the break-room refrigerator. As she walked back to her office, she eyed the flowers. She may not have had any contact with Cal, but he'd definitely made his presence known.

Bastard.

Over the next three days, Monica didn't hear from him. At least not directly. But on Wednesday, he provided a catered lunch for her staff. She texted him a quick thanks. He never responded.

On Thursday, he sent her a beautifully wrapped package, rectangular and only about seven inches long. Was it a bracelet? If so, she was sending it back. Jewelry seemed too personal and inappropriate.

Monica held it up to her ear and gave it a light shake, but nothing rattled. Her pulse faltered as she untied the pretty gold bow. Inside the flat box she found a pen covered in pink Swarovski crystals. It was tacky and sparkly and she adored it.

Oh, he was so calculating. She knew exactly what Cal was up to—trying to soften her up. Well it wasn't going to work. Again, she texted a short thank-you, but didn't receive a response. He probably figured that not answering her calls or texts would drive her crazy. He figured right. Every time she looked at the flowers or wrote with the pen, she thought about Cal.

Friday morning, she received an email that a generous gift had been made in her name. The money would be used to provide health care at a women's clinic in Kenya.

Son of a bitch, he was good.

His diabolical plan actually worked. She couldn't stop thinking about him. Monica had reread his card so many times, she knew his sloping handwriting by heart. He was wearing her down, day by day.

Grabbing her phone, Monica speed-dialed his number. This time, after the fifth ring, he answered. "Hey," she said. Now that she'd heard his voice, she felt tongue-tied and jittery, like she'd mainlined three shots of espresso.

"Monica. What's up?" He sounded casual, almost indifferent.

She grabbed the pink crystal pen and wiggled it between her fingers. "Um, I just wanted to thank you, you know, for everything."

"Of course, no problem." He didn't say anything else.

Monica waited a beat, suddenly unsure of herself. He was interested, right?

She gazed at the flowers Cal had sent, still vibrant and fragrant. On Monday he'd touched her, pinched her nipples, kissed her like he couldn't get enough. Then there were the thoughtful gestures over the last few days—yeah, Cal was interested, all right, but he'd been waiting for her to come to him, then acting aloof when she did. Classic. Well, she wasn't about to fall for that bullshit.

"All right then," she said cheerfully, "take care."

"Wait," he said as her thumb drifted over the End button. "Before you go, there is something you might be able to help me with."

"If possible." Cal wanted to play disinterested? Well she could play twice as hard. *Sure you can. Unless he steps within a fifty-foot radius.*

"Is there a decent restaurant you'd recommend?" he asked.

Everything in Monica's world shifted back into place. This was what Cal had been after all along. A date. Nothing complicated about it. "I suggest you consult a Zagat's Guide."

"I could do, of course, but getting a local's perspective is usually better."

"There's a sushi restaurant in Caesars, a steak bar in

the Luxor, an Italian place at the Venetian. Ask your concierge, he'll give you a list."

"Excellent. Thanks for your help." And then he hung up.

He hung up.

Monica stared at her phone in disbelief. Just when she thought she had him figured out, he'd do the unexpected.

Exactly five minutes later, he called back. "What?" she snapped.

"Monica, will you have dinner with me this evening? You can play tour guide, show me all the sights. I'd be ever so grateful."

"Forget it."

"Splendid. I'll get your address from Trevor and be there at seven. Look forward to seeing you, love."

She didn't have time to say a word, because he'd hung up again. Cal Hughes was driving her insane. Monica planned on telling him so. But first, she needed something to wear.

Six fifty-three. Monica had been checking her phone for the last fifteen minutes while she paced the empty dining room. The tips of her pointy new heels were a little tight and echoed on the tiled floor. Black pumps. Four inchers.

She'd gone round and round with herself about this date so many times, she felt a little dizzy. Or it could be the fact that she was going to see Cal again in…six minutes and fourteen seconds.

This afternoon, she'd finally broken down and called Evan for support.

"We're going out. Cal and I. On a date."

"Just one second." He'd held the phone away from

his mouth. "Hallelujah," he screamed. "Okay, I'm back. So, you've decided to take Evan's advice?"

"Don't talk about yourself in the third person, it's obnoxious. And yes. I'm going to treat Cal like a vaccine. After him, I should either be completely immune to bad boys, or I'll be catatonic. One or the other." Standing by the office window, Monica had run a hand over her navy blue jacket. It was the sassiest one she owned, because it featured four brass buttons. "I think I have a fashion emergency, Ev."

"You're just now figuring this out? Meet you at Nordies at two o'clock."

"I only have an hour and fifteen minutes before my next meeting."

He heaved a dramatic sigh. "I'm not a miracle worker, but I'll do my best."

Evan was already at the store with an armful of colorful dresses when she arrived. He'd shoved them at her and tried to follow her into the dressing room. "I need to see how they fit."

"Out, you perv." Monica slammed the door in his face.

"Fine, but you're the one with the time crunch."

Out of the dozen dresses facing her, Monica tried on three, all muted colors, but they showed off a fair amount of cleavage and were much shorter than anything she'd worn in years.

So now here she stood in the dining room, waiting for Cal in a black tank dress. The material was a little sparkly, but not too much. Her arms and legs were completely bare. Once upon a time, she would have considered this dress too conservative.

Not that it mattered how much skin she revealed. Cal

had gotten an eyeful of her the other night, and Monica hadn't been shy then. In fact, she'd all but shaken her tits in his face.

But tonight was going to be different. Tonight, she was in control. Monica's eyes were wide open, no illusions this time—Cal wasn't the right man for her, and she knew it.

If nothing else, she could listen to that sexy voice and stare at him all night. Cal was like a flower or a sculpture, here to make the world a sexier place. And since she had no intention of getting serious with him, she could just enjoy him while he was in town. Have a little fun. Bad-boy inoculation.

She heard his car door slam at six fifty-nine. *In control. Eyes wide open.*

At the door, she gripped the handle and took three deep breaths before opening it. But the sight of him caused that last breath to become lodged in her throat. She should have been prepared for that face, that body, but Cal knocked her for a loop all over again. He stood beneath her porch light, his green eyes looking a shade darker than normal, more pine bough than fresh spring leaves. Even in the sparse light, he was a burst of warmth and sunshine and fresh air.

The ends of his hair were damp and curled slightly upward, turning the natural highlights to a burnished gold. He'd freshly shaved, and his tanned cheeks looked smooth. Monica wanted to touch them to make sure, but rubbed her thumbnail instead as she resisted the urge.

The tight navy T-shirt showed off his pecs—well developed and perfectly defined. They made her cheeks tighten with heat. Faded jeans—no grease stains—clung to his legs. As her gaze slipped lower, Monica purposely avoided looking at his package. On his feet, brown leather work boots were scratched at the toes.

Cal dressed blue-collar casual, wore it with a comfortable grace, but he was the furthest thing from it. Trust-fund baby. Jet setter. Poshly accented mechanic. She hadn't quite figured him out.

Swiping her tongue quickly over her lips, she glanced up and realized Cal was checking her out just as thoroughly.

His gaze moved over her body, from the bodice of the dress, which dipped a little low, down over her hips. Canting his head to the side, he stared at her bare legs. Although they were too pale, Cal didn't seem to mind. She read the sexual interest in his eyes.

After a few long seconds, he slowly perused her calves and ankles, all the way down to her feet, taking in the dark, pointy heels. Then his glance reversed, moving upward once more. She felt that heated gaze dance across her skin like a drop of water when it hit a sizzling pan. As his eyes rested on her cleavage, Monica stopped breathing for a moment. Finally, he looked her in the eye. "Bloody fucking hell, woman. You have legs. And they're spectacular."

She tucked a strand of hair behind her ear as her gaze bounced away from his. "Thanks." Since working at the foundation, Monica had tried hard to maintain her professional image. But she realized those clothes also made her feel invisible. She liked that Cal noticed and appreciated her body. She felt womanly and sexy for a change. Still nervous, of course, but the flood of anxiety was starting to recede.

Cal held a small pink gift bag in one hand. "If you invite me in, I'll give you this." He gave the bag a little shake.

It took Monica a moment to understand the words. "Sorry." With a quick nod, she backed up and allowed him to enter. "Sure, come on in. Would you like something to drink?"

He openly gazed around the small entryway. The blank ivory walls, the dated ceramic tile flooring. "Beer?"

"Sure. Is a longneck okay? Or I could pour it in a cup, if you'd prefer?" Oh God, she was babbling.

His eyes found hers, and they stared at each other for few seconds. "Bottle."

Would Monica ever get tired of hearing that voice? It made her nipples hard. She spun, her narrow heels catching in the loops of the tan carpet. She managed to right herself, but Cal's arm banded around her, underneath her breasts.

"Okay?" His breath fanned the side of her neck. His body felt warm against her bare upper back, but despite his heat, goose bumps covered her arms.

"Yeah."

He didn't let her go. "You look smashing, by the way."

"Thanks."

"You're welcome." Cal dipped his head and lightly kissed her shoulder. Then he released her.

You're in control. Why had Monica thought tonight was a good idea again? Oh yeah, to prove to Cal that she wasn't bothered by his little games. Right.

Tossing her head, she lifted her chin and strode into the kitchen, mindful of her heels this time. Opening the fridge, Monica plucked out a bottle. When she whirled around, she noticed Cal scoping out her ass. She raised a brow, but he simply grinned.

He took the beer from her hand. "Cheers." He twisted off the cap and took a long draw. The galley kitchen was too confining with Cal in it. They stood only six inches apart. Monica's torso still felt warm from where he'd wrapped his arm around her. He smelled good too—that delicious combination of woodsy aftershave and hot man.

"Why don't we go to the living room?" Monica skirted around him and led the way, parking herself on the far end of the sofa. As Cal sprawled out next to her, there was less than a foot separating their knees. How was this any better? He was still too close. With a beer in one hand and the hot-pink gift bag in the other, he looked sexy and whimsical at the same time.

She twisted her head to glance back at him and eyed the bag warily. "What is it?"

"You have this look of fear in your eyes. What could I possibly give you that would cause such a reaction?" He dangled the strings from his finger. "A snake? A spider?"

"Edible underwear? And I keep telling you, I'm not afraid."

"Keep saying it enough, darling, maybe you'll start to believe it." He glanced around the near empty living room. "Love what you haven't done with the place."

A big-screen TV broke up the blank, textured walls. Threadbare microfiber covered her consignment-shop sofa. She'd bought it in college and never bothered to upgrade. The coffee table, made of pressed chipboard, came from the "as-is" aisle of a home improvement store. "I haven't had time to decorate." Or the interest. After she'd completed her master's degree, Trevor and Allie had given Monica a check with lots of zeros at the end. When her apartment lease ended, a house seemed like a good investment.

"I'm not judging." He extended his arm and shook the bag at her. "Open it."

She plucked it from his finger and, biting her lip, unwrapped the tissue paper to remove a pair of fuzzy pink dice. They matched her steering-wheel cover exactly. Frivolous and silly, they were perfect. "Thank you." She brushed a finger across the rough faux fur and gazed up to find Cal staring at her mouth.

"You're most welcome." He leaned forward and placed the half-empty beer bottle on the coffee table. "I know they're a bit stupid, but I saw them at the automotive store today, and they made me think of you."

He was thinking of her? That made her heart flip. "I love them." As they stared at each other, seconds ticked by, and Monica's smile faded.

Time slowed down, and all of her senses were attuned to Cal. Monica became conscious of her heart picking up speed, of feeling a little light-headed.

He stood and held out his hand. Large calluses dotted his palm. Was he a blue-collar self-starter or an upper-class drifter? He couldn't be both.

She placed her hand in his and stood too.

"What are you going to show me tonight?" he asked.

Everything, she wanted to say. Anything. As long as he reciprocated.

Cal dropped her hand and stuck both his own in the back pockets of his jeans. The move drew the knit material tight across his shoulders. A dark flush stole its way up his neck and cheeks. Monica's eyes darted downward. His cock had grown stiff. He was feeling it too, this pull, this attraction.

"Monica." He said it like a plea.

If they didn't leave right now, this very minute, they'd never make it out of the house. Accepting this date was a big step. She might be ready for sex by the end of the night, but not yet. "We should go."

He nodded, and pulling his hands from his pockets, strode to the door. He opened it for her. As she walked by him and out onto the porch, he muttered something.

"What?" she asked.

"Nothing at all." *I am in for a bloody long, painful night*. That's what he'd mumbled. Didn't bear repeating.

Monica had dazzled him from the moment she'd opened the front door. And by the way she'd taken a dekko at him, carefully checking him out from head to toe, the feeling was mutual. Monica's nervous reaction—fiddling with her hair, meeting his gaze, then dropping her eyes—completely charmed him. And the way she'd stared at his cock just now, with equal parts desire and sheer panic made him want to comfort her. And jump her.

Her dress was lovely. It may have been black, but at least it showcased her figure. Monica Campbell wasn't meant to be a wallflower, sitting on the sidelines in boring suits. Or this dull house. Off-white walls. Unfurnished rooms. Even the carpet was a bland shade of beige. Monica was living in a black-and-white existence, and he hated to see it. She was full of life and energy, especially when she was sparring with him. Sexy as bloody hell. The last few days, not seeing her, not speaking with her, had been difficult, but he kept his endgame in sight. Cal had a mission to bring some color back into Monica's life.

Standing on the porch, Cal waited as she locked the door. The outdoor light provided enough illumination that when she bent over, he had a rather nice view of the backs of her thighs. Her legs were long and slender. Shapely. He wanted to get between them more than he'd wanted anything in a very long time. But that ass. It was a thing of beauty.

Straightening, she turned around and caught him staring again.

"Whoops," he said. "You found me out. But I'm not going to apologize—"

"You never do."

"Because you have a fabulous bum."

"Sure." She shoved her keys into her purse and licked her lips. Keeping her eyes lowered, she used one hand to skim her hip.

"It's true." He took a step closer. Her gaze flicked up his chest and finally landed on his eyes.

Unable to deny himself a moment longer, Cal reached around and cupped her bottom. It was full, firm. Sliding his palm up and down her cheek, he traced the edge of her thong through the silky material of her dress. The mental image of Monica wearing nothing but a flimsy piece of lace had him gobsmacked for a moment. Then Cal ran his middle finger from the curve of her ass all the way up to her hip. "It's a crime to cover up that bottom. You should show it off all the time. Work, home, the supermarket checkout queue. I could write a sonnet about your ass."

"Sir Mix-a-Lot beat you to it." She glanced away, a

little smile playing on her lips. "And back inside, I was guilty of staring as well."

"I wasn't going to say anything, as I didn't want to embarrass you. I'm quite used to people thinking I'm just another pretty face, and I feel slighted." He donned an expression of mock sincerity.

"Poor Cal." She surprised him by draping her arms around his neck. "You want everyone to know you have a pretty mind too?"

"Don't be daft. I don't care a jot about my brain. I just want to be recognized for my muscular physique and extraordinary cock. Is that too much to ask?"

Leaning her forehead against his chest for a second, Monica laughed. "You're quite possibly a narcissist." She glanced back up at him, amusement shimmering in her eyes. God, she was beautiful.

"You call it narcissism. I call it a healthy body image." Cradling her chin with his free hand, Cal bent down and kissed her softly. He fought against pulling her into a tight clutch, because although she'd touched him back, he sensed her wariness. So he let her have control of the situation.

After a moment, Monica deepened the kiss, opening her mouth a bit wider. When her tongue hesitantly brushed his, Cal wanted to devour her, rip that dress right off her. But he kept himself in check. Damned difficult when he remembered what she'd looked like with her breasts popping out of her sexy little bra. Remembered how wet she'd been when he slid his finger along her hot slit. He was desperate for another feel.

Monica slid her arms from Cal's neck and stroked his chest, brushing her fingertips across his nipples. Cal took that as a green light. His hand tightened on her hip before slipping down to her bum, and when she moaned, he let go of her face and wrapped one hand around her nape. She pressed her body into his—it felt bloody marvelous. His cock was rock hard, jutting between them.

Cal wanted to spend the rest of the evening becoming acquainted with every lovely inch of her. He'd strip her down and let his hands get to know her first. Then his mouth.

He walked her backward, until she bumped into the door. Then he pulled his lips from hers. "Let's go inside."

Monica pushed at his shoulders. She dropped her hands, and opening her eyes, stared up at him. "No, we should go." Her voice came out husky and winded.

He was feeling a bit breathless himself. Cal let go of her nape and retreated a pace. Endgame, that's what he needed to remember. *Stick with the plan—ease off.*

Monica's gaze slid past him to the driveway, where the Mustang sat in all its battered glory. "You got it running, huh?"

It took his brain a moment to translate the question. Cal had never been a slave to his prick. At least not since he was a lad. But a kiss and a quick cuddle with Monica took him to the raw edge of desperation. God, he ached for her.

With a deep inhalation, he cast a glance over his shoulder in an effort to concentrate on something other than his hard-on. "I did. It took a new carburetor, igniter, and a great amount of swearing, but I managed." Blowing out a gusty breath, he faced her once more. "So, what do you have planned for this evening?"

Monica walked to the car. "I thought we'd take in the Strip. I'm sure you've seen it, but with all the crazies, every night is something new."

"Can't wait." Cal opened the car door for her. Although he'd had the interior detailed, the black-and-white bucket seats—original, with embossed vinyl—were ripped at the seams, and the less than pristine floorboard showed signs of rust. He should have rented a decent car, something that didn't require an overhaul. But Cal couldn't remember the last time he'd done this properly—gone out on a real date. Next time, he'd have to prepare, even though he was useless at planning.

As Monica slid into the seat, Cal bent down and grabbed the lap belt, fastening it around her waist. "No shoulder harness." His eyes were mere centimeters away from her tits, which were on display tonight, pushed up high and firm. Cal's mouth grew dry as he stared at them. She was so pale, and there was a tiny mole in the center of her chest, directly above her amazing cleavage.

The universe was testing him tonight. With difficulty, he straightened, but his eyes remained glued to Monica's breasts. It would torture him, seeing her body outlined in that tight, low-cut dress, but not able to touch.

"Cal." He yanked his gaze away from her tits and up to her eyes. "Just how extraordinary is your cock, anyway?"

Cal scrubbed his hands over his eyes. "Are you trying to kill me, darling? By the end of the night, my brain will be so deprived of oxygen, I may very well pass out."

Monica tossed her head back and laughed, exposing her throat. He wanted to lick her there, bite the white skin and leave his mark. Monica brought out primitive urges he didn't know he had.

"Where did Miss Prim go, eh?"

"She's taken a backseat tonight. Now get in the car. I'm going to show you Vegas."

Chapter 8

Monica was still on the fence about this date, but Cal had a way of putting her at ease. Or maybe the intense sexual desire that slammed into her system every time he touched her drowned out all other feelings.

The chemistry between them was combustible. The man gave her an eyegasm every time she glanced at him. Sex seemed inevitable.

But his looks were only part of the attraction. That off-kilter smile and his arrogant sense of humor had her melting. She liked bantering with him. She loved the way he kissed—he put everything he had into it, and she felt it all the way to her toes.

Unlike their fumble in the supply closet, the kiss he'd just given her had been gentle. What would he be like during sex? Commanding and forceful or tender and patient? The anticipation caused her hands to shake slightly as she fingered the metal buckle of the lap belt. When his face had been so close to her breasts, she'd wanted him to touch her, taste her. But seeing him frustrated with desire had been pretty satisfying too.

"When was the last time you were in Vegas?" she asked.

"The last time I felt you up in Trevor's garden." Without taking his eyes from the road, he settled his hand on her bare knee. A shot of pleasure coursed through her. And when his rough hand started stroking upward, Monica swallowed hard.

"But your mom..." She had to clear her throat and start again. His touch distracted her. "Your mom has lived here for what, three or four years?"

"I'd meet her in London or Paris. Easier that way." His strong hand rubbed tender little circles along her thigh. Monica parted her legs slightly. He couldn't seem to keep his hands to himself, and that excited her even more.

"Which is better, London or Paris?"

As he turned left onto the Strip, he gave her one last stroke before returning his hand to the wheel. "Depends, really. London is exciting, and of course my garage is there." There was a note in his voice, a wistfulness she didn't expect.

"You and Pix moved around a lot, huh?"

"Quite."

"So what's the longest you've ever stayed in one place?" she asked. "Besides London, I mean."

Cal remained silent. As she stared at his stark profile, highlighted by the bright neon lights and flashing billboards, his expression hardened. He pulled into a casino parking garage and smoothly wound his way up to the fifth level.

He obviously didn't want to talk about it, just like he didn't want to talk about Australia. Even though it was none of her concern, Monica wanted to draw out his secrets and discover everything about him.

Working at the foundation, Monica had met celebrities—mostly local ones. She'd met rich donors and high rollers. But Cal was easily the most interesting man she'd ever come across. And an enigma. He'd traveled the world, had probably been to all the places she longed to go, but he remained grounded and charming and kind.

Kind? How so? He wooed her with dinner and donations and fuzzy dice only to get into her panties. And it was totally working. But that didn't make him kind—that made him a typical male.

After Cal cut the engine, he stretched his arm along her shoulders. "What are you thinking about? I can practically hear the wheels grinding."

"Just wondering what to show you first."

"Liar. But you're in the driver's seat."

"Good, I like it there." She ignored his taunt.

Cal smiled and extracted himself from the car, then walked around and opened her door. Trying to climb out and keep her skirt from riding up to her hips was a hard trick to pull off. Cal's heated gaze latched onto her legs.

"Was this your evil plan all along?" he asked. "Wear something wicked and leave me gagging for it?"

"Maybe. Is it working?"

"What do you think?" he asked. Cal snaked a hand around her waist and guided her between rows of cars to the elevator.

She liked that he couldn't keep his eyes off her. It was intoxicating and made her feel like a temptress for a change.

When they stepped onto the elevator car, Cal stood with his back against the wall and tugged on her waist, drawing her against him until her ass rested against his hips.

For the first time in years, Monica gave over to instinct and shut out reason. Straightening her arms, she shifted them backward to Cal's thighs. She ran her short nails over his long, hard legs. At the same time, she brushed her ass across his cock.

He drew a sharp breath, then let out a low, raspy growl. "Does public sex do it for you? You weren't shy that night in the garden, in full view of the wedding party." Tightening one arm around her, he nibbled behind her ear.

Monica had never fucked on full display, but Cal made every forbidden pleasure sound tempting. "I don't know," she answered truthfully, eyeing the security camera. Sex with Cal—while strangers watched? In all honesty, it turned her on just a little. Not that she'd ever let herself do it.

"Not sure I want to share you with the masses," he said against her neck.

"You can't share what you don't have," she said, sliding her hand along the arm at her waist. "And you haven't had me."

"I live in hope."

The elevator doors opened to a large group of people. Monica grabbed Cal's hand and moved past them. She led him through the casino with its smoky haze and crescendo of noise, past the gamblers and out into the warm night air. They strode by a grown man dressed as a banana, and melded with the crowd.

"When was the last time you came down to the Strip and hung out?" Cal asked.

"Not since I was a teenager."

A mass of tourists and street performers flooded the sidewalk. People flowed in and out of restaurants, bars, and gift shops, while she and Cal walked in comfortable silence. He'd intertwined his fingers with hers, making her hand feel small in comparison.

"You grew up traveling the world. To me, this was home," she finally said. "Not seeing the real Eiffel

Tower, just an imitation." She pointed toward the replica down the street.

"Nothing's stopping you from going to Paris, or anywhere else for that matter."

"I have a job, Cal. I can't just take off."

He stopped and stared down at her. "Allison doesn't give you holidays?"

"I don't take vacations."

"Well, you should. All work, no play, et cetera."

"Are you calling me dull?"

"Never," he said, squeezing her hand. "But you could make room for a little fun."

"I'm here with you tonight."

"And I intend to show you a good time." He bent down and planted a swift, firm kiss on her lips before he resumed walking.

The mischievous look in his eye said he wasn't talking about wholesome fun. No, Cal referred to delicious, sexy, outrageous fun—the naked kind. And it excited Monica in ways she hadn't experienced in ages.

At the corner, three unsteady girls threw their arms around one another and staggered into the street before toppling over like drunken bowling pins. A group of older guys in grass skirts and coconut bikini tops helped them up.

Cal dodged a tipsy couple weaving in and out of foot traffic. "I can't believe Allison let you wander around here as a teenager."

"She never knew, or she would have put a stop to it." Monica took it all in. Two men, one dressed as Batman and the other as Sonic the Hedgehog, had a turf fight near a convenience store. People carried enormous plastic souvenir cups filled with booze, and some drunk kid whipped his dick out and peed in the street. Ah, Vegas.

Cal glanced down at her. "You almost look as if you're enjoying yourself."

She shrugged. "It's been awhile." Mobile billboards advertising strip clubs, night clubs, and entertainers crowded the streets along with party busses and limos. "Like I said, it's home."

She led Cal up to an overhead walkway, taking them from one side of the Strip to the other. "What do you do when you travel? See the touristy sights?" she asked. That might get old after a while. Monica wanted to visit the Tower of London, but she didn't want to see it multiple times.

"It depends on the country." He tucked her into his side, wrapping his arm around her waist. "In Cambodia, I went to Angkor Wat. There are these enormous temple ruins deep in the jungle, covered in carvings. It's bloody amazing."

"What kinds of carvings?"

"Myths, nymphs, monsters, and these violent battles, all told in sculpture." Cal withdrew his arm as he stopped in front of a scrawny kid strumming an out-of-tune guitar. Pulling out his wallet, Cal dropped a bill into the guitar case. "There you go, mate." He picked up her hand and carried on.

Monica glanced back and saw the kid's grin. "How much did you give that guy?"

"Um, I don't know. I wasn't paying attention."

Having grown up with money all his life, something like that probably didn't matter to Cal. That night in the restaurant, he'd shoved a wad of cash at the manager.

This week, he'd donated large amounts of money as if it were no more than loose change in the red Christmas kettle. He hadn't done those things because he was altruistic; he'd done them to get his own way. But that wasn't the case with the street performer.

Monica glanced up at him in frustration. For her own peace of mind, she needed to define him somehow. She had a tendency to label people, put them in a box, and keep them there. Kind of like she'd done with herself for the last four years. There was Good Girl Monica and Bad Girl Monica. Things were easier when broken down into their simplest components.

"I can hear you thinking again," Cal said. "You'd better watch that, or your engine will overheat, and smoke will pour out of your ears."

Car analogies aside, Cal was right. Why did it matter which label she used for him? There was one category he couldn't change—drifter. Cal would shake the Vegas dust from his feet soon and move on to the next place, the next girl. After they had a few nights of fun, Monica would probably never see him again. *Eyes wide open.*

"Okay," she finally said, "what about Switzerland? What do you do there?"

He peered down at her. "Ski. What else would one do in Switzerland?"

"Bank? Yodel? Drink hot cocoa?"

"Well, of course, that goes without saying." Letting go of her hand, he threw his arm around her shoulder. Cal's answers surprised her. Monica thought he'd mention clubs or beaches as his favorite pastimes, but when he started talking about Cambodia and the temples, his face, his body language, became animated. His enthusiasm was infectious, and as he talked, he waved his hands as he described the sculptures.

Switzerland, on the other hand, didn't seem to faze him.

"Okay, name your favorite city," she said.

He narrowed his eyes in thought. "That's a tough one. Maybe Prague. Beautiful gothic architecture. It's lovely at night, staring out over the city. Unless you run into the stag parties honking their guts out in the street, which I'd avoid, if I were you. But there are bridges spanning the Vltava River that offer amazing views of the city. The Prague Castle is like something out of a fairy story. I spent six months there when I was seventeen, working for a surly German mechanic. I helped rebuild a '76 Alfa Romeo convertible. Learned a lot with that car. Red, it was. A pain in the ass to get the parts."

As they stepped onto the escalator and descended to the street, Monica wondered what it would be like to take off, go to a foreign city and live there for a few months, then move on whenever she got the itch. Sounded liberating. But also irresponsible.

Did he have a different woman in every city? "Must be lonely, traveling all by yourself."

Near the street, Cal pulled her toward a low wall, behind a row of bushes. "That sounds suspiciously like you're hinting at something, Miss Prim. If you want to know about me, come out and ask." As he leaned back, he settled her in between his long legs and placed his hands around her waist.

She planted her hands on his chest and gazed up at him through the shadows. "Fine. Do you have a girlfriend in every city, or fuck-buddies lined up all over the world?"

"No and no. I'm not some kind of man slag, shagging my way through Europe. Not since I was a teenager anyway. I just like to see new things."

Monica wanted to believe him. Which made her an idiot. The man was gorgeous, and that hoarse voice was a panty-dropper. He may not shag his way through Europe, but she was certain he had no trouble getting laid.

"Now it's your turn," he said. "What's the craziest thing you've ever done?"

Crazy or stupid? They sort of mingled together until it was hard to separate one from the other. But past stupid behavior was definitely one of her hot-button issues.

Cal searched her face. "We don't have to talk about it. It's not important." He softly stroked her cheek.

Monica shoved at his shoulders and walked backward a few steps. "When I was fourteen, I surfed down a steep staircase handrail. I made it halfway before flying off and fracturing my arm." She jutted her chin in the air, expecting him to call bullshit. For some reason, Cal could read her bluff the way no one else ever had. It made her feel vulnerable, emotionally naked. And she wasn't lying, not really. The arm thing happened, but it wasn't the craziest thing she'd ever done.

He stared at her for a long moment. "Which arm?"

"The right one." She held it up. Her mother had been undergoing radiation therapy at the time and spent most of her days in bed. "Allie was extremely pissed off, but that was normal. I was something of a problem child."

Cal gasped and lightly captured her arm. He stroked his hand from her shoulder to her wrist, leaving goose bumps in his wake. "You, problematic? Say it isn't so."

"It's so."

"Come on, let's find something to eat. I'm starving." Cal wrapped his hand around her wrist and pulled her along. "She warned me off, you know. Threatened to remove my balls."

Monica blinked up at him. "Who?"

"Allison."

Her steps halted, and she glared at the passing traffic. After a few seconds, she glanced back at Cal. "You're not joking?"

Cal peered down at her. "I didn't mean to create hard feelings. I thought you'd laugh, or I never would have mentioned it."

Same old Allie, always sticking her nose into Monica's business. She knew her sister meant well, and Monica had given her enough reason to worry in the past, but would Al ever treat her like an adult? "It's fine," she said. "It's what she does. She's a worrier."

They continued walking another block, then Cal pointed to a bar with twangy music blaring through the open door. "There."

"A country bar?"

"Very American," he said.

"Very corporate. It's a chain."

"What's more American than that?" He gave her a wide grin. The grooves along the left side of his mouth were deeper, higher than the ones on the right side. Monica found herself smiling back.

She let him guide her inside the saloon, and she glanced around while Cal paid the cover charge. Since it was a Friday, naturally the place was packed. Could have something to do with the bikini bull riding in one corner, or the beer pong tournament on the far side of the room.

Cal placed his hands on her shoulders and steered her like one of his cars toward the long wooden bar where the female bartender wore a leather bikini and matching chaps. "What do you want to drink?" Cal yelled in her ear.

"Beer is fine."

Cal ordered two. The leather-clad brunette's smile was an invitation. So were her fake tits rammed into that too-small top. Monica shouldn't be jealous. Cal wasn't her boyfriend. He was on loan until he decided to hit the road to Siberia. That didn't stop the emotion from slamming through her.

Cal stood behind her, his hand resting on her hip, his chest a solid wall against her back. Monica watched his reaction in the mirror behind the bar. He didn't stare at the bartender—he stared down at Monica.

She looked away and grabbed the cups. Cal slid a bill to the woman and took a beer from Monica's hand.

"Cheers." He tapped her glass with his own. He took a sip, then bent down. "Sign says there's a restaurant upstairs. Shall we eat?"

She nodded and let him thread his way through the crowd while she held on to the back of his shirt. When they passed the mechanical bull undulating in the corner, with a barely dressed blond waving her hat at the crowd, Cal glanced back. "Is there a rule saying you have to flash your baps to ride that? If so, bloody brilliant. What will it take to get you up there?"

"A lack of dignity. Let's see you take off your clothes and get up there," she said.

"Maybe after a few more beers, eh?" He began moving toward the stairs.

The restaurant was slightly less crowded. As they

waited for a table, Monica sat beside him on a roughly hewn wooden bench and quizzed him about his travels. Occasionally, she'd throw in a car question.

"Best Chinese food you've ever tasted?" she asked.

"A little place in Boston, oddly enough."

"Favorite convertible?"

He shook his head, pinning his lips together. "That's like asking which is my favorite child. They're all special in their own way, but I have to say the '52 Nash-Healey roadster was a labor of love. And hate. Took forever to renovate that car. It was a stunner. Now your turn. Favorite type of music?"

"Boy bands."

Cal made a face. "Tell me you're joking."

"Hey, I'm a product of my environment."

Through dinner and afterward, Monica spent the next hour and a half listening to Cal. He told her all about his adventures, keeping his stories light and amusing. And there was always a car attached to his favorite places. He'd fixed his first Fiat in Honduras, replaced a broken engine block from a '67 Benz in Menton. On the one hand, she envied all the experiences he'd chalked up, countries he'd seen, people he'd met. Yet she felt a little sorry for him too. Cal never stayed in one place for very long. That had to be rough on a kid.

"What was Pixie like as a mother?" Monica asked, resting her chin in her palm.

"She was less of a mother and more of a partner in crime. She had very few rules, very few boundaries. She was fun." He reached for her hand, rubbed his finger across her palm.

"What about school?" Monica asked.

Nothing about his posture altered, but the atmosphere between them changed. And his finger stopped moving over her skin. "I never went to school."

"Did you have tutors?"

A ghost of a smile touched his lips. "In a manner of speaking. Babcock made sure I did my homework."

"What's a Babcock?"

"She was my nanny, my mum's keeper. Actually, she was like a mother to both of us. She'd make me sit down each day and study. I hated every bloody minute of it, but she wouldn't let me go outside until I finished. We had some heated rows, I can tell you that much." His expression changed when he talked about this woman, softening just a bit. Cal cast his eyes to their joined hands. "Mum was helpless. If Babcock hadn't taken care of the domestic tasks, they wouldn't get done."

"And she followed you all over the world?"

"She was part of the family." Monica wasn't sure if Cal realized his grip on her hand had tightened.

"Was?"

He nodded. "Was."

"I'm sorry, Cal."

He said nothing, merely nodded. "You know, I think it's time to get you on that bull."

Monica understood. He didn't want to talk about Babcock any more than she liked talking about her mom. It only brought back the sadness, reminded her of what she'd lost. "Yeah, that bull thing's never going to happen. Have you ever line danced?"

As Cal stood, he raised one brow. "I have not."

"You've been all over the world, and you've never done the Push Tush? Oh, it's time we did something about that."

Cal was never going to be a world champion line dancer—he could barely remember the simple steps and kept stumbling in the wrong direction—but he sure as hell had fun trying.

That wasn't strictly true. He had fun watching Monica try. In those high heels. Wearing that tight dress. The hem kept riding up higher and higher with each move she made. She'd tug it down, but it didn't stay put for long.

And the way her breasts bobbed up and down—bloody hell, he could stare at them for the rest of the night. While other women wore shorts that showed more ass than they covered and bikini tops that barely fit, they couldn't hold a candle to the beautiful woman next to him. Although Monica hopped around like a kangaroo gone mental, she looked a right treat doing it. As she followed the ridiculous dance moves, she'd bite her lower lip and furrow her brow in concentration. It was possibly the sexiest thing he'd ever seen.

Finally, after more songs than he could count, she turned to him and fanned herself. "God, I'm hot. I need a drink." Her dark blond hair was mussed, and her skin looked dewy. Cal wanted to taste it.

Together they exited the dance floor and headed for the bar. After Monica ordered a cola, she glanced over at him. "I hate to be the one to tell you this, but you were slightly worse at dancing than I was. And I sucked."

He snagged an arm around her waist and drew her closer. "I thought you looked amazing out there."

"Now who's lying?" She grabbed her drink and took a sip, pursing her lips around the straw. Cal immediately thought of her doing the same thing to his cock. God, had he ever been this obsessed with getting a woman into his bed?

After taking a few sips, she offered the straw to him. Cal kept his eyes trained on hers, and as he leaned forward to take a drink, his hand drifted from her hip to her ass. "What are we going to do next?" he asked.

"I want to take a spin in your car."

That did surprise him. "You want a ride in the Mustang?"

She slowly shook her head. "I want to *drive* the Mustang. It is road-worthy, right?"

Cal was protective of his cars, but Monica's blue eyes glimmered, and a slightly reckless tension ran through her as she shoved her breasts against his chest. This evening, right now, she reminded him of how she'd been five years ago. Enthusiastic and curious and full of life. Of course he'd let her drive. He'd let her do whatever the hell she wanted. "Where are you going to take me?"

"The desert. I want to see how fast it can go."

Now this was the real Monica, with the sexy dress and the alluring smile. "Do you know how to drive a temperamental Mustang?"

"I know how to drive all sorts of things, Calum Hughes." She further knocked him for six when she stood on her toes and lightly kissed his mouth.

Before he could wrap both arms around her waist and snog her properly, she slipped away from him and sauntered toward the exit. Cal followed at a more sedate pace, because Monica Campbell looked as good going as she did coming. Was it possible to get a raging case of blue balls after only three hours?

Out on the sidewalk, he hastened to her side. "Admit it, you're having fun."

"I admit nothing." She glanced at him from the corner of her eye. "But going out with you hasn't been a terrible experience."

"Flatterer."

Holding hands, they walked back through the casino where they'd started the night and into the parking garage. It reeked of petrol fumes and cigarette smoke. Smelled comforting. His garage back in London was the closest thing Cal had to a home.

When they reached the car, he dug the keys out of his pocket, but didn't hand them over. "A few instructions: be careful as you start the car. Don't give it too much gas. And as you shift into second, watch the clutch, or it will stall. And if you have to brake—"

"For God's sake, Cal, calm down." She grabbed the keys and walked to the driver's side. "It's just a car."

"That's blasphemous. This is not *just a car*." He mimicked her voice and accent. "This is an American classic, the original pony." He caressed the back fender. "This is a piece of art. Not to be trifled with."

"Do you and the car need a few minutes alone?"

He shot her a narrow-eyed glance. "Not to be trifled with."

She sighed. "Fine, no trifling." Monica unlocked the door and opened it. "Now can we go, or are you going to write a sonnet about the Mustang too?" She climbed in and, leaning over, unlocked the passenger door.

Curling his hands into fists, Cal settled in beside her. As she turned the ignition, he winced. "Gently."

She pulled out of the parking space and drove to the

exit. "This really makes you nervous, doesn't it, handing over your baby to someone else?"

"How would you like it if someone swept into your office and started running the foundation? Careful with the corner." She pulled out onto the Strip and shifted gears. Cal closed his eyes as she ground them.

"I know exactly what that feels like, because Allie does it at least once a week. It's pretty goddamned annoying."

"Watch your speed. Red light." When she didn't brake immediately, he braced his feet against the floorboard. "Red light."

"I heard you." She slammed to a stop at the intersection. "What are you going to fix next? The seats? These springs are out of control."

"If you don't learn how to drive, I'm going to have to fix the bloody transmission. Now when the light turns green, ease up on the clutch."

When she did as he requested, Cal sighed in relief. "That must be bloody frustrating, to have big sister looming over you, second-guessing your every move."

"I'm used to it." They remained quiet as Monica took the highway and drove west.

Cal tried to bite his tongue when she shifted too slowly or didn't open the throttle properly. Once they headed toward a less populated area, he began to relax.

Monica cranked down the window. The loud rush of wind ripped through the car, lashed at her hair. Brushing a strand from her eyes, she let out a whoop. "I love this."

With her head tipped back, she looked carefree and happy. Cal couldn't take her eyes off her.

Chapter 9

Monica felt alive. Adrenaline pumped through her system the faster she drove. Monica's bare foot dropped on the gas pedal, and the odometer started creeping up. Eighty. Ninety. Ninety-five. By now, they were in the middle of fucking nowhere, surrounded by low mountains, rocks, and brush, with a long stretch of road ahead. Stars clustered together in the night sky, looking so much brighter without all the neon to drown them out. Monica wasn't sure how long she'd been driving, but she didn't want to stop.

"How far are we going?" Cal yelled above the wind.

"Eventually, I believe we'll run into an ocean."

Her brain had been quiet for awhile as she relaxed and enjoyed the feel of the car and the sound of the motor. Easing up on the gas, she slowed down. Pulling over to the side of the road, Monica put the car in neutral. The night had begun to cool down, and Cal had turned on the heat, which barely worked and smelled faintly of exhaust. He needed to fix that ASAP.

"I guess we should head back," she said. "We can't keep driving all night." After rolling up the window, Monica attempted to tame the tangles in her hair.

Cal reached over and smoothed back a strand. "We can keep going for as long as you like. California, Canada, circle back and drive to the mountains. Whatever you want."

She leaned her head back and closed her eyes. It sounded so enticing. The old Monica wouldn't have hesitated. "I wish I could. But I have a job and a life. There's the gala."

"Allison's got it under control."

"I'd never hear the end of it." She turned her head, opened her eyes, and found him watching her. "Thank you for letting me drive. I know that was hard for you."

"Just a tad. Want to sit here for a moment longer? Look at the stars?"

After switching off the ignition, Monica unhooked her seat belt. "Yeah, I'd like that."

With one finger, Cal stroked the side of her neck. Monica glanced at him once more. It was tough to see him clearly in the dark interior, but she could feel the weight of his stare. "What?"

"You're so perfect. Beautifully fucking perfect."

He closed the space between them, and when his lips touched hers, Monica couldn't think, she simply reacted and kissed him back. All of the objections she'd had earlier, all of the reasons she'd told herself to avoid this very scenario didn't even make an appearance. Everything about Cal felt right. Honest.

When he raised his head, Monica didn't want it to end. Before she could protest, Cal unclicked his own seat belt.

"Come here," he commanded in that deep, scratchy voice. She was helpless to do anything but obey.

Pulling up the hem of her skirt, Monica climbed over the stick shift and straddled his lap. Her dress rose above her hips, exposing her ass to the night air. Cal's dick, pressing against her lower belly, made the muscles there tighten.

With his arms encircling her, he stroked Monica's back with one hand, sending shock waves of pleasure up her spine, while his other hand rested on her bare hip. He angled his head and swiped his tongue against her neck, circling it over the base of her throat. God, that felt amazing.

Monica grasped Cal's upper arms through his shirt. His biceps flexed at her touch. She longed to stroke him everywhere, touch that hot, solid body to her heart's content.

Fucking in a car—this was familiar territory. The bad-girl side Monica kept locked away was breaking out of the cage again. It terrified and exhilarated her. But she needed to clarify things before they went any farther. With a deep breath, Monica tugged on Cal's hair in an effort to get his attention. "Wait a second."

"I've been waiting five years," he said against the underside of her jaw.

She moistened her lips as he continued to lick her neck. "We're having fun, right?"

Cal pulled back. "I'm having fun."

"I mean, no strings, no expectations—that kind of fun."

He was quiet for a long moment. "Of course. No strings."

It stung, hearing him repeat the words, but they both knew the score. "Good, we're on the same page."

"Same paragraph."

They froze for a second before Cal's hands glided downward to clench her ass. Lowering his head, he tongued the center of her cleavage. She *loved* that.

Rubbing his chin against the top of her exposed breast, he gazed up at her. "Why not red?"

"What?" Monica's hands had wandered down Cal's

solid chest, and she'd been in the process of pulling his shirt free from the waistband of his jeans. Now she froze at his question.

"Why didn't you choose a red dress tonight? You look sinful in red."

"I don't wear red."

"You did. The night in the garden, you wore a red, strapless, shiny thing. Showed off your tits and legs."

He was right. Monica had forgotten all about it. She had only two lasting memories of that night: the pain of missing her mom, and losing herself in Cal. But tonight, this moment, it wasn't about suppressing her inner pain. No, tonight was about letting the old Monica come out and play for a little while, while sensible Monica remained in control. "You remember what I wore?"

"I'll never forget it."

After hearing that, she couldn't get him naked fast enough. Renewing her efforts to tug his shirt free, Monica puffed out a breath. "A little help here, Cal."

He laughed. "You're doing fine on your own. If you don't kiss me soon, I'm going to go out of my bloody mind."

"Is that right?" She'd managed to untuck the hem and slide it upward, revealing Cal's smooth, trim waist. With a smile, Monica teased him with a light, fluttering kiss, her lips barely connecting with his, then lifted her head. "There."

Cal stopped kneading her ass and gave it a sharp slap.

"Ouch." She flinched from the sting. "What the hell?"

"That's for a job badly done. That was not a kiss," he growled.

"What would you call it then?"

"An appetizer." Rubbing her bottom, he raised his head an inch and nibbled her lips. "A job worth doing is worth doing properly."

Monica would place a hefty bet that Cal had heard that phrase often—probably from Babcock. "I'll make you a deal. If I kiss you like I mean it, you have to take off your shirt."

"Fair play."

"Does that mean *yes* in Brit speak?"

Cal's chest shook against her hands in laughter. "In American speak, totally."

Leaning down, Monica kissed him, opening her mouth and letting her tongue brush his before dancing away. Then she did it again. And again. She could spend the rest of the night kissing him, touching him. He opened the door to pleasure and spontaneity. His kisses lit a fire deep inside her. She wanted to fan the flames, crank up the heat. God, it had been so long since she'd felt this good. And as usual, Monica didn't do anything by halves. Not only was she giving herself permission to fondle Calum Hughes, she was doing it under the stars, in a rusty Mustang. It seemed fitting, somehow.

Cal kept a firm grip on her butt, digging his fingers into her flesh and parting her cheeks as he kissed her back. His tongue met hers, twirled around it, then came back for more. The combination of his squeezing hands and firm, talented lips left Monica panting.

As she continued to taste him, she petted his chest, still bothered that she wasn't touching his bare skin. Flicking her short nails across his nipples, she lapped at his bottom lip, then forced herself to break away. "Your turn. Let's ditch this shirt." As quickly as she could manage, Monica pulled it upward until finally her palms met smooth, taut skin.

"Yes, let's." Cal released her ass long enough to slip the shirt over his head. After pulling his arms from the sleeves, he tossed it behind him. Then he slouched down in his seat and shifted Monica's hips, so the center of her pussy rested along the length of his cock.

"Better," she said. Once again, Monica lowered her face to his, darting out her tongue to trace his bottom lip. While her mouth was busy, so were her hands. Exploring his chest, her fingers danced across Cal's warm skin, starting with his pecs. They were sculpted, firm. She regulated her touch, softly skimming, then kneading the hard-packed muscles. It was heavenly, touching him this way. She paced herself, took her time as her hands drifted lower, down the sides of his torso.

Cal expelled a rush of air. "You're a delight, you are. Keep it up, love. Feels brilliant."

"I agree." Monica sank her thumbs between the ridges of his abdomen, following the planes and hollows of each and every one. As her nails lightly scraped over them, Cal gripped her hips, pressing her forward and grinding his erection against her core.

"*Cal.*" Clutching his waist, Monica rolled her hips so that his shaft hit her clit. A few more times, and she'd come. And damn it, she really needed to come.

But Cal clamped down on her hips, holding her still. "Not yet." He pulled her tank dress off her shoulders and down to her elbows, exposing her black satin demi-bra with lace panels. He may not have seen the details, but Cal's hands tracked every inch of fabric, starting with the straps and working his way down to her breasts. He smoothed over the edges of the material, flicking the little tassel that hung between the cups. "I wish I'd fixed the overhead light. I'm a very stupid man."

"You have an assignment for next time," she said.

"Are you promising more car sex?"

Monica maneuvered her arms free from her dress before running her hand over his cheek. His skin felt soft and textured. "I'm not making any promises."

"You will after I get through with you." He reached behind her and, with a quick snap, unhooked her bra. He slid that off her too, and tossed it into the backseat with his shirt.

Monica's nipples puckered when the cool air hit them. She was really doing this—getting naked, fucking Cal on the side of the road. Another car could drive over that hill. She'd be all too visible to a pair of headlights. That possibility was as titillating as it was terrifying. Monica's level of arousal increased at the thought of getting caught.

Cal used his thumb to barely glance across her breasts, making her shiver. She felt confident and sexy with him. Cal encouraged Monica to be herself. When was the last time she'd felt that way, this wild and free?

Using the tips of his fingers, Cal very gently skated over her breasts, from the top to the underside. He repeated the action, and with each pass, Monica grew more sensitive. It almost tickled, but not quite.

"Cal." Aimlessly, Monica's hands wandered over his. She wished he'd pinch her tits, massage them, anything but this light touch. It was driving her crazy. "Harder."

"Like this?" He scarcely increased the pressure.

"No."

He took his hand from one breast and stuck his finger in his mouth. He daubed around her nipple before pinching it, then blew over it lightly. That chilly air meeting her damp skin was delicious torture. "Is that what you had in mind?"

"You're getting closer."

Cupping both breasts, Cal squeezed them together and flicked the aching points. "Better?"

"Rougher."

"Oh, Miss Prim likes it rough, does she?" With his thumbs and forefingers, Cal pinched hard, tugging on her nipples until they were distended and puffy. It nearly hurt. It felt so good.

"*Yes.*" Dropping her head back, Monica grabbed his wrists. With every twist, a hot spark of desire shot straight to her pussy. Her level of arousal was almost unbearable. Monica was wet for him. Throbbing. Empty. The desert wind whipped around the car, causing it to shudder. She shuddered right along with it.

Monica hadn't realized how much she'd needed this—to feel attractive, seductive. Sex had been more of a habit than an exciting adventure over the last year. With Cal, she was on the ride of her life and enjoying every second.

"Calum." Once again, she ground herself against his dick. But it wasn't enough. She wanted more, wanted to feel him stroking inside her.

Bending down, she nipped his chin.

"You're still teasing me," he said. Then, in a move that robbed her of breath, he removed one hand from her breast and plunged it into her hair, forcing her head down to meet him. His kiss was raw and bruising. His tongue invaded her mouth, demanding a response.

Lust wracked her body. Monica wanted him inside of her. Now. She dragged her lips off his, but he didn't relinquish his tight grip. "Need more," she panted.

Cal gave her one last scorching kiss before easing his hand out of her hair. "Time for that dress to come off." It was little more than a wide belt around her waist at this point, but she didn't argue. Monica lifted her arms, and Cal had if off her in seconds.

She savored this feeling—hot and eager, exposed to any potential passersby. Bad Girl Monica was back in action. She didn't even try to deny herself this moment—instead, Monica let her reckless, passionate instinct take the reins. Arching her back, she thrust her breasts out and cupped them, posing for Cal. "How bad do you want this?" she asked.

"Words are inadequate."

She dropped her hands, and despite the darkness, she felt his eyes wandering over her, taking in her tits, her waist, the lacy black triangle just covering her pussy. Starting with her collarbone, Cal's hard palms blazed a trail down her body, over her breasts, across her belly, until he reached her panties. "These need to come off too." Slipping his fingers beneath the waistband, he lowered them.

Monica rose to her knees so Cal could shove them down her thighs. He smoothed his hands up to her hips and gripped them tightly. "Monica, love, tell me you like a good, hard ride. Because I'm not sure how much longer I can do gentle, but I'll try."

She gripped his shoulders, digging her fingertips into

his biceps. Being bad had never felt so delicious. “Don’t bother—I like it hard.”

“Thank God.” Cal bent forward, taking her breast into his mouth. Sucking harshly, he made her gasp.

“I can take more,” she said.

Cal pulled the nub with his teeth, biting down. Then he let go. “Too much?”

Fine tremors coursed through her. “Just enough.” When he did it again, she held on to the back of his neck. “That’s it.”

Cal kept his mouth on her as he placed his hand between her legs. His slid his middle finger inside her slick channel. Monica’s greedy pussy clamped around it as he worked in and out of her. Cal’s attention to her breast never wavered, even as his thumb circled her plump, aching clit. Then he added a second finger. He curved the tips as he pumped them, finding her sweet spot.

Flattening both hands on the roof, Monica groaned. She was so close, and though this felt amazing, she wanted his cock. She rode his hand, and the Mustang bounced with their movements. Her pussy tightened on his fingers as she tried to hold off her orgasm. “Tell me you have a condom.”

When Cal released her breast and withdrew his fingers, Monica bit back a protest.

“I do.” Cal was out of breath. “I want you to touch me first.”

She wanted that too—to clasp her hands around that thick, hard shaft. Slide her fingers over the length of him. Monica fumbled with his belt as he lifted his hips and removed the wallet from his back pocket.

She started to unbutton his jeans, but Cal gently

pushed her hands aside and did it himself, lowering the zipper. He jerked the jeans and boxer shorts over his hips until his cock sprang free.

It was longer than she imagined, reaching past his belly button. Monica folded her hand around it and squeezed, pulling down on the soft skin. She rubbed her thumb across the broad head.

"That's brilliant. Keep doing that."

Monica longed to see him, his chest, the tattoo, his erection. The next time they did this, she wanted light. Gliding her hand up and down his rigid cock, she stroked his chest with her other hand. She loved his skin, hot to the touch and slick with sweat.

The windows turned foggy, and the air felt humid. They were in their own little world, and the only sound was their heavy breathing and Cal's groans of pleasure.

He captured both of her wrists. "Enough. I don't want to come in your hand, Miss Prim."

"Stop calling me that. I'm on top of you. Naked."

"And I'm bloody loving it." He enfolded her in his arms, and his hands smoothed down her back. With a long, slow stroke, Cal dragged his tongue across her nipple. When Monica moaned, he glanced up at her. "Like that, do you?"

"Mmm hmm. Do it again."

"Say please."

Monica thrust both hands into his hair and tilted his head back. "No."

Cal laughed, his breath warm against her tingling skin. Again, he licked her breast, using the tip of his tongue to swirl around it.

"That's so good, Cal."

Fisting his hair, she rubbed herself over the length of his cock. "Inside me." When he didn't stop toying with her, she whispered, "Please?"

"Since you asked so nicely, darling, I'm happy to oblige."

Cal removed a foil packet from his wallet. Ripping the package with his teeth, he rolled the condom over his dick, then grasped her hips. "Ready, love?"

God, yes. Monica answered by lowering herself slowly over the tip. Cal stretched her to the limit. Pausing a moment so she could grow accustomed to him, she took an inch at a time. All the while, Cal gripped her hips with his big, strong hands, holding her steady.

After fully seating herself on top of him, he thrust his hips. Monica clung to his shoulders for support. Her pussy throbbed around him. Had anything ever felt so good? She couldn't remember. But then, she could barely recall her own name.

Cal fucked her at a lazy pace, taking her higher with each long stroke. Monica tried using her hips to increase the speed, but Cal stopped her by lifting her off his dick.

"What?" she gasped, confused and in need. "Don't stop. You said a good hard ride. Those were your words."

"I changed my mind. I want to see how long you can hold out." He lowered her back down, but taking control of her body, refused to let her move any faster. Cal worked her the way he wanted, bringing her to the brink of satisfaction but not letting her fall over.

Monica closed her eyes and enjoyed the feel of his cock pulsing in and out of her. She ceded control, understanding that she'd never had it in the first place. She didn't know what Cal would do next, and that unexpected quality had her shivering with need.

She just hoped he'd let her come soon. "I'm close," she panted.

He rubbed his jaw against her breast. "Want to go fast now, do you?"

"*Yes*, already."

His chuckle sounded more like a growl than a laugh. But he increased the pace by lifting her faster and bucking his hips, ramming into her with swift, deep strokes. That's what finally made her spiral.

"Cal, don't stop. *God.*" Monica's pussy clamped down. Delicious tension ran through her entire body. She couldn't move, couldn't think. She could only hang on and ride out the waves of pleasure filling her. As Cal continued to thrust, another shock wave burst inside her. Closing her eyes, she cried out. Her inner walls clenched in time with her heartbeat.

Finally, Cal came too. Over and over he drove inside her, until his own orgasm left him shaking.

Though their bodies stilled, Monica didn't let go of his hair, just as he kept a firm hold on her waist. They remained there, united, quiet.

Eventually, Cal loosened his hold. Kissing her temple, he stroked Monica's back with one hand. "I want to make you do that again." With a contented sigh, he gazed up at her. "That was even more amazing than I imagined it would be."

"You imagined what it would be like?" she asked.

He softly stroked her hip bone as Monica lifted herself off him. Then he reached around her and opened the glove box. Extracting a package of tissues, he got rid of the condom. "Of course, didn't you?"

"Nope. Never."

"Don't play poker, darling—you'll lose every time."

A smile took over her mouth and didn't want to let go. Of course she'd thought about sex with Cal. For the last five years. And it was better than her hottest fantasies.

They huddled together, with Monica lounging on top of him. Cal's arms hugged her loosely, and Monica smoothed a stray piece of hair from his forehead. She felt so relaxed, with her body curled around his—the close quarters, the dark night, the chirping hum of cicadas in the distance—she never wanted it to end. But her phone vibrated and broke the sensuous cocoon.

Monica had tossed her bag into the backseat. She had to reach past Cal to get it, which left her breast even with his mouth. He nibbled the underside, causing her stomach muscles to contract. "Cal."

"Just turn it off. I like it out here, just the two of us." His hands spanned her ribs and slid up to cup her breasts.

Before she could reach the phone, it stopped its annoying buzz.

"See, isn't that better?" Cal tweaked both of her nipples into points. She began to ache for him all over again.

She pressed her nose to his neck and took a deep breath. He smelled of manly heat and wild sex. She felt great. Vibrant. Full of energy.

Monica liked that Cal didn't treat her as though she were fragile, that he took control. Her ex, Ryan, had been a very attentive lover, but she felt like a freak when she'd asked him to pull her hair one night. He'd given her a look of such shock, Monica had never asked for anything in bed again.

"I'm getting cold," she said, snuggling against him, trying to absorb some of his body heat.

Cal reached into the backseat and grabbed his shirt. He settled it over her like a blanket, then cradled her in his arms. "Better?"

"Yeah." Resting her head against his shoulder, she started to drift off. This was surreal. Cuddling naked in the middle of the desert with blast from the past Calum Hughes. It had been a perfect evening.

But reality came calling when her phone vibrated again, shattering her mellow. As pleasant as it was, they couldn't stay there all night. At some point, they had to go back. "I should get that."

"Tell them to get stuffed."

Monica reached for her bag. Cal's fingers caressed her waist as she pulled out her phone. "Hello?"

"Monica Campbell?"

"Yes."

"This is the emergency room at Las Vegas Memorial Hospital. You're listed as Ryan McMillan's emergency contact. He's been in an accident."

Her heart stuttered. A dozen horror scenes raced through her mind. "Oh my God, is he all right? What kind of accident?"

"He broke his leg, and he's had some pain medication. If you can't come and get him, he'll have to spend the night."

Cal stroked her upper arm. "Who is it?" he whispered.

Monica shrugged him off. "I'm outside of Vegas, but I'll be there in an hour." She hung up and started hunting for her bra.

"What is it, love? Talk to me."

Monica grabbed her dress from the driver's seat and jerked it over her head. To hell with her bra. Hooking her thumbs in the waistband of her thong, she tugged it back into place. "I have to get to the hospital. Can you drive?" She didn't trust herself; she was too shaky.

"Of course."

Monica reached past the steering wheel, bumped her chin on the stick shift, and snagged her shoes next to the pedals. "Thanks."

Cal refastened his jeans. "Who's been injured?"

"My ex. Some kind of accident, they said." Opening the passenger door, she awkwardly climbed over Cal and stumbled out of the car. After slipping into her shoes, Monica smoothed the dress down over her hips. "I have to pick him up now, or he'll have to stay all night."

"Monica, look at me."

She stopped her frantic movements and stared at him.

"I'll get you there," he said. "And he's going to be fine, or they wouldn't release him. Okay?"

She nodded, and the fear darting along her nerves lessened. Cal was right. If it were life-threatening, he'd be in surgery or something. It was just a broken leg. She hoped. "Yeah, okay."

Cal shrugged into his shirt and scooted to the driver's seat. Before he started the car, he pointed at her hair. "You might want to tidy up a bit."

Well, how was that for bloody poor timing? Just when Monica had finally started acting herself, letting her guard down, her bloody ex-boyfriend had to cock things up. This was not how Cal wanted to spend the rest of the evening. This episode had been a prelude.

Cal wasn't done shagging Monica Campbell, not by

a long chalk. In fact, now that he'd had a taste of her, he wanted another go. And another.

As he navigated the highway, Cal shot her a glance. Monica's spine had become ramrod straight. Nervous tension leaked from every pore. She bit on her thumb and stared mutely out the window. Her busy mind worked overtime yet again.

With that one phone call, she'd reverted back to that uptight woman with the unattractive suits. But he'd had a glimpse of the real Monica. The one who drove fast and enjoyed hot sex out in the wide-open desert. And came so hard, she gasped with abandon.

When Monica said she wanted to drive the Mustang, Cal had no idea what a turn-on it would be—the joy on her face, the look of fierce concentration as she shifted. He grew hard all over again just thinking about it. But now Miss Prim was back. Damn shame, that.

Cal focused on driving close to the speed limit. Other than giving him directions, Monica remained silent on the return trip. When he swerved into the hospital entrance, Monica unfastened her seat belt. "You can drop me off at the emergency door. Thanks for tonight, Cal. Sorry it had such a weird ending."

Drop her off? Not bloody likely. He wasn't about to leave her alone with her ex. How long had they been together, and was it really over? Apparently not, since she couldn't run to his side fast enough.

Hold up, was he *jealous*? Was that what this horrible feeling was, pouncing on his chest, working him up until he gripped the steering wheel so hard his fingers cramped? Possibly. Stupid and irrational, but there it was.

"I'm coming with you," he said. "I'm not leaving until I know you're all right."

Monica whipped her head around to stare at him. "That's totally not necessary, Cal. I'll take a cab home. I'll be fine."

He circled the car park until he found a spot. "And yet, I'm not leaving your side."

She shifted her upper body toward him. The yellow haze of the parking lights allowed Cal a tantalizing view of Monica's braless tits in that low-cut dress. Her nipples tightened beneath his gaze. Less than an hour ago, he'd had her naked, straddling him—had been palming those breasts.

"Cal, I had a lovely time, but this is my real life, and I need to get back to it." Monica swiveled and opened the door, then leaped out of the car. With quick, short steps, she walked toward the entrance.

A lovely time—that's all it was? To Cal, it had been brilliant. Illicit, raunchy, amazing sex. He couldn't even form a coherent sentence afterward.

Despite Monica's quick steps, Cal exited the car and caught up, matching his stride with hers. "It was more than lovely. It was bloody fucking fantastic. And what the hell does that mean, your real life? Am I an illusion?" Her choice of words rubbed him the wrong way.

"Come on, Cal, let's not pretend this is something it isn't." She kept walking, kept looking forward.

Cal placed his hand on her elbow and pulled her to a stop. "What we just did is about as real as it gets, love."

"No, it's not." With twisted lips, she finally gazed up at him. "We're having fun, remember? My job, the gala, Ryan's broken leg—they're real life. You're like a trip to Disneyland. Adventurous and exciting, but I know it's going to be over in a couple of days. I have to go." She stood on her toes and kissed his cheek. "Take care of yourself."

Cal had never been so stunned in his entire life. "What the fuck are you on about? I thought we were having a good time, yes, but I didn't realize my cock was simply a theme-park ride. I think I'm insulted."

"You know I didn't mean it like that." She glanced over her shoulder in a self-conscious move. They were closer to the entrance now, and a group of people walked out of the building. "You'll be leaving soon, Cal. Ryan needs me. What am I supposed to do?"

He captured Monica's face in his hands, his thumbs stroking her soft cheeks. "Just out of curiosity, what ride am I?"

She paused a moment. "Big Thunder Mountain?"

Cal grinned. "I can live with that." He leaned down and delivered a soft kiss. He ran his hands down the length of her forearms. "In we go. I've always wanted to see a Vegas hospital. It's been my fondest dream since I was a lad. So, what ride is this Ryan fellow? It's a Small World?"

Her lip curled in a scowl. "Those are the comments you're going to keep to yourself."

He began moving toward the entrance, leaving her behind. "Are you going to stand there all night?" He didn't bother to stop or turn around. But a smile crept over his face when he heard her shoes tap along the pavement as she tried to catch up.

Chapter 10

When Cal walked into the large, square room, it was packed with people needing urgent care—most of them pissed to the gills, if the overwhelming stench of alcohol was any indication. "Don't light a match," he whispered, "or we'll all be blown to bits."

Monica broke away from him and hastened to the front desk, where a man in a chartreuse jacket and white linen slacks intercepted her. Was this Ryan, the bloke with the mussy hair and unfortunate clothing? Surely not, he had two working legs.

Cal strode forward and held out his hand. "Hello, Cal Hughes." A bit on the short side—just under six feet—he wasn't hideous, but Cal didn't see anything special about him either. He wore his bored arrogance like a badge of honor, though. Full of himself. Confidence in one's ability—that was acceptable, but unfounded arrogance simply grated.

"Evan Landers." He inclined his head toward Monica. "Glad you're getting this one out of the house. She works too much."

So this wasn't the ex, then. Suddenly, Evan seemed slightly more tolerable.

"If you're already here, Ev, why did they call me?" Monica asked.

"The hospital didn't call me. I received an incoherent text from Ryan. I thought you were hurt and rushed right over." With a sigh, he grabbed his mobile from his pocket and ran a finger over the screen. "Read." He held it up to Monica.

Ev, ouch. Hurt bad. Memorandum hospital. Monica. Cockatiel balls feet.

She gazed up at him. "What does that mean?"

"I did say incoherent." Evan glanced at Cal. "I am speaking out loud, right? You can hear me?"

Monica glowered, so Cal held his grin in check.

"Is Ryan all right? Why didn't you just call him back?" she asked.

Evan smacked his forehead. "Call him? God, you're a genius. Why didn't I think of that?" He shoved the phone back into his pocket. "I did call him. And I called you. Check your messages, why don't you? Then I left Heather at my apartment—naked and covered in whipped cream, I might add.

"Turns out Golden Boy broke his leg while riding his bike. A hit and run. I'm tagging you in and hoping I still have a chance of getting laid tonight. The dress looks fantastic, by the way. Although a little wrinkled. And where's your bra?" He glanced at Cal. "Good job, you." He bent down and bussed Monica's cheek. "I want details later." Without a backward glance, Evan sauntered to the door.

"Well, he's certainly…"

"A pain in the ass?"

"I was going to say colorful. Don't tell me you dated him as well."

"God, no. He's my best friend. Still not sure why."

Good to know. Evan got to go on living then.

Shit.

Cal had always viewed jealousy as a weakness, a failing in others he'd never understood, so his own reaction astounded him. An overwhelming pressure tightened like a band around his chest, making him feel possessive and petulant. Cal wanted Monica Campbell's complete and undivided attention. He resented this Ryan and his broken leg more than he thought possible.

After Evan left, Monica approached the nurse sitting behind bulletproof glass. "I'm looking for Ryan McMillan. I'm his emergency contact."

The woman's blank face said she'd heard it all, seen even more, and wasn't impressed by any of it. "Let me see some ID."

Monica dug out her driving license. Cal caught a glance at the photo—Monica, unsmiling, in a navy suit and matching blouse.

"Go on back." The nurse buzzed the door. "Room three."

He stayed by her side as they entered the double doors. While Monica searched for number three, Cal tapped her wallet. "You need a new ID. You look like a nun in that photo."

She glared up at him. "I look like a professional woman, which I am."

"A professional for the God Squad."

She stopped at a sliding glass door and knocked softly. A young, pretty nurse in pink scrubs swept the curtain aside and opened the door. "Monica Campbell?"

"Yes."

"He's been asking for you. Come on in."

Cal glanced at Ryan, who lay on the bed, clutching the plastic rails. A black walking cast covered his left leg.

Cal didn't know what he'd been expecting—someone

good-looking or charismatic or oozing charm. But this chap left him thoroughly unimpressed. Evan had called him a golden boy, thanks to all that blond hair, no doubt. One of his rounded cheeks suffered an abrasion. Dirt smudged his canary-yellow biking shirt. He wasn't horrific—women probably found him generically attractive.

Ryan's glazed eyes widened when they landed on Monica. "Monnie," he slurred. "Sorry they called you. I broke my leg."

Monica approached him. "I warned you about this. It's dangerous, riding at night."

He gave her a loopy grin. "You were right." He grasped her hand. "How've you been?"

"Don't worry about me. What are we going to do with you?"

"We gave him a painkiller," said the nurse, "but it'll wear off in a couple of hours. The doctor will be in shortly, and I'll grab some crutches." Before she left, she pulled the curtain closed, giving them privacy.

"Do they know how long you'll have to wear the cast?" Monica asked. Cal watched her face carefully. She seemed concerned but not panicked, as she'd been out in the desert.

"Six weeks. I have to take sponge baths. I don't own a sponge." Ryan finally noticed Cal, standing in the corner. "Hey, do I know you?"

"Ryan, this is Cal Hughes. He's Trevor's cousin."

Cousin? That was his title, after what they'd done in the Mustang?

Ryan took in Monica's sexy, tight dress. "Why are you wearing that?"

She crossed her arms. "Did they catch the guy who hit you?"

"Not sure."

Cal grabbed one of the room's two chairs and placed it behind Monica so she could sit. She nodded a thank-you.

"You don't have to stay, Cal. I'll make sure he gets home."

"Doesn't he have any mates he can call?" Cal whispered.

Monica shook her head. "They're all married with little kids. His brother lives in Colorado, his parents are in Arizona. I'm it."

Resigned, Cal sighed. "Then I'm in it with you." He didn't want to leave Monica stranded and alone. She might need something, and Cal wanted to be here with her—unusual for him. He didn't like to be needed, but Monica elicited strange reactions in him.

Snagging a chair of his own, he sat next to her and removed the remote from the railing that framed Ryan's bed. He turned the TV on, found a sports station, and settled in to watch an American football game while Ryan babbled.

"Remember when we went hiking in the mountains, Monnie?" Ryan asked. "Remember that Thai place we went to every Saturday night?"

"*Every* Saturday night?" Cal asked quietly. "How could you stand the excitement?"

Monica ignored him. She ignored Ryan too. In fact, she remained very quiet, withdrawn.

Finally, Ryan drifted off, and Cal leaned toward her, letting his thigh brush hers. "Are you cold? Want me to find a blanket?"

"No, thanks. I'm fine."

Cal slid one finger over her bare arm. "You've got goose bumps." Then his gaze lowered to her chest. "Your nipples could cut glass."

"Shut it," she hissed and scooted her chair farther away from him. "And you don't have to stay."

Grabbing the armrest, he jerked her chair back, close enough so their legs touched once again. "I'm not leaving. We can argue about it, which I quite enjoy, but it won't matter."

She sighed. "Fine. Don't say anything about tonight."

"I'd bring up our personal affairs? You think that, do you?"

She gazed at him then, and her eyes were troubled. "I don't want to hurt him any more than I already have," she whispered so softly he had to strain to hear.

Cal pushed the hair from her face. "You're very tenderhearted, Monica Campbell. You try to act all tough, but in here"—he let his finger drift to her chest—"you're very kind."

She slapped at his hand. "Whatever."

A moment later, the nurse brought in a pair of crutches, and the doctor followed.

Monica gently patted Ryan's hand. "Hey, wake up."

His eyes fluttered, and he smiled when he saw her. "Monnie."

Cal rolled his eyes.

The doctor leaned against the wall and spoke to Monica. "We've called in a prescription. When he gets home, give him two pills. Make sure he doesn't take them on an empty stomach. He can walk, but he may need help in the shower."

Like bloody hell she'd help him in the shower.

The doctor shook Ryan's hand, and the nurse left to round up a wheelchair. When she returned thirty minutes later, whatever drug they'd given Ryan was wearing off, and he started to whine. Like nails on a chalkboard.

"My knee is starting to hurt. And my head." Ryan rubbed at his temples as the nurse helped him into the chair.

"Buck up, mate," Cal said. "Could be worse."

Monica shot him a glare. "Why don't you go get the car?"

~

Monica looked into Cal's intense green eyes before he turned and walked out of the room. Once she'd known Ryan was going to be all right, she hadn't been able to think about anything but their tryst in the car. Cal's big, work-rough hands on her body, his mouth on her skin. It excited her all over again. Which felt wrong. Especially with Ryan lying there, wounded and in pain.

But being in the desert with Cal—Monica hadn't felt that exhilarated, that sexually charged in years. Ryan, for all of his sweetness and decency, had never taken her to the level of physical pleasure Cal had. She'd tried to love Ryan, tried to make him happy, but in the end, she'd only hurt him. Ryan really was perfect, but not for her. One steamy session with Cal had proven that.

True, she was following her old, destructive patterns, but Monica was in control this time. Still, a part of her wished that what she had with Cal could be something more substantial.

The thought brought her up short. That kind of

thinking had gotten her in trouble in the past, hoping she could change a guy, turning a temporary fling into a real relationship. That was one trap she would never fall into again. Not with any man.

Monica walked next to Ryan as the nurse pushed him to the exit. She gave his shoulder a comforting pat.

Ryan slid a glance in her direction. His eyes were less glassy, his gaze more focused. "I forgot to have your name removed as my emergency person. That guy with you, he's Trevor's cousin? So he's like family."

Um, no. "Sort of, I guess."

Cal had parked the Mustang near the door. He hopped from behind the wheel and jogged over to help Ryan climb into the car.

"In you go, mate. Watch your head." Monica knew Cal didn't like him. She could tell by the way he rolled his eyes whenever Ryan spoke. Even so, he patiently helped Ryan into the passenger seat.

Monica was starting to realize Cal was a stand-up guy. Not one she could depend on for the long haul, but still, good to know.

Cal made sure Ryan's lap belt was buckled, then shut the door. He trotted to where Monica stood at the back of the car. "Ready?"

She paused, turning her head to stare at a couple walking past them. "Thanks for staying with me. You didn't have to do that."

"Do you know the best way to thank someone?" When she glanced back at him, he wore a sincere expression.

"Flowers?" she asked. "Chocolates? Starbucks gift card?"

"I was going to say a blow job, but if you agree to a second date tomorrow night, I'll let it slide."

She breathed out a little laugh. "You're a piece of work, asking me out and talking about blow jobs with my ex sitting three feet away from us."

"Much better than doing it in front of his face, which I know got a bit bungled this evening, but even so, let's be honest, darling, he looks like a bit of a minger, doesn't he?"

She crossed her arms. "Minger?"

"I don't mean to be cruel, but he is rather tragic. You can do better. Unless you only dated him out of pity?"

Once again, Monica found herself wanting to laugh. "You're ridiculous. There's nothing wrong with the way he looks."

"If you say so. What are you going to do with him, anyway?"

"I'll spend the night with him, make sure he's comfortable."

Cal's entire body tightened. Monica glanced at his fisted hand. "It's just for one night." She grabbed hold of it and rubbed her finger across his knuckles, caressing between the bumps until he unclenched it. Cal didn't want her spending time with Ryan. If the shoe were on the other foot, she'd feel the same way, but she had obligations. She'd picked Ryan up, and now she felt responsible for him.

"I know tomorrow's Saturday," he said, "but you need your rest. Your friend Evan said you work too hard."

"Honestly, I'll be fine."

"Of course you will. Don't worry, we'll figure something out, love."

"There's nothing to figure out. I'll handle it."

"Shh." He pressed a finger to her lips.

She swatted his hand away. "Don't shush me. I hate being shushed."

"I know. You were quite vocal in the desert."

Ryan rolled down the window and stuck his head out. "I'm kind of in pain here."

Monica glanced over at him, startled. She'd almost forgotten why they were here. "God, Ryan. Sorry."

Cal walked with Monica to the other side of the car, where she wedged herself into the backseat.

Once behind the wheel, Cal followed Ryan's directions, first to the pharmacy, then to his condo in a well-heeled part of town.

Together, Monica and Cal helped Ryan out of the car, into the house, and onto the sofa.

He looked pale against the dark brown leather. Purple half-moons stood out in relief beneath his eyes and clashed with his yellow shirt. The road rash coloring his cheek had to be sore too. Monica hurried over and propped his broken leg on a few pillows to alleviate the pain. "Are you comfortable?"

"Of course he's not. Poor git looks positively miserable."

"I'm fine," Ryan said. "Thanks for the ride home, Cal, but there's no need for you to stay. I've already inconvenienced you enough."

"Nonsense."

Monica bustled around, bending over Ryan, arranging pillows behind his head. When she noticed he was shooting glances down her dress, checking out her bare breasts, she quickly straightened. "The doctor said you need to take your meds every four hours."

"I can stay," Cal said. He dropped into a chair and crossed his legs. "You go on."

Monica needed to make Ryan something to eat, but she didn't want to leave the two men alone. Cal was acting weird. "Why don't you help me in the kitchen?"

"You know where everything is," Ryan said, looking over his shoulder. Although he was in obvious pain, he threw a strained smile in Cal's direction. "Monica practically lived here, didn't you, sweetheart?"

Oh God. Not a pissing contest. "Cal. Help. Now."

Cal stood and tailed her into the spotless kitchen. Ryan wasn't much of a cook, and neither was she. When they were together, they ate out almost every night.

"Likes things tidy, doesn't he?"

Monica rounded on him. "There's nothing wrong with that. It's refreshing to find a man who can pick up after himself. Listen, I think you should go."

Crossing his arms, Cal leaned his hip against the granite island. "So you want me to leave you here? Alone?"

"Yes."

"Fine." He sighed dramatically. "I was trying to help you out. I thought my presence might act as a buffer, but if you want him pining after you, by all means, I'll go."

"Who are you kidding? You're not trying to be helpful."

Cal dropped his arms and stepped closer. If she took a deep, deep breath, Monica's breasts would skim his chest. "The man's been wounded. I feel nothing but pity for the poor, ugly sod."

Monica took in Cal's tanned skin and slanted smile. Ryan might be more traditionally handsome, but Cal's irregular features appealed to her. "If I didn't know better, I'd say you were jealous."

Cal's eyes drifted to her mouth. "Tell me what you saw in him."

"He's a nice man."

"That's not a recommendation, darling, that's an admonishment. Don't let him hear you say it, he'll never get over the humiliation."

She moved past him to the fridge. "What are you talking about? What's wrong with being a nice guy?"

"Nice guy is code for prat. Nice guys aren't sexy. There's a reason they finish last."

Monica put some deli meat, cheese, and mayonnaise on the counter. She opened a cupboard and pulled out a loaf of bread. "Again, you're ridiculous." But one look at his face said he wasn't joking, not this time.

"A comment like that will hurt him."

"You men, you're all ego."

"Yeah, we are."

As Monica threw together two sandwiches, one for Ryan and one for Cal, she pondered his statement. Ryan's niceness had drawn her to him. But only because he was the opposite of every guy who'd screwed her over. "What's wrong with being a nice guy? Treating a woman with care and respect?"

"Have I treated you with anything less than respect, Monica Campbell?" His rough voice sounded brusque.

"I didn't mean you. Ryan is the type of guy women want to marry. He's long-term material."

Cal moved closer. Monica's nipples peaked against his shirt. "And I'm not?" he asked.

Monica forced herself to glance up at him, to meet his eyes. "No, you're not. You travel all over the world, never stay in one place for long. You don't want to settle down."

"Do you?" The way his green gaze probed her, she felt like he could see all the way to her soul. "You were never honest with him. He doesn't know you at all. Which Monica did you show him? The one who wears ugly clothes that cover every centimeter of skin or the one who likes to drive fast and get naked in the car? Because frankly, the latter is a hell of a lot more interesting."

"Fuck you, Cal," she said between clenched teeth.

As his gaze slowly wandered over her face, his eyes widened. "You should let that fiery side out more often. It's a delight." Then he swooped down, planting his lips on hers.

He didn't lean into her, didn't touch any other part of her body. She could have pulled away at any time. Instead, Monica raised her head so she could taste more of him. All the desire she'd felt in the Mustang slammed back into her, increasing tenfold. Dropping the mayonnaise lid, she grabbed his face, stroking her palms over his cheeks as she kissed him back.

"Monica, everything okay in there?" That distant voice sounded familiar.

Ryan. Shit, how could she stand here in his kitchen, making out with Calum Hughes? Had she lost every functioning brain cell she possessed?

Apparently, yes. Because even now, as she dropped her hands and tore her lips from his, she still wanted more.

Chapter 11

Cal watched Monica's expression change. Her lips, so soft and yielding a moment ago, firmed. Her jaw muscles tightened. She was fighting herself as much as she was fighting him.

"What the hell am I doing?" she asked.

She was talking to herself, not Cal. Nevertheless, he answered. "Having fun. Living your life. Did you really think you'd be happy with him?"

"Coming, Ryan," she yelled and began busying her hands.

Cal grabbed them and held on when she tried to pull away.

"Let me go, Cal."

"Darling, go home. Get some rest or work on your foundation whatnots. I'll take care of him." Cal wanted to clear the anxiety from her eyes almost as much as he wanted to shag her again. "I can see that you're worried and you'll go to work tomorrow whether or not you get a wink of sleep. And truly, he will glom on to this, make it into a reconciliation. He's desperate to get you back—any fool can see that."

Biting her lip, she looked into his eyes, searching. "You're not planning on feeding him too many painkillers, are you?"

Cal grinned. "I'm not planning on it, but I might improvise." He let her pull away this time. When she crossed her arms, he reached out and played with a piece of her hair. Like silk. So soft and deep golden, with light amber streaks. “I’m only joking. Sort of. Come on, let’s go break the news.” Cal dropped her hair and grabbed the plates.

“Let me clean up in here, and I’ll be out in a second.” Monica began gathering all the food and placing it in the fridge. Cal caught a glimpse of its interior as he walked out the door. Even the man’s refrigerator looked tidy. And all health drinks, not a bottle of beer in sight. What kind of life would she have had with a knob like this? Ryan probably got his little-girl knickers in a wad when life became messy.

And Monica Campbell needed mess, chaos. She was meant for driving too fast and wearing nipple-baring lingerie and leaving a man devastated as she walked out of a room. When she’d been writhing on top of him, Monica was a goddess. With her head thrown back, she’d left behind all inhibitions and allowed herself to feel. If Cal possessed a talent for painting, he’d portray her like that. Naked. Wanton. *Intoxicating*.

But with one phone call, she’d lapsed back to that tight-assed demeanor. Why on earth did she hide behind that mask? Why the hell had she dated a man like Ryan? He wasn’t horrible—he was a perfectly nice, boring bloke who would give her a perfectly nice, boring life. Monica was meant for so much more.

Cal walked back to the living room and handed Ryan a plate. “There you go.”

“Thanks. Everything okay in there?” he asked and peeked beneath the top slice of wholemeal bread. “You two were gone a long time.”

"Just making a few plans. You're obviously incapable of being on your own, so I'm staying tonight."

"That's not nec—"

"It is, actually." Cal leaned forward and spoke in a low tone. "Otherwise, Monica will insist on staying herself. She has a big work thing coming up, and you're the last thing she needs to worry about."

Monica stepped out of the kitchen. "Ryan, you ready for your pills?" She glanced down at his untouched sandwich. "Is it all right?"

Ryan's pallor belied his smile. Pain strained the lines near his eyes. "Yeah. Cal's staying tonight. Really nice of him, by the way."

"Are you sure?"

Ryan reached for her hand and kissed the back of it. "Absolutely. It was really nice of you to come for me, Monnie."

God, what a sickening display. Cal forced a smile. "He'll be fine. Take my car, I'll pick it up tomorrow."

Still, Monica hesitated a moment. Then nodding, she headed toward the front door. "I'll call and check on you," she said to Ryan and grabbed her purse. "If you need anything—"

"That's why I'm here." Cal placed his hand on her upper arm and couldn't help but give that satiny skin a couple of strokes with his thumb. Toned, yet so soft.

He escorted her out of the house and walked with her to the car. "Get some sleep, eh?"

"Thanks for doing this."

"You're welcome. Now kiss me one more time." He placed his foot between hers and leaned down.

Monica's lips parted as she gazed at him with wide eyes. "Like you mean it."

Monica's hands rode up his chest, over his shoulders, until she linked them behind his neck. Rising to her toes, she placed her lips over his.

Cal's fingers grazed her hips. While Monica's mouth opened under his demanding kiss, Cal squeezed those globes, had visions of taking her from behind so he could simply stare at it.

Monica fell back against the car door, but she didn't let go of him, didn't stop kissing him. Cal followed, leaning against her and rotating his hips, grinding his cock against her.

She groaned and returned the favor, driving her hips forward, tormenting him, before snapping her head back. "Stop. We need to stop."

That's the last thing Cal wanted to do. But what was the alternative? Taking her in full view of all the neighbors? He must not be thinking clearly, because that didn't seem like the worst idea he'd ever had.

Monica splayed her hands over his chest. "We can't do this here."

"Yes, all right." Closing his eyes for a moment, he clenched his jaw. Regaining his equilibrium was a challenge. When he opened his eyes, he reached out and palmed her breast. "We're not finished, you and I." Then stepping back, he shoved his hand into his pocket—trying desperately to ignore his painfully hard prick—and withdrew the car keys. "Be safe. Remember, don't give it too much gas."

"Yeah, yeah." She held out her hand, palm up. "Will you be nice to him?"

"Yes." He reached out and curved a hand around her waist before delivering one last hard kiss to those full lips. "Go on with you."

"Thanks. I'll see if Evan can stop by in the morning to check on him." She hopped into the car, waved, and pulled out of the drive.

When she didn't give it too much gas, Cal smiled.

Striding back to the house, he remembered his promise. *Be nice*. Cal walked inside and clapped his hands. "So, mate, did you take your pills?"

"Yes, you can go now." With his head tilted back against a pillow and his eyes closed, Ryan waved one hand. "I won't tell Monica you left."

"But I promised I'd stay." Taking care of a sick person wasn't Cal's forte. The memories of Babcock, holding her hand, watching as she grew weaker with each passing day, all came back to him—that utter fucking helplessness. He needed to do something.

"I'll make tea." Babcock always claimed tea was a cure-all. He'd made a lot of tea over the last several months.

"No," Ryan said. "I don't drink it."

"Coffee?"

"No thanks."

Giving up, Cal sank down into the leather chair. "So how did you and Monica meet, anyway? Church social?"

"I'm more interested in hearing about the two of you. Where were you tonight?"

"Joyriding."

Ryan opened his eyes and blinked. "I have a hard time believing that."

"Monica drove my Mustang like she was born for it. As a matter of fact, she didn't drive, she flew."

Ryan's cheeks became parchment white, and dots of sweat beaded his forehead. From pain or anger, Cal couldn't decide. "I don't believe you. Monica doesn't drive fast. She's never even had a speeding ticket."

"How long did you date her, if you don't mind my asking? Because honestly, you don't seem to know her that well."

"We dated for over a year, and I know her very well. If I have my way, Monica Campbell's going to marry me."

Cal's heartbeat hammered in his ears. Monica marry this twat? He forced out a laugh and kept his tone nonchalant. "That might be a little difficult, considering you two aren't dating anymore." He was beginning to dislike this bloke more and more with each passing moment. That small bit of jealousy soon became a fat green monster, sinking its talons even deeper into Cal's chest.

"I don't think so. Monica's afraid of a lot. Commitment, marriage, letting her family down. But I'm not going anywhere. Know that, Cal."

Ryan had one thing right—Monica was very much afraid. But she was afraid of letting go, of being herself, of fucking up. Breaking up with Ryan was the smartest thing Monica had ever done. "Not that my opinion matters, but I don't think you're good for her."

"What are you talking about? We're meant for each other. And if she doesn't care about me, why did she come to the hospital?"

"Guilt," Cal said with a shrug. "Monica's a kind person. And you're a bit of a manipulative bastard, using your leg to try and win her back."

Ryan shifted his ass and winced in pain. "I'm not using it to win her back. Eventually, she'll see I'm the right choice. She's dated guys like you in the past. Guys who don't stick around, guys who break her heart. She might have a fling with you—yeah, I saw her bra on the floorboard of the backseat—but she'll come back to me."

He sounded so sure that Cal almost doubted himself. Ryan's words had a ring of truth to them. A strong emotion bubbled up inside of him. Cal didn't know what it was, but it made him uncomfortable.

Cal wouldn't be around for long, so her choices shouldn't matter to him. But they did. Very much. He'd thought about Monica Campbell over the last five years, and now that he'd seen her speeding down the highway with her hair flying free, had experienced firsthand her demanding, heated sexuality, he couldn't let her reunite with this wet bloke.

Cal needed Monica again, like his lungs needed oxygen.

And she needed him too.

She'd shown him a bit of herself tonight. She'd danced and laughed and shagged. Monica couldn't go back into hiding. Cal wouldn't let her.

For some stupid reason, she'd buried away everything that made her wonderful and unique. Cal wanted to see more than just a glimpse. He wanted full-throttle Monica. And he would accept nothing less.

The next morning in the shower, Monica saw two bruises on the side of her breast. There was one more on her hip, and her nipples had never been this sore. Cal had given her a hard ride, and she'd loved every minute of it. She wanted to do it again. Soon. Now. But Monica had grappled with herself all night. On the one hand, the sex was off-the-charts amazing. But on the other, Cal had a way of sweeping aside all of her arguments and misgivings. And that scared her.

Maybe she was incapable of making healthy decisions. *Defective*. Monica sometimes wondered if she was missing some important genetic component that kept her from wanting normal things out of life: marriage, stability, kids. God, all this introspection depressed her.

As she dressed in a tan suit, Monica drank a cup of coffee. She also slapped on a little more concealer than usual, because the circles underneath her eyes were out of control—tossing and turning, mentally replaying a sexcapade with Calum Hughes could do that to a person.

Monica had gathered her things and was just about to step out the front door when Evan called. She'd texted him, asking him to stop by Ryan's house this morning, but he'd never gotten back to her.

"Details," he said when she answered.

"No."

"You had after-sex hair. Spill already."

With a frown, Monica ran a hand over her head. "Are you going to check on Ryan?"

"God, you're so annoying. Yes, I'll check on Ryan, but I'm not bathing him or taking him to the bathroom. I'll make sure he's alive, but that's it. You know, it's not fair. I tell you everything about my sex life."

"I don't *want* to know everything, Ev. The whipped cream remark last night? Totally uncalled for."

"She reapplied after I got back home."

"Good-bye."

"Wait. Fine, no details, but at least tell me you're

enjoying yourself. I'm begging you, for the love of all that's filthy and wrong in this world, have a good time with tall, dark, and raspy, okay?"

Monica hit the End button as a smile crept over her mouth. She'd definitely had fun last night. Mind-numbing, toe-curling, orgasmic fun. Having an affair with Cal was the best time she'd had in years.

Monica drove through a fast-food place and got another cup of coffee and a bag of breakfast sandwiches—mostly for Jason. He usually came in for a few hours on Saturday morning, and so did Stella. Monica never asked them; they just showed up.

Once in the office, she waved to Stella and headed for the break room. Jason wandered in, red-eyed and wearing the same clothes as the day before.

"Long night?"

"Yeah," he said through a yawn. "You brought food. You must love me."

"I tolerate you," she said, patting his shoulder on the way to her office. Before she did anything else, she needed to check in with Ryan. Monica felt guilty for leaving him with Cal, but she didn't want to string him along, give him false hope.

With her left hand, she toyed with the pink crystal-covered pen and dialed Ryan's number.

"Reginald Wanker's residence," Cal answered.

Monica smothered a laugh. "Really? What if I were his office calling, or his mom?"

"Ah, the lovely Miss Prim. I stayed with him all night. All. Bloody. Night. What more do you want?"

"You could quit calling him Reginald Wanker for starters."

"I could, but I won't."

"How is he?"

"Still alive."

"Glad to hear it." Monica dropped the pen and glanced out the window. "Thank you. Evan's coming over in a bit, so you're off duty."

"Did you drive my car to work today?"

"I drove my own car. Yours is sitting in my driveway. I left the keys in the fake rock by the front stoop."

"Because no thief would think to look there."

"So can I speak to Ryan?"

"He's taking a shower."

"But—"

"Don't worry, I'm standing right outside the door. I'll tell him you called. How late are you working?"

"Probably until six or so."

"Then I'll pick you up at the office. Can't wait, darling. The things I'm going to do to you," he whispered, "will leave you breathless." Then he hung up.

What things? Monica's mind wandered to all sorts of naughty places, and she couldn't keep the heat from rushing to her cheeks. After five minutes of staring out the window at the cloudless blue sky, she finally pulled herself together and got to work. But it was almost impossible to keep her thoughts from straying to Cal's sexy promise. After all, she had a pretty vivid imagination.

Cal rubbed his tired eyes. He hadn't gotten much sleep the night before. The chair was damned uncomfortable, Ryan was a snorer, and Cal couldn't get his mind off Monica.

Around three a.m., Ryan had started groaning, until Cal shoved another pain pill down his gob. Then at eight, Ryan woke again, wanting a shower.

So now Cal stood outside the bathroom door, in case Ryan took a spill. That was as far as he was prepared to go. Bloke could hold his own cock if he needed to piss.

Cal had even grabbed Ryan a set of fresh clothes. After he heard the shower stop, Cal opened the door and tossed them into the bathroom. "Look alive, mate."

"If you call me mate one more time—"

"You'll what?" Cal asked through the closed door. "Bore me to death? Too late. My heart sputters a little more with every word you speak."

When Ryan hobbled out of the bathroom in a T-shirt and a pair of orange cargo shorts—the damned ugliest things Cal could find—he refused Cal's offer of help and hopped down the stairs on his own. Cal held the crutches and tried to steady Ryan's arm, but he shook off Cal's hand and almost took a tumble.

"Careful there. You want to keep the good leg happy. I promised Monica I'd take care of you, so no matter how much of a prat you are, that's what I'm doing until what's-his-face shows up. The one who dresses funny."

"Evan," Ryan muttered.

Cal followed Ryan's slow progress back to the living room. "They've been good friends for a while, then?"

As Ryan sat on the sofa, Cal helped him adjust his leg to a more comfortable position atop a pile of pillows.

"Since college. They're best friends."

"And he's your mate too?" Cal read a great deal from the other man's silence. "Ah, her best friend doesn't like you. Guess not everyone thinks you're perfect for each other." He tossed the blanket at Ryan. He bloody well wasn't going to tuck him in.

Ryan pulled it over his legs and gave Cal a cool look. "Evan never thinks any man is good enough for her. Can't fault him for being protective."

"He liked me." Cal grinned as he crossed his arms over his chest. "I'm going to make breakfast so we can knock you out with a couple more of those pills." He went to the kitchen and dug through the fridge, pulling out a carton of egg substitute and an anemic tomato. Cal searched in vain for butter, but came up empty. Cobbling together an omelet, he cut it in half and plated it up.

When he returned to the living room, Ryan was glaring at a financial news channel. Cal plopped the plate on the coffee table, along with a fork.

Ryan sniffed at the food and eyed him warily, as though Cal had poisoned it. After eating a few bites, Ryan washed down two more pain pills. "Monica said you'd just gotten into town. When are you leaving?"

"As soon as the mood strikes."

"What do you do for a living?" Ryan flipped off the TV.

"Auto repair."

The blighter assumed a smug grin. "And you think that's good enough for her? That you can give her the life she deserves?"

Cal snorted. "No. I never said I was going to give her any kind of life." Monica was a strong, smart woman. She didn't need Cal or anyone else to provide for her.

Fortunately, it wasn't long before Ryan lost consciousness again. Bloody marvel, those pills.

Monica wouldn't rest easy if Ryan stayed here on his

own. Cal didn't want her to worry, so he called the hotel and got hold of Mr. Lawson. The capable butler promised to hire a full-time nurse. Cal should have thought of it last night. Could have saved himself a load of grief.

Satisfied with his scheme, he spent the next two hours trying to doze until Evan pounded on the door. Sporting a pair of bright blue trousers and matching suede loafers, he sauntered into the living room and removed his sunglasses. He glanced down at Ryan with a mixture of distaste and humor. "He could wake the dead with that snoring. How did Monica stand it?"

Cal tried very hard not to think about Ryan touching Monica. The very idea of them together made him want to break something. "I have a nurse coming soon. Round-the-clock care. Can you stay until then?" He was already dialing for a taxi before he made it to the front door.

"Wait," Evan said and followed him outside. "I want to talk to you."

Cal gave the dispatcher the address. Once he hit the End button, he eyed Evan. "What is it?"

"Thanks for taking care of him last night. I'm afraid if she hangs around for too long, Monica will feel so guilty, she'll go back to him."

Cal rolled his shoulders to alleviate the stiffness in his muscles. "He's entirely wrong for her."

"I couldn't agree more." Evan pursed his lips as he scrutinized Cal. "She needs a little excitement in her life, but not too much."

At least Cal and the best mate were of the same mind.

"Here's the thing," Evan said. "Do not, under any circumstances, leave the country with her. Understand me?"

Cal laughed until he realized the man was actually serious. "Where do you think I'd take her, Peru?"

"I'm not kidding. And if you break her heart, I will find you and break your dick." His phone vibrated. "Glad we had this little chat." He walked back into the house and closed the door.

In the last few days, Cal'd had his manhood threatened too many times. What the hell had happened in Monica's past that made everyone so protective of her? Hurt by some man, obviously. But he wasn't going to hurt her. He and Monica agreed they'd have some fun.

If it's just a bit of slap, why are you getting so worked up over her ex?

Bloody fucking hell. He was *painfully* envious of Reginald Wanker. How humiliating. It churned inside his chest like corrosive battery acid.

Cal restlessly paced the street until the taxi arrived. The cab reeked of stale smoke and raw onions.

During the twenty-minute ride, Cal listened to the cabbie's life story and tales of domestic woe, which got his mind off Monica and Ryan. Almost. The fact of the matter was that Monica and Ryan weren't together anymore. She'd spent the evening with Cal. He needed to remember that.

The taxi pulled up to the villa's private entrance. Cal handed over a few bills, hopped out, and waved at the security guard, showing his pass.

He strolled the rest of the way to the villa, enjoying the hot sun beating down on him. He intended on taking a long shower. Then he'd call Monica, retrieve his car, and plan their date. Which may take all day, because plotting things out went against his nature. He'd been raised on spontaneity.

Pixie might be perfectly content in Monte Carlo one day, but have an urge to stay in Vancouver the next. Capricious, his mother. She quickly got tired of a place the same way she grew bored with people. She dropped friends and lovers alike, as she would discarded tissues.

Still, men followed Pixie around the world, their tongues dragging the ground. His mother liked having a fan club. *One on the string and one in the wing*, as she used to say.

Cal had learned much from her entourage of admirers. He had been introduced to Shakespeare by a West End actor, taught to read music from a bass player in Paris, had grown to love Dylan Thomas and Keats and Tennyson from his mother's writer friends. When Pix sat for a famous German photographer, Cal had learned a smattering about art. His knowledge was lax and spotty, much to his erudite father's disgust. It may not have been complete, but Cal's education had been interesting, to say the least.

However, there was one lesson that had been ingrained in him early—*don't get attached*. Not to anyone or anything. Cal had learned to travel light. He had only a few sets of clothes, his car magazines, and his one concession—his tools. He loved his tools, cared for them diligently, maintained and kept them in pristine condition. Babcock used to ship them separately. Once, when he was fifteen, they'd gotten lost on a flight from Brussels to Thailand. Cal had been inconsolable until they finally showed up, two weeks later.

Yet in spite of his history, Cal was becoming attached to Monica Campbell, even though he knew their liaison wouldn't last long. It couldn't, not with his restless nature. Cal had had a few brief, casual relationships over the years with women he'd been fond of, but there was something different about Monica, about her spirit and humor. Still, they'd agreed—no strings. Cal would stay long enough for Monica to break out of her good-girl shell, and then he'd figure out what to do next.

Cal lived a transient life, and he'd always liked it that way. But after seeing Monica and Evan last night, he realized he didn't have anyone like that in his life, not since Babs. She'd been the one person he could rely on. The sense of loss hit him all over again.

Cal stopped at the villa's doorway and rubbed his cheek. Where the hell was all this melancholy coming from? Time to shake it off already. Cal was just fine on his own—a lone wolf, doing what he wanted, when he wanted. Freedom. That's what he had. Other people wished they could fly to Bermuda tomorrow and sit in the sun for three months. Cal could actually do it.

Slipping the key card in the door, he walked into the foyer, taking a second to let his eyes adjust to the indoor light. Then he walked toward his room, past the lounge, and drew to a halt. Batting his eyes a few times, he took in the dirty dishes, wet towels, and fashion magazines littering the floor and the coffee table. He heard a faint, high-pitched voice from a distance and resumed walking toward the master bedroom. As he stepped inside, he heard a one-way conversation coming from behind the lavatory door. With two fingers, Cal plucked a lime-green bra dangling from the corner of the telly. Fairly certain it wasn't his—not unless he'd become a sleep-walking cross-dresser—he knew only one person who could cause this kind of utter destruction.

Chapter 12

"Jules," he called.

An aggressively pink suitcase lay open on the bed, its contents strewn over the room like confetti at Carnival. Surely she hadn't been here longer than a few hours. How could she do this in such a short amount of time? Astounding, really.

The bathroom door burst open and Jules—Juliette Margaret Hughes—emerged. As soon as she saw him, she threw her arms wide open and ran at him. "Hello, big brother, you fucking nutter. Surprised to see me?" Testing his reflexes, she jumped into his arms.

Cal managed to catch her, but staggered backward. He kissed her cheek, then lowered her to the floor. *Surprised* wasn't the word he'd use. *Shocked* more like, and as it began to wear off, Cal realized he saw much more of her than he wanted to. Jules's black bra clearly showed through her transparent pink blouse—which clashed dreadfully with her tangerine skin. She applied her makeup with a generous hand. A little too generous. Her gold sequined skirt was so short, Cal longed to pull the duvet from the bed and swaddle her in it. Even by Vegas standards, her clothing choices were questionable.

"Jules, what are you doing here? For God's sake, is that what you wore on the plane?" Cal was going to have to wallop every asshole who looked at her sideways. And they *would* look.

"No, I flew starkers—of course this is what I wore. What's wrong with it?" She stared down and tugged at her skirt.

"Where to begin?"

"Very funny. Aren't you happy to see me?"

"Natur—"

"Because I had to get out of there. Daddy is cross and shouting all the bloody time. He canceled my credit cards, Cal. I had to borrow money from my biffle to get a plane ticket."

Cal marched around the room and began gathering clothes. But he drew the line at touching scanties. He thrust the bundle into her arms. "What the fuck is a biffle?"

"BFFL. Best Friends for Life. God, what a divvy you are."

"You're dressed like an Essex girl, you know."

Her mouth fell open. "I'm not."

"You are, and it's not attractive."

She dropped the bundle of clothes. "Everyone in L.A. dresses like this, you knob."

Cal sighed. Pulling her into his arms, he hugged her tight. He'd have kissed her forehead, but he was afraid his lips would be streaked with makeup for the rest of the day. "Sorry, you just took me by surprise is all."

Jules hugged him back before glancing up. "You missed me. Don't deny it."

"Of course I did. You're my favorite sister. Does Father know you're here?"

She stepped back. "No. I just left. Not like he cares, banishing me to the pool house and all that."

"And what about your mum? She cares."

"She's a lemming. She thinks whatever Daddy tells her to think."

"Have you given any thought to your court date or the drink-driving charge? Do you think you can just do a runner, and the judge won't notice?"

She rolled her eyes toward the ceiling. "I don't go back to court for a month."

That would explain the six unopened suitcases piled up in the corner. While he was glad to see her, she couldn't stay here. Their father would go barmy and cut her off for good. But how to tell her that without hurting her feelings? "Are you planning on picking up these clothes, or just leaving them in a heap?"

"Listen to you. When did you become so stodgy?"

"I am not stodgy. When did you get in?"

"Last night. Where were you, by the way?"

"Absolutely none of your business."

"It's like that, is it?"

Cal didn't want to talk about his night. Instead, he walked into the closet and retrieved a fresh set of clothes. "Why don't you pick up your clutter in the lounge and order us lunch," he said over his shoulder.

"Don't be daft, Cal. I'll just call housekeeping and let them pick it up."

Babs had taught Cal better than that. He may not be as neat as a pin, but he could certainly pick up after himself. He strode back into the bedroom and removed the house phone from her hand. "You made the mess, you'll clean it up." Without responding to her gasp of outrage, Cal pulled his phone and wallet from his jeans and dropped them on the bedside table, then stalked into the bathroom and shut the door with his foot.

He took a deep breath and stared at his reflection, rubbing a hand over the stubble on his cheeks. He looked a bit shot. No wonder, having spent the night with Ryan, the snore piggy.

His eyes drifted to the marble counter overflowing with feminine shit. Curlers and straighteners and a hair dryer were thrown haphazardly, their wires commingling and dripping to the floor like tentacles. Powder and eye shadow and nail varnish. Bloody fucking hell. And why did she need purple false eyelashes?

Shaking his head, Cal stripped and hopped in the shower. He shouldn't be so hard on Jules. He hadn't seen her in over a year, and he'd missed her terribly. They just needed some ground rules. She wouldn't be staying long, at any rate.

After drying off, he dressed in clean clothes and hastily shaved before strolling to the lounge. Jules had taken care of her plates and towels, and neatly stacked the magazines on the coffee table. As he continued out to the pool, he found her sprawled in a lounger, her shirt off and her skirt hiked up farther than was legal. "God, Jules." He covered his eyes with one hand and sidled to the towel stand. Jerking two from the stack, he tossed them in her direction. "Get decent, will you?"

She sighed, and he heard the lounger creak with her movements. "When did you become such a fucking prude?" After a minute, she spoke again. "You can look." She'd wrapped a towel around her so only the bra straps were visible.

Cal thrust his fingers through his damp hair. "I apologize for overreacting before. I was a twat."

Jules's brows rose over the tops of her pricey sunglasses. "You think?"

"Did you order us something to eat? I'm half-starved."

"Yes, should be here in another fifteen."

Cal perched on the second lounger. He and Jules stared at each other, neither saying a word. The silence grew to an embarrassing length.

She tugged on a curl, let it spring back in place. "So, Australia."

"Yeah."

"Sorry about Babs. I know you were gutted. You could have come to L.A. after she died. You didn't have to stay in Cairns this whole time."

Cal didn't want to talk about it. It was still too raw, even after all these months. "I just needed some time alone. I apologize for missing your birthday, though."

"Don't be stupid."

They remained quiet until Cal's mobile rang, letting him know the food had arrived. It took three men to roll three carts into the villa. Cal signed the check and tipped them. He turned to Jules. "I do hope there's something edible under all these domes." He lifted the silver cloche and discovered cheesecake.

Cal grabbed a fork and tucked in while Jules uncovered the rest. She'd ordered everything from pizza to burgers to onion rings. Not a vegetable in sight.

As Cal ate, he studied her. Jules had changed in the last year, besides the trashy clothes and artistic makeup. She'd always been slim, but now her face had lost some of its roundness, making her eyes seem larger. Her limbs were more lithe, less coltish. His baby sister had grown up.

Other than birthdays, he didn't see much of her. They mostly chatted by video, or texted. Cal's father preferred it that way—after all, Cal was physical proof of the old man's disastrous first marriage. George Hughes didn't like to be reminded of his failures.

Cal gorged on cheeseburgers and chicken strips while Jules picked at a couple of French fries. Once Cal's hunger subsided, he leaned back. "You have to let Father know you're here."

She stood and gathered their plates, setting them back on the carts. "He won't even miss me. After he stopped yelling, he quit speaking to me altogether. He's been issuing orders through Mum for the last few days."

"You can't just run from your troubles."

"You did. You never stay in one place for long, and it's worked for you."

"True, but I've never been arrested, either." One of her blue-shadowed eyes twitched in irritation. Cal fully understood he wasn't the best person to offer advice. Telling her to stay put sounded terribly hypocritical—nevertheless, she needed to hear it. "Look, I know the old man is awful, and you may need a break. But this isn't the way to do it."

Jules crossed to the French doors and stared out at the patio. "I have no money, no credit cards, my license was suspended. What the bloody hell am I supposed to do?"

"I don't know. Look for a job, like a normal person. Go to the animal shelter and sweep up cat hair. Do something productive."

"You don't have a job. Not a proper one. What were you doing this morning?" Jules spun on her heel and faced him. Her brows drew low over narrowed eyes, and her tone was full of icy disdain—so much like their father's it was eerie. "Volunteering at the local homeless shelter, and not falling out of some slutty girl's bed?"

"Watch yourself, Jules," he growled. "I was helping a friend."

"Does this friend have a name, or do you even remember?"

"You know, contrary to popular belief, I'm not a man whore. And she's a very nice woman. Works at a foundation, gives of her time to help others. You could learn something from that."

"You sound like a right idiot. Some slag has you by the cock, and that's why you don't want me here. Admit it. You'd rather I trot back home so you can pull some stupid girl."

"Not true, and don't call her that again. You and I both know how the old man gets. Do you want to be shut out for good? Because if you stay here with me, that's what will happen." When she remained mute, he continued, "He'll do it just to spite me. You need to go home, Jules."

Fat teardrops filled her eyes and spilled onto her cheeks. "You're kicking me out too?"

Oh God. Seeing those tears nearly undid him. Pressing his lips together, Cal stepped around the coffee table and approached her. "I'm not leaving for a while. I promise I'll come visit." He attempted to give her a hug, but she twisted her shoulder and flung him off.

"How long is a while? Three days? A week? Before I know it, you'll be off to Greenland or something, and send me a text six weeks later."

He wasn't a good role model—his father was correct

on that score. Cal didn't know what Jules needed right now, or how to provide it. Damn it, he wished people would stop relying on him. "I won't leave without giving you proper notice, all right?"

"Don't do me any favors. This is because of your Mother Teresa, isn't it?" she asked. "You're not staying here for me, you're staying for her. Typical. You've never cared about me, Cal, not really."

"That's not true. I think about you all of the time." And he did, in his own way. Wherever he traveled, he searched for interesting and pretty gifts. He could have been around more, but his father made it nearly impossible. "I'll try to do better."

Jules shook her head, making the curls wobble. "You're not capable of doing better."

That barb found its mark. Part of him wanted to grab his passport and head to the nearest exit. Being needed by anyone was rather daunting, stifling almost. But right at this moment, the more stalwart side of his nature won by a hair. "Maybe that's true. But I'd still like to try."

"You won't stick around, Cal. You'll be bored silly with this girl of yours in ten minutes," she said with a loud sniff.

No, he wouldn't. Cal felt the truth of that in his gut. He would never be bored with Monica Campbell. How could he be? She sparred with him one minute and kissed him passionately the next. He never knew exactly what would come out of her mouth, and she made him laugh. Monica was a constant surprise.

"I know you don't believe it right now," he said, "but this is for your own good." How many times had Babcock said the same thing to him? Too many to count.

But now, as he stood before Juliette, he knew Babs had wanted the best for him, even if it meant he sometimes hated her for it. And Jules might very well hate him. "I'm sorry, but I'm going to book you on the next flight. It's the sensible thing to do."

Before he could say more, Jules ran out of the lounge. A moment later, she slammed the bedroom door so hard, it echoed down the hall.

Well, fuck. What was he meant to do? She needed to go home. His father would blame him for this, and take it out on Jules. Staying here wasn't an option.

With a sigh, Cal went to retrieve his phone from his pocket, but remembered he'd left it in the bedroom. Jules needed time to calm down, so he used the house phone and dialed his father's number. The housekeeper answered, and Cal waited a good fifteen minutes before the old man picked up.

"What is it, Calum?"

"Good to speak to you too, Father. I believe you've misplaced something."

"I don't have time for games today." The man never had time for games. Even as a child, the only thing Cal remembered about his father were harsh, punishing silences in between heated rows with Pix.

"Jules turned up here last night."

"And just where the hell is 'here'?"

"Vegas. She's fine, by the way."

"Vegas," he sneered. "A funfair for adults. How perfect for you. If you gamble away your grandfather's money, don't come crying to me."

Cal pinched his earlobe. "I'm worried about Jules. She's distraught right now, unsure about her future."

"That's rich, coming from you." Contempt coated his father's words like grease on a filthy engine. "*Juliette* will make a course correction. She's not going to turn out like you, Calum—too much money and too little smarts. She's a bright girl. Send her back home immediately, do you hear me?"

"I will do, but I wanted to let you know what's going on. Since you don't seem to have a clue."

"How dare you? Why don't you go back to wherever the hell you came from this time? Juliette doesn't need you filling her head with nonsense."

Determination stiffened Cal's spine. "I'm not going anywhere. For the time being, I'm staying in the States. And I suggest you stop acting like a plonker. Jules says you haven't spoken to her directly in days. That stops now, do you understand me, Father?"

The old man's breathing was heavy, almost gasping. "If you believe for one minute that you can dictate to me, you're in for a whopper of a surprise."

Cal felt a ping of sadness. How had they gotten here, to this place where bitter words were more normal than courteous ones? "I'm sending her home. She cocked up, and now she needs to face it with you by her side. Do the right thing." Cal ended the call.

Next, he phoned Mr. Lawson and had him book Jules a first-class ticket for later in the evening. At least they'd have a few hours together. If she deigned to speak to him.

With his hands thrust deep in his pockets, Cal strode down the hallway. At the bedroom door, he knocked three times, but she didn't answer. "Jules, I know you're angry with me, but let's talk. Jules?"

When she didn't shout obscenities or call him names,

Cal started to become worried. He tried the handle, but the door was locked. A feeling of dread washed over him. "Jules, let me in. Jules." He listened carefully for movement, but all was silent behind the door.

Cal ran back to the lounge and dialed Mr. Lawson, requesting a key. "I need it immediately. My sister has locked herself in the bedroom."

"I'm terribly sorry, sir," Lawson said in a flat Midwestern tone. "According to the security guard, your sister requested a cab fifteen minutes ago. She's gone."

Bloody hell.

"Deena Adams is here to see you."

Monica glanced up when Stella poked her head in the doorway. "Deena? She's here now? Send her in." Monica stood and smoothed nervous hands over her pant legs.

In her early forties, Deena Adams was a dynamo. As a successful entertainment attorney, she volunteered her legal advice, served as a board member, chaired committees, and worked tirelessly to fund-raise. Monica wished they had three more just like her.

Deena briskly walked in a moment later, a bob of dark blond hair swinging against her jawline. She wore no makeup, and her pantsuit was a higher-end version of Monica's. "Sorry I didn't call first. I was driving by and took a chance that you'd be working today." She held out her hand for Monica to shake.

"Good to see you. Please, sit. Can I get you something to drink?"

Deena propped her briefcase on the chair, checked

her phone, and then speared Monica with a sharp glance. "I only have ten minutes, so I'll keep it brief. I don't appreciate your going behind my back."

Monica was speechless for a second. "Excuse me?"

"I had the media covered. I've talked to all the entertainment reporters, I've gotten us interview spots on three of the top radio stations, and we have a cover story in the style section of the paper, which comes out in two weeks. But you evidently didn't trust my committee to handle the details. Imagine what an ass I felt like when I got phone calls asking me why the foundation coordinator is trying to undermine me."

"That wasn't my intention, Deena. I apologize." Goddamn Allie. This was her fault. Monica trusted the PR committee to do their job, but no, Allie wanted to micromanage. As usual.

Deena checked her phone once again. "Either I'm the PR chair, or I'm not. Pick one."

"Of course you are. We just wanted to be thorough. And I apologize for crossing the line."

"We? As in Allie? Look, Monica, everyone knows the deal. Allie runs the show, and you're just her mouthpiece. But if you blindside me again, I'll quit the board. And frankly, you need me." She picked up her briefcase and nodded. "Good to see you." And then she strode out of the office, slamming the door behind her.

A drive-by bitch slap. That's what it felt like.

Monica fell back into her chair in an angry daze. *Allie's mouthpiece*. The truth hurt. Monica worked hard to show she was up to the challenge of running the foundation. But with Allie pulling her strings, it was a little hard for Monica to prove her competence.

As soon as Deena left, Stella hustled into the office. "What did she want?"

"I stepped on her toes when I contacted the media."

Stella fingered the beads around her neck. "Are you all right?"

"Does everyone on the staff think I sit in here all day and twiddle my thumbs?" Allie's interference was starting to wear Monica down. But what could she do about it? She only had this job because of her sister.

"Oh, honey, anyone who's seen you working day and night knows you're great at your job. When this gala brings in more money than last year, the board will know it too. I was going to head out, but I can stay, if you like?"

"No, I'm good. See you Monday."

It was almost noon, but Monica wasn't hungry. Her stomach tangled into knots of frustration. And if worrying about her professional reputation wasn't enough, she had a date with Cal.

All morning he'd been there, in the back of her mind. She couldn't stop thinking about last night. And not just the sex, although that had been amazing. Just hanging out with him, listening to him talk and tell her stories about all the places he'd been to—it was probably the best date she'd ever had.

In control. Eyes wide open. Right. Monica should focus on work, not Cal.

This gala needed to go off without a hitch. Monica wanted the entire board to see what she could do, how much money she'd raised. And then she'd tell each and every one of them to suck it.

Well, probably not. But she'd sure as hell be thinking it.

Cal questioned a security guard, who couldn't recall the name of the cab company or the number plate. Why the bloody hell was the man in this business, if he couldn't remember important details? Cal requested a look at the surveillance footage, which apparently required an act of God.

While he waited for approval, he called Jules's phone for the tenth time. Straight to voice mail. She was ignoring him.

His father would never forgive him if something happened to her. Cal would never forgive himself.

Jules may be too young to gamble or drink, but that probably wouldn't stop her if she hooked up with the wrong people. Monica knew this town, and she used to be a wild child herself, once upon a time. Perhaps she'd know where to look. That would be a start.

Without wasting another second, he dialed her. "My sister's run off, and I need to find her."

Monica didn't miss a beat. "Here in Vegas?"

"Yes, she arrived last night, we rowed this morning, and she took off in a cab. I have no idea where she is, and she won't answer her phone."

"I'll be right there."

"Monica. Thank you." It had been fifteen years since he'd relied on anyone other than himself. It felt foreign to him. Strange.

As he waited, Mr. Lawson discovered the name of the cab company and had already spoken to the dispatcher. The cabbie had dropped Jules at Planet Hollywood. Cal wasn't sure why, but Monica might know. Good man, that Mr. Lawson. He deserved every cent of the hefty tip Cal planned on giving him.

When Monica arrived twenty minutes later, Cal was waiting for her by the gated entrance. He threw one last look of irritation at the security guard, hopped into the passenger seat, and explained the situation.

Monica nodded. "I'm betting she's at the Miracle Mile Shops. I know it well. It's basically a mall, so I'm guessing she'll feel right at home."

"She can't afford the mall. My father cut up all of her credit cards."

Monica turned her head to look at him. He couldn't see her eyes behind her dark glasses, but she pursed her lips slightly. "I'd check your wallet, if I were you."

"Fuck." Cal dug it out of his jeans. It had been stuffed with twenties and fifties this morning. "She left me three dollars and took two of my cards."

"Tell me what's going on, Cal. I didn't even know you had a sister."

As Monica drove, he gave her a brief history, leaving out the gory details about his father's scathing disapproval. "They moved to California eight years ago. Now she has a DUI, and she'll be twenty-one in three months."

"Oh boy, are you in for a bumpy road." She pulled into an enormous parking garage and eventually found a spot on the eighth level. "Cal," she said, twisting the key out of the ignition, "Jules sounds a little lost. And I know something about that. It's none of my business, but if she takes a lot of shit from your dad, you might want to go easy on her."

He didn't want to go easy on Jules. Cal wanted to

haul her to the airport and toss her onto the plane. "I'll do my best."

"Hey," she said softly, pinning her glasses on the top of her head. "She came to you. When she needed a place to land, you were her choice. So she trusts you."

That took the self-righteous wind from his sail. Cal tugged his earlobe. He could have handled Jules with more tact and patience. "She can't stay here, and I can't very well force her into going back to L.A. I don't know how to rein her in."

Monica patted his thigh. "You can't. She's going to make her own choices. And I'm not saying she should stay here, I'm just saying use your indoor voice when you talk to her. Allie used to yell at me when I messed up, and I would shut down completely."

She trained her blue eyes on him, looking so bloody sympathetic, Cal gave in to temptation. Snaking a hand around her nape, he kissed her. It was hard and brief, left him hungry for more than a taste. But for now, it had to be enough. "Thank you."

She smiled. "You're welcome. Now let's go find your sis."

When they entered the building, Cal stopped and gazed around. For some reason, all the stores had Moorish architectural features and looked as though they belonged inside a Moroccan town. He raised his eyes to the barreled ceiling painted to look like the sky. Cal tried Jules's number once more. "She's not answering."

"She'll turn up. Probably once she's run through your money, but she will turn up."

They wound their way around tourists and past

kiosks, when suddenly, the artificial sky darkened. Thunder boomed.

Monica leaned over. "The rain show. Not that exciting. Come on, security is up ahead."

"Well acquainted with the security here, are you?"

She donned a stony expression. He'd hit a nerve. She'd probably done something minor when she was young, and Allie had no doubt thrown a wobbler.

As they walked, Cal kept a lookout for Jules. Every flash of pink caught his eye. Every dark-haired girl captured his attention. But she could be anywhere.

At the security station, Cal described Jules. The man used his two-way radio to communicate the information to someone, somewhere. They paged Jules's name over the PA system and alerted the various shops that he was looking for her. All pretty fucking useless.

"Why don't we split up?" Monica asked. "You take one side of the shops, and I'll take the other."

Cal nodded. "Yeah."

"Do you have a picture of her? It'll give me something to go by."

Cal scrolled through his phone, glancing at hundreds of photos. Mostly shots of cars he'd worked on, in various states of repair. A few of Babcock, when she was still healthy enough to sit on the terrace and look out at the beach. He finally found a pic of Jules on her nineteenth birthday. She hadn't worn nearly as much makeup then as she did now, and her hair was shorter. She wore a birthday tiara and showed off the sapphire earrings he'd given her as a present.

His stomach dropped. He had picture after picture of the cars he'd worked on, but only one of his sister.

"Here she is." His voice sounded gruffer than usual, thick with emotion. He showed Monica the photo and glanced away. Cal really *was* a crap brother. That seriously needed to change.

"She's pretty. You guys have the same eyes." Monica glanced up at him, scanned his face. "What's wrong?"

"I've been a selfish bastard."

"I would never describe you as a selfish person, Cal." She reached out and gave his arm a quick squeeze. "I'll take this side and meet you in front of the theater."

Cal nodded and moved off. Monica was being very kind to him. He wasn't sure he deserved it.

Cal was a lot of things—handsome, funny, a fantastic lover…but selfish? Not even close. Monica had seen him give money to strangers, and he was kind to everyone. She didn't know the whole story with his sister, but from the way it sounded, they didn't see each other very often. So Cal probably didn't understand that sisters were a pain. Monica had two to prove it.

Over the next three hours, she and Cal tried to divide and conquer, looking in every store, bar, and restaurant. They asked sales people and wait staff if they'd seen Jules. Monica wasn't sure the girl had ever been here. Cal had described his sister's revealing outfit, and Jules's short, gold skirt sounded second-glance worthy. Surely someone would have noticed. But they struck out over and over.

Finally admitting defeat, she and Cal walked back to the car. Monica gazed up at him. His eyes were serious. She was used to seeing him wear a smile, but now, Cal's mouth leveled into a straight line, and his wide shoulders climbed upward, tense and strained. She wished she could reassure him somehow, but she didn't know what to say.

This must have been how Allie used to feel when Monica pulled shit like this.

When Cal's phone rang, he practically ripped it from his pocket and glanced at the screen. "I don't have time now, Mum." Then he froze. "What? She's with you? For how long?" That worried look on his face morphed to anger, hardening his features, turning his eyes into green glaciers. "I'm on my way." He punched the End button. "She's been with my mother most of the afternoon. That fucking little brat."

Chapter 13

Monica held on to his arm. His biceps bunched under her hand. "Cal. Remember, patience."

He turned those cold, angry eyes on her. "I'm brassed off with Jules, make no mistake, but Pixie should have called me hours ago. She's meant to be the adult." He jerked his arm from her grasp. "Do you mind driving me out to her place? I could take a cab, if you'd rather."

She dismissed his biting tone. "Of course I'll drive you." And Monica hoped he'd calm down a little before they arrived. Cal was good-natured and very easy to be around. She had a feeling it took a lot to push him over the edge. Between Pix and Jules, they'd given him a hard shove.

As she exited the parking garage and pulled onto the Strip, she shot him a look. Dusk had set in, painting the horizon in shades ranging from deep pink to light peach. The neon signs popped against the darkening sky. "She may have had her reasons, Cal. Your mom, I mean."

He shook his head. "Don't think so. Pixie is unreliable at the best of times, and self-serving always." He clamped his mouth shut and faced the passenger window. Other than giving her directions, he didn't say another word the entire trip.

When Monica arrived at Pixie's house and rolled past the heavy wooden gates and up the long, circular drive, security lights glowed. Near the house, Paolo waited for them with a little Pomeranian in his arms.

Cal turned to her as she braked. "You don't have to stay, Monica. Go home, do some work, sit in your unfurnished house, and have a good evening."

He started to get out of the car, but she pulled on his sleeve. "Don't pull that shit with me, okay? I don't deserve it."

With a bitter twist of his lips, he nodded. "You're right. I'm taking my foul mood out on you. I apologize. You were brilliant today, calmed me down when I was about to lose my rag. I appreciate it. But don't feel like you have to stick around."

"I'll wait to see if you need a ride."

He smiled then. A wan, tired smile, but it was something. Better than the frown he'd been sporting all afternoon. "Thank you. I'll have to make it up to you somehow."

"You took care of Ryan last night. I'd say we're even."

Cal grimaced. "That's right. Don't remind me." He leaned down and kissed her cheek, then got out of the car.

While he strolled toward Paolo, Monica went to the front door and used the knocker. A maid answered the door and led the way to the large, open living room. This was the first time Monica had been to Pixie's house—the palatial palazzo. Mediterranean architecture on steroids.

The walls, the furnishings, the rugs—all white. The only color in the room was Pixie, lounging on a tufted, modern chaise, thumbing through a glossy fashion magazine. She looked up when Monica stepped into the room. "Hey, Pix."

The older woman's brows rose a fraction, and she unfolded herself from the lounger. "Darling! How are you?" She dropped the magazine and strode forward, taking both of Monica's hands. At five foot five, Monica was hardly statuesque, but Pix made her feel like it. Diminutive in stature with sharp features in a heart-shaped face, she looked a dozen years younger than she actually was. Vitality swirled around her, affecting everything in its path. Monica felt a little more alert just sharing space with Pix. Cal must have gotten the charisma gene from his mom.

Monica accepted Pixie's air kiss. "I'm well. You're looking fab, as usual." Cal's mom wore tight slacks patterned in bold black-and-white stripes. Her hot-pink blouse revealed a risqué amount of cleavage. One more undone button, and her boobs would have been on parade.

Pix flipped a mass of dark hair behind her shoulder. "Oh, Monnie, you're so very sweet. Whatever are you doing here?"

"I brought Cal." Monica stepped closer and lowered her voice. "He's pretty angry right now, so you might want to tread carefully."

Pix squared her shoulders. "He's angry with me, is he? We'll see about that."

Monica began backing up. She didn't want to be in the same room when Cal's heated anger met Pix's haughty demeanor. Sounded like a perfect recipe for disaster. "Where's Jules? I'd like to meet her."

"Game room, down the hall." She flung her left arm in one direction as she looked toward the doorway, waiting for Cal, no doubt.

She didn't need to be told twice. Monica retreated to the hallway, and when she heard the sound of pool balls clacking, she headed toward it.

Her first sight of Jules came as a surprise. The younger girl only vaguely resembled the picture Cal had shown her earlier. Jules's warm brown hair looked longer now, and she'd added a few platinum extensions. Obviously a fan of the spray tan, she displayed too much skin from her neck all the way down to the stacked heels any stripper would be proud to wear. She leaned over the table with her pool cue and lined up a shot.

"Hello. Jules?"

The girl straightened slightly. "Yeah, who are you?" Her brown eyes flashed over Monica and dismissed her. Not waiting for an answer, she bent back over the table, and with a smooth jab, whacked the six ball into the corner pocket.

"I'm Monica, a friend of Cal's."

"Cal's friend? You?" Her perusal was slower this time, taking in Monica's hair, her jacket, her matching slacks, down to her brown flats. "You?" she asked again.

Monica laid her purse on a bar stool. "I'm not sure what you expect me to say." She picked out a shorter cue from the row hanging on the wall and faced Jules. "Want to rack 'em?"

"You're dating my brother? Cal. Calum."

"Yeah." Sort of. Monica would characterize it as hooking up, but she wasn't about to admit that to his sister.

"Saint Monica. You're not what I expected. That suit is a tragedy. Seriously, it's making me want to weep right now."

"Your outfit isn't doing much for me, either." She plucked the triangular rack from beneath the table and tossed it at Jules, who caught it in her left hand.

"What do you two have in common, anyway, you and my brother?"

"Not a lot, actually."

Jules arranged the balls in the right order. "So it's just sex, then. You don't look like the type."

Monica almost laughed. Looks could be deceiving. Back in the day, Monica's slutty behavior had gotten her into more trouble than she cared to remember. And now that she thought about it, sleeping with a guy because he rode a Harley or had ink covering fifty percent of his body or told her she was pretty—it had left her empty. Oh, it was rebellious and exciting while she did it—which made the sex feel even better—but only because she'd been acting out. Waking up the next morning, hungover and staring at a stranger, left her self-esteem bruised and battered. That was the difference between then and now. Cal might be wrong for her, but Monica was having the time of her life. Plus, she liked him. She was even beginning to respect him. He'd been a frazzled mess when his sister disappeared. That said a lot.

Monica's gaze flew over Jules once more. If she had to place a bet, she'd guess that Jules wasn't nearly as brazen as she pretended. This in-your-face look was for shock value. "Cal was worried sick about you today."

Jules rolled her eyes and removed the rack, tossing it back to Monica. "He can't wait to send me home. So he can shag you, would be my guess. Though you don't look that cracking to me."

Monica ignored the dig. "We spent hours searching for you at the Miracle Mile."

Jules's pink lips parted. "How did he know I was there?"

"Lucky guess. You could have answered at least *one*

of his forty-three phone messages." Monica struck the balls, managing to sink just one into the side pocket.

"I don't have to explain myself to you."

Hmm. Defensive. Jules watched as Monica made two more shots, then missed. "No, but you might want to have an excuse ready for Cal though."

"Is he very angry?"

"Yeah. He'll probably give you hell. Siblings are like that. You can yell at each other, terrorize each other, but when it's all over, you hug it out."

Jules took a turn and scratched, sending the cue ball into the corner pocket.

"I wouldn't know. Cal and I aren't like that. He's always jetting off somewhere or holed up in his garage. And of course he was gone all last year."

"Australia, right?" Cal hated talking about it. Maybe Jules could fill in a few blanks.

"Yeah. I haven't seen him in ages."

Monica and Brynn only saw each other every couple of weeks, but Brynnie would be there in a heartbeat if Monica needed her. And Allie, well…Al would take a bullet for Monica. She'd bitch the whole time and never let anyone forget it—probably show off the scar every chance she got—but she'd do it. "So you and Cal aren't that close?"

"Not really." Jules leaned her hip against the table and sighed. "In fairness, Daddy doesn't want him around, but no matter where he is, Cal always flies in for my birthday. Except for this last year, when Babcock was so ill."

"Babcock was sick, huh?" That explained a lot.

"He took care of her."

Monica set the cue on the table. "What was wrong

with her?" She felt a little guilty, asking personal questions about Cal. Not guilty enough to stop, though.

"Something with her heart, I think."

Monica's pulse sped up. "He was with her until the end, wasn't he?"

Jules nodded. "Yeah. She died this past spring. Poor Cal was a wreck. I didn't hear from him for weeks."

He'd said Babcock was like a mother to him. Watching a loved one die—she and Cal had something in common, after all.

Her suspicions were correct: Calum Hughes was a good man. That didn't fit in with the image she'd had of him for the last five years—the bad boy who partied and fucked his way around the globe. He still wasn't partner material, but he was *honorable*.

She glanced up to find Jules watching her intently. "You fancy him, don't you?"

Monica ignored the question. "It's none of my business, but maybe you could cut him some slack. Sounds like he's had a pretty shitty year."

"Well, so have I. I mean, it's not the same, really, but my year hasn't exactly been one for the memory books."

"How so?"

Jules crossed her arms. "Daddy's been nagging me about college. He thinks I'm more clever than I really am, and I hate school. It bores me fucking senseless."

Monica let out a laugh. "I was you, eight years ago."

"Get. Out. You've never been anything like me. Being a do-gooder is as snore-worthy as it gets."

"I hate to break it to you, kid, but I was exactly like you. With better makeup." She raised one brow at Jules's incredulous expression. "I started skipping school and didn't get to graduate with my class. I moved out of my dad's house and shacked up with a loser—the first of many. I got arrested too."

"What happened to turn you into the paragon you are now?"

"I finally got my shit together."

"You don't look together. You look—"

"Yes, I know. Tragic." Monica was getting a little tired of the Hughes sibs railing on her clothes. "I work for a cancer foundation. I'm not going to strut around in tube tops."

Jules snorted. "You might get more donations that way."

"You may have a point."

They both grew silent. Monica thought about Cal and all the pain and loss he must have suffered over the last year. She could relate.

Then she heard raised voices. She and Jules exchanged a glance and both took off out of the room and down the hall.

Cal restlessly circled the living room, his hands fisted at his hips. "Why didn't you call the minute she showed up? How irresponsible can you be?" His voice rose with every word.

Curled up on the chaise, Pixie watched him pace. "I was responsible enough to raise you, Calum."

"Don't fool yourself. Babcock raised me while you played dress-up."

"That's not true," she cried.

"It is true. You went to events and parties and had affairs while Babs did the boring bits."

Cal felt his neck grow hot. Monica had warned him to

stay calm, but when he'd seen his mum sitting there like a bristly cat, anger overrode his best intentions. From the corner of his eye, he noticed Monica and Jules standing near a stuccoed column. He pointed at his sister. "What have you got to say for yourself?"

"Bugger off, asshole." She spun, almost tripped in those ridiculous heels, and clomped up the stairs.

Monica tipped her head to one side. Palms facing the floor, she pressed her hands downward. "Chill out, Cal. Just calm down. Yelling at everyone isn't going to help." She threw a glance at Pix before following Jules up the winding staircase.

Calm? Jules had been here for hours. He'd been bloody frantic all afternoon, and Pix didn't even have the courtesy to ring him. "My sister"—he enunciated each word—"has been missing since noon. I've been worried sick, and you're playing games. As usual."

Pixie unfurled herself and stood, her tiny body shaking with anger. "She begged me not to call you. She absolutely forbade me to call your father, said she'd leave if I did. I finally calmed her down enough to let me get in touch with you. I'm sorry I'm not perfect, Calum. I don't do things the way you would."

He stopped pacing and stared at her for a moment. Then he clapped his hands. "Very good, Mum. Brilliant performance. Quite the martyr. And you're so bloody far from perfect, it's laughable."

All of the defiance left her, and she dropped to the chaise like a deflated balloon. Placing her fingers to her temples, Pix sighed. "I have such a headache."

Cal had no sympathy to give her. "Why did Jules come here? How did she get your address?"

She shrugged one shoulder. "From your phone. She said you were going to send her back to California. If anyone understands how difficult your father can be, it's me. How I lived with that man for eight long years, I'll never know. Jules is lovely. Very tan, that girl. She's welcome to stay for as long as she likes."

Cal pressed his lips together. "She's not staying, and neither am I."

"Oh, do sit down. I'm tired of staring up at you. I'll order us some tea."

"I don't want tea."

"Of course you do. Remember how Babs used to make it? With a little drop of brandy? I miss her too, darling." A smile drifted over her lips, wistful at the corners.

Cal thrust his hands into his pockets. "She loved you, Mum. She took care of the both of us for years. She devoted her life to us, to you. And you didn't come to see her once. Not one goddamned time. I'm ashamed of you." The anger he'd been feeling all day, so scalding it left his throat dry, subsided. Grief crawled its way back to the fore.

"And you better not have filled Jules's head with a load of bullshit. She's not staying here. She's going back to California. She can't just run away and forget her problems."

"Like I did?" she asked. "That's how you see me, isn't it? Haring off and ignoring my problems."

"Yeah, Mum, that's exactly how I see you." It was how Cal saw himself, and he didn't like it a bit. He wasn't sure he could change, wasn't sure he wanted to, but he desired something better for Jules. He didn't want her to suppress her personality, as Monica had done. But

Cal wanted his sister to channel her gifts and become something wonderful.

Pixie gave him a tearful smile. "You and I are more alike than you care to admit."

"Possibly." Cal rubbed his cheeks. He looked at his mum sitting there huddled in on herself, and for once, she looked her age. He always thought of Pix as larger than life, but right now she appeared small, frail almost. "I don't resent you for dragging me around with you. I don't. But I'll never forgive you for abandoning Babcock when she needed you."

"Darling, you still don't understand. I would have been useless to her. I can't even make a decent cup of tea."

She still didn't get it. She never would, his mum. "It wasn't about you. It was about her. Giving her back some of the comfort she'd given you all those years."

"She would have been comforting me," Pixie said, "not the other way around."

Cal slowly shook his head. "You should have been there for her."

"I'm not strong, Cal. I couldn't bear to watch her fade away."

"Then you should have been there for *me*." Until the words left his mouth, Cal hadn't known he'd felt that way. *Abandoned. Alone.*

He couldn't stand here and listen to any more of this. He didn't want her excuses, didn't want her self-pity. He strode out of the room, his work boots making a dull thud against the white-marbled floor. As he took the stairs, two at a time, he grasped the wrought-iron handrail.

Cal felt out of sync. His chest constricted, and heat prickled his skin. Anger and hurt and confusion and bitterness—all rolled into one jumble. Babcock was gone. His mother cared, but in her own limited way. And it wasn't enough. Cal wanted something he couldn't even put a name to. This…lack, it ate at him, leaving him hollow.

At the landing, he heard voices coming from a bedroom down the hall. Cal shortened his steps as he drew near.

"What am I going to do if he kicks me out for good?" Jules's voice cracked.

"Then you'll figure it out," Monica said. "But Cal won't let you down. You know that, right?"

"He's never been there for me—why would he start now?"

Jules needed him. She was in a right poor state if he was her go-to person, but he wanted to help her pick up the pieces and start over. Maybe he could start over too.

Cal peeked through the doorway. They sat on the bed, side by side. Monica pulled something from her purse and handed it to Jules. "Call me anytime. Hey, I know your dad is annoying, but it's because he cares so much." Cal fought an unexpected smile. She may not advertise it, but Monica Campbell was a nurturer. She gave a damn about people. That was possibly her most endearing quality.

"No, he doesn't. He just wants to control me." Jules swiped her nose. "I'm sick of hearing his boring lectures. He's from the Stone Age, so he thinks he knows everything."

"The Rolling Stone Age? Your dad's what, sixty, sixty-five, tops?"

"He may as well be six hundred and fifty the way he carries on." She adopted a deep voice. "*In my day, we went to proper school. In my day, a gap year meant something, not an excuse to pickle your liver. In my day—"*

Monica laughed. "Yeah, I get the picture. My sister Allie's the same way. And living in your dad's house, eating at his table, you're kind of asking for it. That's the way it works."

"Life rather sucks, doesn't it?" Jules asked.

Monica nodded and rubbed circles along his sister's back. "Sometimes. But it beats the alternative."

Cal cleared his throat to announce his presence. "Sorry to interrupt."

Monica stood. "There you are." She glanced down at Jules, who'd lowered her eyes to the floor. "Why don't I go wait in the car, and if you don't need a ride, just text me, and I'll head out." She gave him a smile on her way to the door.

When Monica was gone, Jules glanced up. "At first I thought she was boring. The clothes threw me."

"Me too."

"But she's nice."

Cal smiled. "That she is. Let me preface this little talk by saying if you ever pull this crap again, Father's tirades will seem like a treat. Got it?"

"Yeah. Sorry. I just panicked. He hasn't talked to me in days, Cal. He won't even look at me. It's like I don't exist."

"If you don't like it, become independent. Get a job and take things on yourself. But if you're living at his house—"

"I have to live by his rules," Jules finished. "Mummy says that constantly."

"And what about your mum? Is all this putting a rift between her and the old man?"

"Maybe. I'm not going back. I mean, I will for the trial, but I won't stay there with Daddy freezing me out and Mummy pretending it's business as usual."

"Jules—"

"No, Cal. My mind's made up."

He scanned her face. Behind all that makeup, she was full-on serious. "What do you plan on doing? You have no money—except what you stole from me." Jules had the decency to blush. "You don't have a job or a place to stay. You're due in court next month."

She studied her shoes as if they were terribly interesting rather than hideous. "No need to keep banging on about my situation. I know I'm up shit creek. But Pixie said I could stay here."

"No."

Jules leaped to her feet, squaring off with him. "I can do as I bloody well please."

"Pixie isn't fit to look after that dog Paolo totes around. Staying here is simply out of the question."

"I'm not leaving." Jules crossed her arms.

Cal growled deeply. *Goddamn shit fuck bloody hell.* When had his life become so complicated?

"Stay here. If you move, I'll call Father, tell him where you are, and I'll throw every one of your stupid pink suitcases in the pool."

"What? You wouldn't dare."

"Try me, Juliette. Stay. Here." He turned on his heel and marched down the stairs. As he passed the living room, he noted Pixie wasn't perched on her chaise as usual. In fact, the house seemed empty.

When he flung open the door, the brass knocker clanged, echoing through the night. Monica was leaning against the front fender of her car, staring up at the stars. As he marched toward her, her eyes grew wide.

"I've had it, do you hear me?" He made a slashing line at his neck. "Up to here."

"Whoa," she said. "What happened?"

Cal pointed at the house. "Jules refuses to leave. Refuses."

"I was afraid of that."

"She can't stay here, Monica. My mum would be a worse influence than I am."

"I don't think you're a bad influence, Cal." That little line between her brows reappeared.

"Tell that to my father," he ground out.

"If I ever meet him, I will. So what are you going to do?"

"I have no bloody clue." He parked next to her, resting his ass against her car. "She can't stay here, and I'll throttle her if she moves into the villa."

Monica gazed up at him with a mischievous smile. "I think I have an idea."

Chapter 14

Allie hid her surprise well. Her gaze darted over Monica and Cal, but when it got to Jules, her placid smile slid into place. "Welcome." Allie's gaze swooped over Jules's outfit, but her expression never changed. "Frances will show you to your room. No luggage?"

"I'll bring them 'round tonight," Cal said. "Thank you for this, Allison."

"No problem. So glad to have you, Jules." But as soon as Cal and Jules followed the housekeeper upstairs, Allie dropped the smile and shot Monica an annoyed glance. Then she snagged Monica's hand and dragged her to the drawing room, making sure the double doors were shut before she let loose. "What the hell, Monica? I didn't even know Cal had a sister. A heads-up would have been nice."

Monica took a little too much pleasure in Allie's irritation. It was petty, but kind of satisfying to see Allie caught unawares for a change.

Now Monica sauntered through the room, her fingertips gliding over a Grecian urn. "You like bossing people around. I thought you could put your powers to good use for a change."

"What's that supposed to mean?" Allie asked.

Monica turned on her. "I got a very hostile visit from Deena Adams today."

"What did she want with you?"

"Excuse me? I'm the coordinator. Why wouldn't she talk to me?"

With a sigh, Allie flopped down on the sofa. "You know what I mean. Why was she hostile? I'll call her tomorrow and straighten it out, okay?"

Monica'd always thought the expression *seeing red* was just that. But as it turned out, it was a real thing, because all the knickknacks in the room, every stick of furniture, Allie's face—suddenly, they were all a shade of scarlet. "Are you fucking kidding me, Allie?" Monica's voice was quiet and perfectly calm. Completely at odds with the anger building inside her, like a dust devil swirling its way across the desert.

"What? Why are you mad at me? I said I'll fix it."

"I don't need you to fix anything. I've done nothing but work my ass off for the last two years. I think I deserve a little respect. You don't have to clean up after me like I'm Monica the Fuckup."

Realization dawned in Allie's light blue eyes as they took in Monica's face, her hunched shoulders, her clenched fists. "What's wrong with you?"

"What the hell is wrong with *you*? Deena was pissed because I called all of the media outlets, at your insistence. She thought I was going behind her back, because she already had everything scheduled. Which I believe I mentioned."

Allie stood. "Well, it's a misunderstanding. Why are you getting so bent out of shape?"

"Because everyone thinks I'm your little puppet. And you know what? They're right. You're a total control freak, Al. Why did you even give me this job? You obviously have no faith in my ability."

Looking wary, Allie opened her mouth, then snapped it shut.

Monica folded her arms across her chest. "You're never going to see past all the mistakes I've made. You'll never see me as a responsible adult or give me any credit for turning my life around." Monica dropped her hands, defeated. "You've never forgiven me for anything, have you?"

Allie jerked her head back. "Monica, that's not true."

"Yeah it is. You're the one who sacrificed everything, and I'm the one who made your life hell. You gave me a job, and you and Trevor basically bought my house. When Mom got sick, you gave up everything to take care of us, and I haven't been grateful enough. So I should just shut my goddamn mouth and take whatever scraps you decide to throw my way."

"I don't know what you're talking about." Allie was starting to get pissed off too—her eyes became cold, remote. "We gave you the job because you're capable, and I thought you'd want to honor Mom's memory."

"I'm so damn tired of trying to prove myself to you, Al. You don't think I'm capable, just the opposite. You look over my shoulder constantly. I can't take a meeting without holding your hand. You're always going to see me as that angry, fucked-up kid."

"I told you the other day, Mom would be—"

"Leave her out of it."

"I can't leave her out of it. She's the reason we're doing all this. And you never talk about it," Allie shouted. "You never even mention her! It's like you've forgotten all about her."

Monica's brows slammed together. "Forgotten her?

Because I don't take out my grief and let you play with it?" She moved to the door and glanced back over her shoulder. "This shit at the foundation ends now. No more cc'ing you on every email. No more letting you micromanage every move I make. If you don't think I can do this job, fire me." She threw open the door and practically ran out of the house.

She was tired of feeling like the family failure, tired of backing down, of changing everything about herself, only to find she would never be good enough. It was exhausting.

She'd intended on saying good-bye to Cal and Jules, but she was too upset. Then she heard the door slam behind her. Assuming Allie was following her, Monica continued walking to her car.

"What is it, love? What happened?" Cal's sandpapery voice soothed her.

Monica turned around and let her shoulders droop. "Allie and I just had a blowout. It's been a long, shitty day."

He padded down the stairs and loped toward her. When he stood before her, Monica leaned her head back to look up at him.

"I'd take you home and fuck it all better, but I think I should stay with Jules for a while. Your twin nephews have roped her into a game of hide-and-seek. I think she's a bit out of her depth with them."

Monica smiled. "They're a handful."

Cal placed his hands on the curve of her hips. "I don't know what I would have done without you today. You were brilliant."

"Thanks. I'm glad I could help." Monica spread her hands on his upper arms, tightening them to get another feel of those biceps.

"I'm sorry our plans didn't work out tonight, but I'll make it up to you tomorrow." He swayed toward her and lowered his head. His lips were only a whisper away. "I'll pick you up at the office. Six thirty work for you?"

"What about Jules?"

"I think she needs a dose of Trevor's company. She'll appreciate me a little bit more after a few hours with my cousin."

Monica started to laugh, but Cal captured her mouth with his own. As his lips moved over hers, he grasped her possessively. Monica's arms found their way around his neck, where her fingers dove into the short layers of hair above his nape. His heat, his kisses, his rough touch left behind a trail of desire. Monica wanted him again. But too many obligations kept getting in the way.

Cal's hand softened and trailed down to cup her ass. Then he lifted his head. "Damn it, why do we keep doing this out in the open? Come on, let's go have that shag in the garden."

Great suggestion. But his sister. Her sister. "Not practical." Another difference between now and five years ago—back then, Monica wouldn't let anything stand between her and what she wanted.

"Practicality is highly overrated."

She leaned forward and placed a kiss in the center of his sturdy chest. "I'll see you tomorrow night."

"Be ready," he said. "I'll have something special planned."

"I thought you didn't make plans."

"You're an exception to my rules, Monica Campbell."

She raised one brow. "Rules? I thought you didn't believe in those either."

"Perhaps you're reforming me."

~

Monica sat at her desk and rolled her crystal pen between her thumb and forefinger. She should've been working, finishing up cost projections for the next board meeting, but she didn't have it in her. Cal would be here in half an hour, and she couldn't wait to see him.

She needed a reprieve from another hectic day. Although Monica hadn't received any unexpected visitors, Ryan had called, thanking her for coming to the hospital. He'd wanted to talk longer, drag out their conversation, but Monica had cut it short. Then his flowers showed up. A dozen red roses—so...expected compared to Cal's colorful, over-the-top arrangement.

Maybe Cal was right and Ryan wanted a reconciliation. That wasn't going to happen, but she hoped he'd come to that conclusion on his own.

And Monica hadn't heard from Allie, either. She felt pretty awful for the way she'd lashed out, but Monica had tried reasoning with Allie before. Her sister never listened. Maybe Al was finally taking her seriously, allowing Monica to handle the day-to-day operations of the foundation. Or she could just be giving Monica the silent treatment.

After fifteen minutes, Monica gave up the pretense of working and shut down her computer. Grabbing her purse, she walked down the hall to the bathroom. She was the last person in the office, as usual. In the mirror, Monica primped a little bit, fluffing her hair and applying a coat of lip gloss, then trekked back to her office.

She'd just tossed her purse in the bottom drawer when she heard the outer office door creak open, and a moment later, Cal walked in. "Hello, love. Did you have a good day?"

Would she ever grow accustomed to looking at him? That first glance always stole her breath away. As her gaze slid over him, she sauntered to the front of the desk. "It's getting better."

He wore dark slacks and a navy shirt. Her eyes were drawn to the V at the center of his collarbone. She slid her gaze up his throat to the tilted grin. When she looked into his eyes, they crinkled in the corners, causing her heart to pound. "How was your day?"

"Long. Jules talked nonstop as I worked on the Mustang. My ears are still ringing." He yanked on his earlobe.

"So did you really plan a date, or are we winging it tonight?"

"I have something very special planned." He rubbed his hands together and gave her a wicked smile.

"Dinner? A movie? You're going to let me drive your car again?"

"Wouldn't you like to know?" Cal strode forward, his thigh muscles flexing as he moved.

She wanted time to explore those thighs, run her fingers up and down his legs and slowly feel her way to his long, thick shaft. Monica had a few plans of her own.

Her gaze trailed over him, all the way down to his feet. Instead of work boots, he sported loafers. "You have tassels."

Cal stopped and glanced at his shoes. "Do you have something against tassels? Because I rather like them. When they're attached to nipples, they're even better."

She kept staring at his feet. "They're cute."

He walked another couple of steps until he stood in front of her. "Cute?" He reached out and fingered the collar of her black blouse edged in lace. "Is this from the Italian Widows collection? Quite fetching."

She tried to smack at him, but he caught her hand and brought it to his lips. His eyes remained on hers as he kissed her palm.

"I actually wore a skirt today, instead of pants. I should get credit for that."

Cal glanced down at her legs. "It falls well past your knees. Are you trying to seduce me with your ankles?" He pulled her toward him, causing Monica to lose her balance and grab his upper arm for support.

"Cal." Her smile fell away when she saw the heat in his eyes. Their one night together had been at the forefront of her mind for the last two days. The Mustang, his fresh, clean scent, his hard dick inside her…it replayed in her head over and over.

Cal leaned down and brushed his lips across hers. "I want you right now."

Monica nodded. "I'll grab my stuff and we can get out of here." She tried to pull her hand out of his grasp, but he wouldn't let go.

"Right now." His gravelly demand caused her stomach to flutter.

Monica's gaze flew around the room. "We can't. Not in my office."

"Everyone's gone for the night. The place is shut down tight."

"No. Not here." Tugging her hand back, Monica shook her head.

With an indifferent expression, Cal shrugged. "Of

course. We'll go back to mine, assume the missionary position, and keep the lights off. Very good."

He was playing with her. She knew he was playing with her, and yet she couldn't leave it alone. That damned last-word thing. "Just because I don't want to use my desk doesn't mean I do boring sex. And I didn't notice you complaining the other night."

Cal raised his brows. "Who said anything about the desk?"

That left her speechless for a moment. "Then where?" Curiosity overrode her sense of propriety. "I'm for sure not doing it on this floor." She winced at the industrial gray carpeting. Looked scratchy.

"Not the floor." Cal reached out, his hand landing on her chest. His tanned fingers plucked open two of her shirt buttons.

Monica froze to the spot, helpless to stop him. She was *not* having sex in her office. But the very thought of it caused thrills of excitement to skitter throughout her body. "Up against the wall?"

"Everyone fucks against the wall. Where's the imagination in that?" He placed a finger at the base of her neck and lazily traced to the third button.

Monica watched its progress and stared in fascination as he flicked open two more, revealing the scalloped, lacy edge of her bra. The tops of Monica's breasts were bare, pushed up high and firm in the scarlet demi bra. She'd worn it with him in mind.

"Red." His lips parted, and Cal's chest expanded as he inhaled.

He was pleased. No, not pleased—aroused. She really needed to wear this color more often.

As Cal stared at her breasts, Monica's heart pounded. Her panties grew wet. With one sexually charged look, he could draw that kind of response from her, make her body hum with desire. After a full minute, Cal dragged his gaze from her cleavage, up to her face.

Monica's gaze bounced away. "You said you liked the color."

"Seeing you in that, it's better than Christmas."

She started to laugh, but when Cal used his finger to follow the upper curve of her breast, it turned into a gasp. "I'm not having sex in the break room," she said as he finished undoing the buttons visible above the waistband of her black skirt. "I'd never be able to eat in there again." Her voice was a breathless whisper.

"Not the break room." He used both of his hands to untuck her blouse and then peeled the edges back, revealing more of her pale skin. "The other night in the Mustang, I never got to see you naked. Tonight, I want to see everything." With the pads of his fingertips, he brushed over the satin smoothness of her bra strap, then followed them downward and cupped her breasts. Her nipples immediately budded beneath his touch.

The suspense was killing her. Not the desk, not the floor, not the wall. "Where?"

"Where what?" Cal continued to lightly stroke her. "You mean where would I fuck you in this office?"

Monica licked her dry lips. "Yes."

"First, I'd strip every bit of clothing off you." He pushed her jacket and blouse over her shoulders and down her arms, leaving them hanging from her wrists. He bent down and swiped his tongue across her breast.

"And then, I'd grab your ass. Have I mentioned how much I love your ass?" He licked her again.

Was she really doing this? In her office, her professional sanctuary? *Yes*. Her bad-girl self wanted to come out and play again, and even though it felt dangerous, Monica wanted to walk on that fine edge. With Cal.

Her breasts felt full and achy. Her nipples strained against the red satin. "What would you do next?"

Cal knelt down before her. He slid his hands around to her bottom, where he kneaded her cheeks through the lightweight wool skirt. Gazing up at her, he leaned forward and nipped her naked waist.

He didn't play nice, and she loved that. Monica sucked in a breath. "Watch it. I bite back." Her jacket and shirt still dangled from her wrists, constraining her, keeping her from touching Cal—and she really needed to feel him right now. With jerking movements, she pulled at the cuff until she managed to shrug out of the restrictive clothes, dropping them to the floor. Using both hands to capture his head, Monica ran her fingers over his fine, short hair, sifting through the blonder strands.

Cal glanced up. "I look forward to it."

She was so turned on, she could barely catch her breath. "What would you do next? If I let you fuck me here."

"Well, next, I'd reach under your skirt." He let go of her ass to gather the material in his fists, yanking it up, exposing her legs. He stopped and grinned when he saw her thigh highs. "Stockings. Miss Prim, you are full of surprises."

"You don't know me as well as you think you do."

Cal lifted her skirt up past her panties. Satiny red panties. "Perhaps. And I'm amending the naked part. I'd let you leave on the stockings, because they're sexy as hell." Compliments from Cal, delivered in that husky voice, turned her into mush every time.

His fingers circled the border of the silky thigh highs. His hands were close, so close to her swollen clit. Just another two or three inches, and he'd be right there. "Touch me, Cal. Please?"

He grinned. "I will. Eventually." When Cal's tongue darted across her bare leg, near the top of her stockings, it put his face right in front of the triangle covering her pussy.

"Okay," Monica said, "I surrender. The floor works. Yay for office sex." Her knees trembled, and she started to lower herself to the carpet. But Cal held her up.

"No." That one word locked her knees into place.

"What? I'm on board here. Clear off the credenza or something, and let's go." A few minutes ago, it had seemed out of the question. Now she was desperate for him, her body needy and ready for release.

"Who has sex on a credenza?" he asked.

He ran his hands along her outer thighs and wiggled his thumbs past the elastic and underneath her panties. Then he slid his middle finger against her slit. Oh yes. Restless, achy, Monica bit back a moan. Back and forth, his touch so light, so whisper soft, she had to fist his hair, using it as an anchor to keep her upright. Monica's hips jutted forward.

"Take your skirt off." Cal's thumb circled her clit. It was swollen, pulsating, begging for his touch.

Without hesitation, Monica reached around and unzipped the back of her skirt. "That feels amazing.

Don't stop." But he did. And very gently, Cal removed his hand from her pussy. When Monica groaned at the loss, he let out a small laugh and helped her wiggle out of her skirt until it landed in a heap at her feet. She also toed off the ugly black flats, until she wore nothing but her underwear.

"Now the bra," he said.

She wasn't going to hurry this part. He'd been teasing her, now it was his turn. Bowing backward, Monica thrust out her breasts. She grinned when every bit of his attention honed in on her tits. His lips parted slightly, and his green eyes darkened.

"This bra?" she asked. Gliding a finger along the lace-edged cup, she inclined her head to one side. "I don't know. I'm beginning to wonder if this is a good idea after all. You haven't told me where we'll do it."

Suddenly, Cal's hands clamped on her hips. "I've been remiss, darling. I'll spell it out in detail. After you're naked."

Although heat flooded her pussy, she pretended to think about it. "No, I need the details first."

Cal's jaw slid to one side, and his eyes narrowed as he gazed up at her. "All right then, I'm going to spin you around to face that window. You're going to press your hands against the glass, and I'm going to take you from behind."

Monica's eyes fluttered over his face. Cal was serious. She swallowed as she turned to look at the large, unadorned glass. Her office faced an empty parking lot and a darkened medical building.

She swung her head back to face him. "If we get any closer to the window, someone could actually see us.

For real." They'd be open to scrutiny. There may not be anyone in the other building, but she didn't know that for sure. And if someone were up high enough, they would probably be able to see her right now, standing here in her underwear. Oh God, that shouldn't make her heart thump in excitement. It shouldn't make her pussy clench just imagining Cal standing behind her, pounding into her, leaving her exposed, vulnerable. But it did.

"All the windows in the building across the way are dark," he said. "The chance that anyone will spot us is remote."

"But possible. No, it's too risky." She didn't sound convincing, even to her own ears.

"You're shaking, and your knickers are soaking wet. It excites you, doesn't it, that risk?"

She didn't bother lying. "Yeah." Monica wanted to go there. Dangerous sex with Cal—she could become addicted to this. Or she could get caught, and her life would be ruined. It almost seemed worth it, acting out this exhibitionist fantasy.

Cal said nothing, letting her make the call.

But it wasn't much of a risk, not really. She hardly ever saw lights on after dark, and she worked late every night. "We could turn off the main light." That was reasonable. A compromise—semipublic sex, but dark enough to provide some protection.

"No, I want to watch your reflection when you come. And, Monica"—he snagged her panties and pulled them down to her knees—"you will come. Hard." He looked into her eyes as he continued removing the scrap of material from between her legs.

Her cunt throbbed in response. "Is that a guarantee?"

She bent over and held on to his shoulder while she stepped out of her panties. He tossed them aside, and now she stood before him, her pussy bare, clad in nothing but sheer thigh highs and a screaming-red bra. Monica had never been this aroused. Calum Hughes knelt at her feet, his gaze so scorching, she felt the heat of it on her skin.

"It is." Cal palmed her ass, his grin lilting a little higher. "Now take off the bra."

"No. Not until you're naked too." He wasn't the only one who wanted a show.

Cal released her, and while still on his knees, unbuttoned his shirt. As he pulled it off his shoulders and down his tight, muscular arms, she got a glimpse of his tattoo. Celtic knots wove their way around each other, connecting to form a larger pattern.

Monica traced her finger along the ink work at the top of his shoulder, following the intricate loops as if they were a maze. She *loved* that tattoo. "Where did you get this?"

"Ireland."

"Does it mean something?"

"Probably." Cal rested his hands on her waist. "You're wearing a bra and no knickers. Doesn't that seem odd to you?"

When he kissed her stomach, Monica threaded her fingers through his hair once more. "You're still wearing pants. They need to come off."

Cal gracefully rose to his feet. He kicked off his shoes and discarded his socks before shucking out of the dark slacks. "Anything else I can do for you?"

Monica stared at his boxers. Navy blue. His hard

cock strained the material. "I'm sure there is, if you put your mind to it." She stepped toward him, close enough so her breasts brushed against his smooth chest. Tucking her finger inside the elastic waistband, she gazed up at him. "Time to lose these."

"I think the bra should go first." Cal played with the strap, adjusted it to one side, then, bowing his head, ran his tongue across her neck. Wrapping his hands around her upper torso, he deftly unsnapped her bra and slid it from her shoulders. Slowly.

As the cups fell away from her breasts, Monica watched him, watched every expression that drifted across his face. He appeared almost reverent as he peeled it down her arms, exposing her fully.

"You're beautiful everywhere, Monica Campbell."

He made her feel beautiful. The way he looked at her, the way he cupped her breasts and stared at them, like they were the most amazing things he'd ever seen. When he scraped his thumbs across her nipples, Monica ran her short nails along his forearms.

"You like it harder than that, don't you, love?"

There was something so hot about being with a man who knew exactly what she needed and was willing to give it to her. Biting her lip, she didn't speak, merely nodded. So Cal obliged. He squeezed the underside of her nipples. Gently at first, then gradually Cal kneaded them harder in his big hands. Monica loved this rough play. It heightened her arousal, left her craving more.

Pulling and twisting the engorged points, Cal eased off, then started all over again. He worked her up until she was so wet, so needy, she could hardly think.

Monica's eyes drifted shut as she tilted her chin upward. That felt delicious, his hands on her, but still, she wanted more. "Your turn. Shorts off."

"Not yet. I'm not done with you." He released her nipples and bent toward her, taking one between his teeth, biting just hard enough to make Monica cry out. Then he lapped at it before latching his mouth over her breast and sucking.

Monica's hands ran mindlessly over Cal's upper back. Her pussy was so ready for him. *Need*. Her entire body hummed with it. "Cal." He continued to suck, and she felt the pull of it all the way to her clit. "*Calum*."

Finally, he raised his head. His cheeks were ruddy, his lips parted. Monica planted her hands on either side of his face and pulled him down for a kiss. Cal's tongue brushed against hers. She sucked it, nibbled at it. Cal responded by biting her upper lip, groaning deep in his chest. She liked that she had this effect on him, glad she wasn't the only one feeling this powerful lust that had taken over all reason.

Finally, Cal pulled away. Panting, he jerked his boxer shorts off, releasing his thick, long dick. Monica stared at it. She wanted to touch, lick, stroke every single inch of him. She wanted her hands on that warm, smooth skin. Wanted to wrap herself around him and breathe him in.

Grasping his cock with one hand, Monica rubbed the soft skin along his hard shaft, following a thick vein up to the tip. A drop of precum beaded at the surface. Brushing it with her finger, Monica spread it over the head. She removed her hand, and glancing up at him, worked that same fingertip in her mouth, twirling it along her tongue, her eyes wide.

"Monica." She loved the way he bit out her name, his impatient, guttural voice striking a chord deep inside her.

Placing her hand on the base of his cock, she knelt before him. Lowering her head, she swirled her tongue across the broad tip.

Cal scrunched his eyes closed. A tic in his jaw betrayed a shaky grasp on his self-control. He was close, and she'd barely touched him. Still, she couldn't help but tease him a little more.

"Do you like that?" Rhetorical question. She smiled as she lapped upward, along the length of him. Then, taking him in her mouth, she sucked gently. Cal's cock twitched against her lips.

"Darling, I have plans," he said. "Plans that involve taking you from behind, watching you in the window as your tits sway back and forth."

The tip of Monica's tongue darted over his slit, granting her another taste of salty liquid. She still hadn't relinquished her grip at the base. She liked feeling this way, playful and powerful, while Cal stood almost helpless, a slave to her mouth, her hands. She could take him now, like this. But she wanted him inside of her, wanted to feel this magnificent cock ramming in and out of her, to feel him from behind. And as he watched her in the window's reflection, she'd be watching him. She wanted to be naughty with him, possibly revealing herself as he took her in full view of anyone who could be walking by.

She let go of him and rose to her feet. "You should make plans more often."

"I've been thinking about fucking you all bloody

day." He leaned down and nipped her chin. "I love that little cleft." Then he snatched her around the waist and lifted her up, until her face was level with his. "Kiss me."

Wrapping her arms and legs around him, Monica complied. With Cal's cock wedged between them, she planted her lips on his, stroking her tongue into his mouth. She'd had boyfriends in the past who didn't like to kiss after she'd gone down on them. Cal wasn't like that. He was earthy, sensual.

She broke away. "Condom?"

"Right." He stared hard at her lips.

Monica swept her hands across his shoulder blades. His skin—tanned and smooth over powerful, striated muscles—warmed her palms. Monica angled her head and licked that tattoo, curling her tongue along his taut bicep. She smiled up at him. "I've been wanting to do that since I first saw you working on the Mustang."

"You should have done. It's quite an icebreaker. The condom's in my trousers. That means I'm going to have to put you down."

"But you'll get to fuck me. Seems like a good tradeoff."

"A very good tradeoff. You'll have to unwrap your legs from around my waist, though."

Monica stroked his cheek. "In a second. One more kiss."

"One more," he agreed.

There was nothing gentle about it, and Monica needed that. Needed the way he devoured her, his tongue thrusting against hers, his lips almost brutal in their intensity. He sucked her bottom lip as he lifted his head. Finally, he let it go. "All right now, legs down."

Monica unwrapped her calves from his lean hips, and Cal dropped her to the ground. He snagged his pants, quickly dug in the pocket, and removed a condom and rolled it on. Then taking her shoulders, he spun her around, just as he'd promised, and marched her forward.

Monica searched the building across the way. No lights, no sign of movement. This was insane. *Insanely hot*. She glanced at herself, barely recognizing the naked, sexy woman with messy hair and puffy lips.

"Bend over, Miss Prim. Hands on the glass," Cal ordered. Monica obeyed, and with her feet in a wide stance, she bent over, but kept her head tilted up so she could see him. This was the craziest thing she'd done in years, and it scared her. But titillated too. Cal did this to her—freed that part of her she never thought she'd see again.

In the glass, Cal's reflection looked like a naked, hot specter. Meeting her gaze, he ran his palm down her spine—then he gave her ass a not so light tap.

Monica shrieked at the unexpected swat. She liked it. The afterburn caused the walls of her pussy to tighten. "After this, you won't be able to call me Miss Prim."

Without warning, Cal thrust once, burying himself deep inside her. Grasping her hips with both hands, he yanked her backward. "Oh, you'll have to do more than this to lose the nickname."

Monica had no idea what he had in mind, but she was down for it. The tendons in his neck strained as he began to move, slowly.

"You feel so good." He bit out the words.

"Faster."

He shook his head. "No."

"Damn it, Cal. You took it slow last time."

His smile rose a notch. "And I'm going to take it slow this time too."

Keeping his steady pace, Cal pumped his cock inside of her, drew it out, then slid back home. The friction drove her crazy, and yet he never changed the momentum. She didn't know how he could stand it, but she'd get even. He was punishing her for some reason, and she'd return the favor. One of these times, Cal would be the one begging her for release. Monica was going to enjoy that.

Using one hand, he reached out to massage her breast. She longed to touch him back, but kept her hands plastered against the cool glass.

The pressure inside of her kept building as Cal glided back and forth. Her pussy became slicker with every minute that passed. She was so close. The added stimulation of watching him fuck her pushed her to the brink.

"Cal, please. Please. Harder. I need it. You promised."

"So I did." Dropping her breast, he used that hand to grab a fistful of her hair. Cal dug the fingers of his other hand into her hip.

When he started pumping deep and fast, Monica almost lost her balance. "Harder."

His grip dug into her skin. He hung onto her hair like a rein. This was exactly what she liked.

Cal's arms flexed as he slammed into her. When he thrust his hips forward, Monica's breasts swayed, just as he said they would, and he watched them with complete concentration.

Monica came then, crying out. She closed her eyes as powerful sensations coursed through her, curling up through her clit, causing every muscle in her body to clench. On and on it went, tunneling through her, making her dizzy as she held her breath.

Cal continued to fuck her until he came too. He let out a hoarse yell, and his body shuddered as he paused for a moment, thrust again, then jerked her hips back against him. "Monica."

His cock spasmed, and Monica's muscles tightened around it. A smaller, less intense orgasm rocked her. Monica's hand slipped down the glass, but Cal's firm hold kept her from falling. Aftershocks sizzled through her as he continued to drive into her.

Once his own orgasm subsided, Cal stilled. Loosening his grasp on her hip, he unclenched his fist, letting go of her hair. Stroking a hand down her shoulder, Cal continued to rub her back, his hand warm and soothing against her skin.

She didn't think he could top their last time in the Mustang, but he had. He'd pushed her, challenged her, and now he touched her with such tenderness, she melted a little bit.

They remained in place, both breathing hard for some minutes. Finally, Cal removed himself and stepped away. Monica's legs shook as she lowered herself to the floor and lay on her side, completely spent. Cal discarded the condom before stretching out next to her.

"You are brilliant." He brushed the back of his hand across her cheek.

She gave him a tired smile. "You're not so bad yourself."

"Not so bad? I delivered on my promise, love. I made you come. Hard. I could feel your cunt tighten around me." He gave her hair a gentle tug.

"I could have been faking, you know."

Before she could take her next breath, Monica found herself on her back with Cal lying on top of her. His eyes glimmered a bright green. "You were faking that rousing, bloody fantastic orgasm, were you?"

"No," she admitted. "I wasn't faking." Monica reached up and lightly slugged his shoulder. "You're a real champ in the sex department. Do you want a trophy or something?"

"Yes, I do. A trophy would do nicely."

Monica burst out laughing. "God, you're so arrogant."

He grinned back. "But a brilliant lover." He lowered his head and nuzzled her neck.

"Yes," she said, then sighed. "You're a brilliant lover."

Cal lifted his head. "That's all I'm saying." The smile died from his lips as his eyes shifted to the building next door. "Shit."

"Oh no." Monica tried to turn her head to look, but with Cal on top of her, it was impossible. "Can someone see us?"

"No, we're too low. But the cleaners are arriving next door. They just walked into the building."

"Shit," Monica echoed.

"Stay here, they can't see up this far. I'll grab our clothes and hit the lights, and we'll run into the hall."

The danger of getting caught, of someone seeing her naked, sent a frisson of fear shooting through her system. It had been thrilling fifteen minutes ago, but now, once the heat of the moment had passed, Monica realized how stupid she'd been. What if Stella or Jason had come back to the office? What if one of the cleaning crew down there had whipped out a phone and taken a video? God, she was an idiot.

Cal crept low as he scrambled for their clothes. With his arms full, he ran to hit the overhead lights, then using the clothes as a shield, he walked quickly to her desk and shut off the lamp. Now they were in the dark. Monica closed her eyes for a moment and mentally kicked her own ass. Why was she so reckless? *Defective*.

Cal opened the hall door, letting a dim glow filter into the room. "Come on, love."

Monica rolled over and rose a few inches as she peeked out the window. A first-floor office showed light behind closed blinds. Although she didn't see any movement, she kept low and duck-walked across the floor and out into the hall. Cal pulled her office door closed behind her.

After burying her head in both hands, she muttered, "What was I thinking?"

"You were thinking how amazing the sex would be. How adventurous. And it was." She heard the clothes drop to the floor, and then his warm hands covered hers, prying them from her face a second later. "Monica, if I'd seen any sign of life, I'd have turned you around so fast, you'd have been dizzy for days. I wouldn't let anyone see you compromised. It was just a bit of harmless fun."

Harmless fun had gotten her into trouble in the past. Harmless fun had gotten her knocked up by a guy she'd barely known. Harmless fun was her downfall. And guys like Cal were the catalyst.

She bent down and started sorting through the clothes, tossing his into a pile near his feet. Standing, she turned her back to him and stepped into her panties, hastily tugging them up her legs. When she slipped into the bra, Cal secured the hooks for her.

"I'd have kept you safe," he whispered in her ear. "I'll always keep you safe. Do you understand?"

She didn't believe him. Cal was a cut above every other man she'd dated, but she didn't trust him. As soon as she'd start to rely on him, have feelings for him, he'd leave.

You're supposed to be in control this time, Campbell. Cal hadn't twisted her arm in there. Monica had been willing to take the risk. But instead of feeling empowered, she felt like she was speeding downhill without any brakes. Crashing was a foregone conclusion.

Chapter 15

Cal felt an overwhelming need to reassure her—and he meant every bloody word. He wouldn't let any harm come to Monica Campbell, not if it were in his power to prevent it.

Twirling her around by one shoulder, Cal placed a hand on her lower back and yanked her closer. A lock of her hair bounced against his chest, giving off just the barest hint of lavender. Before Cal could stop himself, he plunged his free hand through the intermixed shades of honey and golden-brown, gripping it tight at her scalp.

Staring down into her beautiful, troubled face, he looked her dead in the eye. "I wouldn't have let anyone see you. Do you believe me?" Monica's light blue eyes grew wide, and Cal forced himself to loosen the grasp on her hair. Why was he behaving this way, like a lunatic? "Do you believe me?" he demanded.

After a moment's hesitation, she lifted one shoulder. "It doesn't matter—I shouldn't have done it."

Of course she should have. She'd been in the moment—she'd smiled and teased him and enjoyed herself. And he was right there with her, every bloody step of the way. This was the Monica she was meant to be—a risk taker, a woman who enjoyed wild, uninhibited sex. But he couldn't convince her of that. Not right now. She had a bad habit of fucking him stupid, only to regret it moments later. Her postcoital remorse was hell on his ego.

Cal dropped his hands with a sigh. "Come on, love. Let's get you dressed." He plucked her shirt from the floor and held it open for her. Giving him one last worried glance, she shoved her arms into it, hastily rebuttoning and covering up that gorgeous red bra.

No doubt about it, Cal was a derrière man, but Monica's tits were stunners. Her rosy nipples—big and luscious as cherries—made his mouth water.

"Are you going to get dressed?" She nodded at him as she slipped into her shoes.

"I'm pondering. I look so good naked, I should bless the world and walk around like this all the time, don't you agree?"

She gave him an exasperated look and grabbed the skirt from his hand. "Seriously, you have an ego problem."

"I was just thinking the same thing."

Her words may be chastising, but he could hear the amusement in her voice, though she averted her face to hide any evidence of it. He liked that he could make her laugh. He'd definitely made her smile in that office a few minutes ago.

When she'd knelt down in front of him, right before she'd taken him in her mouth, Monica had given Cal the sauciest grin. Then she'd taken command of his prick, stroking and licking. Hell, he was getting hard all over again.

Telling his cock to behave itself, Cal pulled on his clothes and stuck his feet into the tasseled loafers. He'd asked Mr. Lawson to fetch him some shoes from one of the shops. Cal didn't care what they looked like; he simply wanted Monica to see him in something other than shoddy boots. Now he felt faintly ridiculous.

He glanced up. Monica had caught him staring. "Tassels are for wankers, aren't they?" he asked.

"No. You look very nice." She lowered her eyes, almost as if she were embarrassed to give him a compliment. Then Monica opened her office door and scurried to her desk, where she gathered together all of her work gadgets.

"Hungry?" he asked, propping his shoulder against the door frame.

"Cal, I'm just going to call it a night and go home." She was running scared—afraid of him. Afraid of herself.

"I understand. Sex with me can be exhausting. You're most likely done in, poor pet."

She threw him a warning glance. "I need to work."

"Of course, and it has nothing to do with that fact that you let down your proverbial hair? You've had your fun, and now it's time for self-flagellation."

She kept her eyes down as she shoved folders into her bag. "I have board meeting drama, and the gala's six weeks away."

"So naturally, you won't eat until then."

Heaving a sigh, she finally looked at him. "Do you ever shut up?"

"Occasionally. But only when I'm sleeping or eating pussy." He smiled at her gasp, whipped out his phone, and put a call in to Mr. Lawson. "We'll be arriving in half an hour. Have dinner waiting on the terrace, will you?" When he hung up, Monica looked at him with raised brows. As she hefted the bag onto her shoulder, Cal walked forward and took it from her.

"I told you I made plans. Dinner will be waiting for us. You'll love it."

She left her office and walked next to him through the short hallway. "You really think you've got me figured out, don't you?" At the suite door, she flipped off the lights, leaving them momentarily in the dark.

"Not completely, but I'm learning as I go. By the way, just to give you fair warning, I plan on fucking you again tonight. But I'll taste you first." Then he opened the outer office door and allowed Monica to pass through.

"Just to give *you* fair warning, I'm going home after dinner," she said, locking up with a snap of her wrist.

Cal said nothing as he trailed her to the lift. He didn't look at her either, but kept his eyes trained on the arrows above the doors.

"And what's a taste, anyway?" she asked. "A taste sounds very brief."

"Would you like me to explain in further detail?"

"No."

He waited.

"Maybe."

The doors opened, and they climbed on. Monica pressed the *L* button and clutched her purse in front of her. Cal's eyes kept straying to her, taking in her mussed hair, her swollen lips.

"Yes," she said. "Explain."

"In this scenario, we'll both be naked, of course."

"You seem to prefer it, being God's gift and all."

"Quite. I'll use my hand first, to make sure you're wet. Once you're ready, I'll slide one finger inside you. I'll work up to three, but it's a process. Then I'll lick your outer pussy lips. You'll be begging me by then, but I won't let you come, not yet. Not until I've parted you and licked you like a ripe peach. Eventually, I'll nibble your adorable little love button until you go wild. That's my idea of tasting. You probably thought I meant sampling."

Monica's cheeks were pink now, her eyes bright. Her chest rose and fell at a rapid rate. "Love button?" she said, sounding out of breath.

"Would you prefer joy buzzer?" He grinned as she rolled her eyes. He nearly groaned when she licked her upper lip. Though she would probably deny it, she enjoyed their banter as much as he did.

The bell dinged, and the doors slid open. They walked in silence to the parking lot. "I'll follow you in my car," she said.

"Oh, what a shame. I was going to let you drive the Mustang again."

She hesitated. "Give me the keys."

Cal pulled them from his pocket and dropped them into her hand. He still wasn't comfortable letting someone else take the wheel, but tempting Monica was worth it.

She climbed in the car and started the engine. "Just out of curiosity"—she gazed at him from the corner of her eye—"what's your idea of sampling?"

As Monica parked in front of Cal's place, a valet appeared out of nowhere. The service here was impressive. She'd always wanted a peek inside one of the villas, and she'd probably never have another chance.

Cal placed his hand on her lower back, guiding her up the walk. "I worked up an appetite, how about you?"

"Dinner," Monica said. "That's all I'm agreeing to." *For now*. She just wanted to state it for the record, but her delivery was weak. Even Monica wasn't buying her flimsy denials. She and Cal would be having sex again before the night was over. After hearing his ideas on tasting versus sampling, she couldn't think about anything else.

"If you say so." His agreeable tone said he wasn't taking her seriously either. She hadn't really given him a reason to. Every time they were together, she meant to say no, but her legs fell open instead.

Cal unlocked the door and nudged her inside. Monica walked past the threshold and stood in the foyer, taking in the detailed pattern on the tiled floor, the marbled walls, the modern crystal chandelier that looked like dandelion seeds. "This is gorgeous."

"It's not on par with Trevor's place, but it'll do in a pinch, eh?" He grinned down at her.

"If one doesn't mind slumming," she joked. Monica fought against reaching up and touching the left corner of his mouth. That crooked smile got her.

Cal relieved her of her purse and bag, setting them next to the front door. Then he took her hand. "Come on. Food's outside." He sped through the living room, tugging her behind him.

"Wait." Monica dragged her feet. Her quick glance around the living room gave her an overall impression of warm walls and sumptuous furniture—a mixture of old-world dark wood and modern design. "I want to see it all."

"Later. I'll show you everything, I promise." He pulled her to the French doors.

"Do you always keep your promises, Calum Hughes?"

He stopped then and looked over his shoulder. She'd only been joking, but his eyes were somber. "Yes. Always. Don't you?"

Monica hadn't kept the promise she'd made to herself, the one about steering clear of good-time guys with sex on the brain. And she hadn't kept the promise to her mom, either. Monica didn't plan on following her heart anytime soon. "No, I don't always keep my promises."

Cal studied her for a long moment. When he smiled, the left side of his mouth stayed on an even keel with the right. "What a pity. Now, come along."

Cal led her outside and onto the terrace. This wasn't Trevor's winding English garden, but it was beautiful. Hanging flowers and topiary bushes dotted the perimeter of the pool, where tendrils of steam rose into the night sky. Lit from within, the bright blue water cast shimmers that danced along the tan French pavers at her feet. Outdoor heaters flanked either side of the candlelit table set for two, and a buffet cart stood to one side.

Still holding Cal's hand, Monica looked around. "This is amazing."

"Reminds me of another garden. Another night," Cal said.

She turned to him. "What if Allie hadn't interrupted us that night? Would you have been so eager to see me again, or would you have avoided me like the flu?"

"After what we did an hour ago, how can you ask me that question?" With his back to the low light, Monica found it impossible to read his expression.

Five years ago, Cal had been a dangerous bad boy

looking for an easy lay. "I think if we'd fucked that night, you wouldn't remember my name."

He squeezed her hand. "I'm not the same man I was five years ago, but I'd have remembered you, Monica Campbell. You're unforgettable." With his free hand, he stroked her cheek and bent his head. His lips stopped inches from hers, but he paused. "Would you have forgotten me?"

"Yes."

"Liar," he said on a breath. He rained tiny kisses over her lips, her chin.

"How have you changed?" she whispered.

Cal straightened. "I'm older, wiser. More devastatingly handsome than ever before."

Monica sensed a depth to him that he hadn't possessed five years ago. Maybe it had happened over the last year with Babcock's death. Losing a loved one could do that to a person. When her mother died, it had changed Monica. The grief and loss made her more careless than ever.

Monica shook off the guilt and sadness that crept in every time she thought about her mom. Allie's accusation yesterday had hit the mark. She didn't like talking about her mom, or thinking about the times they'd shared. It was just too damn painful. Monica decided to embrace this night with Cal. Her past, the present—it would all be waiting for her tomorrow.

He let go of her hand and pointed with his chin to the food cart. "Go see what treats I've got for you."

She opened one chafing dish, then laughed. "Fried chicken?"

"You Americans seem to love it. After all, you've put that military colonel in charge of it."

"Funny." She moved on to the next dish. "Mashed potatoes." The next were filled with cornbread and green beans and some kind of casserole. "Cal, do you have Vegas confused with the Deep South?"

He laughed. "No, but I told the chef to make something all Americans love to eat." He paused. "We can send it back. We can order takeaway if you like, or go to a restaurant at the casino."

He pulled his phone from his front pocket, but Monica grabbed his sleeve. "This is wonderful. I was only kidding."

He seemed unsure of himself for a split second, then the old taunting grin returned. "We could hop a jet and go anywhere you want. You know how we trust-fund knobs are, any whim fulfilled."

"Cal." The atmosphere had changed. This had been a sweet gesture on his part, and Monica wasn't sure what she'd said or done, but the self-deprecating humor had a hint of bitterness to it. Cal always poked fun at himself, in his own way. His arrogant statements weren't meant to be taken seriously. But this jab, this one was real. She wasn't sure how to fix it, so she glossed over it. "Please tell me there's chocolate?"

Cal's shoulders relaxed slightly. The tension that filled the air a moment ago disappeared. "Of course there is. Do I look like a fool? Wait, don't answer that." He moved behind her, slid his arms around her waist, and rested his chin on her shoulder. "Really, if you want something else—"

"This is like a fantasy. A picnic in the moonlight." She turned and gave him a small reassuring kiss. Cal let her go and stepped back.

Monica handed him a plate and filled hers with some of everything, along with a chicken leg. "When we were little, Brynn and I used to fight over the chicken legs. I always wanted both, but my mother made us share."

"What was she like, your mother?"

"Motherly."

As Monica sat down, Cal took a seat across from her. Shaking out his napkin, he raised one brow. "We can talk about something else. There's always the weather. Or sports. How do you like Chelsea's chances this year?"

"Is that a soccer team or something?" Monica picked up her fork and took a bite of creamy mashed potatoes. *Mmm, buttery*. "This is delicious."

Cal tutted. "Football, not soccer. You Americans. Do you still miss her?"

Although the day had been warm again, the evening air started to cool down. Even with the portable heaters, Monica shivered. "Every day. But I don't want to talk about my mom any more than you want to talk about Babcock. It hurts."

His gaze locked on hers. "Agreed." He poured them each a glass of wine.

"What's the best French wine you've ever tasted?" she asked.

"To be honest, I have a hard time telling a good cabernet from a bottle of plonk. I'm more of a lager man. I'd rather go to Stuttgart for Oktoberfest than French wine country, although it's beautiful there." Cal sat back, his eyes skimming over her.

Monica felt self-conscious when Cal watched her eat the chicken leg as daintily as she could manage.

Covering her mouth with a napkin, she laughed. "Stop staring at me. You're making me nervous."

"It's fun, making you blush. You're comfortable being totally naked in front of me, but if I watch you eat, you get embarrassed."

Monica froze for a moment as the truth hit her. She not only didn't mind being naked in front of Cal, she loved it. Loved the way his eyes grew a deeper green and remained glued to her body, taking in her slightest movement. She felt sexy and alive. She wanted to feel that way again, right now.

She'd been chastising herself since they'd scuttled out of the office, and while it had been a stupid move—fucking in front of a picture window—it had felt incredible at the same time. The fear of getting caught and the feel of Cal buried deep inside her—it had been the best sex of her life. Carefree. Daring. She thought she'd put all that behind her, but Cal opened the door to her bad-girl ways. And she liked how he made her feel. So how was Monica supposed to mesh her old self with her life now?

God, she was tired of going around in circles, overthinking. She simply wanted to shut down her brain and *feel* again. Cal did that to her. And as scary as it was, Monica wanted it one more time. Just for tonight.

She threw her napkin on the table and glanced back at the French doors. "Is your butler coming back?" She wanted Cal to take her again, here in this setting, this garden.

"Not unless I tell him to, why?"

"Then I'm going for a swim." Monica kicked off her shoes, then with exaggerated movements, she stripped out of her jacket.

That got Cal's attention. He licked his lips as she held up one arm and unbuttoned her cuff. She repeated the movement with her other sleeve. When she reached up to unfasten her blouse, she paused. "Should I keep going?"

"If you don't, I'll do it for you," Cal said.

Monica wagged her finger. "Uh, uh, uh. This is my show." She turned her back to him, and with painstaking progress, undid one button at a time. Occasionally, she glanced over her shoulder and shot him a grin. When she was done, she clasped the edge of her blouse and eased it, ever so slightly, down her shoulder.

Cal's eyes were fixed on her. He held his body motionless. "Don't stop now."

This was what she wanted. To captivate him. To be powerful and sexual and let herself go. She could do this with Cal.

She slipped the other side down the opposite shoulder, but not very far. Monica only revealed her upper back, then turning to the side, she shoved a hand through her hair and watched Cal's Adam's apple bob as he swallowed.

With a wiggle of her hips, she slipped the blouse from her shoulders and let it fall on the patio. Then raising her arms above her head, she undulated her torso. Monica stopped when his eyes met hers. She hadn't done this in so long. Monica felt more at ease with Cal than any man she'd ever been with.

Next, she unzipped her frumpy skirt. Nothing about her clothes was sexy, but the way Cal watched her, she felt like the hottest woman alive. "Want to see more?"

Scrubbing both hands over his face, Cal groaned. "You're tormenting me on purpose, aren't you?"

"Does that sound like something I'd do?" With exaggerated movements, she slid the skirt over her hips before kicking it aside. Thrusting her shoulders back, she reached behind her and released the hooks of her bra. First she let the straps fall but kept the narrow cups in place with her hands.

Cal leaned forward, his gaze glued to her breasts. His breathing picked up speed. "I'm right on the edge, darling. Do you want me to beg?"

Monica affected a pout as she slipped off the bra. With one finger, she circled the areola of her right breast until her nipples grew hard. "Maybe later." She fingered the front of her panties. "See how wet I am? All for you, Calum."

He scraped his chair back and stood then, tearing at his shirt in his haste to remove it. "Do you have any idea what you're doing to me?" He strode forward and stretched out his hand to palm her breast, but Monica moved out of reach.

Biting her lower lip, she shook her head. Her hair whipped around her jaw. "You keep torturing me, I say turnabout is fair play. *Mate*."

"Ah, but you want my touch." Cal shed the rest of his clothes and stood there, staring at her, his cock hard, ready. Wrapping his hand around it, he gave it a long stroke. Monica watched, captivated at the sight of Cal moving a hand up and down the length of it.

Monica slipped her thumbs in the waistband of her panties and wriggled them over her hips, revealing her mons, a little bit at a time, until she wore nothing but the black thigh highs.

Cal's gaze drank her in. "You are the most beautiful creature I've ever seen."

She grinned. "Better than an Austin Healey?"

He nodded, his expression serious. "Yes."

High praise indeed. She wasn't sure if she believed him, but it was a lovely compliment. Slowly, she peeled off one stocking, and straightened before extending her arm and dropping it on the patio.

"You're almost there. Keep going." Cal gave himself one more stroke.

By drawing this out, Monica was punishing herself. She wanted his hands on her skin, his mouth on her clit. He'd promised to taste her, after all. Her backside grew cold as she shed the second stocking.

Keeping him in her line of sight, Monica sauntered to the pool, swaying her hips with each step. As she glided down into the water, it sloshed against her ankles, calves, thighs. Cal remained on the terrace, staring after her. "Are you coming in?"

"Most assuredly."

The water rippled against her stomach. "Feels good. Nice and warm." When the water reached her chest, Monica turned and bent her knees, sinking lower as she watched Cal wade in. His delicious muscles contracted as he moved toward her.

"I know what will feel even better." He walked closer, and she moved farther away, toward the wall. The pool wasn't large, and she could stand at the deepest end and still keep her chin above the water.

Cal approached her, bracing his hands against the pool edge, and pressed his body against hers. Whipping aside her hair, he nipped the outer shell of her ear. "I like it when you're spontaneous."

Monica laced her fingers behind his neck. "I didn't mess up your plans, did I?"

"No," Cal growled against her ear. "Getting you naked was on the short list. I was planning on a shower too, but I'm nothing if not accommodating." Gazing into her eyes, Cal cupped her face with one hand, then kissed her.

This kiss felt different from the others. Over the past few days, Cal had kissed her in passion, and he'd used light, butterfly pecks, but this one...this one felt purposeful. Almost serious. As the thought popped into her mind, Monica wasn't even sure what that meant. She pushed the notion aside. *Feel, don't think.*

She liked Cal's hard body slick against hers, liked the way he made her hot and achy, made her breasts crave his touch. When she was with him, Monica felt wide-awake, as though she'd been sleepwalking through life these last four years.

Chapter 16

Cal gazed down at her flushed face. Monica's fuller upper lip garnered most of his attention. Her tits, bobbing just below the surface of the water, were a very close second. Plunging his hand into the hair at her nape, he tilted her head back and sucked on that bloody upper lip. It drove him crazy every time she so much as licked it.

When Monica's hand circled his cock and squeezed, every logical thought he had disappeared.

Cal continued to suck and bite her lip, but let go of her hair and handled those full, round tits. She liked it when he got a little cheeky with them, but Cal tried not to handle her too roughly. He didn't want to cross the line from stimulating to painful, but he'd seen the faint bruises from the other day. He'd have to be more careful in the future.

As he torqued her nipples, twisting them, pulling them out, pinching them just hard enough, Monica used both hands to stroke his cock. The water provided added sensation. Her hands were slippery as they slid up and down his shaft. Bloody fucking fantastic, it was.

His hands gripped her breasts one last time before he nabbed her wrists. "No more. I want to taste you." Holding her by the waist, Cal lifted her out of the water and set her on the rim of the pool. Between the half-moon and the soft lights shining around the garden, Monica's pale skin glowed. Her nipples hardened in the cool air. She was so slim, her waist curving inward and giving way to fuller hips, rounding down to that splendid ass.

Cal gazed up at her. She was breathing hard, waiting to see what he'd do next. He appreciated her anticipation.

"Spread your legs, darling."

Leaning back on her hands, Monica propped her heels on the concrete and spread her knees wider. Cal now had a very nice view of her pussy. Only a small triangle of hair remained on her mound, and the rest was bare. He ran a finger over the outer lips, and Monica shivered.

"Even your cunt's lovely."

Her body was ripe and inviting, every pale centimeter of it.

She watched as Cal spread her lips apart and fluttered his middle finger over her wet slit. Pressing down on the top of her mound, he worked his finger inside her.

"You said three."

"I said it was a process." Cal slid a second finger into her tight sheath, curled both of them upward, scissoring them back and forth. Monica was getting there, her arousal evident by the moisture coating his fingers as he continued to stretch her.

"That's…that's pretty good. Just like that." Leaning her head back, Monica bit her lower lip.

"Pretty good is for amateurs."

She lowered her chin to grin at him. "So you're a professional finger-banger?"

Cal smiled back and slithered the third finger inside of her. That wiped the grin off those pouty lips. They formed an *O* as he glided in and out. She was more than ready to come, but Cal would use his mouth this time. After all, he'd given his word.

When he slowly removed his fingers from her body, Monica's eyes popped open. "Don't stop."

"I have plans, remember?" Cal lowered his head to swipe his tongue along the edge of one outer lip. Her legs twitched, and a breathy moan escaped her while he sucked on it, gently, carefully. After a few seconds, he stopped to gaze at her. "Do you like that?"

Monica nodded.

"Want more?"

"Yes, please." A hint of a smile played on her lips.

"Oh, I do like good manners when I'm tongue-fucking. Nicely done, you." Unlatching his arms from her legs, he parted her and started lapping her inner folds, savoring her sweet, rich taste.

He used a steady rhythm, laving his tongue up the length of her, then swirling it around her swollen clit. As he licked her, occasionally his eyes drifted up to gauge her reaction. Monica's face had softened in pleasure, her light blue eyes becoming stormy.

When Cal's tongue slid inside her, Monica's hips bucked off the ground. She threw her head back, and he studied the long line of her neck—down to that tiny mole in the center of her chest. He continued to dart his tongue in and out of her, taking his time. Cal wasn't in a hurry, didn't intend on stopping until she came so hard she couldn't walk properly.

Monica drew gasping breaths and exhaled soft groans. When he used his thumb to rim her tight little puckered hole, her body stiffened, and she started to yelp, but stopped herself. Monica clutched a handful of his hair as she came, her pussy convulsing around Cal's tongue. She shoved her hips toward him, pulled his head closer. From the corner of his eyes, he watched her toes curl. Good. She was enjoying herself, then. He took a great deal of pride in making her lose control.

Cal didn't stop until she went completely limp and her grasp on his hair loosened. He pulled his tongue from inside her and gave her one last swipe. Grazing both hands over her calves, he kissed the curve of her ass where it met her thighs, then bit down.

"You're killing me." She closed her eyes, her chest heaving as she panted. Monica remained quiet for so long, he nipped her ass again.

"Are you all right, love?"

"I give up, okay? I admit it, you're bloody brilliant."

Cal wanted to shout in victory, but he settled for a grin. "This is what I've been trying to tell you."

She laughed and sat up, stretching out her hands to rest on his shoulders. "Did you say something about a shower?"

Cal hauled himself out of the water. "It's enormous. Could double as a car wash. You should really fuck me there."

"I really will—just make sure you have a condom."

He bent and placed an arm beneath her knees, then scooped her up. She seemed very preoccupied with protection. "I'm safe as houses, you know—been tested and all that. You aren't on the pill or something?"

Monica slung her arm behind his neck. "I just like to take precautions. And I can walk."

"I'm aware. This is more fun." He wouldn't question

her about the safety issue. She wanted him in a condom; he'd wear one. Hell, he'd wear two. Anything to get inside her once more.

Cal strode into the house, leaving wet footprints along the plush carpet and the marble floor in the hallway. As he walked, Monica fingered the side of his neck. Once or twice, she bit down on his shoulder. He liked it a little rough as well. "You keep that up, we won't make it to the shower. I like it when you bite me."

She licked his earlobe. "Like this?" she whispered, then pulled the skin between her teeth.

"Just like that, Miss Prim."

"When are you going to quit calling me that?"

He stopped in the bedroom doorway. "Does it really bother you?"

"I just wondered what kind of debauchery it takes to shake that nickname."

"When we've reached it, I'll let you know." He walked over to the bedside table, where he lowered her slightly. "Grab the condoms, would you?"

Monica opened the drawer and snared a string of them. "Is this enough?"

"It'll do for starters."

As she clung to his neck, Monica's gaze roamed over the suite. "This room is humongous. How's the bed? Hard or squishy soft?"

"You can try it for yourself. I plan on fucking you there too."

"You and your plans."

He carried her to the bathroom and maneuvered sideways to allow them both through the door. When he set her on her feet, Monica spun in a circle.

"This is bigger than my bedroom." She ran her finger along the smooth lip of the glass sink.

Why was she so thrown by the opulence? Trevor's house was expansive, each feature singular, and filled to the rafters with antique bric-a-brac. Using the loo was on par with a visit to the British Museum.

"Is this how you live in London?" She glanced up at him, caught him staring at her breasts.

"No. I have a small flat above the garage. One bedroom, no telly."

Monica walked into the shower and glanced at the buttons. "Do I need an engineering degree to turn this on?"

Cal stood behind her, pressing his prick against the small of her back. After tossing the pack of condoms on the stone bench at the end of the travertine shower, he programmed the temperature and turned it on. Eight jets of pulsating water flowed over them from all directions. "It takes a little practice. You'll have it in no time."

"You're not going to be here long enough for me to figure it out. So which do you like better, the one-room flat or this place?"

Before he could respond, she turned in his arms, ran her hands down his chest. When she reached for his cock, he forgot the thread of their conversation. In fact, he forgot to think at all.

As he walked her backward, Monica still played with him. With both hands, he pushed the wet hair off her face.

"Feel good?" she asked, gripping him firmly.

"Very good."

He backed her up to a wall, and with a vice-like grip on her hair, kissed her hard, the way they both liked. His tongue wasn't gentle now, but demanding as it tangled with hers. And she responded. Monica always responded, reciprocating in kind. Not just a willing partner, she was an active one as well. He admired her boldness.

Monica turned her head to the side and let go of his cock. Cal kissed a trail from her ear to her neck, licking at her skin and sucking gently. Monica grabbed a bottle of shower gel sitting within a niche in the wall. As he continued to lap water from her silky skin, she poured some into the palm of her hand, releasing a lemony sandalwood scent. Rubbing her hands in soapy circles over his chest, she used her short fingernails to flick his nipples.

Cal raised his head. "Again."

Monica's laugh was low and seductive as she complied. "You like that?"

"What do you think?" He angled his hips forward, pressing his cock against her lower belly.

"I think your dick just got a little harder." Her slick hands continued their journey over his pecs and down to his stomach. Her fingers caressed each abdominal muscle and darted into his belly button.

Cal leaned his forehead against the top of her hair. "It did, and it's feeling very left out right now."

"Ah, that's such a shame. But it's going to have to wait a bit longer, because I'm not done touching the rest of you." She worked her fingers over the V-shaped indentions above his hips, but instead of soaping up his prick, as he wanted, she moved up to his arms. "I've been wanting some one-on-one time with these muscles since I saw you working on the Mustang."

"Is that right? I couldn't tell. Those sunglasses you wear hide your expression."

"Yep. I was checking you out. Especially your ass. You looked good bending over the hood of the car."

Cal fought to breathe normally as her fingers trailed along his biceps. "My ass is one of my better parts."

"I think all your parts are equally delicious." She seemed fascinated with the tattoo. Most of the soap had been washed off, but she lightly ran her fingers over it. "So you got this in Ireland? It must mean something."

Cal closed his eyes, his heart thudding at her soft, languid touch. "The knots are eternal, never ending. Like nature, they keep going on without us. Or some such nonsense." Oh God, he should have kept his mouth closed. He came off like a prat trying to explain it. He wasn't anything more than a car fanatic sounding pretentious.

Monica peered up at him. "Nature, huh? Like those jungle ruins you talked about? That temple in Cambodia? Humans leave their mark, but nature keeps trying to take it back."

Cal's eyes flew open, and he scanned her face. She didn't appear to be mocking him. In fact, she gazed up at him with a serious expression. "Yes, exactly." The moment stretched on as they stared at each other.

Monica blinked first. "And ink raises your hotness factor, so there's that." She grinned and licked the curve of his bicep.

"Of course. One needs to keep one's hotness factor in mind at all times."

Monica poured more shower gel into her hands and finally—thank God—worked it over his cock, leisurely, with long, slick strokes. Straightening his arms, Cal placed his hands on the tiled wall and threw his head back, enjoying each pass of her hands.

She worked him until his self-control nearly snapped. "Monica." At the sound of his grating plea, she eased off, placing her hands on his hips before reaching around and caressing his ass.

That was better. Her hands on him, sliding over his skin, the warm water hitting him at every angle—it felt amazing, but he could hold on as long as she wasn't wanking him off. "I'm going to have to touch you soon. It's rather imperative."

She leaned forward and licked his nipple. As she gazed up at him, her wet lashes clinging together, her cheeks pink from the humidity, Monica shook her head. "But I'm not through."

He reached down and grabbed her wrists. "It's my turn. I insist." He let go of her long enough to snatch the bottle and pour a generous amount into his own palm. Then he began sliding his way over her breasts. His hands were slick against their fullness and skimmed over her nipples. She gasped, and he did it again. He let himself play with her. He hadn't spent nearly enough quality time with them. Not as much as he'd like, at any rate. They were firm and heavy in his hands.

Monica guided her fingers along his forearms. "That feels so good. Don't stop."

He bent down, and taking her nipple in his mouth, suckled until she cried out. "Cal." Releasing her, he smiled against her breast.

He traced a path to her waist, then over that ass he couldn't get enough of. With his middle finger, he followed the seam of her bottom and teased her little hole some more, slipping the tip inside. Lord, she was tight.

"Cal." She rested her chin on his chest.

"If you want me to stop, tell me now."

"No, I like it."

Cal worked his finger in a little farther. Monica retaliated by licking a circle around his nipple, then flicking it with her tongue.

He monitored her breath. She was panting, but relaxed, not clenching around him.

Cal lightly glided his finger in and out of her while she wrapped one leg around his thigh. She smoothed her palms down his back, propping her hands at his waist. When she started breathing a little harder, he increased the pace. She may lose her Miss Prim moniker after all.

"Cal, I want you inside of me. Now."

So demanding, his Monica. Never afraid to ask for what she wanted. At least not where sex was concerned.

Tenderly, Cal removed his finger from inside her. He reached to the stone bench and retrieved a condom packet, hastily rolling one on and letting the package flutter to the shower floor.

Lifting her by the waist, Cal settled her back against the wall. Before he could thrust inside of her, she stopped him by tugging on his hair.

"Hey, I want it hard this time." She linked her ankles behind his back and fingered the side of his neck. "None of that steady-wins-the-race business."

He laughed at her use of the old expression. No, Monica definitely wasn't shy about what she wanted. "I'm sorry, love, do you think you're in control here?"

She nodded. "Yep. In the office, you had it your way. Now I want it hard and fast."

"Like a good car."

"If that analogy works for you."

Cal reached down and positioned his cock at her tight entrance. With one swift thrust, he drove inside her. God, that felt good, being inside Monica Campbell. Having her stare up at him with passion-filled blue eyes, with her lips parted, her face damp, her hair a tangled, wet mass—Cal couldn't remember when he'd seen anything more lovely.

"And what if I decide to go slow?" With an unhurried movement, he withdrew almost all the way before easing back into her inch by inch. "Like this."

"Then I'll die of old age by the time I come."

"With a car, sometimes you have to start off at an even pace." He continued his slow retreat before stroking into her pussy once more. "You have to take it easy before you get her onto the open road."

She raked her nails down his back. "Damn it, Cal, I'm not a fucking car."

"No, darling, you're not." Cal closed his eyes. He couldn't stare down at her, look at her tits squashed tight against his chest, or he'd start hammering into her. Teasing her was agony. But so delightful, he wanted to hold out for a few minutes more. "You're a sexy, exciting woman."

"And you are a well-hung stud of a man. That voice of yours," she cooed, "it makes me want to get on my knees and suck you dry. It makes me want to bend over and let you have your naughty way with me while you slap my hot ass."

Cal stopped and opened his eyes. "I know what you're trying to do."

"Is it working?"

Cal let go of her hip and grabbed one of her breasts,

pinching her nipple hard. "Yes." He slammed his mouth over hers and began doing what she'd asked. He pounded into her, pulling out and plunging back in, digging his hand into her hip. He had to remind himself to be a bit gentler with her and relax his grip. Cal didn't want to damage her lovely skin.

Monica Campbell made him lose all reason. Filling her, thrusting into her—it felt so right. Made him block out all of his problems, all of his worries.

He sank into her, retreated, then did it again. She took every stroke, absorbed each thrust. Cal wanted her to come first, but bloody hell, he was close. Gritting his teeth, he tried picturing Monica in one of her somber suits. God, even that was a turn on, because he knew exactly what she wore beneath those drab clothes. Sexy red bras. Fuck.

Cal clenched his jaw and continued working in and out of her. Harder, faster. Filling her up. Fucking brilliant, that—being balls deep inside Monica Campbell. He didn't want it to end, yet he needed release.

He let go of her nipple and slid his hand between her legs. Using his thumb, he flicked her distended clit. Back and forth, he grazed it. Still, he kept up the pace, driving into her without losing his rhythm. A difficult maneuver, but Cal was determined to give her the ride she deserved.

With a cry, Monica dug her nails into his shoulders and came. Now Cal allowed himself to come too. Helpless, he clamped down on her hip. With a flood of pleasure crashing through him, Cal pressed his lips against her hair and groaned. So good. So goddamned good.

Screwing his eyes shut, he continued to plunge into

her, even after he was empty. And he remained inside her as he tried to catch his breath.

After a few minutes, his brain jolted back to life. "Well, was that hard enough for you? Any harder, and I might have knocked us into the next room."

She nodded against his shoulder. "That was fucking awesome," she muttered.

That might be the nicest compliment he'd ever received.

He supported her legs while she unwound them from his hips, then set her on her feet. "I concur. And that's the quote I want on my sex trophy."

Monica rested against the wall and laughed. Placing one hand on his chest, she gazed up at him. "I could walk before, but I'm not sure I can now. You may have to carry me to the car."

Cal felt a little shaky himself. "Let me get you a towel." If he had his way, she wouldn't go home tonight. And he wasn't above using bribes to get her to stay. He shut off the shower and stepped out. A lemon-scented fog clouded the room and coated the mirror.

After discarding the condom, Cal grabbed a thick white towel embroidered with the casino's initials and took it back into the stall. Monica stood exactly where he'd left her, slumped against the shower tile. "There's something you're forgetting." He bent down and started with her ankles, drying one leg, then the other. "I have chocolate cake."

"I probably don't need chocolate cake."

"Don't be ridiculous, everyone needs cake. And I have a huge fluffy bed that needs to be broken in."

"I think I'm broken. I can hardly move."

"That's because I'm so fucking awesome." He

continued to rub the backs of her knees, up her thighs, over her hips and belly. He took extra care when he got to her breasts, massaging the soft, textured towel over her nipples a few times. They beaded at the attention.

"I'm pretty sure they're dry, Cal."

"I do like to be thorough." Cal motioned for Monica to turn around so he could dry her hair. She spun and flattened her hands against the wall. He squeezed the water out of the ends and patted at her scalp. When wet, her hair transformed into a much darker shade of blond, almost brown, but not quite. He kissed the top of her head and inhaled deeply. Her lavender shampoo mixed with the lemon scent surrounding them. Divine.

"You never answered me before," she said. "Which do you like better, this place or your one-bedroom flat in London?"

He didn't know why it mattered, but she had something on her mind. He didn't have to see her face to know it—he could hear it in her voice. "This is nice, obviously. But the flat in London is fine too. I don't get too worked up over accommodations." He moved the towel over her shoulders, down her spine, and gave her ass a good rub.

"That's because you're used to staying in places like this. They don't faze you anymore."

Cal's hands slowed. "Allie's been married to Trevor for years now. Aren't you used to places like this?"

"Not really. I grew up in an older neighborhood. Our house was falling apart, literally."

Unsure how to proceed, Cal continued stroking her back. If he asked too many questions, she might stop talking. Yet this was really the first time she'd volunteered any personal information, so he couldn't let it go. "Why is that? Couldn't afford to fix it?"

"No. My mom's medical bills were out of control. That's why Allie and Trevor started the foundation, to help people like her."

Cal finally understood her, a part of her anyway. Monica was a sensual person, with carnal appetites she tried hard to ignore. His poor darling must have a bitch of a time reconciling both sides of herself—the self-sacrificing philanthropist and the lustful thrill-seeker. And this dichotomy somehow tied in with her mother's illness, although he wasn't sure how, exactly. "Staying in places like this makes you feel guilty, doesn't it?"

She didn't say anything for a minute, and Cal thought she might change the subject. But then she swallowed. "I always feel guilty when I think about her."

His hands stopped moving. "I feel that way about Babcock. By the end, she was unconscious most of the time. When she died..." He couldn't even say it out loud, it was too monstrous.

"You were relieved?"

Cal dropped the towel. He wrapped his arms around her waist and buried his head in the crook of her shoulder. "Yes."

"Me too," she said. "She suffered for so damn long."

Cal had been carrying that disgrace with him for months now. To hear Monica admit the same thing took away some of the shame. "It's because we loved them, I suppose."

"It still makes us awful people."

He nodded. "Perhaps."

Monica shrugged her shoulder. Cal took the hint

and moved back. She cleared her throat. "I should be getting home."

"Absolutely." His carefree tone sounded strained, but he carried on. "After dessert. You're not going to make me eat chocolate cake alone, are you?" He didn't wait for her to argue again, but simply left the shower and walked out of the room.

Monica watched Cal walk away. And for the first time in a very long time, she didn't feel alone.

Monica's mom had been sick for years, but when Allie talked about Trisha Campbell, she spoke only of the good times. Brynn would occasionally bring up a particular event, like the year all three girls got bikes for Christmas. Allie had received a purple ten-speed that made Monica so jealous, she'd stomped her foot and wrote a letter to Santa that morning, demanding an upgrade.

Nearly every memory Monica had of her mother was tainted by guilt and remorse—about past mistakes, about being resentful when her mom had been too sick to pay attention to any of them. But most of all, about feeling relieved when her mother slipped away. The years of suffering were finally over. And Monica was so glad.

While her family cried their eyes out, Monica remained dry-eyed. She realized, somewhere in the back of her brain, that her reaction wasn't normal—that she was a horrible person. That's when Monica's life had spun out of control, which left her feeling even worse.

Allie was right—Monica rarely mentioned Trisha Campbell, usually left the room if her sisters started reminiscing. She rarely discussed her mother with Evan. Yet for some reason, she'd opened up to Cal.

And Cal, of all people, understood.

Monica stepped out of the shower and grabbed the hair dryer from beneath the countertop. Cal's leather shaving bag sat next to the sink. She unzipped it, pulling out his brush. Mason Pearson. Jeez, even his man accessories were high-end.

She needed to get out of here, go home and hide under the covers for a while. She'd opened herself up to Cal, and he'd seen too much. Monica didn't feel vulnerable baring her body, but she'd just revealed a piece of her soul, and that frightened her.

First she dried her hair, then rubbed at the faint mascara smudges beneath her eyes. She grabbed the robe hanging next to the door and took a deep whiff. Cal. The lemon shower gel mixed with his woodsy scent. She shrugged into it and cinched the belt.

She was going to march into that bedroom and get firm with him. She needed to go home, back to her life, where she didn't get banged doggie-style in her office, where she didn't share her deepest secrets. With her head high, she opened the bathroom door.

But then she saw him, lying in the middle of the deep red sheets, holding an enormous piece of chocolate cake and two forks. And he was still buck-ass naked.

That lopsided grin melted her determination. Every single bit of it.

He patted the space next to him. "I'll hold the cake, you run and jump." He lifted the plate in the air and nodded encouragingly.

Letting out a laugh, Monica ran four feet and belly

flopped onto the bed. He was correct yet again. Soft and inviting, the mattress cradled her. Like a marshmallow. She felt as if she might sink right down into it.

"See, what'd I tell you?" he asked.

"You're annoyingly cocky. If I admit you're right, you'll become insufferable."

"I'd never be insufferable. I'm far too charming."

"See? Cocky." She took the fork he offered and cut a tiny piece of cake. Cal didn't take his eyes from her mouth as she ate it. "Oh God. This is so good."

"I told you so. I'm always right. It should get boring, but it never does." He crossed the space dividing them and licked the corner of her mouth. "You missed a crumb. And I have an idea about this cake. But first, you'll have to take off the robe."

Chapter 17

The next four weeks passed by in a blur. Monica hadn't heard a word from Allie. And it bothered her. She didn't feel good about the way they'd left things. Monica had every right to be angry at Allie's constant interference, but she could have handled things differently. Somehow. She could have kept a hold on her temper, for starters.

At the office, Monica worked nonstop on the gala, shored up donors and sponsors, and tackled every crisis that popped up. She had two run-ins with Marcus Stanford, reiterating her position on his wife's charity, and explained, for the millionth time, why the staff weren't there to wait on him, type his letters, or photocopy his shit. But she said it nicely and with a smile.

Monica also spent a part of her days avoiding Ryan McMillan. He texted every afternoon, called each morning—which she declined—and sent gifts. Right now, the break room contained Belgian chocolates, flowers, and mini-muffin baskets. Ignoring him wasn't working. She needed to have *the talk*. Eventually. Maybe after the gala, when things calmed down.

With everything else going on, Monica hadn't done any work with the international grants. She'd pretty much given up her goals of changing the foundation's agenda. Maybe in another year or two, but probably not. Still, every once in a while, Monica would take out the folder and read over the research she'd compiled. Then she'd chastise herself for wasting time and shove it back in the drawer.

On a happier note, after only three days in town, Jules had wandered into the office and volunteered her time. Apparently, talking Cal's ear off while he replaced an exhaust system wasn't as thrilling as she'd hoped it would be. Monica immediately put her to work on the silent auction.

Cal's sister had the vocabulary of a truck driver and an opinion on everything, and she freely shared both. Jules's clothes still rated a nine on the skank scale, but she'd toned down her makeup and removed the extensions from her hair. They started a routine of eating lunch together, and Monica grew fonder of her by the minute.

Jules had made herself at home in Allie's mansion. She loved Allie's fussing—weird, but true—thought Trevor was a god, and played with the twins every afternoon.

"Do you know what your cheeky little nephew, Zack, did?" she asked, lounging in Monica's guest chair. Today, Jules had packed her boobs into a short white dress that had to be at least one size too tight, and stomped around in a pair of monster heels. "He took my phone while I wasn't looking and added this farting app. So every time my phone rang that day, it sounded quite rude. The boys thought it was hilarious."

Monica smiled. "Yeah, you gotta watch Zack. He's the sneaky one."

"They miss you." Jules cast her eyes to the window, sipped on her iced coffee, and failed to appear nonchalant. "You could stop by the house, you know. Take an evening swim or a stroll around the garden."

"Don't even," Monica said. "You know Allie and I aren't speaking."

"Which is rubbish, if you want my opinion."

Monica started tapping on her keyboard. "I don't. When you fix your relationship with your parents, I'll take your advice. Until then—"

"Right, get back to work. I'm here for free, you know. It's not like I'm getting anything out of this."

Monica glanced up as Jules tromped to the door. "Actually, I'm sending your lawyer a letter, telling him how helpful you've been. He's going to pass it along to the judge."

Jules turned. "Really?" Her eyes narrowed. "Did Cal put you up to this?"

"No. And by the way, are you coming to the villa tonight?" A couple nights a week, Jules ate dinner with them. Cal enjoyed his sister's company. They teased each other mercilessly. It made Monica miss Allie, just a smidge. Before Monica had taken the job at the foundation, their relationship had finally been in a good place. Monica wished they could go back to those days.

Jules sighed dramatically. "No. It's spaghetti night at the Blake house, and I promised the twins I'd be there. Thomas says he can stuff four meatballs in his mouth at once. We'll see." She left the office, slamming the door behind her.

As soon as Jules left, Monica began plowing through her to-do list like a woman possessed. In the last few weeks, her life had been divided in half. During the day, she was all business, but she no longer stayed late, and she didn't work on weekends. Once six o'clock rolled around, Monica blew through the office door...and straight into Cal's arms. Now, she devoted her nights to pleasure.

They'd eat dinner on the patio, then make love in the pool...and the living room, the kitchen, the foyer. And every night she'd lay in his bed, engulfed in his arms, listening to him talk about his travels.

"What about Egypt?"

"Rode a camel to see the pyramids. I was...twelve, maybe? Camels are disgusting animals. Give me a Mercedes Gullwing any day."

"Great Wall of China?"

"I've seen it. But do you know what's really fascinating? The Shaolin monastery in Dengfeng, and the nearby martial arts school. Seeing these vast demonstrations, masses of children going through their motions, like a choreographed dance."

She'd asked him if he'd ever hit the clubs on Ibiza or partied on the beaches in Barcelona.

"When I was younger. That gets old after a while. Temples, ruins, talking to people in the marketplaces—much more interesting."

"Favorite place in Africa?"

Cal remained quiet for a beat. "Safaris are marvelous. Sleeping in a tree-house suite, watching the animals in their habitat was amazing."

"What about the poverty?"

"Awful. The conditions in some of the countries are deplorable. No sanitation, no clean water. It's heartbreaking. That's not what you want to hear though, is it? You want to hear the good stories, the exciting places."

Monica rolled over to face him. "No, that's not all I want to hear. I know what conditions are like in developing countries, Cal. I may not travel, but I can read." She propped herself up on one elbow. "They need medicine, doctors, more clinics."

"Didn't mean to insult you, love. I apologize."

She sighed. "It's okay. I just wish the foundation would branch out a little."

"Allie wouldn't go for it?" he asked, kissing her chin.

"No. And she's still not speaking to me right now."

Cal rubbed his hand along her back. "You two will sort things out. It's what you do."

"And what about you and Pix? When are you going to thaw that wall of ice between the two of you?"

Instead of answering, Cal told her about the time he sat in a café and watched rain fall on the Seine, and what St. Petersburg Square looked like at sunset. Monica pictured herself there too, dreamed about it. The more he talked, the more she wanted to see the world. What was it like to climb to the top of the Eiffel Tower? Or see a real Venice canal? It was a lovely fantasy.

Listening to Cal's sexy voice as he weaved stories of small, quaint villages and exotic, far-off cities was addictive—everything about him was addictive. His touch, his kisses, his smile. She'd never get tired of him, but she could never let herself get used to him, either. Every night, Monica walked a tightrope, allowing herself to open up to Cal, but not too much. It was a difficult balancing act, and Monica had never been good at balancing.

One evening after she got off work, Cal drove her out to Henderson. He'd seen one of his cars up for sale at a recent auction and contacted the new owners, a wealthy couple who lived in a square box of a mansion. They housed their collection in the most ostentatious garage

Monica had ever seen—black-and-white slate flooring, climate controlled, and rows of vintage cars that stretched on for days.

Cal stopped next to a red Ferrari. "What do you think?" he asked, bending near the front fender and tugging on her hand until she hunched next to him. "See these lines? Look at that delicious curve of the front panel." He actually petted the pristine grille.

"And you restored this?"

"Most of it. My lads at the shop helped. V-12 engine, three hundred horsepower. Gorgeous." Cal moved to the driver's side door. "Get in. See what it feels like."

Monica slid into the leather seat. Luxury. This was the ultimate. Even the interior was beautiful—a padded leather dashboard, a polished wooden steering wheel. It felt cool and smooth beneath her fingers.

"Isn't she something?" Cal asked. "I had to create my own jigs for the suspension parts, and molds for the back panel, but it was worth the effort." He rubbed his fingertips across the sleek roof.

"If you keep talking like that," Monica said, "I'm going to get jealous of a car."

Cal bent down, leaning his hands on the open window. "You should hear how I talk about you. Your chassis is stellar."

"Are you referring to my ass again?" She shot a quick look to the corner of the room, where the tall, balding owner stood watching them. "What's his deal? Does he think you're going to steal something?"

"They only built twenty of these. I don't blame him for acting proprietarily. Just finding the parts for this beauty took a massive amount of time and work."

"What did it look like before this transformation?" she asked.

"A woman in Hamburg inherited it from her father-in-law, and it just sat there, collecting dust and corroding in an old barn. Wasn't even covered up properly. Can you imagine?"

"Ah, poor orphaned Ferrari." But it *was* stunning. The overhead lights reflected off the glossy, candy-apple paint. It was sex on wheels. "I wish I could drive it."

"So do I." Cal stroked it one more time. "Anyway"—he straightened and helped her out of the car—"I thought I'd show you what I can really do. I haven't made much headway on my Mustang, not as much as I'd like, at any rate. Without the equipment in my shop, it's been a challenge."

"Well, this is impressive. You're kind of amazing, Calum Hughes."

For once, he didn't come back with an arrogant quip. He just smiled, a little shyly. "Thank you, but it was a team effort."

Before they left, Monica talked the couple into buying tickets to the gala. While the wife wrote out a check, the husband pointed at Cal. "I've been searching over ten years for a '57 Aston Martin. Would love to add one to my collection."

"I'll be on the lookout," Cal said. "I'd love to work on one, as well, but they're damned hard to find. As soon as I get back to London, I'll put out the word."

Monica smiled and accepted the check, but she'd overheard Cal's conversation, and it put things into perspective. Monica tried not to actively think about Cal leaving, but he would, and soon. Just because they were having a good time didn't mean he'd stick around. On the drive back to Vegas, Monica reminded herself this was supposed to be fun. No strings, that was their agreement.

"Penny for them?"

"What?" She glanced over at him. Sitting behind the wheel, he always looked self-assured.

He picked up her hand and kissed it. "You're thinking terribly deep thoughts over there. You grow very quiet when you're thinking. Want to talk about it? Are you worried about the gala? The board meeting? That's coming up in a couple of weeks, isn't it?"

"I was just mentally running through my to-do list for tomorrow." She rattled off a few mundane tasks, guaranteed to bore him in three seconds.

Monica might like sleeping in Cal's arms every night, hearing all about his adventures. She even liked listening to him talk about European sports cars. But Cal wouldn't stick around, not for her, and probably not even for Jules. Leopards didn't lose their spots. Look at her. Monica had had her shit together until she'd run into Cal, and now she was almost back to square one—falling for the wrong guy.

No, not falling. *You're in control this time, remember?* Monica could separate her feelings from sex, right? Men did it all the time. Thank God she'd had this wake-up call before she'd done something stupid, like stumble into love with Calum Hughes.

Cal was frustrated. Not sexually, of course. He and Monica shagged more often than rabbits. It should be embarrassing, the vast amounts of sex they had, but he was too contented to care. They'd christened every room in the bloody villa more than once. The linen closet had been a little cramped, but worth it.

No, his frustration lay solely with Monica herself. Since their visit to see the Ferrari a week ago, something had been troubling her. He wasn't sure what had occurred that night, but she'd changed. Not outwardly. Sexually, she was as willing and responsive as ever.

Just five minutes ago, she'd sucked him dry and seemed to take great pleasure in watching his response. Monica had lightly skirted her tongue along the bell end of his cock, then flitted little licks up and down his shaft. When she finally took him deep in her throat, Cal toppled over the edge of sanity, thrusting his hands into her hair in an effort to guide her, force her to go faster.

But Monica had released him and shook off his grasp. "This is my show, Hot Rod. Hands to yourself." She'd started doing that too—calling him Hot Rod. It was kind of charming.

"Why are you talking? Your mouth should be full."

Puckering her lips, Monica lightly blew across the tip. His prick jerked at the feel of her warm breath, and Cal clenched his teeth. "You're slaying me, love. It's brutal."

"Death by slow fellatio? I've never heard of it."

"It's a thing," he defended. "Look it up."

"I don't need a backseat driver. Keep your hands to yourself."

"Fine, no hands," he'd ground out. "But turnabout is a bitch—you remember that, Miss Prim."

She smiled up at him. "You're going to pay for that." She took him in her mouth again, and every time he got close, she'd back off. Monica played this game well, goddamn her.

As he neared orgasm once more, Cal had been panting hard, clutching the sheets. Sweat covered his brow. He wasn't going to beg her for release—he had too much pride. But he had to clamp his jaw shut in order to keep from shouting, *"Hurry the fuck up and let me come!"* Perhaps she'd read his expression, because ultimately Monica increased her speed, bobbing her head, taking him deeper while her hands pumped the base of his cock.

When he finally came, he shot into her mouth. Long streams of it. She took it all and kept going, milking him dry, giving him possibly the most intense orgasm he'd ever had.

And now he lay here, completely spent, yet still frustrated. No, the sex hadn't changed—it was this part afterward that had altered.

She lay spooned against him, her head propped on his outstretched arm. Cal brushed his thumb over her stomach, waiting. Waiting for her to talk, to ask him questions, to say something…anything. But Monica remained silent. If he asked what was troubling her, she'd chide him, tell him she was thinking about tomorrow's tasks.

Bullshit.

Cal knew when she was lying. Always. So he quit asking, because he hated it when she fobbed him off. Resented the bloody hell out of it, actually.

Intimacy. That was the missing ingredient. They'd had intimacy before, and now it was gone. Monica used to talk to him after sex. She'd opened up about her mum a little bit. He'd told her about his fight with Pix, his concerns for Jules.

Monica may be doubling down on the sex, but her heart remained guarded. She held an important part of herself back from him, and Cal didn't know why.

"Want to hear about the elephants in Sri Lanka?" he whispered, then kissed her neck.

"Next time," she said.

Cal's ego felt a bit bruised from that one. Why did a lack of intimacy worry him anyway? That was for twats and people in real relationships. He and Monica were all about sex. They'd made a deal from the beginning.

As Monica fell asleep, Cal stayed awake long into the night, thinking about where he'd land next. His garage manager, Otto, was pressuring him to come back to London and get his ass to work. But Cal didn't know if he wanted to head to England in the middle of winter.

He could go to Hawaii and surf. Or he could fly up to Alberta, watch the northern lights. But none of it appealed. Trouble was, Cal couldn't picture himself anywhere but here. Lying next to Monica, smelling her sweet scent as he cradled her in his arms each night.

What if he and Monica came to a new arrangement? Still have fun, of course, but perhaps they could be... *What? What would you be, muppet, exclusive?* Yes, exactly. Exclusive. So what if he flew back to London for a few weeks or even months? He could come and see Monica in between. Visit Jules to make sure she stayed on course. Long-distance relationships—people did them all the time.

He wouldn't be able to go haring off on a moment's notice, but so what? They wouldn't live in each other's pockets either, like Trevor and Allie. Not everyone had to. He and Monica were independent people. They didn't have to get married or live in the same place all the bloody time. They could have their own lives, but still be committed to each other.

Yes, this could work. Cal congratulated himself on his sensible idea and fell asleep around three a.m.

When he opened his eyes, bright sunshine flooded the room. Monica sat on the end of the bed, pulling on a black stocking. The bed bouncing, that's what had awakened him. Thought he was in the middle of an earthquake there for a minute. "What time is it?"

"It's eight seventeen. I'm so late. My stupid phone died."

Cal sniffed and threw back the covers. "I'll have to drive you home. We left your car at your place." Rubbing his eyes, he staggered to the closet and grabbed a set of clothes. He took them back to the bedroom and caught a glimpse at Monica's bare thigh as he shoved his leg into a pair of ripped jeans. She stared at him as well.

"What?" he asked.

"You're not going to wear underwear?"

"I thought time was of the essence. We need to get you home to change. Do you really want to have a talk about my lack of smalls right now?"

She shoved her feet into the sensible black pumps. "No. And you don't have to take me anywhere. I've called a cab."

"Nonsense. I'll have you home faster. You can show me the back roads." He slipped a T-shirt over his head and shoved his feet into a pair of ancient athletic trainers. "All ready."

Monica finger-combed her hair and walked down the hall. "You men have it so easy."

"No time for a diatribe on my sex," he called after her. He picked up the bedside phone and dialed Mr. Lawson. "Have the car ready out front, would you, and cancel Miss Campbell's taxi? We're in something of a hurry."

Monica fluttered back. "My purse, my bag." She made a circuit of the room, stopping to check under the bed.

"You dropped them on the sofa last night." He took her by the shoulders and shepherded her to the foyer. Her hair was a mess, she wore no makeup, and her clothes had been wadded up on the floor all night. She looked wonderful.

Cal darted into the lounge and grabbed her bags, then followed Monica out the front door and down the stone path. The Mustang waited for them, a valet at the ready, holding open the passenger door.

Cal grabbed a bill and shoved it in the man's hand. "Ta." He hopped behind the wheel, let Monica give him side-road directions, and sped ten miles over the speed limit the entire way.

When he arrived in the driveway, he killed the engine. "Go change. I'll make you a cup of coffee, yeah?"

She turned to him, clutching her bag with both hands like it was a bloody good luck charm. "You don't have to do that."

"Monica, my love, why are you wasting precious time arguing? You need to fix that hair."

Her hand flew to her head and patted it. "Great." She climbed out of the car and ran inside the house.

Cal got out at a slower pace. Life would never be boring with Monica Campbell. Walking through the front door, he heard the shower running upstairs. He'd been inside her house only a few times, and it was every bit as sad and colorless as he remembered.

Striding to the kitchen, he found the tiny four-cup coffeepot. He opened a few cabinets. All empty, except for one that held paper plates, plastic glasses, and disposable travel cups with lids. It housed the coffee can and filters too, along with stir sticks and little packets of sugar.

As the coffee brewed, Cal checked all the other cabinets and drawers, finding only plastic utensils. Even Cal's flat in London had proper cutlery. An expired carton of milk and two shriveled apples hid in the refrigerator. This entire house lacked permanency. She lived like a squatter. This was a place to sleep, like a hotel, except even hotels hung bad artwork on the walls.

Monica walked into the kitchen a few moments later. Today's bland color: gray. Gray pantsuit, gray button-up blouse, gray shoes.

He poured a cup of coffee, doctored it with a packet of sugar, and handed it to her. "Here."

Was the rest of the house as dismal as the first floor? Was the bedroom this tragic? He had to know. Without a word, Cal walked past Monica and charged up the stairs.

"Where are you going? Cal, what's wrong with you?"

She dogged his steps as he peeked into the two small bedrooms on the second floor. A few unpacked moving boxes lined the walls, but the rooms were absent of furniture. Then he strode into the master bedroom.

It was equally as appalling. An unmade bed—sloppy,

his girl—no headboard, just a mattress and box spring and plain white sheets. Blinds covered the windows, not curtains. There were no personal touches whatsoever. No books, no knickknacks, nothing that said Monica Campbell lived here.

"Cal, get out."

He thrust his hands deep into his back pockets while his gaze spanned the room, and after taking everything in, settled on her. "I've seen hotels in Bolivia that have more personality than this. The clothes I get. I despise them, even though I understand them. But this?" He removed his hands and flung an arm outward. "You need pink pillows and pretty bedding and pictures of your family. Where's a photo of your mother?"

"Get out of my room." She set the cup down on a bedside table. She only had the one.

"Where's your mum? I haven't seen a picture of her or your sisters or your father in this entire house."

"I haven't had time to decorate. I keep telling you that."

"I'm not talking about decorations. I don't know a single woman who doesn't put her own stamp on a place. Darling, no one's too busy to prop a family photo on the dresser."

She held up her hand. "Do not compare me to all the other women you know. You need to leave so I can go to work."

"What do you imagine I'll do here alone, steal your cache of paper plates?" Cal tried to come up with a reasonable explanation for this pathetic house. But really, the house was just a symbol—like her clothes, like her job. The only time Monica spoke of anything personal was after sex, when her impenetrable guard lowered ever so slightly. Occasionally, she'd share a story about her mother, about her childhood with Allie and Brynn. But even then, Monica never revealed more than morsels, little bits of herself doled out in tiny increments. She always left Cal eager for more, but the minute he asked a personal question, she'd clam up.

Monica Campbell bought hot-pink, fuzzy steering-wheel covers. That was frivolous. She wore frilly bloomers and bras that made his cock stir to attention just thinking about them. But they were hidden beneath her conservative suits. She'd dated Ryan What's-his-tits, a bloke so utterly devoid of charm, even his own mother must loathe him. Cal would bet his trust fund the man had never given Monica the type of rough, raunchy sex she needed. Yet she'd stayed with him for a year.

Monica Campbell's entire life was a well-constructed lie.

Cal walked past her to the closet, ignoring her sputtering. Surely she had to own something besides knickers, something that revealed her true nature.

He turned on the light. For a walk-in closet—even a small one—she had very few clothes. All suits, mostly trousers, in every shade of hideous. In the back hung three long dresses covered by plastic dry cleaner's bags. For her charity galas, obviously.

"Cal." Monica now tugged at his arm. "I'm serious. Get the hell out of my closet. Get out of my house."

"Why? There's nothing here, is there? Not one bit of the real you." Cal had never been so angry in his entire life. A sensuous, funny woman lay beneath all that fucking gray. "Whatever the hell you're wearing under that ugly suit, that's the real you. What color is it today? Purple? Bright blue?"

"Stop it," she yelled. "I don't have to justify myself to you."

He strode past her, out of the closet, and stopped in front of her dresser. He began yanking open drawers and grabbed handfuls of colorful lace. "This"—he shook a hot-pink bra at her—"this is who you are. Colorful and sexy and whimsical."

Monica marched forward and jerked the scanties from his hands. "What the hell's gotten into you this morning?" She shoved them back in the drawer and slammed it shut. "When I let you give me a ride home, that wasn't an invitation to insult me or paw through my personal shit."

He slowly walked toward her, and Monica skirted around the dresser, retreating until her shoulders hit the wall. Her wide eyes registered shock, but it quickly turned to anger as he kept stalking toward her.

"I've tasted and touched every single part of your body," he said. "But you don't want me looking in your bedroom, your closet. There's not one personal item in this entire god-awful little house. Why are you *hiding*?"

Monica shoved at his chest with both hands, but he didn't move. Wouldn't move, not until he had an answer.

"Why are you doing this? I'm not hiding. This is me. This is the real me." She sounded desperate, as if she were trying to convince herself as well as him.

"Are you really that thick?" He studied her, puzzled by her implausible assertion that this Spartan room, these dull colors, were a reflection of her true spirit. They were just the opposite. Camouflage. "You're living a lie. I don't know if it's for Allie's benefit or your own. Like that fake Statue of Liberty on the Strip, this character you're playing is a cheap imitation of the real thing. And the real Monica is brilliant."

"Shut up." She shoved at his chest again, harder this time. "Don't criticize me for being a responsible adult, something you could never manage. And don't talk to me about living a lie, because when life gets tough, Cal, you run in the opposite direction. You don't exactly confront things head-on—you haven't talked to your mom in weeks. So who's the one hiding, you or me?"

Cal's eyes narrowed. "Well, I never claimed to be something I'm not."

"Fuck. You. I don't owe you any explanations." Her breath came in shallow gasps as she stared up at him. Twin pops of color brightened her cheeks.

"The hell you don't. You act like one person when you're in my bed, and another person when you're out of it. Will the real Monica Campbell please stand up?"

"There's an easy solution. I'll never be in your bed again."

"Really? Are you having me on right now? You want me every bit as much as I want you." Now he was breathing heavily, as if his lungs couldn't take in enough air. He and Monica simply stared at each other, the anger palpable between them.

Then they lunged at each other. Monica threw herself at Cal, ripping at his shirt. He returned the favor, grabbing her blouse and tearing at the buttons. Red-and-white polka dots trimmed in white frills. That's what she wore beneath the bland gray costume.

She leaped into his arms, and he caught her, stumbling backward until the mattress hit his calves, then he tumbled down and rolled over, pinning Monica beneath him.

Angrily, he kissed her as he yanked her shirt from her trousers in quick, impatient movements and finished ripping open her blouse.

Monica fumbled with the hook on her slacks, and Cal lifted his head. Nudging her hands aside, he helped her lower them down her hips.

She pulled on his collar, scraping his neck with her nails in the process, and jerked at his T-shirt. "Take it off."

Cal sat up and stripped out of the shirt—she'd ripped the neckline, but the rest remained intact. After dropping it on the floor, he moved back on top of her.

Things often got frenzied between them, but this felt different. Raw and primal. Monica dug her nails into his sides. Cal kissed her too hard and grabbed fistfuls of her hair.

Curving her body around him, she wiggled her fingers into his back pocket and pulled out his wallet. "Condom," she said, gasping for breath.

"Get one, and hurry up." He didn't want protracted foreplay. He wanted to fuck. Hard. Take every bit of his frustration out on her. Unzipping his pants, he wrenched them low enough to free his cock.

In seconds, he had the condom on and placed himself at her entrance. In one powerful stroke, Cal rammed inside her. As he moved, his eyes met hers. Her light blue irises appeared glassy, and her pupils dilated. Cal held her gaze as he pounded in and out of her.

Biting her lip, Monica lowered her eyes until they drifted shut.

Cal stopped moving. "Look at me." He waited until she complied. This time, her eyes weren't unfocused—they were full of rage. "Say my name."

Her lips pinched together. "Asshole."

He gritted his teeth in a semblance of a smile. "Almost. Try it again."

She hesitated. "Calum."

"Again," he grated, pulling out of her, then driving back inside.

"Calum."

He continued, bucking his hips over and over. She felt so good, so tight.

Monica reached down to rub her clit. Every time her eyes would start to close, he'd stop moving. After the fourth time, her gaze never wavered.

For once, he came first. Burying his head in the crook of her neck, he continued thrusting until his balls emptied. Monica came then, shuddering beneath him. Her legs twisted against his, her trousers bunched at the ankles.

Afterward, he didn't move, but kept his full weight on top of her. When his heart resumed its normal pace, Cal rolled onto his back and stared at the ceiling. Neither spoke for several minutes.

"I don't know what you want from me, Cal," she finally said. "But I'm not going to turn myself inside out for you. You're not worth it."

"No, I'm not. But you are." He turned his head to look at her. Her hair, so perfect a few minutes ago, had become mussed again. He shifted to the side, propped his weight on one elbow, and stared down at her. "I've seen a lot of terrible shit in this world, Monica. Truly heartbreaking stuff that I can't banish from my head, no matter how many beaches I see or how many ruins I visit. Beauty and ugliness go hand in hand. Pleasure and pain coexist, and it all seems so fucking random. But you…you've buried the best part of yourself in this life that you hate, and it's unnecessary. It guts me."

"Okay." She sat up and scooted to the edge of the bed before standing. "We've dissected me. Now it's your turn." She tugged up her pants, jerked at the zipper, and pulled together the tattered edges of her blouse. "You think if you keep moving, never settling in one place, nothing can hurt you. So you wander around without any purpose, without putting any thought into your life at all. And you throw money at people in order to feel better about it. Except it doesn't work, Cal. Because you can't outrun all the shit you feel inside, all the isolation and pain. And by the way, I'm not one of your cars. I don't need fixing or restoring or whatever the hell you do. I'm not broken. Now get out."

Chapter 18

How dare he? Monica stood in front of the bathroom mirror, attempting to untangle the knots from her hair. How dare he accuse her of living a lie? She was living like a responsible, rational human being. She had an important job. She had a home, a family. What did Cal have?

He wandered around, looking at the world but never being a part of it. He never talked about friends, he didn't like to discuss his mom, he hadn't seen Trevor in years. Cal was a loner. Monica dragged the brush through a snarl near her scalp and flinched.

Why did he care how she lived? Their relationship was all about the sex. In six months, he probably wouldn't even remember her.

All right, she didn't believe that, not exactly. After all, Cal remembered everything about their first meeting, down to the color of her dress.

But if she thought for a second he cared about her… Of course he cared about her, in his own way, and she cared about him—they were friends with bennies. It didn't go any deeper. Nor did it give him the right to come in here and start insulting her, questioning her.

Giving herself one last glance in the mirror, Monica took a deep breath and opened the bathroom door. No sign of Cal. She should be relieved he wasn't there, forcing her to talk, but the empty room made Monica feel more alone than she had in weeks. With Cal, the piercing isolation left her. But now it flooded back in spades.

Their argument felt final, somehow. Maybe that was for the best. She and Cal wanted different things out of life. *Eyes wide open, remember?* Yeah, Monica remembered.

She changed clothes before trotting down the steps and grabbing her bags. The house seemed so quiet, the silence hurt her ears. She dug out her keys and hurried to the garage. Monica didn't have time to examine her life right now, even if she wanted to. She was running almost three hours late.

On the drive, she hit rush hour, and as she sat in traffic, automatically reached for her coffee cup. Shit. She'd left it on the nightstand when she and Cal were in the middle of their knock-down drag-out.

Right before they'd had sex. Angry sex. Monica closed her eyes and remembered the look on his face when he'd told her to say his name. There had been a harsh, cold gleam in his green eyes. His mouth thinned into a firm line, his jaw clamped down tight. He'd been pissed off and commanding. It had turned her on. Cal barking orders with that grumbly voice had made her wet. Of course, when he was playful and gave her a crooked smile—that revved her up too.

It dawned on Monica that she'd just made a car analogy. Terrific.

Forty minutes later, she arrived. Pulling into the parking lot, Monica found a spot in the back row. She hustled into the building and when she stepped into the main office, every head turned in her direction.

"So I'm late one morning."

They continued to stare.

"Was it my turn for doughnuts or something?" Monica set her computer bag down on Carmen's desk. "Seriously, what's going on?" she whispered.

"Where have you been?" Carmen hissed.

Stella burst out of the hallway and rushed toward her. She cast her steely gaze over everyone. "Move on with your lives, people." As one, the staff turned away, even Carmen.

"The shit's hit the fan, kid," Stella said.

"What's happened?"

Rubbing her forehead, Stella sighed long and deep. "Allie's waiting in your office. The ballroom flooded last night. We have no venue for the gala."

Shit. Shit. Shit. Monica hauled ass down the hall and nearly ran into Jules coming out of the break room.

"Run for your life," she said. "Allie's in a rage. On the drive over, she wore this hideous, frightening smile. I nearly shit a brick just sitting next to her."

"I'll handle it. Thanks, Jules."

Stella stayed on her heels. "I'll interrupt in ten minutes with a cup of coffee. Good luck."

Monica hadn't seen Allie in weeks. This was the worst possible circumstance for a reunion. Taking a deep, fortifying breath, she opened the door to find Allie standing in front of the window, "Hey, Al. I just heard the news." She walked across the room and tossed her purse in the bottom drawer of her desk.

"I tried to call you six times last night. Were you too busy with Cal to answer your phone?" Allie didn't turn around.

"My phone died, sorry. And my personal life is still off limits. Now give me the details."

"There's not much to tell. The ballroom flooded, there's extensive damage. They don't have anything else available, and we're going to have to cancel the gala."

Allie spun around, her eyes accusatory. "If you don't want to talk about Cal, let's discuss the foundation, shall we?" She tossed a folder on top of Monica's desk.

The file she had been compiling on international grants and cost projections for medical equipment. The same file she'd shown Trevor. "Were you rifling through my desk?"

"It belongs to the foundation," Allie said. So snotty. So superior. Always playing the big sister. *Marcia, Marcia, Marcia.*

All Monica's self-recriminations over the past few weeks blew away. This was why she'd been so angry. This right here—Allie's sanctimonious, I'm-so-fucking-perfect attitude.

Fury, hot and sharp, lanced through her. She ripped open the middle drawer, shoved her hands inside, and started pulling out lip gloss, pencils, paperclips, and dropped them on top of the folder. "Here. Take these too. All of this crap belongs to the foundation." She found a stray peppermint. "And don't forget this." Then Monica grabbed her purse and upended it, dumping everything until the bag was empty. "I have a few tampons, some loose change." She threw her wallet at Allie, who caught it deftly in her right hand. "Receipts, my credit cards. Hey, how about I cc you on my bank statements?"

Allie tossed the wallet on the desk. "While you're doing pointless research, we have a gala to cancel. But I'm so happy you were having a great time with Cal last night."

"You're right. I shouldn't have a life. I should be on call 24-7 in case the *ballroom floods*. I should have anticipated that."

Allie nodded at the green file, peeking out from under the debris. "What about that? What were you planning on doing with all that third-world grant stuff?"

"Does it matter?" Monica plucked it out and dropped the folder in the trash can. "There."

"What were you planning on doing with it?" Allie repeated.

"I thought the foundation could start branching out, make a bigger impact, have an international presence."

"We're not in this to make a name for ourselves. We're in this to help people."

"That equipment and training could help people, Allie. And you still don't understand—foundation work is a competitive sport. If we don't start making some big moves, we'll get left behind."

Allie's brows dipped together. "You make fundraising sound mercenary."

Monica started cramming stuff back in her purse. "It is. For every dollar we get, some other charity goes hungry. It's a cutthroat business. Donations have risen by seven percent this year. I *worked* to make that happen."

In the last two years under Monica's leadership, the foundation had grown. She'd added events and luncheons. She'd put together packets and presentations to get larger donors involved. Last year, they'd had their first walk-a-thon, and next year she wanted to add a bike race. It didn't bring in very much money, but it upped their profile in the community, which was vital for survival.

Allie sat in the guest chair and crossed her legs. "You know how much money it takes for projects like that?"

"Yes," Monica snapped. "I know exactly how much. I did a shit ton of research on it."

"That's not our vision," Allie said. "We help individuals pay for treatment. That's our purpose."

Allie kept using "our" and "we" as if Monica had any say in the matter. She didn't. Allie might include her in fund-raising minutiae, but Monica had no voice. "Maybe we should change *our* vision."

"Monica, you probably don't remember when Mom needed that experimental treatment—you were too young."

"I was fifteen, Allie. I remember."

"Dad went ass deep into debt to pay for it."

"I know that too." In fact, the board had hired a marketing team who had come up with brochures and ads that featured Trisha Campbell's story, distilling their mom's beautiful life into a thirty-second sound bite—turning her from a wife and mother into nothing more than a statistic. Monica wanted to celebrate her mother's life, not grieve her death repeatedly. Allie always did this, made it seem like she was the only one who remembered what their mother had gone through. But Monica and Brynn had been there too.

"It doesn't matter anyway," Monica said. "If we have no venue, we have no gala. No gala means we can't offer more than a handful of grants next year." Monica began gathering up all the paperclips on her desk.

"We need to get busy," Allie said. "We have to cancel all the sponsors, the vendors, call all the attendees and the press. This is a disaster."

What a shitty day—first her nuclear blowout with Cal,

and now this. Monica had put too much of herself into this gala—she couldn't just give up. She dropped the paperclips back on the desk. "You know what? We're not canceling that gala. Not without trying to find another location. I've worked too damn hard to bring in donations. If we don't pull this off, we'll be out in the cold."

When a knock sounded at the door, both Monica and Allie turned toward it. Stella tiptoed into the room, bearing two cups and a carafe of coffee. "Sorry to interrupt. Who needs caffeine?" She set the cups on the desk. Her gaze bounced between Monica and Allie. "So are we canceling?"

"Not yet." Monica glanced at Allie as she said it.

"I've called an emergency board meeting for tomorrow to explain the situation," Allie said. "Even if we do find an alternative venue, less than two weeks isn't long enough to replan this event."

"I disagree. I'm up to the task. Are you?"

"Fine, I'm in, but only if we find a suitable replacement site and the board agrees. But I have to tell you, Mon, I don't think it's going to happen. I don't want you to get your hopes up."

"Have you talked to the hotel manager?" Monica poured herself a cup of coffee and added sugar. It was a three-pack kind of morning. "Does he have *any* rooms available?"

Allie shook her head. "No, he's all booked up. I even had Trevor try and convince him, but it was a no-go."

Monica turned to Stella. "Tell the staff to stop what they're doing and call every hotel, every casino. Think outside the box on this one—museums, the Cactus Garden. Try everywhere and anywhere."

"You got it, honey." She took the coffeepot and marched out of the office.

Monica dropped her purse on the floor. "Are you going to stay and help, or do you need to get home?"

"I'll stay. We should divide locations alphabetically. Do we have a white board?"

There weren't any apologies, no postmortems on their fight. But working together on this gala thing, maybe they could call a truce. At least for now.

Monica took another sip of coffee. It was going to be one long-ass day.

Cal finally calmed down. It had taken an hour-long drive in the desert to accomplish it, but the anger he'd felt upon leaving Monica's house dissipated.

She'd said some ugly things to him—mostly true—and kicked his ass to the curb...which he deserved.

Monica claimed he had no purpose in life, that he was running from himself, that he couldn't confront things head-on. She was partly right.

Cal's purpose had been cars and motors. Starting from the bottom up, he enjoyed repairing damaged machinery, bringing it back to life. He was good at it, loved it. But it didn't consume him the way it used to.

And he wasn't running from himself either, not exactly. He just didn't feel at home anywhere, a misfit. Might as well have a bit of travel, see new and interesting things. But now, it sounded rather dismal. Lonely.

That bit about confronting things head-on, well, Monica was dead wrong on that score. Cal had confronted her just this morning, face to bloody face, and they'd wound up in a stonking row. Tackling it that way had been a stupid move, admittedly. Direct and honest didn't work with Monica—she was too wrapped up in her own lies. Not that she'd ever admit it. Predictably, she'd gotten her hackles up. He couldn't blame her, the way he'd carried on. But seeing Monica in that house, with her paper plates and her bare walls, depressed the hell out of him. No, it enraged him.

At night, he held Monica in his arms—the woman who made him smile and challenged him and asked a million questions about the world. Then every morning that woman disappeared in a puff of smoke, and Miss Prim took her place. And when Monica had become less communicative in the last week, Cal felt as though she were shutting him out.

Something or someone had forced her into the role of a drab moth. She was anything but. Monica Campbell was bright colors and loud music, and yes, she was caring and considerate too, but so terribly unhappy. He didn't know whether it was because Allie peeked over her shoulder every five minutes or that the foundation reminded Monica of her mother—but he wanted to fix it.

Then she'd accused him of treating her like one of his battered cars. Again, she had a point. When he'd seen her that first day at Trevor's house, Cal's only thought had been restoring the bright, bubbly girl he'd kissed five years ago. Now Cal was invested; he'd grown to care about Monica. She wasn't just a project.

She didn't owe him any explanations, not really. It was her life to waste, and even so, he wanted to be part of it. Now Cal would be lucky if she ever talked to him again.

He looked down at the gift bag in his hand. She definitely couldn't talk to him if she didn't have a phone. So he'd bought her an upgraded one. With a bright pink case.

As he continued stalking to his car, the midmorning sun peeked over his shoulder. When he reached the Mustang, Cal's own phone vibrated against his hip. Hoping it was Monica, he glanced at the screen with a sigh. "What is it, Paolo?"

"You have not spoken to Pix," he said.

Monica's words came back to him. No, Cal wasn't in a hurry to see Pix—there really wasn't anything left to say. His mum could live her life, and he'd live his. *So this is what you call living, mate? Fighting with the few people you care about?* But this wasn't about Cal and his life, this was about Pixie abandoning Babcock.

"I don't know what you expect me to do, Paolo. Pixie and I had a row."

"And?"

He couldn't do it. Not today. Cal couldn't stand any more confrontations. He wanted to lose himself in the Mustang's transmission. Working on cars had always been Cal's therapy. He needed it today, before the women in his life sent him 'round the bend.

Monica finished her fourth cup of coffee. While it kept her alert, it didn't help her nerves. Allie made her batty. She insisted on sharing Monica's desk, and they'd been calling every suitable spot for hours now, with zero results.

Standing, Monica stretched her arms over her head. "I need a break. Ten minutes."

Allie crossed off another hotel. "We're not going to find a place on such short notice. It's never going to work."

"I like your optimism." Monica grabbed her coffee cup and left the office. It had been like that most of the day—Allie complaining, insisting they cancel the gala. It gave Monica a headache.

Stella found her in the break room, a gift bag in her hand. "This just came for you."

Another gift from Ryan? She hoped to hell not. Monica took the bag and pulled out a bright pink phone and a note.

I'm an asshole.

She smiled at that. This was Cal's apology.

He'd been way out of line this morning. She'd said some really hurtful things to him too. Monica had been on the defensive. He claimed she was living a lie. Was he wrong? She still couldn't merge the two separate sides of herself—maybe she never would. But that wasn't the same as living a lie.

Monica gazed down at the brown pantsuit she'd changed into after he'd left that morning. So maybe she *had* gone overboard when she'd done a complete one-eighty—she had her reasons. And she probably didn't need to look like a pilgrim to do her job well. Fair enough.

She couldn't think about it right now though. She had to figure this gala thing out, ASAP. After refilling her cup, Monica made her way back to her office.

In between listening to Allie making calls, Monica

set up her new phone and synced it, discovering she had twenty-three voice-mail messages.

She deleted all six of Allie's automatically. No need to put herself through that. She deleted Ryan's messages as well. One from Cal, apologizing, asking if she liked the phone. As arrogant and cocky as he was, he had a side of him that liked to be reassured. It was sweet and unexpected.

Everything about Cal was unexpected. Like this morning. His anger had sprung out of nowhere, but he was furious that she was living in a virtually unfurnished, blank house. He'd said she needed color and pillows and curtains. He was right. She'd been living like a guest in her own house for months, but she didn't have the energy to do anything about it. She wasn't even sure she liked that house.

Allie glanced over, her eyes focusing on the gift bag. "Who's that from?"

"Cal sent it to me."

Allie's full lips rolled inward. "So is this serious? This thing with Cal?"

Monica shrugged. "We're hanging out." This morning hadn't been fun. It had been powerful and intense, like a thunderstorm—all sound and fury, leaving a flood of emotional destruction in its wake.

"I wasn't sure about him at first," Allie said, "but I like him. He's sweet with Jules, and he's been letting the twins help him fix the Mustang. He's very patient."

"We're not serious." Monica's stomach clenched. She wished things were different with Cal, but she couldn't expect him to turn into someone else, someone who stuck around. That wasn't fair.

"I just worry."

"You don't need to, Al. I'm a grown woman."

"Listen, I know I come off all nosy—"

"And bossy," Monica added.

"But—"

"And condescending."

Allie narrowed her eyes. "It's only because I love you and I don't want to see you get hurt." She leaned back in her chair. "You have the worst taste in men. Except for Ryan, of course."

"You couldn't be more wrong, Al. Ryan was the wrong choice for me. We would have been miserable." Monica knew it was true, had known it all along, but she'd kept trying to make him fit, like a too-tight designer shoe from the sale rack.

"What was so wrong about him?" Allie tilted her head to one side. "He had his shit together. A job. A life. He wanted to marry you."

Monica stroked the pink phone with her thumb. "He didn't mind that I wear gray pantsuits."

Allie's frown deepened. "I don't understand."

"It doesn't matter. Come on, let's get back to work."

At one thirty, Allie called it quits. She stood and grabbed her purse. "I'm so sorry, Mon, but this is a bust. We did everything we could."

Monica rose from her desk. "We haven't exhausted every possibility. We need to look for offbeat places. Can Trevor call in a few favors?"

"I'll ask, but I think you need to face the fact that it's over. We'll try it again next year."

There had to be one place in Vegas still available. "I'm not giving up."

Allie walked to the door. "Your time would be better spent figuring out new projections for next year's goals. There's going to be a hell of a lot less money to work with."

After Allie left, Monica snarled at her computer. More projections, more numbers and spreadsheets. It made her head pound that much harder.

She needed to call Cal, thank him for the phone, but she was reluctant to talk to him just yet. Her anger had faded, but she was hurt by his accusations. Monica did the best she could to prove to Allie and the rest of her family that she'd changed. Why was that so hard for him to understand?

As she worked up the courage to call him, her phone buzzed. Ryan again. Grabbing her purse and her new pink phone, she walked to the outer office and stood next to Stella's desk, waiting as the older woman wrapped up her call.

Stella hung up and shook her head. "I've crapped out. Not a place in town that's available on the date we need. So what's next?"

"We brainstorm. I need to run an errand, but I'll be back in an hour. Hold down the fort?"

"You may have to admit defeat on this one, kid."

"I may. But not yet."

Monica had a ton of work to do, but she couldn't put off Ryan any longer. It was time to cut ties, once and for all. She couldn't accuse Cal of not confronting life head-on and then be afraid to do it herself.

As Monica drove, Cal's words about hiding kept coming back to her. Hiding what, her racy underwear? That was just something she indulged in. It made her feel good, but it wasn't an insight into her psyche.

Cal didn't know her, not really. They'd been hooking

up for a few weeks—that didn't make him an expert on all things Monica. *Evan agrees with him*. Well, Evan dated bimbos, so he wasn't the most reliable source of advice.

She pulled her car into Ryan's driveway and closed her eyes. She hated to go through this again. It had been hard enough the first time, seeing the disappointment and understanding in his eyes. She felt cruel, but she couldn't let him continue to hope. *Rock, meet hard place*.

Getting out of the car, Monica walked to the house and rang the bell. She heard uneven thumping on the other side of the door. Ryan's crutches.

When he saw her, his face lit up in pleasure. "Hey, what are you doing here?" He leaned forward to kiss her, and she swiftly gave him her cheek. He thumped awkwardly backward, allowing her to enter the house.

The place looked as neat and tidy as ever, and his laptop sat open on the coffee table. "Have you been working?"

"Oh, yeah. Quarterly taxes."

Monica gripped her purse strap. "Where's your nurse?"

"I sent her home after the first day."

"Then how have you been getting along?" Now she felt terrible. She should have called more often, made sure he had everything he needed.

"Hey, don't worry." His gaze scanned her face. "I've been fine. I can manage getting around, and I've had my groceries delivered. I'm good." He grinned, all handsome and perfect and blond.

Hobbling over to the couch, Ryan dropped onto it with a wince. Monica grabbed a pillow and shoved it under his leg. "When was the last time you took a pain pill?"

"I don't need one." He grabbed her hand. "I'm fine. Sit down and talk to me."

"Ryan."

His grin slowly faded. "You're not here to check up on me, are you?"

Monica forced herself to meet his eyes. "I'm so sorry."

"So, it's really over. You and Cal, you're together?"

Monica's hand lifted to the top button on her blouse. "It's… Who knows?"

"I thought if I gave you enough time, you'd miss what we had. That you wouldn't feel so panicked and get that look in your eyes."

"What look?" Monica frowned and dropped her hand.

He patted the sofa next to him. "Sit down for a minute."

Monica hesitated, then sat, perching next to him. "What look?"

"When I'd talk about the future, your eyes would start racing around the room, like you were looking for the nearest exit. I thought you were just wary, but that's not it, is it?"

Oh God, he'd nailed it. Every time Ryan had talked about moving in together or getting married, Monica wanted to change the subject. Was her reaction specific to Ryan, or did she feel that way about commitment in general? What if Cal started talking about the future?

Stupid question. Cal didn't make plans. He was a live-in-the-moment kind of guy.

"Did you ever love me?" Ryan asked. He didn't wait for her to answer before he spoke again. "I thought you just didn't like to say the words, the same way you never talk about your mother. The same way you never talk about the frustrations with your job or the fact that you're so hard on yourself."

All of it was true. Yet Monica talked about those

things with Cal. She opened up to him in ways she never had with anyone. Not even Evan. She felt safe with Cal. She could show him all of herself, and he didn't judge her for it. Except this morning. He'd judged the hell out of her then.

"You're really good at hiding what's going on inside of you, Monnie."

Monica's pulse beat against her throat. "I don't hide," she snapped.

He reached out and rubbed her knee. There was nothing sexual in his touch. "I'm not accusing you of anything. It's just the way you are. Remember the philharmonic?"

She'd bought Ryan tickets to a performance of Mozart's most famous symphonies. Agony. Sheer boredom for three endless hours. "It was fun." *Liar*. Cal's accent rang in her ears.

"You hated it. I knew that, but you wanted to make me happy. I thought that was a sign that you loved me."

Monica began picking the clear polish from her thumbnail. It occurred to her that what she'd done with Ryan was what she'd done with every man in her life. She warped herself into their version of the ideal woman. From her first boyfriend and his love of monster trucks to Ryan's passion for Mozart. *Defective*. No, not just defective—seriously, *seriously* messed up.

"I'm so sorry. I never meant to hurt you, Ryan. I wanted you to be the one."

"I know." His smile was tinged with sadness. "You tried really hard. I should have gotten a clue when you bought that house."

"What do you mean?"

"Monica, four months ago I asked you to marry me. You said you had to think about it, and the next week, you bought a house. Your own house, without even discussing it with me."

She stood and walked around the room, wrapping her arms around her torso. "My lease was up. I bought it as an investment."

"Sweetheart, if you can't be honest with me, at least be honest with yourself."

She whirled around and flung her arms down. "I'm not lying to myself," she yelled. "I wish everyone would stop saying that." She clapped her mouth shut. *Oh God.* Monica took a gulp of air. "Sorry."

Ryan gazed at her with a puzzled frown. "That's the first time I've ever heard you raise your voice."

"Really?" She paced to the door. "Because I yell at Allie all the time." And Cal. She wasn't afraid to yell at Cal. She stopped moving and glanced back at him. "I wanted to say yes."

"It would have been perfect. I'm here. I love you, Mon. We could make this work. Can you say the same about Cal?"

Monica shook her head. "No, I can't. But I've decided I don't want perfect. It's too much pressure." Her entire world turned on its axis. She didn't want this tidy life with a man who wouldn't pull her hair during sex or talk to her in a rough, posh voice. That's not who she was. Never had been.

He leaned his head against the cushions, looking more tired and pale than when she arrived. "If you change your mind—"

"I won't. I never meant to hurt you." Monica

stumbled out of the house. She felt numb, yet her mind spun in circles.

Sitting in her car, she dialed Evan. Her call went straight to voice mail, and she left him a rambling message that didn't make much sense.

As she started the car, a terrible dread filled the pit of her stomach. Suddenly, Monica didn't know who the hell she really was. She wasn't the girl she used to be—flighty and irresponsible—nor was she the mousy woman she portrayed herself as, the one who worked day and night in order to avoid having a real life. So where did that leave her? Who was she now?

Would the real Monica Campbell please stand up?

Chapter 19

Monica drove back to the office and continued her efforts to find a place for the gala. But her mind kept wandering back to the argument with Cal and her conversation with Ryan.

At four fifteen, she turned off her computer. Allie was right, it was over. Time to start crunching numbers for next year. All her plans, everything she'd worked for had been shot to hell because of a broken pipe.

She'd almost called Cal three times this afternoon, but each time she'd talked herself out of it. Now that she'd given up for the day, she grabbed her phone and dialed his number.

"I'm sorry," he answered.

"I know. Me too. Thanks for the phone."

"What's wrong, love? Is this about the gala thing? Trevor mentioned it."

"Partly."

"Meet me at the villa."

"I'm heading there now." She didn't even hesitate. When Monica ended the call, her hands were shaking. She didn't know why she felt so nervous. This was Cal, the man who made her laugh, made her come until her knees trembled, the person she confided in. When they were together, a weight lifted off her shoulders, and she could relax. He may not be around tomorrow, but she needed him today, right now.

She shoved everything in her bag and left the office, waving to Stella and Carmen on her way out.

When she arrived at the villa, she handed her keys to the valet and walked to the front door. Cal stood there, waiting.

His hair was damp, and he wore his usual T-shirt and faded jeans. Walking toward him, she didn't say a word, but he must have recognized something in her expression, because as soon as she cleared the doorway, he scooped her up in a one-armed hug.

"I'm sorry," he whispered against her lips. "I'm so sorry."

Monica clung to his shoulders. "I don't want to talk."

"All right." A vague, fractured thought ran through Cal's head: something troubled her, more than just work problems. But as soon as she slid her mouth over his, all thoughts ceased.

When he reached out and thrust his hand through her curtain of hair, he noticed his fingers trembling ever so slightly. Cal slipped his tongue between her full lips, and she met it with her own. He wanted her out of the suit. Without it, she'd have nothing left to hide behind. He wanted to see her in the red-and-white polka-dot bra once more. This time, he'd appreciate it.

He tore his mouth from hers and lowered Monica to her feet. "Get out of these clothes," he growled, and began ripping them from her. He wasn't gentle, either. As he yanked the jacket from her shoulders, Monica shrugged it off her arms and threw it to the marble floor. Cal didn't wait for her to finish unbuttoning her silky brown blouse. He grabbed the two halves in both hands and ripped it. It was offensive and hateful. She didn't utter a word of protest, just yanked it off, as if she couldn't stand the material touching her skin.

The red bra made him smile, and as he stared at her breasts, her nipples puckered. Cal ran the palm of his hand from her slender neck, over her tits, and down to her belly button. Her taut stomach flexed beneath his rough hand. She inhaled sharply when he ripped at her waistband. "These trousers need to come off."

She fumbled with the button, and they fell to the floor. After kicking them away, she arched her back, angled her chin a little higher.

"You are so lovely." As Cal's gaze rose to those beautiful breasts, his heart ratcheted up.

"Cal."

Her voice brought him out of a trance. He looked into her eyes, those crystal-blue eyes. They'd glazed over with desire, but there was something else in their depths. She needed something from him, but damned if he knew what it was. "Tell me what you want, Monica. I'll give you anything."

"Just you."

Cal locked an arm around her waist and pulled her up against him. With her sweet breasts crushed against his chest, he walked her into the lounge. His cock became painfully hard, and staring down at her wasn't helping. The full tops of her breasts rose above her bra and bounced with each step he took. When her tongue darted out and licked that full upper lip, Cal groaned.

With one hand slung around his shoulder, Monica

gazed up at him while she absentmindedly fingered his tattoo with her other hand. "Hey."

He stopped in front of the sofa and met her gaze.

"About this morning—"

"We'll say no more about it." That didn't seem to appease her. Whatever bothered Monica, he knew she'd never open up to him until she felt relaxed and sated. And she'd come to him for that. Cal felt humbled and challenged at the same time. He wanted to make her forget all of her problems, if only for a while. If she wanted sex, he'd oblige.

When he dropped her on the sofa, she let out a little squeal. Divesting himself of his jeans and boxers, he didn't take his eyes off her.

Monica reached around to unhook her bra.

"Leave it on."

"Why?"

"Because you look fucking hot in it."

"I look fucking hot out of it," she said, a smile tugging at the corners of her mouth.

"That's my line, and you absolutely do. Now leave it on." He ripped the shirt over his head and kicked his trousers to the side. His cock jutted out, stiff and ready. When Monica's eyes lowered to it, he reached out and gave it a stroke. "But take the knickers off."

She pulled her gaze away from his shaft, her eyes darting over his face. Angling her gorgeous ass upward, she wiggled her panties over her hips, down her legs, and tossed them next to his jeans. Then she lay back against the tapestry pillows and placed her arms above her head.

For a moment, Cal thought he might come on the spot. Bold, exciting, thoroughly sensual—this was his

Monica. She didn't show this side of herself to anyone but him.

Cal bowed toward her and rubbed his hand along her thigh. Her breath faltered at his touch. His hand glided higher. Then he grabbed her legs and yanked her closer.

She half yelled, half laughed. "I didn't see that coming."

"Good. I like to keep you guessing."

"I've noticed."

He lightly pinched her hip before caressing her waist. Then, situating his hips between her legs, he planted his fists by her head as he held his weight off her. Cal's cock bobbed between them, resting on her belly as his body skimmed hers. Her bra barely scratched his chest, but her nipples pebbled against his skin. "I'm in a bit of a quandary, love."

She ran her short nails down his chest. God, that felt nice. "What's your problem?"

"I'm trying to decide if I want to kiss you, taste you, or fuck you. Actually, I going to do all three—I'm simply pondering the order." He lowered his head, his lips a mere whisper from hers. "What's your opinion on the subject?"

She answered by grasping the sides of his face and kissing him. Weaving her hands through his hair, she thrust her tongue into his mouth at the same moment she wrapped one leg around his waist. Cal's eyes drifted shut as he lowered his hips and ground his cock against her soft skin.

Monica tugged on his hair until he raised his head. "Kiss, taste, fuck."

Cal ran his tongue over the seam of her lips. "Deal. But I get to decide when I'm done kissing you."

Monica's fingers wandered over his shoulders. "You drive a hard bargain."

"I do." He thrust his cock against her again while he nibbled at her lips, kissed the corner of her mouth. Monica moaned, tightening her leg around him in an effort to rub herself against his almost painful erection.

She turned her head to the side and gently bit down on his jaw. "Kiss me, damn it. Like you mean it."

He leaned back. "Hungry for me, are you?" Her eyes narrowed in irritation, which made him smile. Then he kissed her properly, the way she liked.

She rewarded him by stroking her hands up and down his back, digging her nails along his spine. Monica knew what he liked too.

Cal lowered himself on top of her. He longed to fuck her, right now, like this—without a condom. But she was terribly conscientious about it. Another secret of hers—one he'd uncover eventually.

Softly, his lips coursed a path from her mouth to her neck, raking his teeth over the spot right below her ear. She gasped and bucked her hips against him. "More of that."

He nipped her once more before trailing his mouth over her shoulder, down to the tops of her soft breasts. Taking another look at her tits through the fanciful fabric of her bra, he licked her nipple through the satin cup. He moved his hand from her waist to toy with her other breast and rubbed his thumb over her already hard nipple.

Monica's breath turned choppy and uneven as he sucked even harder. "So good."

He glanced up at her. "Like that, do you?" He

snatched one bra strap, then the other, pushing them down her shoulders. The cups fell below her tits, framing them. Monica yanked her arms free, and when he latched onto one nipple, biting down ever so gently, she held his head in place.

"Calum. Calum."

He liked hearing her say his full name. Was going to insist she use it more often.

He left her breast and kissed his way to her belly, using his tongue to swirl a pattern across her tender flesh. Monica's leg became slack around his. Placing his hands on either side of her knees, he forced her thighs farther apart.

Monica propped herself up on her elbows and watched him. Only lust registered in her eyes. No worry, no doubt—just the same hot need that consumed him.

Trapping her gaze with his, he positioned his mouth at her pussy. With one lash of his tongue, he licked in between her plump folds, and his eyes drifted shut. "I love the way you taste, Monica Campbell. Sweet and salty and fucking delicious."

He opened his eyes and watched her head drop back. "Calum."

He sucked one of her smooth outer lips, using very little pressure. When he parted her with his hands, he lapped a circle around her clit. It was swollen and obviously sensitive, because she jumped when he flicked it. He loved eliciting responses from her, discovering what she liked, what made her gasp.

With his lips, Cal brushed light, feathery strokes up and down her slit. He fought hard not to lose himself in her taste, her silky texture, but he made sure he kept in tune with her, measuring her reaction, her breathing. She was panting now and close to coming, so he backed off a bit, applied less pressure.

"Cal. Calum. Please."

His tongue darted inside her, fluttering up and down. She liked that too, and her breasts rose and fell rapidly.

"Don't stop doing that," she said.

He continued, reveling in her response, making her mindless with need. She yelled as she came a moment later.

Cal didn't stop his movements, but kept up the pace, licking inside her. Another wave wracked her body, and she groaned, pulling at his hair. As that second orgasm rippled through her, Cal felt more powerful than he ever had.

After a long minute, Monica's body went slack. She released her hold on him, and he eased away from her.

"Seriously fucking awesome," she said, her eyes closed.

Cal stroked the side of her hip with one hand. "Don't fall asleep. We're not through."

Her eyes drifted open, and she grinned. "Can I take my bra off yet?"

"No." Cal moved off her, but came back a moment later. He held a condom in one hand as he pinched her nipple, then kissed the side of her neck and worked his way to her earlobe. He bit down, and Monica sighed with pleasure.

Cal positioned himself on top of her once more. Her body fidgeted under his. "Want me to put it on for you?"

Cal kissed her temple. "No, you'll only torture me. And you'll enjoy it."

"Only a little, and you'll enjoy it too." Monica

laughed, grabbed the foil packet out of his hand, and ripped it open.

Cal stole the condom back and rolled it on himself. She was still grinning as his gaze traveled over her face. "Where did those freckles come from?" Cal smoothed a finger above her eyebrow. "You're never out in the sun."

"I hate them."

"They're adorable."

Monica framed his jaw with both hands, her smile becoming more wistful. She stroked her thumb over his lips and placed a tiny kiss on his chin. "What's your middle name?"

His brows dipped as he stared at her. "Why?"

"Because I want to know."

"George. Terribly sexy, I know."

"Please fuck me, Calum George Hughes," she said.

"So formal." Cal adjusted his hips and slid inside her, but he didn't thrust immediately. They stared at each other for a long moment. The late-afternoon sunshine slanted through the room, bathing her face in a warm glow. Monica Campbell was possibly the most beautiful woman he'd ever encountered, and he was lucky enough to be balls deep inside her.

Cal began to move slowly. He wanted to savor this, make it last. He couldn't ever recall a feeling quite like this one—as if he and Monica were connected, and not just physically. He would sound a complete knob if he uttered that thought aloud.

He licked the little dent in her chin. He loved that dent. Cal wanted to take it slow this time, fuck her gently, but this wouldn't satisfy her for long. Monica liked it hard and fast. He'd give that to her. Eventually.

But right now, he wanted to draw it out, prolong the pleasure for both of them.

"More," she demanded.

Cal gave her a hard kiss, but kept up his steady pace. He pulled out almost all the way and then slid back into her. Over and over again until she bit his shoulder.

"I hate you," she panted.

"Do you really?" Cal pulled out of her entirely.

"Okay, maybe *hate* is not the right word." She tried to place her hands on his shoulders, but he moved out of her reach and rose to his knees.

"I should say so." In a swift move, Cal hooked his hands around her thighs and pulled her ass toward him. He draped her legs on either side of his chest until they stuck straight up in the air. He stroked his hands up and down her calves, over her shins. "Your turn. What's your middle name?"

"Taylor."

Positioning himself at her entrance, Cal slid back inside her. "Monica Taylor Campbell." He embedded himself all the way, stretching her to capacity.

When he pulled out, she opened her mouth to protest, but he rammed back inside her, filling her again. "Monica Taylor," he ground out. "So fucking tight."

As he worked in and out of her, her breasts jiggled slightly. He watched them, couldn't take his eyes off them. With both of his arms hooked around her legs, he thrust back and forth. When he sensed her urgency, he placed his hand on the top of her pussy, and with his thumb, found her ripe little clit. He brushed it—once, twice—then she came.

"Cal. Oh God." She scratched at the back of his hand.

Monica closed her eyes, and her pussy tightened around his cock.

Cal continued to pound hard while stroking her. Occasionally, he'd swivel his hips, providing a different sensation, a hot friction. Her walls clamped down on him, testing his endurance. A fine sheen of sweat covered his chest and arms. "Fuck. I want this to last." He clenched his jaw. "Going to come, love." He stopped playing with her and wrapped his hand around her other leg, then he picked up the pace, slamming into her faster than before.

Cal came with a hoarse shout, his hands gripping her thighs like they were the only things keeping him steady. His cock jerked inside her, and she shuddered around his shaft, draining him.

Once he stopped moving, Cal planted a kiss near her ankle, his breath harsh from exertion. "Amazing."

He pulled out of her and gently lowered her legs. Cal dropped a little kiss on her shoulder, then slid off the sofa and onto the floor.

Monica sat up and simply took him in. With his chin resting on his forearm, he looked beautifully masculine. He smiled at her—a drowsy, blissful half grin.

Something about the tilt of his lips tore at her heart. Monica's day had gone downhill from the time she'd opened her eyes this morning, but it had all fallen away when she'd stepped into his arms this afternoon. They weren't just having fun—well, she wasn't. How Cal touched her, like she was special—that meant everything.

Oh God. She didn't want this. Not now, not with him. He was going to break her heart, and she'd handed it to him on a platter. Shit.

The realization brought Monica out of her peaceful haze, making her scramble off the sofa and reach for her underwear. She grabbed her panties and pulled them on. Cal settled his hands over her upper arms.

"Monica. Look at me, love. What's happening right now? You're thinking again."

"It's just been a hell of a day."

He stared at her, his light green eyes dancing over her features like he could read her thoughts, but then his expression changed to one of boredom. Cal slid his hands down her arms before relinquishing his hold. "Oh, dear," he said with a yawn. "Look who's lying again. How original."

"Shut up." She slipped her bra over her shoulders and adjusted her breasts.

"I'm not looking to get in a row right now. I'm still basking in the afterglow. Give me a few to work up a lather, and then we'll have a go." He stood and threw away the condom before walking to the liquor cabinet. He poured a finger's worth of whiskey. "Cheers." He tipped his glass before taking a sip.

Flicking back her hair, she faced him. He was still naked and semi-hard. How was that possible? "I'm not lying, I've had a shiteous day."

He picked up the restaurant guide and perused it. "Of course not, darling. You're living your truth." His dry tone raised the hair on the back of her neck.

Marching over to him, she plucked the menu from his hands and tossed it on the floor. "I'm not having this argument again." Her gaze fell to his penis. She couldn't fight with a naked man. "Put some clothes on."

He smirked. "Makes you nervous, does it? My being in the buff?"

"Yeah. I'm trembling."

"You were ten minutes ago. Yes, you've had a bad day. But that's not what this is about, so please don't insult me. You've been upset since you set foot in this house. If you're still tetchy about this morning, say so."

"I'm not tetchy. I'm not even sure what that means."

But he was right. Again. Monica lied about everything—she lived behind a persona she'd created. She'd been running so hard from the mistakes of her past that she'd done a U-turn in her life, and now she was as screwed up as ever. But the lie was comfortable, and the truth seemed almost paralyzing. Buried deep inside, under all the responsible behavior and professional demeanor, Monica's wild child remained alive and well. And she liked being let off the chain. Monica reveled in hot sex with Cal. She loved the freedom it gave her, the excitement. The emotion.

She'd been lying about her feelings for him too. Monica thought she could handle a no-strings sexual relationship. All of her peppy self-talk about being in control and eyes wide open was bullshit. She'd fallen in love with Calum George Hughes. How could she be so damned stupid? Loosening the tight reins on her old ways had led to this—love. Of all the men she could have chosen, she'd picked Cal Hughes, a man who never stuck around. A man she couldn't count on. All those years of playing the good girl, dating appropriate guys, living a straitlaced life—blown to bits.

Suddenly, her body was on fire, as though every nerve ending burned beneath her skin. Beads of sweat dotted her forehead. Monica felt as if her heart might burst through her chest at any moment. Pain, sharp and biting, ripped through her torso. All of these revelations at once—they were too much. Maybe she was having a heart attack. This was what dying felt like. "I have to go." She spun away. "I have to get out of here." She began gasping for air. She couldn't breathe.

He plucked her up in his arms and walked to the overstuffed love seat by the window. Sinking down, Cal held her as she struggled.

"Let go. Let me go." She pushed against his chest and tried to rise, but he tightened his hold.

"No. You're having a panic attack. Deep breaths." When she ignored him and tried to break free, he gave her a little shake. "Deep breaths. Come on. In." He held her gaze with his own. "And out. Again." He breathed with her. *Inhale. Exhale.*

After three or four minutes, Monica's heart began to slow down. With a shaky hand, she pushed her hair away from her face. "What's wrong with me?"

Cal stroked her back. "You're just scared, that's all."

"I don't know what the hell you're talking about." But she was lying, of course. She couldn't seem to stop herself. In truth, Monica was terrified of him, of herself, of her feelings.

She pushed off his lap and stood, feeling a little woozy and so embarrassed, she turned away. Who acted like this? Who had a panic attack after the most amazing sex ever? God, she was a freak. *Defective.*

"Monica." He waited until she slowly turned back

around. "Let's stay right here, eat dinner, talk. After that, you can go if you want." He stood and approached her slowly. With infinite care, he reached out and stroked a hand down the length of her hair. "Okay?"

When she didn't pull away, he enfolded her in his arms, hugged her tighter in his embrace. Monica hugged him back. Closing her eyes, she took a deep whiff of him and struggled to remain calm.

Then Cal stepped back. "I'll get dressed." He strode over to where his clothes lay in a pile and pulled on his boxers and jeans. He held up his T-shirt. "You want?"

She nodded, and he lobbed it at her. Dark green—the same shade as his eyes when he was angry—and it smelled of fabric softener and Cal. Monica pulled it on. The hem hit her above the knees, and the sleeves fell below her elbows.

Her feelings for him frightened her. That's why she'd freaked out. She'd never felt like this. Not even with Aaron—the asshole who'd abandoned her in Mexico—and she'd been ready to leave her friends and family for him.

Calum Hughes was the real deal. He loved his sister, and he'd cared for Babcock in her final days. But he'd leave. If not tomorrow, then next week, or next month. Cal would take off for Bora Bora or Nepal, and she'd be stuck here in Vegas.

Not stuck. You have your family, your life.

But what kind of life did she have? Was she going to spend the next five years trying to prove herself to Allie and people like Marcus Stanford? The next ten or fifteen? Just the thought of it left her drained. And for what, a job she hated?

Monica covered her mouth with one hand. *She hated her job.* She hated working at the foundation.

Shit. That panicky feeling threatened to rise up inside her and take over once again.

A look of concern filled Cal's eyes. "You all right?" He walked over to her, raised his hand to touch her shoulder, but Monica moved out of reach.

"I hate my job," she said in a rush.

"Yeah, of course you do."

"No, I hate my job. I need this job."

Cal crossed to the mini-fridge hidden in the bookcase and grabbed a bottle of cold water. "Why?" He handed it to Monica.

"Because it's who I am. Allie depends on me. I have to show her I'm responsible. I owe it to my mom."

"Let's take those one at a time, yeah? It's not who you are. You hate it."

Monica paced to the sofa and sank down. She twisted the cap off the bottle, taking a long drink. She knew Cal wouldn't criticize her, and because of that, he was the only person she could talk to. "Yeah. I hate it. But I can't let them down."

Cal sat next to her. His long fingers stroked her bare leg. "One thing at a time. You hate it."

She nodded. "I hate it." After several minutes, she smiled and breathed out a little laugh. "It sucks so hard. I hate the numbers and reading grant applications and having Allie question every decision. I like working with the donors, though."

"How does it feel to admit it?"

Her gaze sought his. "Scary."

"That's okay. If you're scared, you're alive. You said you have to prove yourself to Allie. Why?"

Monica flung the bottle onto the coffee table.

"Because she's my sister. Because I've fucked up so much in the past. Because I have to show her that I can do this."

"She's your sister. She's not living your life for you. You fucked up in the past? So what? Everyone has."

She shook her head. "Not like me."

He scooted to the edge of the couch and faced her. "What's the worst thing you've ever done? Most horrific?"

She opened her mouth, but nothing came out. She was too ashamed.

"Did you run a red light? Wear two different socks by mistake? You're a good person—what could you have done that's so terrible?"

Where to begin? "I was thirteen when my mom got diagnosed. She was sick for a long time. I felt..." She stared at the fireplace grate and shrugged. "I felt like she left me, even though she was still there. Allie quit school and came home to take care of us all. As my mom got worse, so did I. I made life hard for everybody in the family." It was hard to admit that. Painful.

Cal continued to stroke her face. "You were a child."

"I was a brat."

"All children are brats. No exceptions. They're messy and they smell bad and then they go through puberty. Don't know why they're all the rage."

Monica didn't laugh. "After she died, I went off the rails. I drank too much. I toked up, took too many pills. I woke up next to strangers, Cal, and sometimes, I couldn't even remember what I'd done with them." She took a deep breath and studied his face. He didn't look shocked or surprised or disappointed. "Four years ago, I met a guy, and after two dates, I let him drive me to

Mexico. In the morning, he was gone, and so was all my money. I had to call Evan to come and get me."

After a minute, Cal lifted his hands, palms upward. "All right, so you have terrible taste in men—present company excluded, naturally. And you committed a few youthful indiscretions. You trusted the wrong people."

"I got pregnant."

Chapter 20

That one shocked him. His face went slack for an instant before he covered it up with a neutral expression. "I see." He remained silent, waited her out.

"Are you going to ask what happened to it?"

He placed his hand over hers. "Only if you want to tell me."

Monica took a shaky breath. "After Evan picked me up and brought me home, I just sort of checked out. I stayed in bed for days. I was ashamed and felt so goddamned stupid." She tugged her hand back and curled her legs beneath her, pulling Cal's shirt over them to cover herself. She'd never felt so vulnerable in her life as she did right this minute. But Cal wasn't looking at her with disgust. There was nothing but sympathy in his eyes. The lines of his body were tense, but he leaned toward her, as if he were barely holding himself back from reaching out. Seeing that compassion made her want to throw herself into his strong arms and never let go.

But Cal wasn't hers to keep. So Monica sat up and lowered her feet to the floor. "A month later, I was still a wreck, but I found out I was pregnant. I knew I had to turn my life around. I had someone else to think about besides myself. I had to get my act together and quit making selfish choices. Then I lost the baby." She tucked her hands under her thighs, suddenly cold despite the warmth of the low-setting sunlight beaming through the window.

"I'm so sorry, love."

"Yeah, well, it's probably for the best. I'd have made a lousy mother."

"That's simply not true," he said. "I've never met anyone as caring as you. You try to cover it up, but you have the most tender heart of anyone I've ever met."

With her jaw set, Monica slid him a sideways glance. "It was karmic justice."

"What do you mean?"

Monica scrubbed her hands across her eyes. "I told you, Cal, I was relieved when my mom died. I lost my best friend, and I was *glad*. I'm not a good person at all, I'm awful. When I lost my own baby, it broke my heart, but I deserved it. I deserve every bad thing that happens to me. That's why I work for the foundation. I couldn't go back to being that thoughtless, rebellious girl. Not after miscarrying. Not after making such a mess of my life. My mom would have been mortified by my behavior. I let her down."

"Come here." When he held his hands out to her, Monica fell toward him. She buried her face against his solid chest. Then Monica Campbell, the girl who didn't cry at her mother's funeral, began to sob.

Cal hated feeling helpless. His poor Monica. She'd been in pain for so long. Holding her close, he rocked her gently in his arms and let her cry.

Monica was still suffering from grief and guilt. He couldn't make that go away, but he knew firsthand how brutal and exhausting it was to watch a loved one die. He'd gone through it as an adult for eight months. Monica had been a needy child, enduring it for five long years. Of course she felt abandoned. A perfectly natural emotion.

And she hadn't taken a job at the foundation because she needed to prove something to Allison. It wasn't about responsibility at all. Monica was trying to atone for her perceived sins. That fact was so bloody obvious, he didn't understand why no one else saw it.

Once her sobs slowed, Cal continued to stroke her, to soothe her as best he could. "I didn't know your mother, but she managed to raise three beautiful, smart daughters. I think she'd want you to forgive yourself."

She glared at him and pushed out of his arms. "You don't know anything. I shared one piece of information with you—"

"Bullshit. You shared your biggest secret with me. Want to know mine? My biggest secret?"

"No." She scooted away from him and tried to stand, but Cal snared her arm and pulled her back down.

"Babcock didn't want me to know she was ill. She swore my mother to secrecy, but I found out from Paolo. I flew to her immediately. She was dying—congestive heart failure after way too many cigarettes over the years. And I *hated* her for that—for leaving me and for not seeing the doctor until it was too late, and for keeping it a secret.

"She shrank, Monica. Literally, she seemed to cave in on herself. By the end, there were days when she barely remained conscious. And Pixie never came to see her once."

Monica drew a shaky breath. “I’m so sorry.”

“After she died, I’d get up every afternoon and head to the beach. Then sit and drink a beer every night. I’ve literally done nothing for the last five months.”

“You were grieving, Cal. You stayed with her until the end. That’s heroic.”

“But I didn’t want to be there.” Guilt flooded him, along with shame and self-loathing. “There were days I resented the hell out of her. She was meant to be the strong one.”

“Would you do it again?” she asked.

“In a heartbeat. When you were a teenager, you were overwhelmed by it all. And you didn’t deserve to lose your baby. Bad shit just happens.”

They sat in silence. Time slipped by until full dark descended. Cal felt a bit lighter. Talking with Monica helped. He could never have told all that to anyone else. Not Jules, not Pix. Only Monica.

After a while, she wiped at her eyes with the back of one hand. “I should go. I shouldn’t have left work early.”

“You should stay. You haven’t had dinner yet.”

She gave a little laugh. One that held no humor at all. “I’m not really hungry.”

“I am.” He stood and walked to a lamp in the corner, flicking it on. The light drove away some of the shadows. Then he walked back to Monica and grabbed her hand. “You can watch me eat. Seafood or steak?”

“You’re super rich,” she said with a sniff. “Why not get both?”

Placing a hand on either side of her face, he leaned down and kissed her forehead. “Good idea.”

“I’m not very good company right now.”

"Do I look like I need you to entertain me? I want you to stay." When she appeared unsure, he caressed her cheek. "Please, Monica Taylor Campbell? Don't force me to eat alone."

She gazed up at him, her bloodshot eyes so sad he couldn't bear it. "Okay."

"Excellent. Go get a shower, and I'll order dinner." He turned her around and gave her bottom a light pat. If she'd insisted on going home, Cal would have followed her and sat in her driveway all night, just in case she needed him. He wanted to be her rock.

Monica would never believe that of him. She was too jaded by her past to have any faith in what Cal said. *So don't tell her, you git—show her.*

How? Cal had no experience with relationships. Any time he stayed in one place too long, he'd immediately start feeling restless. He didn't know how to be a partner. And he couldn't offer her any guarantees.

Thrusting his hand in his pocket, Cal did what Babcock would have done in a crisis. She would have cooked his favorite comfort foods and told him stories of her childhood in Cairns, near the reef. Cal didn't cook, so he dialed Mr. Lawson and ordered everything he could think of to tempt her. He could tell her about zip-lining across the jungles of Peru or the giant Buddhist prayer wheel in China.

As he waited for her to get out of the shower, Cal stepped onto the terrace and called Pix. He rubbed at his eyes as he waited for her to pick up.

"Calum," she answered. That was all she said, all she needed to say. He heard her pain, and it echoed his own.

"You let me down, Mum. You let her down."

"I know. I wish I could make it up to you, but I can't. I assumed you called to tell me good-bye. I'm rather surprised you've stayed in town this long."

After the revelations Cal had shared with Monica, he should be throwing everything he owned in a bag and hightailing it to the airport. *Don't get attached*. He'd lost sight of the one lesson that had served him well, and become smitten with Monica. He didn't know how long he'd stay, but he wasn't ready to leave her yet.

"No, but I'm flying to L.A. with Jules next week. She has her court appearance."

"Oh. Wish her luck for me?"

"I will." Cal hesitated, didn't know what to say. Dealing with his emotions—it was all slightly embarrassing. "I'll talk to you when I get back?"

"Thank you, Calum."

He ended the call and turned to see Monica standing at the entrance of the French doors. The lights from the living room silhouetted her. She still wore his shirt. It hung over her trousers, making her appear tiny. She'd draped the jacket over her forearm.

"Sorry to interrupt."

"You weren't. I was talking to Pix. You were right this morning, I've been avoiding her." Cal wiggled a finger at her. "You didn't have to get dressed on my account."

"I'm leaving." She said it with such finality, it was a punch to his solar plexus.

"What?" With long strides, he walked to her. Her eyes were still red, her face free of makeup. She looked younger and more vulnerable than she had five years ago. He brushed a stray hair from her cheek. "I ordered a vast amount of food. I wasn't sure what you wanted."

She shrugged. "I'm still not hungry."

Cal wrapped his hand around hers and laced their fingers together. "I thought we agreed you'd stay."

Monica tugged her hand from his and took several steps backward. "Cal." She swallowed and rubbed her palm over her hips. "I really… I care about you. A lot."

"I care about you too."

"That's why I have to leave. I think we should end this. And I'm serious. I don't want you calling me or sending me gifts. Let's just make a clean break."

"What are you on about?" With narrowed eyes, he took a step forward.

She didn't back up. Instead, she extended her arm to keep him away. "I know you can't stay in one place for long. It's not who you are. But that's what I need. I need someone in my life who won't leave."

"Because I can't give you any guarantees, you want to end it altogether? In typical Monica fashion, you're running scared." His harsh tone dared her to deny it.

"Yeah. That's it in a nutshell."

"The truth. How novel."

"If I get in any deeper with you, I'm going to wind up hurt. I'm protecting myself. You of all people should understand that. That's why you never settle anywhere—so you don't have to get close to anyone."

"Don't do this, Monica. We have a connection, you and I."

She dropped her arm. "Can you promise you'll be around next month?"

Cal turned away and looked at the urn full of bright red flowers. He glanced back, met her eyes. "No. But I'll fly back to Vegas at regular intervals. We can still be together."

"You've had me pegged from the beginning. I have been afraid. Afraid of making stupid mistakes and letting Mom down, letting Allie down." Monica's eyes darted away as she cleared her throat. "I'm not sure about much in my life right now, but I know I want more than regular intervals. I don't deserve it. I know that, but I want it."

"Monica, I'll give you everything I have, darling."

"On a part-time basis. When it's convenient for you."

Cal couldn't argue with that. He couldn't promise her tomorrow, let alone forever.

"Before she died"—Monica crossed her arms and glanced away—"my mom told me to follow my heart. She said it wouldn't let me down. I thought it was the morphine talking, because my heart leads me in the wrong direction every time." Nibbling her lip, she sniffed. "But I don't think I've been listening to my heart. I've been listening to my fear."

His steps ate up the distance between them. Placing his hand beneath her chin, he raised her face until she looked at him. "That's what you're listening to right now—fear."

"No." Tears filled her eyes. "Look at me. I haven't cried in years, and now I can't stop. You run from everything too, Cal. It's who you are, and I'm not judging you, but I don't want to be a part of it either." She grabbed his hand and kissed his palm. "I have to go."

He stood silent as she walked away. Cal opened his mouth to call her back, but what for? He didn't have anything lasting to offer her. And she did deserve more. More than an uneducated sod like him.

Not for the first time, Cal wished he were a better man.

He'd never felt so utterly alone. Not even when he'd lost Babcock. And he had no one to blame but himself.

~

Sitting in her car, Monica ran her hands over the fuzzy steering-wheel cover and glanced at the pink dice Cal had bought her. Had she made a terrible mistake?

She was tired. Mentally. Emotionally. Monica had never been so open with anyone the way she had been with Cal. It sucked her dry.

Walking away from him was the hardest thing she'd ever done. The easy thing would have been spending the night in his arms. Every night, as long as he decided to stick around. And Monica would do whatever it took to keep Cal happy, to keep him by her side, because that's who she was. Today had been chock-full of revelations, none of them particularly pleasant, but she'd learned one thing—she was tired of making herself over to please other people.

Cal tortured himself because he'd wanted to leave Babcock. But he'd stayed because the woman who raised him had been sick and dying. Australia was a onetime deal. Monica couldn't depend on him. He'd admitted it himself.

She needed to figure out who the hell she really was, without worrying about Cal leaving or when he would come back. *If* he'd come back. So Monica ended it, and shattered her own heart in the process.

She wasn't sure what to do next, where to go. She couldn't go home and lie on the bed where she and Cal had had sex this morning. God, was it only this morning? Today seemed like an eternity.

She reached into her purse, grabbed her phone, and speed-dialed. "Hey, can I come over?"

Twenty minutes later, she kicked on Evan's door, juggling a bottle of Patrón, a carton of ice cream, and her computer bag.

When he answered, Evan's gaze bounced over her, then he snatched the bottle from her hand. "I'll get you a spoon."

Once they'd settled on his sofa—purple suede—he swirled the tequila in his glass and raised one brow. "I have fortification. Now spill."

Monica blew out a breath. "I hate my job. I'm in love with Cal—I didn't get vaccinated. I got the disease. Your advice is the worst. And the ballroom flooded, so the gala's off. My life is a shitpile." She scooped a spoonful of Chocolate Therapy ice cream into her mouth. It wasn't therapeutic and would probably go straight to her ass.

"My God, it's you," Evan said before leaning over and kissing the side of her head. "Monica Campbell, my best friend. She's back, ladies and gentlemen," he said to the muted actors on TV. Then he toasted her and took a sip.

"No, Ev, I'm not the same. I don't even know *who* I am."

"Self-awareness is completely overrated. So, you're in love with Cal. He seems like a decent guy."

"He's not forever material, but damn, I wish he were. He's so funny and he's smart and his smile is lopsided. He's an artist with cars. But I want it all, Ev. I want the ring and the 'til-death-do-us-part crap. How can I be happy, wondering when he's going to bail?"

"You've got it bad." Evan scrunched farther down on the sofa, propping his yellow-socked feet on the glass coffee table. "Why do women need forever?"

"I think I have issues."

"*No*," he gasped, "not you." He took a sip of Patrón and wiggled his toes. "Monnie, my friend, we all have issues."

"I mean with my mom. When she got sick, I felt scared and alone, so I started looking for affection in losers, thinking if I could conform into what they wanted, I'd be worthy. I even did that with Ryan."

"Oh God, stop, I'm begging. All this navel-gazing is going to make me drink until I pass out, then my eyes will be puffy tomorrow. Look, I date crazy orange women with big, fake tits. Probably because my dad paraded cocktail waitresses and showgirls in front of me during my formative years. You work with what you have. But, Mon, I know you." He set his glass on the table and turned to her. "I *know* you. You've never been in love before now. Maybe Cal is good for you."

She shoved the spoon into the ice cream and set the carton next to his glass. "I just broke up with him. Not that we were really together."

"Despite your criticism of my advice, I'm going to leave you with one more nugget of wisdom. If you find love, grab it. You don't know when or if it will come around again." Fine lines fanned out from the corners of his brown eyes. For once, he wasn't being a smart-ass.

"I can't think about it anymore tonight. I've got a board meeting tomorrow and a gala to cancel. How about you? How's Hope?"

"Heather. We broke up. She hated my clothes and accused me of being color-blind. And why don't you just have the gala at Allie's house? She's got that fricking mansion. The garden is big enough to hold everyone. Have tents or whatever out there."

She stared at him. "That's insanely brilliant."

He shrugged. "I have my moments."

So the next question—give Allie advance notice, or bring it up at the board meeting? Allie would feel pressured at the meeting, less inclined to say no. Monica was determined to make this event happen by any means necessary. She could ask Allie's forgiveness later.

"Can I take a shower?" she asked. "And borrow some sweats to sleep in?"

"Like I own sweats." He waved a hand toward the hallway. "You know where everything is. Go on, and I'll make up the sofa. I'm not giving you my bed."

"Thanks." Monica tapped the side of his face with her palm and headed down the hallway.

"Hey," Evan called.

She turned around. "Yeah?"

"It's all going to be all right. Your sucktastic life, I mean."

"Sure it is." Evan must have been drinking something stronger than tequila if he really thought that. Nothing ever turned out okay. Not her mom, not her job, not her terrible decisions with men. Although Cal didn't feel like a bad decision. He felt just right.

But if Monica had taken a chance on Cal, she'd never be secure. Even though he'd offered her regular intervals. That was a big compromise for him. But security was important to her. *More important than spending time with the love of your life?* Whoa. Who said Cal was the love of her life? Except that he kind of was.

Cal was unlike anyone she'd ever met. She couldn't pigeonhole him, couldn't put him in a box. Just when she thought she might have him figured out, he would reveal something new and wonderful about himself. And the sex was off-the-charts amazing. She couldn't imagine letting another man touch her ever again, let alone make love to her. Monica wanted only Calum.

So where did that leave her? Monica should have opted for the tequila—maybe then her brain would stop dashing back and forth and the pain in her heart would dull to bearable levels.

In Evan's bright aqua bedroom, she chose a pair of sea-green boxer shorts and a Ralph Lauren T-shirt from the dresser drawer. After grabbing a quick shower in his guest bathroom—Gucci towels, naturally—she shuffled back to the living room.

"Do you need another blanket?" Evan asked, carefully unfolding the zebra-print duvet.

"No, I'm good. Thanks, Ev." He patted her arm as he headed to his bedroom. Monica climbed beneath the Egyptian cotton sheets. They weren't as soft as the ones in Cal's villa.

She pulled the silk duvet up to her chin and looked out over the Vegas skyline. Neon lights as far as she could see.

Monica stared at them until the sun came up.

Monica Campbell was naked—not a bloody stitch. She lay between his legs, her hair trailing over his hips. She smiled right before her mouth slid over him, taking the length of him deep in her throat. Heaven. Then she gazed up at him and started buzzing.

Cal pried one eye open, realized he'd been dreaming. Monica wasn't here. She'd left last night, broken things off for good.

He fumbled around for his phone on the bedside table. "What is it, Jules?"

"He's had a heart attack." Her voice sounded tremulous.

Cal sat up, his heart still pounding from the dream. "What? Who?"

"Father. Mummy just called. I have to get back home immediately."

Shit. "Are you still at Allie's house?"

"Yeah. Will you go home with me, Cal?" She sniffed. "I need you."

"Of course, but slow down. How serious is it?"

"I don't know." She cried in earnest now.

"Is Trevor around? Let me speak to him."

"I'll get him."

"Jules? It's going to be all right." He hoped that was true. For her sake, for his stepmother's. When Cal had failed to return Jules to L.A., his father had been positively livid. Cal wasn't sure what kind of welcome he'd receive from his stepmother, either, but he'd stick by Jules's side and see her through.

A moment later, Trevor's cool voice said, "Terribly sorry about this, Cal. Is there anything you need? I could book you a private flight."

"Yes, actually. Thanks for that. And Trev, if anyone asks, *I'll be back*. Do you understand, mate? I'm not leaving for good."

"I won't get rid of the Mustang, if that's what you're implying."

"It's not. Get Jules to the airport, and I'll meet her in less than an hour."

Suddenly, he was very glad he'd spoken to Pixie the night before. If anything happened to his mum and they hadn't made up, Cal would never forgive himself. Although he'd never have his father's approval, none of that mattered now. His father might be dying, and Cal wanted to say good-bye.

He threw back the covers and nabbed the clothes littering the floor. *Monica*. He reached for the phone to call her, but remembered she never wanted to see him again. But no time for that now, he needed to get to Jules.

Four and a half hours and countless tissues later, Cal and Jules arrived at the hospital. His little sister was a mess, her eyes nearly swollen shut from crying so hard.

In the waiting room, his stepmother, Tara, sat in a corner. Jules ran to her, throwing her arms around her mum's shoulders. Cal stopped in the doorway and stared at them. Unequipped to deal with this kind of thing, he never knew what to say.

As he walked toward them, he held his hand out to Tara and flung his arm around Jules's shoulders. "How is he?"

His stepmother was a very quiet woman. The exact opposite of Pix. "He's going to be all right. He's had a mild heart attack and needs a pacemaker."

Cal closed his eyes in relief. "That's good news."

"The doctor says if he doesn't slow down, the next one could do him in."

Not so good news. The old man would never slow down—it wasn't in his nature.

Cal settled Jules in a chair, then he bent down in front of Tara and patted her knee. "How are you holding up?"

Wispy blond hair framed her face. Her skin looked pasty, and dark rings circled her red eyes. "I'll be fine. Thank you for bringing Jules home."

"You're welcome." He glanced between the two of them. Poor Jules looked pale, scared. "Tea. That's what we all need." He gave what he hoped was a reassuring smile and went hunting for some. Babcock's cure-all, sans the brandy.

He found the cafeteria, bought three cups, and laced the weak brew with lots of sugar and milk. He carried them back to the waiting room. Cal felt completely useless. But maybe just being here, sitting next to Jules and holding her hand—maybe it helped.

He fought the urge to call Monica. She would know what to say, what to do in this type of situation. She was good at that. He *needed* that.

Monica Campbell hadn't been out of his life for twenty-four hours, and he missed her so much he ached with it.

~

Monica shook hands with all the board members. Even Stanford. The meeting had gone well. Allie's English garden would hold the event this year. Monica had a ton of work ahead of her, and she was glad. It would take her mind off of Cal.

She hadn't stopped thinking about him since she'd left the villa the night before. Was leaving Cal the right thing to do? Because it felt wrong on every level.

Deena Adams sauntered over and nodded. "I owe you

an apology. You're not just here to rubber-stamp your sister's decisions. Whatever help you need to pull this off, let me know."

"Thanks, Deena."

Monica gave Stella a thumbs-up as she walked to her office. Once she closed the door, she glanced over at the portrait of her mother. Those damned tears burned the backs of her eyes. She missed her mom so much. Before she'd gotten sick, Trisha had been the glue that held her family together. Allie did her best to fill the role, but it wasn't the same.

Monica grabbed a tissue, dabbed her eyes, and had just sat down when Allie blew through the door.

"You get off on blindsiding me, don't you? First Jules, now this."

Monica shrugged. "Yeah, a little bit."

"Hosting it in the garden is kind of brilliant. Congratulations, Sis. Come on." Allie waved her arm. "I'm starving, and we need to hammer out the details. Might as well do both at the same time."

Allie was being a good sport about all this, so Monica didn't complain about her lack of appetite. She grabbed her purse and followed Allie out of the office. On the way out to the car, Monica donned her sunglasses. The morning sun seemed unusually bright. Or maybe her eyes were overly sensitive from all the crying.

"Everything all right?" Allie asked. "You aren't gloating, and that worries me."

"Yep. I'm fine."

Allie stopped walking and turned to her. "I'm sorry that I made you feel incompetent. That was never my intention. You're really good at this job."

"Thanks. And I'm sorry I yelled at you. It's just that you're always so damn perfect. How am I supposed to live up to that?"

"I've never expected you to be perfect, Mon."

"Actually, you do." She resumed walking toward her car. "You always expected Brynn and me to follow your every order, to the letter."

Allie finally moved. "Do I really act like I'm perfect?"

How to answer that? Cal would tell her not to lie. "Sometimes. You were the good daughter, and I was the bad one. We all get it."

"You weren't the bad one." She hopped into Monica's passenger seat.

"Well, Brynn wasn't the bad one. So that just leaves me." Monica didn't say any more until they reached the restaurant.

"I'll try to ease up," Allie said. "Come on, I'll buy you a cup of coffee. You look like you need it. Are you sure you're okay?"

No. Not even. Monica missed Cal. She wasn't sure she'd ever be okay again. "I don't want to talk about it."

They exited the car, and as they walked toward the entrance, Allie patted Monica's back. "You never do. I'm sorry I gave you a hard time about Cal too. I shouldn't have interfered. I just want to protect you." She held up a hand as if Monica were about to argue. "I know you don't need it. You've made so much progress in the last few years, I didn't want to see you slip back into old patterns. But I was wrong."

Normally, Monica would snarl about being an adult and handling her own life, but not today. Besides, she was very close to tears. Again.

"When you talk to Cal," Allie said, "tell him I'm sorry to hear about his dad."

Monica froze midstep. "What?" she whispered.

"You didn't know?"

"Tell me."

"He and Jules left for L.A. this morning. His dad had a heart attack."

Monica clung to the column near the restaurant door for support. "Is he going to be okay?"

"I..." Allie shook her head. "I don't know." She placed her arm around Monica's waist and led her inside.

"Table for two," Allie told the hostess. She helped guide Monica to a table and waited until they were alone. "Mon, talk to me. Are you all right? You look like you're going to be sick. Why didn't you know about Cal's dad?"

"Poor Cal. Poor Jules. It just happened this morning?"

"Yeah. Why don't you call him?"

"We're over."

"What? I thought you two were doing well." Her eyes narrowed. "Did he dump you? That son of a bitch. I warned him."

"No, I ended it."

Allie's head snapped back. "Oh." When the waitress stopped by, Allie ordered two cups of coffee. "Why?"

"I'm in love with him. I didn't mean for it to happen. I thought I could handle a fling, but Cal is just so...fantastic."

"Does he love you?"

"He cares about me, but he can't stay in one place for long. He's not made that way." She glanced at Allie, took in the tight seam of her lips. "Just say it and get it out of the way."

Allie shook her head.

"You told me so. You told me not to get involved with him. I didn't listen. Say it." Monica crossed her arms on the table, dropped her head, and began sobbing.

Allie awkwardly patted her head. "Monnie. Stop, honey. Please. You never cry. This stupid man is making you cry."

When Allie sniffed, Monica glanced up. Allie blotted her eyes with a paper napkin, taking care not to smudge her mascara. "I hate seeing you this way. You're breaking my heart."

"What else is new?" Monica mopped her chin with the back of one hand.

When the waitress brought the coffee, she stopped short. "Everything all right here?"

"More napkins, please," Monica said.

The woman scurried off and returned with a two-inch stack.

After several minutes, Allie stopped crying, and Monica finally dried up too. "God, this is embarrassing. I'm like a leaky hose. Also, now's probably not the best time to tell you this, but at the beginning of the year, I'm quitting the foundation."

Allie sputtered and choked on a sip of coffee. "What? I told you I would ease up."

"I hate that job, Al. I'm sorry. I won't leave until you find a replacement. I just can't do it anymore."

"Is this about your international grant idea?"

"No. But it might be good for the foundation. You should keep an open mind."

"So you're really leaving? For good?" Allie asked. "What will you do for work?"

Monica shrugged. “I don’t know. I only know what I don’t want. But hopefully, I’ll figure it out as I go along. I’m going to call Jules, see if her dad’s all right.” She grabbed her phone and stepped out of the restaurant.

“Hello?” Jules’s nose sounded stuffy.

“It’s Monica. I just heard about your dad. Is he going to be all right?”

“Yeah, he’s going to be fine. Here, I’ll let you talk to Cal.”

Chapter 21

When Jules shoved the phone into his hand, Cal had no idea it was Monica. "I don't mean to bother you," she said, sounding stilted. "I heard the news and—"

Cal tightened his grip on the phone. "No bother. It's very kind of you."

"Allie just told me, or I would have called sooner. Is he going to be all right?"

"Yeah, he's going to be fine, as long as he takes it easy. That may require heavy sedation." She remained silent. They'd regressed in less than a day. She didn't chide him, didn't chuckle…just silence. "I'm only joking. We're going to take proper care of him, of course."

"I'm so sorry, Cal. If there's anything you need…"

He needed her. Turning away from Jules, he closed his eyes. "I have it under control. Thank you for calling." Now he sounded odd and formal.

Monica hesitated. "You're welcome."

There were a million things Cal wanted to say, but they weren't the words she needed to hear.

"If you change your mind, call me. Good-bye, Cal."

She hung up before he could say anything. Why had he let her walk out that door? Why hadn't he followed her? *Because you can't offer her tomorrow. You don't even know where you'll be next week.* Cal had always equated his ability to take off anywhere, at any time, with freedom. Now it just felt pointless.

He thrust the phone back at Jules and mumbled something about coffee. He could use a few minutes alone. Had Allie told her the rest of it—that he was planning on going back to Vegas? Did Monica even care? She'd called Jules, after all, not him. He had a sinking suspicion that he'd fucked up badly. The thought of never holding her again left him empty.

He made another trek to the cafeteria and brought back sandwiches and crisps. Tara placed the unopened food on a side table, but Jules nibbled on hers.

"Did you and Monica have a row or something?" she asked.

"Yeah, something," Cal answered. He glanced at the telly and pretended to watch the news.

The next few hours passed slowly. Cal made himself useful by checking in with the nurse every hour. Finally, Tara was allowed a five-minute visit.

When she returned to the waiting room, she looked ill. "He's working himself into a fuss. His blood pressure is too high." She sank down in the chair and placed one hand over her eyes. Tara relied so much on the old man, Cal didn't think she'd make it through the day without him. "He's worried about work and about Jules's upcoming court date. He simply won't lie still."

"He'll be all right, Mummy. Won't he, Cal?"

"Of course." He squeezed her shoulder. "Father will pull through this. Don't worry about court—I'll contact your attorney and see if he can postpone your appearance until next month." She gazed up at him, looking so terribly young, her brown eyes wide and searching as they met his.

"Thanks for being here. Knobface."

He leaned over and kissed her temple. "I'll go see if I can settle him down, all right?"

Cal found a young, pretty nurse, and using a hefty dose of charm while stressing his accent, Cal talked her into giving him five minutes with the old man.

Cal wasn't sure what to expect when he walked into the room. But the robust, arrogant father he knew appeared old, weak. His skin matched the white pillowcase, and his hair looked much thinner than Cal remembered. The old man's cheeks were sunken, and the tubes and wires running from his arms and chest weren't encouraging. It brought back memories of Babcock.

George Hughes was a colossal prat, no question about that. As he lay there, immobilized by the equipment attached to him, he barked at the nurse trying to take his blood pressure. He demanded to see the doctor and kept asking for his mobile. "Now, damn it. Why won't you people listen? I need my phone. Where is my phone?"

"You're not getting your phone," Cal said. "You've had a heart attack, you geezer."

George's white brows dropped so low they threatened to cover his eyes completely. "Get this man out of my room."

Cal shot the nurse a grin. "I'm the son. Lucky me, eh? I'll try and get him to behave." She unwrapped the cuff and shot him a sympathetic glance before leaving the room. "They don't like you," Cal said. "You're being a twat."

"What are you doing here? Come to dance on my grave, have you?"

"No, I'm a terrible dancer. No rhythm at all. I probably get that from your side of the family. And you're not dying. Yet. But keep it up with the yelling and the threats, and you'll be stuck here for days. Is that what you want?"

Screwing up his lips, causing deep wrinkles to pucker around his mouth, George looked out the window. "Don't know why you care. No one invited you here."

"Not strictly true. Jules asked me to come with her."

George placed his hands on the guardrails. "If you're here to suck up, you're in for a rude surprise. You're not even in the will, you know." He glanced back at Cal with an expression as icy as his tone.

Like Cal gave a toss. "And here I thought Pixie was the dramatic one. Listen, Jules has been worried sick. Tara's nerves are shot. They're worried about you. Tell me what needs to be done, and I'll take care of it."

"Why should I trust a layabout like you?"

Cal shifted his weight onto one foot. "Because you and I have something in common."

"What, our last names? I'm not even one hundred percent certain you're really mine. Your mother wasn't faithful, you know."

"Ooo, nice. Come on. Get them all out of your system." George remained quiet. "I'm talking about our fondness for Juliette."

"Am I supposed to thank you for showing up here and doing your duty?"

Cal leaned both hands on the footboard. "God, no. That would ruin our delightful dynamic. I just want you to calm down, leave work to your assistants, and get better. And do stop yelling for your mobile. It's not happening." Cal moved around the IV drip and opened the table drawer, removing a pad of paper and a pen.

"You're loving this, aren't you?" George watched Cal's movements. "Seeing me weak like this."

Cal rolled his eyes. "Not really. I don't hate you. I'm not wild about you, either, so don't go crazy."

George snorted. "The feeling's entirely mutual."

So they didn't hate each other. Not exactly a touching moment, but Cal would take it.

"See to Juliette's court date," George said. "Call my secretary and have her reschedule my appointments. Tell her to prioritize anything pressing and pass it off accordingly." He continued to rattle off a long, detailed list, and Cal wrote it down. "Did you get that? It's all important."

"I've got it." Cal stood and shoved the list in his pocket. "I promise you, I'll take care of it." He turned to leave, but George's voice made him retrace his steps.

"Calum, I might need a nurse when I get out of here. I don't want Tara taking care of me. That's not how it's meant to work. Find someone qualified. It'll put her mind at ease."

"I'll find the best nurse in Beverly Hills."

George sighed. "Perhaps you're not as useless as you look."

Cal threw back his head and laughed. "That's possibly the nicest thing you've ever said to me."

"Don't let it go to your head."

He patted his father's foot. "Get some rest."

The day had passed so slowly. Throughout the afternoon, he made tea runs and spoke three times to his father's secretary. Competent woman. Emotionless. The perfect match for George Hughes.

Now Cal stood by the window, staring down at the dark street below. Not many cars at this time of night. In the window's reflection, he watched Jules stir. She opened her eyes and rubbed her neck.

"Any news?" she asked.

"No. Why don't you let me call for your driver? You and your mother should go home and get some sleep. Real sleep. You'll feel better for it."

"No, I don't want to leave."

He understood her reluctance. Cal had never left Babcock. Not for one day. Near the end, he'd been terrified to leave her side, afraid she'd die without him there. Cal hadn't wanted to sit at her bedside, vigilant, waiting for the end. It had been agonizing, yet he'd done it. He'd held her hand in the final moments. Maybe that had given her a bit of solace. He liked to think so anyway.

Jules came to stand next to him, and he placed his arm around her shoulders. "He's going to be fine."

"He's been so stressed since my arrest," she said.

"It wasn't your fault, Jules. You heard the doctor say a lifetime of unhealthy habits was most likely the cause."

"Still, I didn't help." She flung an arm around his waist. "I've given it a lot of thought, and I'm going to plead guilty to the drink-driving charge. Take responsibility for my actions and whatnot. Monica turned her life around—so can I."

He kissed the top of her head. "Of course you can. You could rule the world, if you set your mind to it."

"Maybe I'll become world empress tomorrow. For right now, I'm going to stretch my legs a bit. Do you fancy a coffee?"

"Yes, thank you."

Jules held out her hand, palm up. "Money?"

He snagged a bill from his wallet. "I want change."

"I want bigger tits. What's your point?" She walked out of the waiting room and disappeared down a corridor.

A few minutes later, Tara stirred, and her eyes flickered open. She glanced around, then she blinked, owl-like, at Cal. "Where's Jules?" Her accent was working-class plastered over with new money and willpower, but occasionally her roots came through, like now. At first it had surprised him, his father's choice of a trophy wife, but when Cal stopped to think about it, he realized Tara's father was extremely wealthy. That made up for a lot. Even for a snob like George Hughes.

"She went for coffee."

"Thank you, Calum, for being here. I don't know what we'd have done without you today."

"Of course." Over the last twenty-one years, Cal had barely spoken more than a few dozen words to the woman. Her job as Father's wife was purely decorative, but she seemed to care deeply about the old man.

"Did you tell your mother about George?" she asked, a little too casually.

"No, not yet."

"He refuses to speak of her, you know. I've always wondered why he married her in the first place." Tara realized she'd blundered, and her cheeks burned bright. "No offense."

"None taken." Cal sat across from her. "I've often wondered the same thing. They have absolutely nothing in common."

"They have you," she said.

"You know Father's opinion of me." How Cal was

an uneducated wastrel who'd never amount to anything. He couldn't really argue with that assessment. After all, what had he contributed? Making the world a better place, one restored car at a time? Hardly life-changing.

Perhaps Monica Campbell and her charitable ways were rubbing off on him. Cal admired Monica's drive, the fact that she'd gotten her life in order when she had fallen pregnant. That one still gutted him. That she'd gone through that pain and kept it locked away inside of her. Everything made sense now—her complete transformation. He finally got it.

Tara leaned forward and shyly touched his knee. "For what it's worth, Calum, George is wrong about you. He always has been. You've got such a good heart, and you adore Juliette. It's never been my place, but I've tried to turn him around."

Cal's smile felt twisted, bitter. "No worries. Father can have his opinion. I've never let it bother me." Huh, and he'd accused Monica of being a liar. Of course it bothered him. Hurt like bloody hell.

Pix had been an unconventional mother, but she loved him utterly. Although limited in her capacity for feeling empathy, she was great fun, just not terribly useful in a crisis. Between his parents, Pix came out on top. She may have dragged him from pillar to post, but having Pixie Hughes as a mother wasn't so bad, in the scheme of things.

"I shouldn't have let Father keep me away from Jules. I'm quite mad about her, you know."

"You're not going to start crying like a little girl, are you?" Jules's voice sounded behind him. He turned to find her walking toward him, two cups of coffee in her hands. She gave one to Cal and one to her mother. "I'll go get another." She rubbed Cal's arm. "And I love you too, you giant wanker."

Paolo's pleas replayed in his mind. Seeing his father look so ill, thinking about Babcock—he should really make things right with his mum. Cal nodded to Tara and, excusing himself, walked down the hallway. He called Pixie and filled her in, giving her the details of George's condition.

"Your father is a very angry man, Cal. That's bad for the heart. And he ate too many sausages. That will do it to you, which is why I never let Paolo eat red meat."

"Sausages are pork."

"Isn't that red meat? Ham is pink, surely. What about you, are you all right, darling?"

"I'm fine, Mum."

"Please give Jules a hug for me. I'm terribly sorry the two of you are going through this, and you have my deepest sympathies." She sounded like a greeting card, but Cal knew it was her attempt at showing concern.

"Will do. I love you, Mum."

"And I, you. Call me if you need anything at all. Anything, Calum, I'm quite serious." He didn't know what she could possibly do, but at least she made an effort.

He felt better, having made his peace with her. Now if he could make things right with Monica. He missed her terribly, but what was he meant to do? Despite her wild, impulsive nature, Monica Campbell was a forever kind of woman, and Cal didn't make promises he couldn't keep.

Chapter 22

WORKERS AND MOVERS AND CATERERS SWARMED through the garden. They nearly careened into one another as they furnished three tents, strung thousands of lights, hammered on a dais for the string quartet. The gala would be much less formal than the event Allie had originally planned. Monica couldn't believe they'd pulled it off in less than two weeks. So why couldn't she muster some sort of pride or satisfaction?

Monica ran a hand over her tired eyes. She hadn't been sleeping. She'd been living at the mansion, not only because it was convenient, but because she didn't want to lie in her own bed. The last time she used it, she'd been with Cal. He seemed to be all she could think about. Her days were miserable, her nights unbearable. Monica had made a mistake, breaking it off with him. A terrible, painful mistake.

"Things are coming together." Allie stood next to her, the ever-present binder in her arms. She'd morphed into a bossy, busty general, ordering everyone around the garden and making sure all would be perfect for the big night. She was totally in her element.

"Yep," Monica said. "Looking good."

Allie gazed at Monica's profile, but Monica avoided eye contact. Seeing her sister's compassion only made her feel worse.

"Mon, I say this with love—you look like shit."

"Thank you," she said, keeping her eyes on the men carefully threading lights through the rosebushes. "And I say this with all due respect—fuck off."

"Still surly, I see. Do you have a dress yet?"

She turned to Allie. "Can you just beat me to death with that binder so we don't have to have this conversation again? I'm wearing something from last year. It's fine."

Instead of snapping a retort, she rubbed Monica's shoulder. That damn compassion again. "Go get some rest, Mon. We have this thing under control."

Monica cleared her throat and looked away. She couldn't rest, and yet, she was exhausted. Not just from all the work or the sleepless nights—she was exhausted from grief. How was she supposed to get over Calum Hughes? The man had driven back into her life with that shitty Mustang. He'd told her about cities she'd never heard of, he'd called her out on her bullshit, and he'd made love to her like it meant something. Now Monica was nothing more than a puddle of useless, gooey sorrow.

"Seriously," Al said. "Go take a break."

Monica nodded and dodged men moving tables as she made her way to the house. Pandemonium ruled in here too, with florists and cleaners bustling through the hallways.

She took the stairs two at a time. No one was allowed up here—Trevor's orders. He was very put out with strangers fucking up his routine. His words. Repeated often.

Monica didn't want to go back to her guest room. She'd spent hours on that bed, tossing and turning, miserable without Cal.

She darted into the salon instead. It was her favorite part of the house and overlooked the garden. She stood at the window, watching everyone come and go. And felt completely alone.

When the door opened, Monica turned to see Trevor enter. A pained look crossed his face as he glanced at her. He advanced farther into the room and withdrew a handkerchief from his jacket's inner pocket. "Here. Mop up."

Monica touched her cheek. Shit. She'd been crying again. When was this going to stop? She used to be so strong. *Closed off*. Maybe, but closed off was a lot less humiliating than this. "Thanks."

Trevor stalked to the booze cart and poured two measures of alcohol. As she sniffled and wiped her eyes, he walked back and handed her a tumbler. "Drink that." He sank down on the sofa and sipped his own.

"What is it?"

"Brandy. Now, what's got you all wobbly?"

"Don't want to talk about it." She took a sip, and it went down smooth. "Is this old?"

"Older than you and I put together. Now talk. Or you'll force me to fetch Allison, and neither one of us wants that. She'll smother you, and she'll put me to work."

Monica shuffled to the opposite tufted Chesterfield and flopped down. "I'm just…you know." She shrugged.

"Ah, of course. Now it's all so clear."

She took another sip, enjoying the alcohol scorching a path down her throat. "Cal."

"Quite."

"I love him. Like, head-over-ass love."

"Mmm. My condolences."

She glanced at him, took in his tailored suit, the blue silk tie. He and Cal couldn't be more different. "I broke it off with him."

"Yes, Allie said as much."

She sipped her brandy and began to loosen up. She hadn't been eating, and the alcohol hit her quickly.

"Does he love you?" Trevor gazed at her through cool gray eyes, studied her like she was one of his silver saltshakers in the glass case downstairs—with impersonal, mild interest.

"I know he cares about me. Or he did. But I haven't heard from him in days."

"Cal had a rather unconventional upbringing."

"I know that."

He raised one brow. "Do you? Then you know his father's never shown an ounce of affection. Pixie is… well, Pixie. Anything that doesn't affect her directly doesn't hold her attention for long. Cal was mostly left to his own devices."

"He had Babcock."

"Know about her, do you?" He paused with his glass halfway to his lips.

"Yeah. He was with her until the end. He's a good guy. But he doesn't stick around."

"And you want what, true love conquering all"—he motioned with one finger—"happily ever after, and all that rubbish?"

Monica leaned forward. "Watch yourself. You sound a little cynical there, Trev. Since you're married to my sister, that's not reassuring."

"I'm cynical about everyone else, never Allison." His eyes turned to ice. "She's a fucking miraculous aberration. But we're not talking about her. We're talking about you. What if Cal can't promise forever? You're obviously miserable without him. But you've been miserable for years, so what else is new?"

She opened her mouth to protest, but what for? "I'm quitting the foundation." She swallowed the rest of the brandy in one gulp and began coughing as Trevor watched.

"Good," he said, once she finally stopped. "I'm not one to give advice, and God knows I'm not one to take it, but that job is not right for you. You and Allison could use some distance." He stood, drained his glass, and rebuttoned his jacket. "I guess you can make up your own mind about Cal, but he did stress that he'd be back."

"What?"

"When he left for L.A., he said, *if anyone asks, I'm coming back*. Perhaps that was meant for you. You've always been an all-or-nothing person. Maybe there's room in your life for a little compromise?" He strode to the door and left her sitting alone.

Compromise. Balance. Yeah, she could use some of that. And if she was this miserable without Cal, maybe she could take him on his own terms. Seeing him in intervals...maybe that would be enough. She could make it be enough.

~

Cal threw down the wrench and wiped his hands on a plush white rag—a monogrammed rag that used to be a hand towel in its former life. In the last few days, he'd performed tune-ups and changed the oil in the Bentley, the Rolls, the Mercedes coupe, and the Range

Rover. There was nothing left for him to do. Not a bloody thing—unless he wanted to tear each car apart and rebuild them, piece by piece. It might very well come to that. He'd never been so…not bored. Restless? Agitated? Yes, all those things, but the root cause felt more like hopelessness.

Cal had become a shell of a person, walking around this vast, stupid estate—listless, with nothing to do but think. All the sunshine, the mild weather—it should have recharged him. Instead, it had the opposite effect.

He bent down and shut the toolbox—if one could call it that. After his father came home, Cal had gone out and bought the basics. George didn't own so much as a screwdriver, let alone a torque wrench. Cars were Cal's therapy, but unfortunately, even that wasn't working right now. But really, what else was there? Play tennis? Swim? Sun himself by the pool? How did Jules stand it out here? Los Angeles held no appeal for him. At least in Vegas he could buy his way into a game of poker or work on the Mustang.

And be close to Monica.

Right. That. She was the reason this horrible, morose feeling had taken him over. How he missed her. Her smile, her scent, her plump upper lip.

Shit. He'd made a pact with himself. No thinking about Monica. No sense in dwelling on what he couldn't have.

Cal walked out of the garage and stared up at the sky, where white clouds resembling cotton wool drifted to the east. Lowering his head, he glanced at the vibrant garden Tara had planted at the back of the house. Gardens reminded him of Monica. Cal ground his teeth. God, if only he could think about something else. Anything else. But memories of her—her soft, pale skin, her lavender-scented hair, her infectious laughter—flooded his brain every other goddamned minute.

Grabbing the keys to the Range Rover, he stalked back to the garage. He needed to get out. Go for a drive. Somewhere. Anywhere. He simply couldn't stay locked up one more minute.

Cal started the engine and circled 'round to the front of the house. His father got a little better day by day. He'd be able to go back to work in a few weeks. Cal would be free then. Able to jet off to Budapest or spend the winter in Key West.

Oh, who was he kidding? There was only one place Cal wanted to visit. *Visit*. That was the problem. Monica wanted something much more permanent than the occasional meet up. She didn't want him on a part-time basis. She'd made that clear. So why didn't his brain get the message?

When his phone vibrated, Cal's heart began to pound. It did every bloody time, and it was never her. He glanced at the screen. His father. Again.

"Yes?"

"Come upstairs." Then he rang off. No explanation. He didn't ask; he commanded. And Cal obeyed. He didn't want to be the one to send the old man back to hospital.

Slamming the car in reverse, he drove to the garage and climbed out. He was trapped here. Like an animal in a zoo. *Like Monica in her office*.

Cal rubbed the bridge of his nose. He really needed to think about something else. A '72 Iso Fidia—a car he'd dreamed about since he was sixteen. He could dwell on that rather than Monica's voice and her fuzzy steering-wheel cover, and the way she made him breathless every time she walked into a room. *So stop already, you wanker*. If only it were that easy.

Cal strode inside the house. The air felt cool and smelled a bit stale. He took the curving stairway to the second floor and down the long, wide hall to his father's bedroom. George had been ensconced in there for nearly two weeks and was chomping at the bit to get back to work.

The household had descended into chaos when George first got home. Cal had caught him on three separate occasions looking over stock profiles. The man couldn't stop himself, and as a result, his blood pressure was still far too high. But the old man eventually made a bargain with Cal. George could talk to his secretary for ten minutes each day, if he agreed to stop disrupting the staff's schedule and quit hounding Tara about every domestic decision. That seemed to do the trick.

Cal stood in the doorway. "You rang?"

George waved him in. "Yes, come. Sit. I want to show you something, and I think you'll be pleased."

Doubtful. George held out a folder, his expression rather smug.

"What is it?" Cal asked.

"I said sit down. Read it for yourself. Your mother did teach you how to do that much, didn't she?"

Suppressing a sigh, Cal moved to a bedside chair and lowered himself. He stretched out his legs and crossed one boot over the other. Then he snatched the folder and skimmed the first page. Irritated, he lifted his gaze to his father and shook his head. "No. This is not happening."

"You haven't even read the bloody thing."

"I don't want to be in your will. Give it all to Tara and Jules." He tossed the file on his father's legs.

The nurse, dressed in plain blue scrubs, walked into the room. "Time to take your vitals," she said in a singsong voice.

"Woman, can you not see that I'm busy right now? Come back later."

This one was older and less nervous than the previous five. She ignored the old man by grabbing his wrist and studying her watch. George tried to pull out of her grasp, but she held on tight.

He snarled at her, then turned his focus back to Cal. "Look, I can admit when I'm wrong. Fortunately, it doesn't happen often. But you've been here for Tara and Juliette, and I'd like to show my appreciation. It's merely a token."

"Send me a fruit basket. I don't need your money, and I don't want it."

George rolled his eyes, and as the nurse attempted to wrap the blood pressure cuff around his arm, he slapped her hand. "Get away from me. I'm trying to have a conversation here."

Cal glanced up at her and smiled. "Can you give us five?"

She shot George a hateful glance. "I'll give you ten." She marched out of the room, mumbling under her breath.

"Making friends wherever you go," Cal said.

"I pay people. I don't need friends. So what are you going to do with yourself after all this?"

"I don't know, really." Without Monica, Cal felt worse than when he'd stayed in Cairns, puttering around the beach all day. He felt rudderless. Lost without her.

"You could stay in California," George said. "It's not too bad, you know. Perhaps we could find something useful for you to do, rather than play with cars all day."

When Cal was eighteen, he would have loved to hear that sentiment—if not those exact words—from his father. But Cal had made his own way in the world, was respected in his field. The old man might not understand that, but it didn't matter. Calum knew who he was. "No thanks. I'm glad you're feeling better, Father." Still pale, George appeared older and frailer than his years. That disapproving man from Cal's memories had now become less of an ogre and more human.

"Suit yourself. I was only trying to do the right thing. Now take this file on your way out."

Cal left the room, tipping his head to the nurse in the hallway. Downstairs in the pink floral living room, he found Jules.

"I thought he looked better today," she said. "Is he still being an ass to the nurse?"

"As ever." He sat and tossed the file on the coffee table. He sighed heavily and glanced at the roses in varying shades of pink and white in a small glass vase.

"God, I'm tired of hearing that," Jules said.

Cal glanced up at her. "What?"

"You, sighing constantly. Like a leaky tire. Have you called her?"

Not wanting to talk about Monica, he stood, retrieved the folder, and headed to Father's study. Jules padded after him.

"Have you?"

"It's none of your fucking business, Jules. Leave it." Cal had never spoken so harshly to his sister. He turned, and another sigh escaped him. Damn, she was right. "I'm sorry. I don't want to talk about it."

"No shit. But it might help, you know. Instead of moping around here all day, like some brooding, wet bloke. You've lost weight. You can't sit still. You're bloody miserable. You're in love with her."

Cal stopped at Jules's words. "No, I'm not. What nonsense. Two grown people can share admiration and mutual respect. That's all it was."

"Uh-huh." Jules crossed her arms. "So you don't miss her?"

Of course he missed her. She was vital, like sunshine or fresh air. "It's complicated, Jules. At your age, I don't expect you to understand it."

She laughed then. "My age? Monica's only five years older than I am. I'm not a child, and I can see how you're pining away for her."

"You've been watching too many romantic movies," he accused. He turned around and continued walking. *Pining*. What a word. Yes, he craved Monica. Longed to feel her touch again. Catch a glimpse of her lovely face. He needed her. Desperately.

Oh God, he'd been *pining*.

When he stopped again, Jules ran into his back. "Ow. Why can't you just admit the truth? You're in love with Monica Campbell."

Just hearing her name caused his chest to swell, his pulse to race. Could it be? What else would explain this ennui, this feeling of utter, dismal hopelessness?

Bloody fucking hell. Yes. That's what this horrible,

gut-churning feeling he carried around day and night was about—love. He'd never felt this way before, tied up in knots and unable to think about anything except her. He'd been too foolish to recognize it.

The poets and songwriters had their heads firmly up their asses. There was nothing glorious or transformative about this feeling. It was anguish, pure and simple. "I'm in love."

"I know." Jules walked around him and parked in his path. "You get this dopey expression every time I mention her, and the rest of the time, you're quite stroppy."

Of course he was stroppy. He hadn't been with Monica in almost two weeks. And it wasn't just the sex, it was the companionship and hearing details about her day. Holding her in his arms at night. "I'm in love. God, this is wretched."

"It doesn't have to be."

"It does, actually. She wants nothing to do with me." He moved around her and walked into the formally appointed office. He threw the folder on the mahogany desk. When he pivoted, Jules stood right in front of him, gazing up at him with eyes coated in purple eye shadow. "Leave me alone, brat. I can't take it today."

"Why did she break it off with you? Were you mean to her?"

"No, I wasn't mean." He'd begged her to stay. Memories of their last conversation haunted him. Cal had insisted he couldn't promise forever. He rubbed his forehead. Forever with Monica Campbell. That sounded like nirvana, but it was impossible.

She had a job—she couldn't just pack up and leave whenever she wanted. *She hates that job*. Even so, he couldn't expect her to traipse after him. And Cal had been a complete fool to think a long-distance relationship between them could work. How could he hie off to Caracas and leave her behind? The very idea was ridiculous.

Pocketing his hands, he gazed down at Jules. "I don't have anything to offer her. I don't have a regular job or a proper home or anything resembling stability."

"So get all those things. What else have you got going on? A very busy surfing schedule?"

"If Monica cared about me, she'd have called. She's the one who broke it off."

Jules laughed so hard she snorted. "You're such a twat. She's waiting for you to make the grand gesture."

Cal kicked out at a chair leg as he stalked to the bookcases. First editions, lined up neatly. "She said not to contact her. Not to send gifts. She clearly doesn't care about me."

"Oh, Brother. You and your lame gifts."

Now that was just insulting. He jerked his hands from his pockets and shook a finger at her. "I put a lot of thought into every gift I sent you, Juliette. Besides, I travel, and Monica doesn't want a long-distance situation. She was very clear about it."

"Take her with you."

Cal paced to the door, thrusting his hands in his hair. Monica wanted to travel more than anything. Still, that job represented commitment to her family, to her mother's memory. She wouldn't walk away from it, not even for Paris.

"You're scared," she said.

Terrified, more like. Afraid Monica would throw his offer right back in his face. But even if she never agreed to take him back, Jules was right—he had to try. "A grand gesture, eh?" What kind of grand gesture would impress Monica Campbell?

George's health was relatively stable—he had the best nurses and doctors at his disposal. Jules's court date had been rescheduled. Cal had time to fly to Vegas, but how was he supposed to win her over? Monica wasn't impressed with money or status. What could he possibly give her that she didn't already have?

Chapter 23

Monica looked out over the party. Enormous tents lit by hidden spotlights and swathed in fabric dotted the garden like mushrooms. Every tree branch and bush had been wrapped in lights. Classical music played softly in the background. Portable heaters were scattered throughout, in case it got chilly.

People seemed to be enjoying themselves as they wandered around the garden, noting the trellises and fountains, the grotto and the waterfall swimming pool. Low chatter filled the air. The evening was warm, inviting…magical. The only thing missing was Cal.

But Monica had come to a decision yesterday. As soon as the party was over, she would head to L.A. She'd already booked her flight. She had an overnight bag packed and waiting in the guest room. Someone had to make the first move, right?

Maybe having it all wasn't a realistic expectation, not with someone like Cal. But Monica loved him enough that she'd take whatever time she could get with him.

"We did it," Allie whispered in her ear.

Monica turned to find her sister standing next to her, holding two glasses of champagne. Trevor stood behind Allie, tall and foreboding as his cool gaze took in the sight.

"Good God, what happened to my garden?"

Allie slapped the back of her hand against his chest.

"We'll put it back the way we found it." She wore an off-the-shoulder light blue dress with lots of sparkles. When she handed Monica one of the glasses, Allie's eyes widened. "You broke down and got a new dress? You look beautiful."

Monica glanced down at her cleavage. "Is it too much?" She'd gone shopping last night, dragging Evan along for a second opinion. The fire-engine-red dress immediately made her think of Cal. Amazingly, it fit her without any alterations. Tight and strapless, it flared out at her knees, mermaid style. The price tag nearly made her pass out, but she had to have it. Besides, Monica couldn't remember the last time she'd worn anything this formfitting. At least that's how she justified the expense.

Allie pursed her lips as her eyes scanned Monica. "I'd say it's just enough. But you're not going to be able to hide in a corner tonight."

"Yeah, I'm tired of hiding. It's boring." She sipped the champagne and took in a deep breath. The sweet smell of roses wafted on the air and mixed with the rich smell of meat coming from one of the tents. "I'm not sure how we pulled this off, but it's better than the ballroom."

"It is lovely," Trevor said. "Although having my privacy invaded by all these people is tiresome. You're going to have to make it up to me in some creative way, Allison."

Allie reached up and kissed his jaw. "I can do creative," she almost purred.

"Oh God, you two. Gross." Monica looked away.

"We're a good team, Monnie," Allie said. "Sure you want to quit?"

"I'm sure." Monica had never been more sure of

anything. She'd put together a job description for her replacement, and at night, when she couldn't sleep, Monica had revised her own résumé. She hoped she'd find something that suited her, where she could deal with real people instead of numbers.

Now Monica needed to get her personal life on track. What if she showed up in L.A. and Cal didn't want to see her? Her stomach lurched. If he didn't care for her, at least she'd know. She wouldn't spend the rest of her life wondering about what-ifs. From now on, Monica planned on following her heart.

Her dad, Brian, and his wife, Karen, stepped out of the house and onto the terrace. As they made their way over, their eyes flickered around the garden. They'd just flown in from Texas the night before and hadn't seen all the work that had gone into the transformation.

"Hey, Dad." Monica hugged him, then kissed Karen's cheek. "I'm glad you guys made it."

"We wouldn't have missed it," Karen said. Dressed in a conservative silver gown, Monica's stepmother looked lovely. Over the years, she'd grown on Monica, and Brian loved her to distraction. That had been hard on Monica at first, but she'd come to terms with it.

"Girls." Brian cleared his throat. "This is so nice. Your mom would have loved this."

"She would have told us not to make such a fuss, but I think she'd have been pleased," Allie said. "In about ten minutes, I'm going to give my speech, and then I'll bring you up on stage to say a few words, Mon."

Monica nodded. "Sure."

Brynn walked toward them and cast a glance over her shoulder. She wore a long ivory dress. More Renaissance

Faire than charity fund-raiser, but she looked pretty. "Hey, Trev, do you know that guy? The really tall one?"

He flicked a glance over her head. "Never seen him before."

Allie craned her neck to look past Brynn's shoulder. "The beefy guy staring at your ass?"

Brynn's cheeks turned red. "Yeah."

"I've never seen him before either," Allie said.

Monica tried to be a little more subtle, but the man's gaze was unwavering. "Nope, but he's cute. You should stop long enough to let him catch you."

Brynn shook her head. "He's not my type."

Trevor buttoned his suit jacket. "I'll go speak to him at once and tell him to keep his eyes in his fucking head."

Brynn grabbed his arm. "No, don't. I'm going to lose myself in the crowd." She glanced at Monica. "Looks great. Good job." Then she slipped away and melted into the shadows.

Out of the corner of her eye, Monica spotted Evan. How could she miss him in that bright blue jacket? She crossed the garden and stood next to him. He'd nabbed a handful of canapés and couldn't shove them in his mouth fast enough.

When she reached him, he leaned down and brushed a kiss on her cheek. "You look good in that dress. Very fuckable."

Monica raised one brow. "That's the look I was going for. At the gala in my *mother's honor*."

"Sorry, I call 'em like I see 'em." He snared a champagne flute from a passing waiter. "I think your dad's wedding was the last time I was here."

"Yeah, I wanted to thank you for the garden idea. You're a genius."

"You're just now figuring that out? I've been telling you that for years."

Monica briefly rested her head on his shoulder. "I also wanted to thank you for telling me the truth about my sad life. I kind of love you. Like a brother, so don't get all creepy."

"Is one of us dying?" he asked. "Because otherwise, this shit's getting uncomfortable."

She glanced up at him. "Always with the jokes. I'm going to L.A. tonight. I'm going to put my heart on the line, Ev. I'm so scared, I can't even think straight."

He gazed down at her, his expression serious for a change. "That sounds potentially disastrous or very exciting."

"I know."

He squeezed her shoulder. "Good luck. Call me tomorrow. Let me know how it goes. And Monnie, if you need me to come to L.A., I'll be on the next plane."

"I was hoping you'd say that."

"You know I'm always here. Like Batman and Robin, kid."

Monica nodded at the girl near the bar who licked her hand, knocked back a shot, and sucked on a lime wedge. Nowhere in nature did skin appear that shade of orange. "I assume that's your date."

"Of course. Speaking of which, that was her fourth tequila shot. I need to stop a train wreck. Break a leg with the speech."

Monica gave him a hug before returning to her family.

"Okay," Allie said, blowing out a breath. "Speech time. Wish me luck." She handed her glass off to Trevor.

He kissed her temple. "You'll be marvelous, darling. You always are."

Allie wended through groupings of people, stopping to chat on her way to the podium. When she stepped up on the dais, the music stopped, and she tapped on the microphone. "Thank you for coming tonight."

As everyone clapped, Monica made her way forward. She wasn't a big fan of speaking in public. But all she had to do was give a simple thank-you to the staff and the board, and it would be over. Her gaze bounced off Marcus Stanford and his busty wife. Perhaps Mrs. Stanford should be less concerned about junk food and more concerned about injecting toxins into her blank face. *Ouch*. That was bitchy. Monica put it down to nerves.

Allie rambled on a bit too long, then she announced Monica. Holding up the hem of her dress, Monica climbed the steps, hoping she wouldn't fall.

Allie smiled and handed her the mic. As Monica stared at the crowd—Vegas's richest and a few infamous—she blanked. Her mind stopped working. She stood, statue-like, for at least a full minute, maybe more.

When Monica said nothing, murmurs broke out over the crowd. This had never happened to her. She opened her mouth to speak, but nothing came out. Monica stared out at a sea of faces and remained silent.

Evan raised his brows. Trevor lowered his. Marcus Stanford smirked.

Out of desperation, Monica said the first thing that popped into her head. "Patricia Campbell isn't a statistic."

The murmurs stopped and everyone became silent, waiting.

Monica cleared her throat. "We talk about survivors

and victims of the disease. Well, my mom wasn't a victim." She took a deep breath, unsure of what to say next. So she decided to go with the truth for a change. "She was a fighter. Cancer didn't define who she was. My mom laughed too loud and liked hair metal bands. She had this wicked, biting sense of humor. And she fought to live, from the day she was diagnosed until the day she died.

"She believed in me, when I didn't believe in myself. My mom was my best friend, and I still miss her. I want to thank you all for being here tonight, and for honoring her memory with your donations. Thank you so much."

Monica was about to lose it. She shoved the mic back in Allie's hand, who looked as surprised as Monica felt. But she also felt free. Free of the guilt she'd carried around for so long. Her mom loved her. She wouldn't have held Monica's stupid decisions against her. Why had it taken her so long to realize it? Patricia Campbell wasn't a saint, but she'd been an amazing woman.

Monica hustled to the steps, intent on getting the hell out of there. She wanted Cal's arms more than ever. She took strength from him; she felt cherished when he held her tight. Monica only hoped like hell it wasn't too late to win him back.

She was brilliant, his Monica. Cal was proud of her. His brave girl spoke about her mother in public, and looked lovely doing it.

That dark scarlet dress was made for her. The silk hugged her curves and outlined those stunning breasts. In the back, it clung to her ass, accentuated it. No more

Miss Prim. The dress was as bold a statement as that speech had been. Monica wasn't hiding anymore.

She kept her head lowered, her steps quick as she sped to the back of the garden. Cal followed her. When she almost reached the pond, he grabbed her hand, pulling her to a stop.

With a gasp, she twirled around and gazed up at him with wide eyes. "Oh my God. Cal, what are you doing here? I thought you were in California."

He smiled. "They have these amazing contraptions called planes. I know how we left things, but I had to be here. This was your big night. You were fucking awesome up there." Cal couldn't remember being this anxious. This hopeful. He wanted to touch her, but refrained. She might have changed her mind about him. She may not want forever. She may have washed her hands of him completely. God, he hoped not.

"Thanks." Monica tucked her hair behind one ear. "I can't believe you came. And you're wearing a tux."

"Only for you. So, am I a good surprise or a bad one?"

"Good."

Thank God. "That was an incredible speech. Was it hard, talking about your mum?"

"Very. I didn't plan it." She placed a hand in the center of his chest. "Cal—" She glanced around, nodded to a few gawkers. "Let's go somewhere private." She took his hand and led him to the back wall.

He had to tell her how he felt, right now, before he lost his nerve. "Listen, I know I've been an idiot, but I'm in love with you. Have been all along, but I was too blind to see it. Now, I know you may not feel the same way, and you're perfectly justified. But I only just realized I love you, so in my defense, I think you should give me another chance."

As she turned to face him, Monica's lips quivered slightly. "You're in love with me?"

"I am. I missed you, darling. So terribly."

"I missed you too. Like crazy."

He placed his hands on her waist. "Truly?"

"Truly. I love you too."

Now Cal smiled as well. "Say it again."

"I love you, Calum George Hughes."

He stepped closer, wrapping his arms around her. "You look so beautiful, I'm almost afraid to touch you."

"Trust me, I won't break."

He swept her into his arms, kissing her tenderly. God, he'd missed her. Her sweet smell, her honey-blond hair—which was swept to one side tonight, making her look like a glamorous movie star from a bygone era. Cal had never seen a sight more beautiful than Monica Campbell.

She pushed at his shoulders until he lifted his head, but he didn't loosen his hold. "I texted Jules every day and got updates on your dad."

"Did you? That little monster never said a word." He shook his head. "I don't want to talk about either one of them right now." She felt good in his arms, and he planned on never letting her go again. "You wore red."

"It made me think of you. I was going to fly to L.A. tonight."

His fingers stopped moving across her hips. "Were you? To see me?"

"Yeah. I quit my job, and I wanted to tell you in person."

"How do you feel about it? That job meant everything to you."

She played with the studs on his shirt. "No, you mean everything."

Cal touched her cheek, drifted his fingers along her jawline. "I don't deserve you. You're so lovely and clever. You're out of my league, in every respect."

"That's not true at all. I know you won't stay forever." Cal opened his mouth to stop her, but she kept going. "I'm not asking for a lifetime."

"Darling, stop."

"I'm not making any demands. And I'm not sure how it will work, but I want to be with you. I love you." Her words ran together in a jumble. "Because if you—"

"Monica, stop talking, please. I have something important to say too."

Monica's mouth snapped shut. For all of two seconds. "I finally tell you I'm ready to accept your terms, and you tell me to be quiet?"

He pressed a finger over her lips. "Monica Taylor Campbell, I'm not going anywhere without you. Ever. You are it for me. Home is where you are. I promise you this—wherever you are, that's where I'll be. And you know I always keep my promises."

Monica tapped his finger out of the way and, grabbing his face with both hands, brought it down to hers. "Say it again," she murmured against his lips.

"I love you." He walked her back several yards, until she bumped into the garden wall. This was where they'd had their first kiss five years ago. Full circle, red dress and all. There were no lights here, and the music and chatter seemed distant.

He lowered his head, and when his lips touched hers, Cal's hands roamed over her, latching onto her ass. He rained tiny kisses across her lips, her dimpled chin, her cheeks. "We never did get our garden shag," he whispered against her ear.

"Forget it."

"I'm still registered at the villa." He continued nibbling her neck, her shoulder. He couldn't stop touching her. "How about we head there after the party?"

"Deal," she said. "And by the way, you're not going to be able to move by the time I get done with you, Calum Hughes."

"Do not tease me," he said against the swell of her breast.

"I'm not sure which to do first—fuck you, suck you, or ride you like a mechanical bull."

He raised his head. "Oh *yes*, giddy up. We can stop on the way, and I'll buy you a cowgirl hat."

When she laughed, it sounded divine. This was his Monica—wild and untamed, sexy and secure. He kissed her again, and when Monica spread her hands over his chest, it felt so right. Yes. This was where he belonged.

Before he could get too carried away, Monica pushed him and ended the kiss. "I should get back to the party. And Brynn will want to see you. If we can find her. You know how she hates crowds."

Cal cupped her face with both hands. "First, I have something to show you, but I don't know if you can get a proper look at it out here."

"I've seen it before. It's impressive."

Letting go of her, he laughed and reached into his jacket, pulling out a thin stack of pamphlets. Then he grabbed his phone and turned it on, using it as a flashlight so she could see them.

"What are these?" She glanced up at him. "Imaging machines?"

"More compact than a regular machine, and they use less power. I bought three of them."

"Why?"

"Well, if you hadn't come to your senses, I was going to bribe you."

"With medical equipment?"

"Exactly. Two women's clinics in Africa and one in India need these desperately. I thought you might like to deliver them in person."

Monica gasped, covering her mouth with one hand. She stared up at him with wide eyes. "You bought imaging machines."

"Yes, I did. I thought they'd make a smashing wedding gift. You *are* going to make an honest man of me, aren't you?"

"You're the most honest man I know. You're it for me too."

"I know how important your family is to you. We can stay here in Vegas, if you'd like, and buy a house nearby."

"I want to travel, Cal. I want you to show me the world. Can we start with Paris? No wait, London. I want to see your garage."

"Anywhere, it doesn't matter. As long as I'm with you."

Keep reading for a sneak peek at the next book in the Beauty and the Brit series

HIS TO KEEP

IAIN CHAPMAN LISTENED AS HIS LAWYER EXPLAINED about the new economic regulations, zoning details, and ecological classifications that had just been enacted. But as Stan droned on, Iain became more agitated. "For fuck's sake, Stan, cut to the chase and tell me how all this is going impact the land we want to develop. Preferably in English." Iain couldn't take one more acronym. NEDA, CDBG, SBA, USGS. It was giving him a bloody headache, it was. In his right hand, he rubbed a pair of red dice back and forth. It was a habit Iain had acquired over the years, one he couldn't seem to shake.

Stan Daniels sighed deeply. He seemed to do that a lot around Iain—who had probably paid for the three-thousand-dollar suit the prat was wearing. So he could save his sighs for other clients, because Iain wasn't having it.

"Cut the drama, mate. Just give me the highlights already."

"Let the man talk, Iain. It's why we're paying him,

innit?" From the window overlooking the busy street, Marcus Atwell turned to face them, all the while stroking his chin—a sure sign he was worried. But that was nothing new. It was when Marc started playing with his floppy hair that Iain knew real trouble was brewing.

"What this means," Stan said, "is you'll pay more in taxes, shell out more for inspections, and have to jump through more governmental regulation hoops. Get used to it."

"How much more are we talking about here?" Iain asked.

"A couple million, give or take."

Iain pushed back his chair and stood, pocketing the dice as he walked across the room. "That sounds like pocket change to you, does it?" Stan came from money and had gone to a fancy Ivy League school. Probably grew up using hundred-dollar bills to wipe his privileged ass.

"Do we really have to do this today?" Stan asked. "It's pocket change to you too, Iain. You have a multimillion-dollar project you want to implement. This is a drop in the bucket."

"He's right, Iain," Marc said. "We're not the poor lads from Manchester anymore. It's all a matter of perspective."

At the credenza in the corner, Iain poured coffee from an antique silver pot. Drinking from the delicate china cups always made him feel faintly ridiculous, but it added to the traditional British decor. No sense in having four-thousand-dollar Chippendale chairs only to drink from a cheap ceramic mug. Presentation was important. And two million really wasn't much in the bigger scheme of things, but he didn't take any of it for granted. Not a bloody penny.

"Send us copies detailing the changes, and cc my project manager, yeah?" Iain sipped his coffee—strong, black, bitter. He glanced over at Stan. "Was there something else? I'm getting billed for every moment you stand there looking like a twat."

The bald man smiled. "I don't charge for looking like a twat. That one's on the house." He bent to pick up his briefcase. "Always a pleasure, Iain."

"Fuck off."

"Nice seeing you, too." Stan nodded at both men and left the room.

Once he was gone, Marc paced the floor. "She's coming this morning?"

"Yeah. Should be here in a few."

"We don't need to do this," Marc said. "There are other investors. We could develop the properties slowly, take our time."

"And we may have to," Iain said with a shrug, "if this doesn't pan out."

"It probably won't. Brynn Campbell might hate you on sight—and I wouldn't blame her, because you're a bit of a blighter, truth be told. And if she finds out you set her up, she could turn Trevor Blake against us."

"It'll work, trust me. Hiring Brynn's firm is a stroke of genius. We need a fresh partner for this project. One with deep pockets. Who better than Trevor Blake? And if we're really lucky, Brynn's other brother-in-law, Cal Hughes, might throw in with us. Those two have loads to spare, good business sense, and Trevor's name carries weight in this town. I went over every other angle I could think of, and Brynn Campbell is the weak link."

"It feels wrong, using this girl to get to her relatives. Seedy, yeah?"

"It's called networking," Iain said. "No different than

glad-handing at a cocktail party or going to a charity dinner in order to meet serious players. It's just business."

Marc stopped treading over the hand-loomed rug. "Whilst I'm not convinced that this is our best solution, the course she's teaching might actually do you some good. Your leadership skills are a bit lacking, aren't they?"

Iain paused, the cup midway to his lips. "What the bloody hell are you on about?" Iain was leadership personified. He had the portfolio and bank balance to prove it. "There's nothing wrong with the way I lead, mate. I get results."

"You do," Marc agreed. "But you also hack off a lot of people. And those you don't offend are scared shitless of you."

"Good." He didn't give a damn if people feared him, as long as they did their jobs properly. This wasn't a popularity contest. No one got a prize for congeniality. "If they don't like working here, they're free to quit."

"Which explains our high turnover rate. You could stand to be a little nicer to people. Wouldn't kill you none, would it?"

"I expect people to show up and do their jobs. In return, we pay them very well at the end of each week. I'm not their mate. End of."

"The accounting department nearly piss themselves every time you walk into the room," Marc said.

"And?" Nothing wrong with that. At least his employees respected him.

"My gran used to say you catch more flies with honey than with vinegar."

"That's daft, it is. Why would I want to catch flies?" Strolling to his chair, Iain carefully set the cup and saucer on his desk, then tugged on the bottom of his waistcoat before resuming his seat. "This scheme is going to work. Brynn Campbell will give me a pointless lesson, I'll be charming, she'll be charmed, and in turn, I'll ask her for an introduction to Trevor Blake. In the meantime, you make sure our proposal is sorted, yeah?"

"I'm on it, but I still say your management style could use an overhaul."

"Bugger off. By the way, how's Melanie? Haven't seen her in weeks."

"Fine." Marc combed his fingers through his hair, leaving it more disheveled than before. "Things are fine."

Something was definitely going on there, but if Marc didn't want to talk about it, Iain wouldn't pry. None of his concern, as long as it didn't interfere with business. "We can't afford to have you distracted right now. I need you focused on this project."

Marc's blue eyes turned glacial. "Since when have I ever cocked-up on a project? I'll do my bit, you do your part. But if we're relying on your *charm*, we could be in real trouble."

"Funny," Iain said to Marc's retreating back. The door shut with a click behind him.

Management training nonsense—Iain couldn't think of anything more useless. And his *management style* didn't need an overhaul. He and Marc had built this company from nothing, in spite of a crap economy. Fine, Iain was sometimes harsh with his employees, but if they couldn't handle it, they probably didn't belong here. Besides, he didn't get his jollies from being cruel. Everything he did, every decision he made, was for the benefit of Blue Moon.

A few moments later, Amelia knocked on the door

and slipped into the room. "Iain, your appointment's here." Ames was a lovely woman—professional-looking in a conservative black dress. No one would ever guess that they'd met in a strip club.

Iain had been a bouncer, Ames a bartender. When the business started taking off, he'd brought her onboard full time—steady hours, full bennies. With her disarming warmth and bright smile, Amelia made his visitors feel welcomed. In fact, they were so comfortable by the time they entered his office, they'd lowered their guard. And Iain took advantage of it. She was the honey and he was the vinegar. Flies, indeed.

Until now, he hadn't realized he'd been fondling the dice once again. Shoving them into his pocket, he stood and donned his jacket. Then he smoothed the lapels and straightened his tie. When Amelia didn't move, he glanced up at her. "What's the problem?"

She shook her head. "No problem."

"Then why are you still here?"

"Iain, your trainer's a woman."

He hadn't told Amelia about his plans for Brynn Campbell. His assistant would disapprove, and then she'd nag. No, it was better that he and Marc keep this scheme to themselves. "So?"

"She's very pretty. And she seems so nice. Just for once...don't be yourself."

He reared his head back at her words. "What the bloody hell is wrong with everyone today?" Attacking his leadership skills, questioning his ability to be civil. Iain could do civil...when he put his mind to it. "I'll be myself, thank you. If you don't like it, sod off, Ames."

She wagged her finger. "Yeah. That's what I'm

talking about. Do the opposite of that." When she disappeared through the door, he faced the window and looked out at his three-million-dollar view. Three-point-two-five, if one wanted to be technical. And when it came to money, Iain was always technical.

The morning sun slanted through the tinted window. If he stood at the right angle, he could catch a glimpse of jagged brown mountains in the distance. The palm trees lining the street below swayed in the breeze, reminding him that he was in the middle of a desert. He never grew tired of seeing this. Nothing in Vegas was real—it was all a facade. The buildings, the people—all transitory. And Iain loved every bloody bit of it.

He heard the door open, and after a long pause, close. Her footsteps were hesitant and light across the gold onyx floor.

"Hello." Her voice was soft, feminine. Young.

Iain slowly turned, a smile fixed on his face. But as he locked eyes on Brynn Campbell, unexpected desire slammed into his gut like a sucker punch. The pictures in Iain's file didn't do her justice. Ames had called her pretty, which was also inadequate. Bloody gorgeous more like.

Iain thought he knew everything about Brynn Hope Campbell, from her shopping habits to her tax returns. He knew what hobbies she favored and the classes she'd taken in college. But nothing had prepared him for meeting her in the flesh.

His gaze moved over her, taking in her slight frame. Then his eyes swept over her again. And a third time. With every pass, he noticed something different. The color of her hair wasn't merely brown—it was tobacco brown with burnished gold highlights. Her eyes weren't ordinary blue—they were navy. She wore leather flip-flops. Her toenails were varnished the same shade as her turquoise necklace. She carried a black binder in one hand, like a schoolgirl.

Lightly tanned, her skin glowed along high, smooth cheekbones. Her features were dainty, fragile—a lovely setting for those big, dark eyes. Her chin drew to a sharp point below a mouth that was too wide for such a delicate face. *Innocent.* The word floated through Iain's mind, but he immediately banished it. No one was innocent—not in this town.

Brynn was on the petite side, but her legs appeared long and slender. The white, loose blouse flowed over her torso, skimming her small tits. The V-shaped collar left her neck and throat bare. Iain's gaze fell to the wedge of visible golden skin. He wanted to see more. No, that wasn't true. Iain was a greedy bastard—he wanted to see everything.

She'd pulled her wavy hair into a low ponytail, but a lone curl refused to be confined and brushed against her jaw. She appeared almost fey. A wisp of a woman who might blow away with the gentlest breeze.

And he needed to focus.

He moved toward her and buttoned his jacket, keeping his gaze trained on her. "I'm Iain Chapman."

"You're British." She made it sound like an accusation.

"Observant, aren't you?"

She opened her mouth, but didn't speak. Taking a breath, she tried again. "I try to be. Pleased to meet you, Mr. Chapman. My name's Brynn Campbell." She stared at his silver tie like it was the most fascinating thing she'd ever seen. She was timid, but he found that charming. And for the first time, doubt robbed him of his certainty. Was this was the right course of action? A simple introduction to Trevor Blake, that's all he was after. Right?

"Call me Iain. I've been told I require a management makeover. Are you the woman to give me what I need?" He hadn't intended the innuendo, but he didn't apologize for it either.

Her gaze fluttered from his throat to his eyes. "I'm not sure. To be honest, I'm not really a teacher. I just write the curriculum."

He knew that, of course. Had paid Cassandra Delaney a few thousand extra to have Brynn teach the class personally. "I'm not much of a student, so I'd say we're well matched." When her eyes swept over his face, he smiled. But Brynn didn't smile back, as most women would. In fact, she stared at him with a faint frown on her generous lips.

Well, this was new. Iain was used to women flirting with him. And he wasn't foolish enough to believe they were attracted to his delightful personality. Although he did all right in the looks department, his face wasn't what lured women, either. No, Iain's main draw was his fat bank account. He was fine with that. Made things simpler. Everyone walked away happy. There were no expectations, no fuss. No emotional ties.

But this woman wasn't acting like the others, and he couldn't say why that intrigued him so much.

Brynn Campbell wasn't his type at all, and yet he was utterly enchanted by her. She didn't wear her sexuality like armor. She was small, nearly flat-chested, and dressed as if she were attending a music festival rather than a business meeting. With copper bracelets stacked on her slender wrist, she wore tattered jeans and very little makeup. And the way she watched him with those wide, wary eyes…

When he took a step toward her, she tensed. What did she think, he was going to make a lunge for her? He never dreamed she'd be so skittish. Or that he'd find it so compelling. Something in the way she tensed like prey made him feel very much the predator.

He found he liked that feeling quite a lot.

A knock sounded at the door and Amelia peered in. "Would you like some tea, Miss Campbell?"

Brynn glanced over her shoulder. "That would nice, thank you."

While she was looking away, Iain took the opportunity to study her breasts. The blouse was deceptively sheer. Tilting his head, he tried to see through the crinkly material, but he couldn't even detect the outline of her bra. It was maddening and enticing at the same time. As soon as Ames shut the door, Brynn faced him again. And caught him staring.

Swallowing audibly, she raised the black binder, clutching it to her chest and blocking his view. "Why don't we get started?" she asked.

"Yes, why don't we?"

She stared at him for a beat, then Brynn squared her shoulders and stuck one hand in her purse. She pulled out a pen, and opened her book to the front page.

Iain tried to get a peek at what she jotted down, but she snapped the notebook closed before he could read it. "Are you taking notes on me, love?"

Brynn angled her head to look up at him. "If I were

your employee, your suggestive glances might be considered actionable."

"Actionable, how? Like we'd clear the desk and have at it?"

Her brows drew together and formed a small V. "That comment would definitely qualify as actionable."

He leaned down, caught a whiff of perfume—vanilla and something floral. "Pretend you never heard it." Iain breathed her in. *Absolutely delicious*.

Her lips had parted slightly, but she didn't move away. Brynn Campbell might be wary, but she was also interested.

"The key to running a successful business," she whispered, "is keeping a professional attitude. Sniffing me probably isn't professional."

"And here I thought the key to running a successful business was making money. Shows how fucking little I know, eh?"

"Do you always use that language?" Brynn opened her notebook and scribbled again. "With employees, I mean."

"Yeah. I don't believe in censoring myself." He still hadn't moved away, was still leaning toward her. Her shallow breaths caused her chest to rapidly rise and fall, and that became the focus of Iain's attention. Her breasts were so tiny, he'd be able to suck on the whole damn thing. The thought made his mouth water.

"Um, *I* don't feel very comfortable when you look at me like that."

Iain reached out, his finger grazing a red splotch on the side of her throat. This hadn't been part of the plan, but hell, he was improvising. "I wasn't trying to make you feel comfortable."

"Oh." She paused. "*I* feel that, together, we can create a work environment that is both productive and respectful. *I* don't feel respected as a colleague right now." She stepped back two paces, leaving Iain's hand dangling in the air before he let it fall to his side.

Blimey, she was serious. And so lovely, it almost stole the breath out of his lungs. Iain felt an unwilling smile pull at the corners of his lips. "Are you quoting from a book, or something?"

Brynn nodded and cleared her throat. "A manual, actually. *Leading by Example: A Partnership in Effectiveness*."

"Sounds boring enough to send me to sleep."

"I wrote it." She enunciated the words, pointing her chin upward. He'd pricked her ego a bit. It was always vital to know as much about one's opponent as possible, and Iain had just learned that Brynn Campbell took pride in her deadly dull work.

"Brilliant. Then we can dispense with the lessons. Give me the short version, and afterward, I'll take you to lunch." What Iain really wanted to do was take Brynn to bed. He wasn't sure if she could teach him anything about leadership, but he was almost certain he could teach her a thing or two about pleasure.

And from the looks of her, she needed it desperately.

Acknowledgments

To the usual suspects—you wonderful minxes: Thank you for your constant support. We've been scattered like dandelion seeds this year, but you ladies are always there for me.

To Mary Altman, my editor: Thank you so much for all your encouragement. I appreciate the time and dedication you give to a project. Working on this book with you was a wonderful experience, and I loved every minute of it.

To Dawn "Cover Queen" Adams: You nailed it. Thank you, thank you, thank you.

And to my husband, Jeff: I couldn't do it without you. Love you. Thank you. Mwah.

About the Author

As a girl, Terri L. Austin thought she'd outgrow dreaming up stories and creating imaginary friends. Instead, she's made a career of it. She met her own Prince Charming and together they live in Missouri. She loves to hear from readers. Visit her at www.terrilaustin.com.